THE HORSES KNOW

LYNN MANN

Coxstone Press

THROUGH HER, I EXPERIENCE ME
IN A WAY I DON'T DO ALONE.
MY LOVE AND THANKS GO OUT TO HER
FOR ASSISTING MY JOURNEY HOME.

Amarilla Nixon

ONE

Awakening

I wanted to be one of the Horse-Bonded from the moment I found out who they were. I was seven years old, it was a hot summer's day and I was playing with my dolls under the kitchen table while my mother and my aunt kneaded dough above my head.

'It's Holly's Quest Ceremony tomorrow, there'll be tears in that household tonight,' said Aunt Jasmine.

'I can't understand the whole business myself, why Holly would want to just up sticks, leave all her family and friends behind and forego any chance of having a family of her own one day, and all because a horse has chosen her,' my mother replied.

'She's always been a restless soul and I think she'd have found it hard to settle down anyway, even with her talent for bone-singing. I think this is the best thing that could have happened to her. And just think, another Horse-Bonded from our village! She's the second in as many years, it must be something in the water,' said my aunt.

I crawled out from under the table and clambered up onto one of the worn but homely wooden chairs that surrounded the flour-dusted table. 'Mum, what's Horse-Bonded?' I asked, making swirls in the flour with my finger.

'Oh, Amarilla, sweetheart, it's just when a horse and a person stay

together all of the time and they talk to each other without needing to
speak out loud. Horses are very clever and wise, and some of them
choose a person who will look after them and in return they teach their
person things,' said my mother.

'What kind of things?' I asked.

'The Horse-Bonded don't always tell us non-bonded folk, but if a
Horse-Bonded and his or her horse pass through the village, then any
quarrels between neighbours are taken to them and they always settle
things in a way that leaves everyone happy.'

'And sometimes,' said my aunt, 'there is a bonded pair that makes a
very big difference wherever they go, and they become famous and their
names go down in the Histories, like Mettle and Jonus. Just think, Holly
and her horse might go down in the Histories.'

'Oh, Jasmine, don't go putting big ideas into my little Amarilla's
head,' complained my mother. 'Holly has to find her horse first and then
we'll probably never see or hear from her ever again, just like with
Fionden after he went. Two years since his Quest Ceremony and not one
visit to see his dear mother, how she copes I have no idea.'

'How will Holly find her horse?' I had shifted to kneel on my chair so
I could lean over the table and stare into my mother's flour-smudged
face.

'Amarilla Nixon, either sit on that chair properly or get down from it,
I will not have you climbing all over the furniture,' she scolded.

'But I want to know how Holly will find her horse. Can I go and ask
her?'

'She's likely to be very busy preparing to leave, Am,' said Aunt
Jasmine kindly. 'Give me five minutes to finish up here and then I'll tell
you all about it while my dough rises.'

As I sat on my aunt's knee in our sunny garden, she told me that
Holly had felt "the tugging" a few days earlier. She had been assisting the
Master Bone-Singer of the village, to whom she was apprenticed, with
the Miller's son, who had broken his finger. It was lucky she was only
assisting, in my aunt's opinion, as before the healing was finished, Holly
stopped singing and fell silent, leaving her Master to sing the bone back
to full strength alone. She later explained that she had, all of a sudden,

felt another mind touch hers and it had started to tug at her, gently but insistently. She lost all sense of what she had been doing as she focused on this foreign sensation and within a few minutes recognised it from the description she had been given as a child, just as it was now being described to me. She stood up, thanked the Bone-Singer for the opportunity he had given her and then informed him that her horse was tugging at her and she needed to go home to prepare herself to leave and find him.

'But how will she find him?' I said.

'After her Quest Ceremony, she'll start walking in the direction the tugging is coming from and carry on until she meets him coming the other way.'

'What will happen at her Quest Ceremony?' I asked.

'Why don't you come tomorrow and find out for yourself?'

We went back inside, where my mother was peeling vegetables for dinner.

'I'm going to Holly's Quest Ceremony with Auntie Jasmine tomorrow. Are you coming too?' I asked her.

My mother glared at my aunt. 'Really, Jas, you know how I feel about people running off into the sunset on nothing more than a whim, and I don't want Amarilla being a part of it.'

'Firstly, it's a lot more than a whim, as you well know and secondly, you will be there too; the whole village should be there to wish a person well when they leave on their quest. It's an exciting time and we all should be there to wish Holly well.'

That night, as my thoughts drifted just before sleep took me, I saw her in my mind for the first time – a black and white horse whose blue eyes were encircled by a thin strip of black skin which enhanced their unusual and vivid colouring. Her long eyelashes matched the brilliant white of her coat and her forelock was black, but streaked with silvery white. I went to sleep seeing her face and had dreams of meeting her one day, although I felt as if I already knew her.

The following morning, my parents, my two brothers, my sister Katonia and I made our way to the house that Holly shared with her family. As we walked along the cobbled road past the multitude of two-storey stone cottages with their slate roofs, all very similar in appearance to ours, more and more families joined us on our way, including my aunt and her husband, Jodral.

My brothers, Robbie and Con, walked along in front of me, chatting animatedly. Every now and then they would laugh and then look around immediately to see if my mother was watching them, and I wondered what they were plotting.

Robbie was fourteen, dark-haired and mischievous, and always managed to be where there was trouble, usually without being obviously involved. He was always encouraging auburn-haired, twelve-year-old, quieter Con to join him in his mischief and the two of them were inseparable. Everyone said Robbie and Con were just like my mother and my aunt all over again, a fact which Robbie always tried to use to his advantage when being yelled at by my mother.

I walked hand in hand with Katonia, who was two years my senior. She and I were alike enough to obviously be sisters, both slight in build, brown-haired and blue-eyed. We had always been close, as Katonia was a natural little mother and doted on me from the moment I was born. As I grew older, we became each other's preferred playmates and her confident character always protected my more introverted one.

My aunt caught up with Katonia and me. 'Girls, your mother tells me she hasn't given you anything to hang on Holly as she passes you. I had a feeling she mightn't, honestly, my sister really should relax sometimes, but anyway, here you are, a metal horseshoe each that I got from Hayden this morning and some made from grasses that I made myself last night.'

Hayden was the village Metal-Singer. He could sing metal into almost any shape, from the tiny, fingernail-sized horseshoes, each with its own tiny hook, that Katonia and I now held, to garden and farming tools and even the large field gates.

'What are they for?' asked Katonia.

'When Holly leaves her house, her family and close friends will be waiting for her at the front door. They will each present her with something for her back-sack that will aid her on her quest; hunting equipment, bedding, a cookpot, food, that sort of thing. The rest of the village will form two lines opposite each other from Holly's house, all the way down the road to the end of the village. As Holly walks down the corridor of people, we'll all say goodbye and wish her well. And we hang these,' she said, holding up her own handful of tiny horseshoes, 'on Holly's clothes and back-sack, wherever there is room for them, as she passes us. They hold all our love and good wishes, and will protect her from harm as she travels to meet her horse.'

'Will everyone hang things on her?' I asked, picturing Holly lost under a mountain of ornaments.

'No, Am, some people will throw flowers and the Healers will walk behind her and sing her as close to perfect health as they can, as their gift. The point of the Quest Ceremony is for everyone who knows Holly to give what they can and wish her well. It's the least we can do after all that the Horse-Bonded do for us and your mum does agree deep down, no matter how much she protests.'

It wasn't long before we saw the ends of two lines of villagers, just as my aunt had described. My brothers took their places next to the Baker and his wife, and Katonia and I joined the lines next to them.

We waited and waited. My brothers grew bored and flicked bits of dirt at each other, then at the Baker every time he turned away to look down the line, and finally at my sister and me, until I wailed to my mother, who scolded Robbie and Con into behaving themselves.

Just as the sun started to gain strength and beat down on us, and my mother started up about how she knew she shouldn't have brought her children and in another ten minutes she would be taking us home, I heard laughing and shouting in the distance. As the shouting got louder, I could hear voices I recognised wishing Holly well and congratulating her. Then I saw her. She was bent over slightly and people were throwing little flowers over her head and reaching out to touch her as she passed. She wore brown leggings and knee-high brown leather boots, a beige shirt with brown, sparkling buttons and a red neck scarf. On her back was an enormous sack with some pots and blankets tied to the outside of it. Little ornaments dangled from her blond hair, her clothes and her back-sack. As she got closer I could see horseshoes made from metal and grass, such as we had, others made from glass and some made from what looked like bits of coloured fabric. Four Healers tailed her, singing in droning tones as they concentrated intently on her back.

'We're proud of you, Holly,' called out the Baker's wife. 'All the best, love.'

'Good luck, Holly,' shouted my brothers in unison as they hung horseshoes in her hair.

I quickly hung my horseshoes onto the blankets tied to her back-sack as Katonia said, 'Good luck, we hope you find your horse very soon.'

'Come home to us soon, Holly, and stay safe, you make sure you find that horse of yours before one of those Woeful finds you,' said my mother.

'Mailen!' my father said sternly. 'Holly, you'll be fine, ignore my wife, she just worries for a living. Here you go, love.' He added his horseshoes to the arm of her shirt.

More good wishes followed as Holly moved down the line and then she was gone.

'What's a woffle?' I said. Katonia looked mystified.

Robbie said, 'Woeful are monsters who live in the woods. They stalk their prey before leaping on them from the trees and tearing their throats out.' He held his hands up with his fingers curled as claws for added effect.

'Now, Robbie, you don't want to be frightening your sisters with monster stories, you'll give them nightmares,' said the Baker. 'Mailen, Frank, I think your children are feeling the effects of the heat, you might need to get them home.'

My mother came hurrying over. 'Right, everyone, home now for lunch, and if you two,' she said to my brothers, 'think that now means in an hour's time, after you've followed the Bailey girls home and stuck cleavers on their backs, then you are wrong. And you'll leave all the cleavers you have stuffed into your pockets by the roadside, right now.'

'Mum, Robbie said the woffle live in the woods and tear people's throats out. They don't, do they?' I said.

'Oh, he did, did he?' She glared at Robbie.

'You can't tell me off for telling the truth and I know it's true, because we are learning about the Woeful at school, that's woe-full, Am,' said Robbie. 'In the next six months, everyone in my class will be tested to make sure we can sense them and when we've passed, we'll FINALLY be allowed out of the village without an adult.'

'That does NOT mean that you have to go around frightening younger children. You weren't taught about the Woe... I mean creatures until now for a very good reason and if I catch you trying to scare your sisters again, you won't be leaving the village without an adult whether you pass the test or not. Do I make myself clear? And that goes for you too, Con, whatever your brother has told you.'

'Yes, Mum,' they droned in well-practised unison.

'Now, girls, I want you to listen to me,' my mother said. 'Whatever your brother told you is nothing to worry about. You have your family and the whole village to protect you, and you are safe. Do you believe me?' I looked at Katonia and we both nodded.

'Good, now let's get back for lunch.'

Half an hour later, we all sat around the kitchen table, our chatter and laughter bouncing off the stone walls of the large, sunny kitchen as we helped ourselves to salad, bread and cheese.

My father knocked loudly on the table and said, 'Right, everyone, I think we should all raise a glass to Holly and her horse.'

As I copied my family, I remembered the black and white horse with blue eyes who had entered my thoughts the previous night. I felt confused; I'd never seen her before, yet somehow, I knew her. And I also knew something else.

'When I grow up, I am going to be Horse-Bonded,' I announced, 'and my horse will keep me safe from the Woeful.'

My mother put her hand to her forehead. 'I never should have let Jasmine fill her head with the Horse-Bonded,' she said. 'Now look what's happened. Curse Holly and her wild ways. And you, Robbie, with your talk of the Woeful.'

'You were the one who brought them up when you were talking to Holly,' retorted Robbie. 'I only told her what they are.'

'Mailen, calm yourself, love,' said my father. 'Each of our children has had the same reaction when they learnt of the Horse-Bonded and you've been nigh on hysterical each time. Look how things have turned out; Robbie will apprentice to an Earth-Singer next year and I know he will work hard. Con will no doubt follow in his footsteps, and Katonia will of course achieve her ambition of becoming a Rock-Singer, as well as having her own home and family like you. And I'm sure that when our little Am is older and decides what she will be good at, then she too will succeed.'

'But I've already decided what I'll be good at. I will be good at taking care of my horse after she tugs me. I am going to be one of the Horse-Bonded and my horse will be black and white with blue eyes, I know it, I've seen her,' I said.

'You see?' squeaked my mother. 'My Amarilla is going to leave us. I knew one of my children would, I always knew one of them would, oh Frank didn't I always say one of them would? You talk to her, I need to go and lie down.' With a sob, she left the room.

My father said, 'Don't worry, Am, your Mum is tired and just needs to rest for a bit. Why don't you help Katonia clear away, and when the boys and I have washed up and had a chat about topics of conversation that are suitable to have at family times,' he glared at Robbie, 'we'll all go and play cricket outside.'

My father was a skilled Rock-Singer whose voice and intent could lift rocks to a height that few others of his profession could match. I heard it said often that it was his affinity for rocks that gave him his stability of character and never-ending patience with my mother, which was fortunate once my personality began to assert itself. From that day forward, to my mother's anguish, horses and the Horse-Bonded were my sole interest. I knew that a horse would one day tug me, and I knew exactly what she would look like.

TWO

Obsession

*D*uring the years that followed, my shyness was forgotten as I interviewed as many villagers as I could for any information they could give me about horses or the Horse-Bonded. I worked hard to improve my writing so that every tiny piece of information I gleaned could be recorded for future reference.

As I grew older and learnt to use the school library, I scoured the Histories for stories of the Horse-Bonded. I learnt that the first Horse-Bonded to exist was one of the Ancients, a man named Jonus. With the aid of his horse, Mettle, he was instrumental in establishing the new way of life, or "The New".

Before The New, the Histories tell us, humans lived very differently from the simple, largely harmonious way that we do now. We live in relatively small, self-sufficient communities and most things we need can be made or grown using the power of the mind, or a strong back and sound work ethic. During "The Old", everything was provided by machines.

Animals were farmed indoors with machines controlling their feeding, movement and hygiene. Food plants were likewise propagated and harvested indoors, where the climate and light source could be completely controlled at all times. No disease was permitted in the clinically sterile conditions and the genetically modified produce provided the optimum nutritional value.

Worldwide, people lived crammed on top of each other in countless, impossibly tall buildings that made up vast cities. No one was permitted to live outside the cities, since their safety could then not be guaranteed. "Safety and Comfort" was the promise to the people from the governments.

Transport vehicles ran on rails up to each and every building and were controlled by machines, since accidents could happen were humans to drive themselves. One simply entered one's destination at the control panel and then sat back until arrival at the desired destination.

Exercise of any form was not permitted outdoors as safety to one's person could not be guaranteed, so children played in each other's homes or at organised, indoor play venues. Adults could only exercise at machines, in the safety of either the home or a communal, policed gymnasium.

Animals were not permitted to be part of human communities since their behaviour could not be guaranteed and they were therefore deemed dangerous. When the law banning pet or zoo animals was passed, all animals were rounded up and dumped outside the tall, impregnable city gates to fend for themselves.

Eye and hair scans took place at the entrance to every building and vehicle, so that the position of every citizen could be constantly monitored in the interests of safety.

Records were kept of all families and food was rationed accordingly, so that no obesity or ill health could occur due to bad eating habits. Families lived their lives around work or school, exercising and socialising with "appropriate associates"; it wasn't considered safe for people of different races, religions or social classes to mix, as differences of opinion could occur and that could compromise the safety of the individuals concerned.

The Histories show that the more measures that were taken to ensure safety, the more people tended to look for reasons to feel frightened and unsafe. This trend was mirrored at the level of governments, and the level of mistrust between nations grew.

Certain individuals began to recognise the source of the growing anxiety and paranoia, and started to step apart from it. They came from all nationalities, races, religions and social classes, and yet they are all recorded as having experienced the same sudden yearning for a life of which none of them had previously had any notion or experience. They wanted to live a life that allowed their instincts to guide them, safe or not. They wanted to be surrounded by other animals, by trees, grass, sun, rain and wind, not concrete, machines and carefully conditioned, safe air. Gradually, in ones, twos and occasionally small family groups, they began to leave their homes and their cities.

It wasn't as hard to leave as they had been led to believe it would be. The criminal underground that has existed in any human community since time immemorial until The New, was well established and well organised. At the promise of being awarded everything the emigrants were leaving behind—their apartments and all the possessions they couldn't carry with them—the Kindred, as they were known, happily bribed and threatened where necessary to get their charges out of the city gates to freedom and the great unknown.

Without exception, the Ancients walked as their instincts guided them, until they could no longer feel the weight of the oppressive societies they had left. And their instincts led them to each other. As they welcomed each other with joy and relief, they began to realise of what they were a part. They had ignored all of the caution and fear with which they had been indoctrinated since birth, and followed what a feeling inside urged them to do—and they had found other people who had done the same. The Histories tell of the way their hearts and souls sang with the joy of their new lives, at least in the beginning.

All of the fledgling communities agreed, independently of each other, to live according to what their intuition told them was right. And so it was that these Ancients became the founding fathers of The New. A potential now existed for humans to evolve away from a way of life where decisions were based on fear, towards one where decisions were guided by the inner wisdom and strength possessed by each and every person.

But it was hard. So hard. The food they had managed to save and bring with them didn't last long and they had never had to produce food for themselves before, let alone build shelters or even make fire. Intuition led them to eat food that nature provided and they learnt to hunt and gather seeds to sow for later seasons, but it took time to get the first farmland to be productive. They had to salvage ploughs from long-abandoned farms, and find, round up and train donkeys and oxen to pull them, so that further land could be cultivated. The initial, hastily erected shelters didn't last the first storms and had to be rebuilt time and again. People pulled together and tried their hardest, but cold and hunger can do things to a weary mind. Bit by bit, doubts began to creep in.

Jonus was among those trying to find a way to build a sturdy, weather-proof shelter in his community. His group were on their fifth attempt and although their new ideas seemed to be working much better, everyone knew they hadn't achieved what they sensed they needed. They were, as ever, hungry, and tempers were flaring. It was during a break for water one morning that Jonus was tugged. He had no idea what was happening of course, and assumed hunger was responsible for him imagining that he could feel another mind pulling at his own. Days later, unable to form a single thought and driven almost to madness by the now fierce tugging of his mind, he ran from his place of work towards where he judged it to be emanating. Two days later he found Mettle, a sixteen hand, grey stallion, heading in his direction.

The Histories tell of how Jonus returned to his community a few days later with Mettle at his side. He explained that Mettle had told him that the horses who yet remained on the planet recognised the effort the humans of The New were making to evolve their species, and they wanted to help. They weren't prepared to serve humans in the ways in which they had been willing in the past, but some horses would choose individual humans with whom to work and those humans would then be a source of wisdom and strength to their fellows.

Jonus said that according to Mettle, they would find the answers to their building problems in memories buried deep within each and every one of them; memories of a race that had lived many millennia before and which had built enormous four-sided structures, each face of which was a triangle.

That night, two members of the building team had the same dream. They dreamt of groups of dark-haired, nearly naked, bronze-skinned men and women who sang together. They focused on massive blocks of stone as they sang and gradually the blocks began to rise to impossible heights, until they were placed to rest beside their equally large neighbours.

A few days later, the first Rock-Singers set to work.

Mettle and Jonus travelled from community to community, spreading encouragement and using precise wording to help people remember skills long lost to the human race, but present still within the human psyche. Their aim was to ensure that The New survived, and the Histories would come to show that they achieved their goal.

Other Horse-Bonded and their horses were also mentioned in connection with noteworthy historical events to which they had contributed, and I was fascinated by every mention of them.

It wasn't long before my reading and writing skills far surpassed those of my friends at school, so driven was I to read and note down everything that would prepare me for when my horse summoned me. My yearly school reports began to indicate the extent of my obsession:

"Amarilla is an extremely intelligent child and learns quickly, however attempts to broaden her interests are proving futile," was the comment at the bottom of one of my reports. I remember it well because my mother, understanding exactly to what it referred, repeated it over and over again in an increasingly high-pitched voice, until my father poured her a glass of wine and assured her she would feel much calmer sitting on her chair by the fire.

Subsequent reports carried a similar theme:

"Amarilla writes well, however she fails to recognise that there are topics worthy of her creativity other than horses."

"Amarilla's attempts at drawing are always interesting and she is a devoted student. I think the piebald horse with blue eyes has now been sketched from every possible angle."

"Amarilla is good at her sums when she is applying herself. I do, however, spend a goodly part of many lessons redirecting her attention from her daydreams to her work." And,

"Amarilla's knowledge of the Histories is admirable in a student of her age, however her written accounts of them tend to show effort only when there is mention of horses and the Horse-Bonded – a shame."

By the time I was fourteen, my father knew to be home before I was on the last day of the school year, and to ensure that my mother had a glass of wine in her hand. For my part, I knew to leave my report on the kitchen table and then make myself scarce until the evening, by which time my mother would have ranted, my father would have consoled, and we would all be back to normal again.

'She'll grow out of it, you know she will,' I overheard him tell her for the hundredth time. I was sitting in the bushes by the back door, waiting for the explosion that would signal my mother had finished reading this year's report. 'And anyway, it will all come to nothing unless a horse actually chooses her and what are the chances of that?'

My stomach turned over as my father voiced my biggest fear. Despite having had such strong images of my piebald, blue-eyed mare for the last seven years, and despite my dreams of her as I stared out of the window at school – how the sun caught every single silvery-white tail hair as she flicked flies off of her gleaming black and white coat, how she pricked her ears and flared her nostrils at any new sound, focusing her intense, blue-eyed stare towards it until she was satisfied as to its source – what if, and I whispered this even within my mind, what if she weren't real?

But then I felt a sensation I had first experienced a couple of years previously; a whispering passed by my mind. It wasn't a tugging – at least it didn't match the description of it that I'd been given – it was the faintest sense of her passing me by, much as two people pass by on opposite sides of the street. My heart soared as I knew afresh that she existed and that when the time was right, she would call me.

'But even if a horse never tugs her,' my mother's voice jolted my attention back to their conversation, 'she's wasting so much time obsessing over it all that she's missing out on preparing for her future. All her friends are testing for the different Skills to see if they show aptitude. Nate's already chosen his path as an Earth-Singer, give him a few years and he'll be out with Robbie and Con, singing the earth full of air, then singing it into furrows ready for seed, and what will our Amarilla be doing? Drawing horses, practising husbandry on the donkeys and driving herself mad waiting for the tugging that may never come?'

'Our Amarilla will come around now she sees her friends choosing their futures, you'll see,' said my father.

I began to see that there was something I could do that would please everyone. I exited the bush and went into the kitchen. My parents turned in their seats at the kitchen table as I entered the room. My mother opened her mouth to begin berating me and my father looked at me quizzically, obviously wondering why I had approached my mother by choice when she was far from calm.

'I've decided to test for the Skills,' I said quickly. 'I know everyone else was tested in the last few weeks of school and I'm late putting myself forward, but maybe if I go and ask, one of the Testers will agree to assess me tomorrow? After all, we've only just broken up, the holidays haven't really started properly, have they?'

'Oh, Amarilla,' my mother said, rushing towards me with her arms outstretched. 'I hoped and prayed you'd see sense but you seemed so determined.'

My father heaved a sigh of relief. 'Amarilla, your mother and I are thrilled. I will go and ask the Testers if they will agree to your suggestion.'

'Dad, you only need to ask Nerys,' I said, referring to the Tester of the Healing Skills. 'I want to test for the Skills that will aid me once I am bonded.'

My father took in a sharp breath and held it. My mother, however, had clearly decided to focus on the fact that I would test for the Skills. 'Frank, please go and ask Nerys now, I absolutely can't bear to wait until later. Oh, our Amarilla will be a Healer! I can hardly believe it, a Healer in the family, wait until I tell Jas.' She gave me a last hug and rushed off to give her sister the latest news.

My father took one of my hands in each of his and squeezed them gently. 'Amarilla, my beloved daughter, you are very wise. Not only have you decided to test for a path that will give you a future if you aren't ever tugged, I said IF,' he added, as I rolled my eyes, 'but you have also made your mother very happy. And for that, we are all eternally grateful.'

We both dissolved into laughter and he hugged me close to him, before releasing me and departing to go and find Nerys.

THREE

Healing

*I*t had seemed like the best thing to do. If it transpired that I showed any aptitude for any of the Healing Skills, my parents would be ecstatic, I would be learning a Skill that would help me to care for my horse and I wouldn't be the only one of my age not training in one of the Skills or Trades after my final year at school.

Back then, it was customary for children to be tested for the Skills at fourteen even though they still had another year left to complete at school, so that their minds would have a year to open to the idea of their chosen path. It also gave those who tested for the Skills, but showed no aptitude for them, a good amount of time to consider in which Trade they would like to apprentice. Often, children chose to train for the same Trade as their parents, foregoing their Skills testing, but there was never any pressure put on children to choose a particular path. A child's own intuition was trusted to guide him or her towards the path to which they were best suited.

My father found Nerys to be more than happy with the idea of testing me, so the following day I arrived promptly for my after-breakfast appointment with her. I knocked on the door of the testing room and entered when bid. I saw that three of the walls were stone, but one was made of glass. There were no floorboards in front of the glass wall and a low table stood on the exposed earth.

Nerys was tall and slim with long, straight grey hair tied back in a tail. 'Amarilla, what a very pleasant surprise this is,' she said. 'Are you testing for everything, or have you sensed that one of the Healing Skills might be for you?' Her hazel eyes warned against any attempt to pull wool over them.

'Just the Healing ones, as they'll be of most use to me once I'm Horse-Bonded,' I said.

'I guessed as much. Let's hope you show some aptitude for one of them then, shall we? I think we'll start with the herbs. Come and sit with me at the table. We'll be sitting on the earth as you are going to be using your senses to choose between these herbs and it helps to begin with if there's nothing between you and where they sprang from,' she said cheerfully.

As I sat down on the bare earth and crossed my legs, I saw that there were ten different herbs on the table, none of which I recognised. I began to feel nervous, which must have shown on my face.

'Don't worry, I'm sure you'll be good at something,' Nerys said. 'Now, I want you to look through the glass, out across the fields and into the woodland beyond. As you look, let your senses go out there with your vision. Smell the earth and the plants, feel the breeze, hear the rustle of the leaves. Taste what you smell, hear, see and feel.'

I surprised myself by finding it easy.

'Got it?' she asked and I nodded. 'Good. Now I want more of you out there. Let only a small part of your mind stay with your body, the rest of your awareness needs to be out crawling between blades of grass, moving up tree trunks and along branches, wisping between the leaves, filtering in and out of air pockets in the soil. Be the trees growing, the smaller plants reaching up towards the light, the seed splitting to allow the shoot to emerge. Actually be them.'

I had a definite sense of being the trees, smaller plants and shoots. I told Nerys this and she smiled.

'You're doing very well. Your awareness of your mind is surprising for someone your age,' she said. 'Now I want you to perform the same exercise, but with the herbs in front of you. They were picked only half an hour ago, so they're still full of life and vitality and that should make it easier for you to tune into them. Look at the herbs in turn. Extend your senses and then as much of your awareness as you can towards them, into them, through them.'

I tuned into each of the herbs as much as I could and my head began to ache. I nodded to let Nerys know I had done as she had told me.

'Right, now, the common cold. Feel as if you have one. Feel the sore throat, headache and congestion. Concentrate on the congestion. You can't breathe through your nose, your whole face feels as if it's solid and throbbing. Take that feeling to each of the herbs you have tuned in to and tell me if any of them lessen the congestion feeling. Take your time, Amarilla, don't rush.'

I did as she instructed. By the time I got to the fifth herb, my head felt as if it would explode, but I had experienced no lessening of the sense of congestion I had created, so I carried on. I reached number seven, a small herb with tiny leaves and little pink flowers. I tuned into it and married it up with the congestion I could almost physically feel now. Something shifted; all sense of congestion disappeared and so long as I was tuned into the little pink-flowered herb, I couldn't for the life of me recreate it.

'Number seven?'

I was rewarded with a beaming smile. 'Wonderful, that's just marvellous. Well done, Amarilla, very well done,' Nerys said. 'We'll try another.'

'Is my head meant to ache like this?'

'Oh, that always happens when you're not used to using your mind this way, the more you practise, the less you'll ache. Now which of these herbs would you suggest for a bad bruise? Go through the same steps as before and take your time.'

By the time I had correctly identified the herbs used to overcome bruising, fever, earache and menstrual cramps, I was as exhausted as Nerys was delighted. 'I think we can say you have a strong aptitude for herbalism, the like of which I haven't witnessed in any other student to date,' she said. 'Go home and get some rest. Get rid of your headache and you'll be fresh for tomorrow.'

'Tomorrow?'

'Well, normally I'd test you for all three Healing Skills together, but I'm afraid I rather got carried away with your ability with herbs, so I think we'll need to leave bone-singing and tissue-singing until tomorrow.'

Judging by the pounding in my head, tomorrow was going to be too soon.

I arrived home to find both of my parents anxiously waiting for me.

'Darling, how did you get on?' my mother asked. 'I hope you concentrated and did your best, because you'll never get accepted for training if you just daydream out the window and Nerys is being so good to us, testing you during the summer break…'

'Mailen, let Am speak. Amarilla, how did it go?' said my father.

I told them what had happened and as my mother listened, she leant further and further towards me until she was barely seated on her chair. 'Oh, my little girl, I knew it, I knew you could do something worthwhile with your life, now tell me again from the beginning. Leave absolutely nothing out.'

'She's tired, Mail, she's got bags under her eyes, let her rest,' my father protested.

'Nonsense, some things are far more important than sleep, Frank, this is our daughter's future we are talking about, now, Am dear, from the beginning.'

'Dad, it's okay,' I said. 'You go back to work, I don't mind telling Mum again, honestly.'

My father sighed. 'See you this evening then, sweetheart,' he said, laying his hand on my shoulder as he passed behind my chair. 'Try and get at least some rest.'

After my mother had finally finished grilling me, I had a few hours to myself before I was needed to help with bread-making. I took myself outside and lay down on the grass beneath our old oak tree. My head was still too full of the day's events to allow sleep to come, so I closed my eyes and visited my favourite subject. I saw my piebald mare grazing in the summer sunshine, her coat flecked by damp patches of sweat. Every now and then she stamped a foot to shake off a fly, or reached round with her nose to dislodge a biting insect from her torso. I felt the now familiar whisper fleet tantalisingly past my mind and I revelled in the sure knowledge that somewhere, she existed.

Then, from nowhere, the whisper popped and became far more definite. I reached for it with my mind but the more I reached, the more I seemed to push it away, until I could no longer sense it at all. Puzzled, I opened my eyes and sat up. What was that? There was nobody I could ask and I had learnt from long experience that mentioning horses to my family and friends would be met with distress, amusement or boredom. There was only one way to try and work out what had happened.

I lay back down and closed my eyes again. I tried to relax my mind and forced myself not to try and reach out to anything. Gradually, I fell back into my daydream and pictured my horse's face in the minutest detail I possibly could. I saw the whorl of white hairs in the middle of her forehead, her beautiful white eyelashes, her pink muzzle with its fine coating of tiny silver-white hairs and long whiskers, her pale blue eyes, each surrounded by a circle of soft, black skin in her white face. I even saw the look of focused irritation before each stamp of her foot or swipe at the biters on her body.

And then I felt it again. Instead of the faint whisper passing me by, I had a definite sense of her. I found I could maintain the awareness of her and she would stay near me, but if I reached out to her with even the tiniest portion of my mind, she'd pull away from me and be gone. I was happier than I'd ever been in my life. I must have fallen asleep at some point, but when I woke to my mother's voice calling me to come and help her, I still had a smile on my face.

By the time bedtime arrived, my mind was churning. What had changed? Was it something in me that had changed and made me more open to my horse? Was it because of the testing? Or was she changing somehow? Was she okay? Was she trying to reach me? No, it couldn't be that, if she needed me she would just tug me and I'd go to her. So, what happened? My mind went round and round in circles as the night hours passed.

When Nerys saw me the following morning, she wasn't pleased. 'Amarilla, did you rest as I instructed you to yesterday?' she asked.

'Yes, well that is no, not really. Mum wanted to hear all about it and that went on for a while and then I didn't get much sleep last night for some reason.'

'Your mother, ah,' said Nerys. 'Well we'll say no more about it, but after today's session I'll come home with you and tell Mailen all about it while you escape, that is, I mean, go and relax. I suppose I'm not surprised you didn't sleep much, I shouldn't have pushed you so hard yesterday. Today we'll see how you get on with bone-singing and tissue-singing.' She indicated that I should sit at a table near the door, on which sat several bones and some fluid-filled jars containing what appeared to be kidneys, a heart and some other indefinable tissue.

'Yesterday, you learnt to sense which herbs would resonate with, and ease, which conditions. With the Singing Skills, you will need to be able to sense the energy vibration of a patient's healthy bones or tissue and identify where there is any divergence from that healthy vibration, which will indicate fracture or disease. You will then learn to produce a sound that will resonate with the injured bone or tissue so you can send your mind to the affected area along the pathway you are making with your voice. Once you can do that, you can heal the fracture or disease with your intention. Understand?' Nerys asked.

'I think so.'

'So, you can understand then, that a Herbalist is merely an intermediary between herb and patient; it is the herb that does the healing. With Bone-Singers and Tissue-Singers, on the other hand, it is the Healer who performs the healing and this is why bone-singing and tissue-singing require much longer apprenticeships. It is a long time before an Apprentice is allowed to assist her Master in finding and making the appropriate sounds, and an even longer time before there is any question of an Apprentice applying intent.'

'How long are the apprenticeships?' I asked.

'Bone-singing and tissue-singing apprenticeships average around six years, depending on the ability and temperament of the Apprentice. Herbalism apprenticeships average around three or four years, again depending on the individual, but I do know of one student over in Mountainsfoot who did his in two and a half.'

I knew that Horse-Bonded were usually tugged by their horses once they were adults, but I also knew that something with my horse was changing and that there was a good chance she would tug me well before I reached adulthood. I made up my mind. 'Nerys, I'm sorry for wasting your time this morning, but I've decided I don't want to test for the Singing Skills, I'd like to be a Herbalist. And I'd like to start my apprenticeship now.'

'But, Amarilla,' Nerys protested, 'won't you at least try the other two Skills so you can choose between all three? I'm sure you'll have aptitude for either one of them, just look at how quickly your sister took to rock-singing.'

'I would really like to be a Herbalist,' I insisted. 'I took to it well enough yesterday, didn't I? And the apprenticeship is so much shorter.'

Nerys was only seconds in figuring it out. 'You don't want to do a long apprenticeship because you think your horse will tug you in the next few years. You want to start now because then you should finish aged around seventeen, possibly even sooner with the aptitude you showed for it yesterday. You do realise that it is extremely unusual for a horse to call for a person until they are adult?'

I was grateful that she was questioning when, rather than if, my horse would call for me. 'I know, but I know my mare will tug me sooner. She's changing, I can feel her.'

Nerys regarded me thoughtfully. 'I think you'd better tell me all about it,' she said finally.

And so I told her everything. How I had started to see images of my horse in my mind from the day I learnt of the Horse-Bonded. How for the last couple of years I had felt a whisper of her when I thought of her, and then how yesterday I had felt her change.

Nerys looked at me searchingly. After some minutes had passed, she said, 'I've never heard of this happening to anyone who has been bonded. It sounds like a child's fantasy, but I believe you. Your performance yesterday in the herbalism testing was exceptional. I have never seen a student take to it so quickly and with so little instruction, and the earache test isn't usually attempted at this early stage, let alone passed. You are clearly very sensitive and the fact that you've been using your mind to sense your horse since you were so young explains how you had so much awareness and control over it yesterday. I did wonder how that was possible.'

Gratitude and relief overwhelmed me, and I burst into tears. Nerys came to sit next to me and put an arm around my shoulders. 'I understand why you want as short an apprenticeship as possible and why you want to start now. Please stand.'

I did as I was asked. Nerys stood opposite me and placed both of her hands on my shoulders. 'Amarilla Nixon, by the light, do you agree to apprentice yourself to me, Nerys Hicks, and only me, until I deem you worthy of the title Herbalist?'

'Nerys Hicks, by the light, I agree to apprentice myself to you, and only you, until you deem me worthy of the title Herbalist, or until my horse tugs me, whichever is sooner,' I said, hoping she wouldn't be angry.

Her eyes widened momentarily and then, stifling a smile, she said, 'Apprentice Nixon, I accept you under those terms.'

'Master Hicks, how do I tell my parents about me leaving school early to start my apprenticeship?'

'I'll come home with you now, so your parents can sign your apprenticeship forms, and I'll tell them,' said Nerys. 'I'll tell them that their daughter, whilst having more knowledge of horses, the Horse-Bonded and the Histories than any other student I've had the fortune to meet, doesn't tend to apply herself particularly well at school – and yet is the most naturally gifted Apprentice Herbalist I've ever come across. I have a feeling that the idea of her daughter becoming the youngest qualified Herbalist in the Histories will be enough to quell any objections Mailen might have.'

I noticed she didn't mention any objections my father might have; she obviously knew my parents very well.

FOUR

Apprenticeship

*M*y parents agreed readily to my leaving school and beginning my apprenticeship a year early, although my mother insisted that I at least enjoy the summer break with my friends first and begin my apprenticeship when they went back to school.

By the time the first day of my apprenticeship arrived, I was nervous. I entered the stone building which housed the healing rooms and knocked on the door of Nerys's office. She flung open the door.

'Morning, Apprentice Nixon, bright and early I see, very good. Right, we'll get you straight into things. Come with me.'

I followed her into a small room next to her office.

'This is your herb journal,' she said, laying her hand on a thick, hardbound book, 'and that is your herb dictionary.' She pointed to a thinner, soft-backed book.

I picked up the journal and leafed through it. Each page was headed with the name of an ailment but was otherwise blank. "Constipation" read the top of the first page I stopped at, followed by "Hair Loss", "Hay Fever" and "Rheumatism". I frowned, confused.

'Don't worry, the pages will soon be filled in. This book,' Nerys said, picking up the dictionary, 'shows all of the plants we have so far identified as being useful in healing. There is a detailed drawing, as well as a description of when it flowers, where it can be sourced and anything else you need to know. Your job for now will be to work your way through the dictionary, finding examples of the herbs, and then you will need to take each ailment listed in your journal and describe which herb or combination of herbs you can sense will help the affliction. You will learn firsthand what the different herbs are, where you can find them and at what time of year, and what they may be used for. Any time you need any help or advice, my door is open. For the coming weeks, you will need to restrict yourself to herbs that can be found within the village as you haven't yet been given permission to venture beyond without an adult, and I will be busy with some of the other Apprentices. After that, I will need to give you the lesson that you will be missing at school, which will enable you to leave by yourself. For now, it's just you, your senses and the plants. Apprentice Nixon, your work has begun.'

She whisked from the room, leaving me with my two books. I felt daunted but slightly excited. *I'm doing this for you,* I thought out to my horse and imagined that she could hear me.

I found that sourcing herbs wasn't a problem; the four-inch-thick journal was where difficulty lay, as I had to go to each page, understand the ailment and its symptoms, try to create a sense of it in my mind and then test each of the herbs I had found so far to see if any of them would ease the symptoms in any way. And there were an awful lot of ailments listed, many of which I had never heard of, let alone had any chance of being able to create a sense of. I took my concern to Nerys.

'Don't worry, just tackle the ailments you already know, they will be enough for you to be going on with and when you run out of those, you will be ready to join me as an observer in my treatment room. As different patients come for treatment, you'll be able to tune in and get a sense of the energy vibration of their ailment. You will then be able to recreate it on your own,' she said.

A month or so later, I had sourced all of the herbs that could be found in the village and farms that immediately surrounded it. I hadn't identified what they all could be used for, but I found that I could only spend part of each day creating ailments and tuning into herbs, before my head ached too much for me to continue, so I would spend the rest of the day sourcing more herbs and learning how to store them properly. I was ready to venture further afield and that meant asking Nerys to teach me about the subject that was avoided in all households that held children under the age of fourteen; the Woeful.

Since the first time I had heard their mention, the only way I had found of soothing the churning in my stomach whenever the Woeful entered my thoughts was to think of my horse. I had a well-practised routine. I would push thoughts of anything but her to one side and then picture her in the minute detail that always seemed to come to me. The way the white part of her coat was so white that the rays of the sun appeared to cling to her so that she shone even brighter. The way she would lift her head suddenly from grazing, ears pricked and nostrils flared as she sensed potential danger lurking in the trees beyond. The way all of the muscles of her body would tense ready for flight. The way she would prance around the other horses now and then, showing them how lucky they were to have her as part of their herd. It was always as if I were actually standing watching her. And then I would feel her, just at the edge of my mind. As time went on, I realised that she was always there; I just had to clear my mind so that I could sense her. I thought of her now and relaxed as I knocked on Nerys's door.

'Enter,' she called out.

I stepped into her office and took a deep breath. 'Master Hicks, I would like to be able to leave the village to source more herbs. Please would you teach me about the Woeful?'

'I see those brothers of yours have been unable to contain themselves, Amarilla, when did you hear of the Woeful?'

'At Holly's Quest Ceremony. Robbie only told me because he heard Mum warn Holly about them. He said they stalk their prey from the trees, and then jump on them and rip their throats out.'

'I can see how Robbie would pick up on those particular details, but I can assure you there is a lot more to it than that. The Woeful should not be regarded as monsters, but rather as creatures to be pitied. Come and sit down with me over here.' She indicated two soft armchairs over by the unlit fireplace. 'With your knowledge of the Histories, we have a head start. You are, of course, familiar with The Old?'

I nodded. 'I know how the people of The Old used to live. They thought that if they controlled everything, it would mean their lives were safe and comfortable.'

'Correct,' Nerys said. 'They thought that if they isolated themselves from anything or anyone who was different from them in any way, there would be no conflict, no chance of any danger and they would have safe and happy lives. They did, of course, fail to realise that the very conflict they tried so hard to avoid by controlling their external circumstances, was present INSIDE each and every one of them. The more they tried to control the world outside of themselves, the more frightening it became that their sense of unease and anxiety didn't abate. And so, they tried to impose ever more control, presumably thinking that at some point the fear and anxiety would disappear.

'But it didn't. The cities became centres of mental instability and illness and the fear and suspicion that existed between individuals was present on an even larger scale between cities and between nations. Everyone was fearful of everyone else. And fear drove the governments to do unspeakable things. Creating the Woeful was one of those things.'

'What are they?' I asked in a small voice.

'They are the descendants of a group of beings that the people of The Old referred to as Enforcers. The Enforcers were created by scientists of The Old, who genetically modified human embryos to produce an army of super-beings, if you will. They introduced genes from eagles to give their creatures talons at the end of their fingers. They used genes from various apes to produce a stronger, more compact body shape capable of scaling buildings and they also appear to have introduced genes from one of the larger cats, judging by the fangs they managed to produce.'

She produced a drawing of a creature that frightened me and at the same time left me feeling very sad. It looked like a human being but was hunched in posture. The features Nerys had mentioned were all apparent and it was also covered in sparse, brown hair, over what appeared to be brown armour.

'Why do they have hair on the outside of their armour?' I asked.

'That isn't armour, it's his skin. The thinking seems to be that the scientists must have introduced a gene from something with an exoskeleton, a crab or lobster, maybe. Anyhow, the result they produced is what you see. Extremely tough but flexible skin, almost impenetrable.'

I was horrified. 'Why did they do this?' I asked in a whisper.

'Fear and control. The same motivation for all other decisions made in The Old. The Enforcers were produced to do just as their name suggests, to enforce all of the rules and measures the government put in place. Anyone violating any of the rules was eliminated by the Enforcers, in the interests of public safety.'

'But how did they make the Enforcers do what they wanted?'

'Computer chips, linked to computers in main control centres, were placed in each and every one of them at birth. The computers were able to process everything the Enforcers saw, heard and did. Orders were issued by the computers according to the strict protocol with which they had been programmed. Disobedience was impossible. Any deviation from their instructions resulted in pain beyond belief and the Enforcers learnt quickly to obey orders without delay.'

'But how did the Ancients manage to leave, with Enforcers on the loose?' I asked.

'They didn't exist when the Ancients first started to leave their cities. It was decades after the first Ancients had established their communities that fresh refugees from the cities brought word of these new beings. After their widespread introduction to the cities, the slow but steady stream of people leaving the cities and arriving at The New communities was reduced to a mere trickle and eventually it stopped altogether.'

'Why didn't I find mention of them when I was reading through the Histories?'

'School books don't contain their mention anywhere. It has always been felt that knowledge of the Woeful, and therefore knowledge of what humans have been capable of in the past, should not be acquired until children reach an age where they can fully understand the implications of it. Not to mention, of course, sparing young children from nightmares, which your Robbie was warned about. You do understand the implications of what I am telling you, don't you?'

'Humans are capable of doing horrible things?' I said.

'Yes, but the point is that fear can drive people to do things that in the cold light of day, they would never consider doing. The people who did this were human beings, just like us. They would have known that what they were doing was wrong but they chose to listen to their fear instead. The lesson to learn here – and it's one that the horses have repeatedly asked their Bond-Partners to share with us all – is this. However afraid you are, whatever situation you find yourself in, always listen to your intuition and follow it. Never make your decisions based on fear. This,' she pushed the drawing towards me, 'is what can happen.'

'Do the Woeful really live in the woods?' I asked.

'Encounters with them have always been in the woods, but no dwellings have ever been found. It seems they tend to roam around, living from day to day, hunting and gathering their food as they go.'

'Why don't they attack us in the village?'

'Nobody knows. When the humans of The Old eventually destroyed themselves, there was little left of their cities. We have to assume that when the computers that controlled them perished, the Enforcers were free to do as they wished. All the evidence points to them avoiding human contact since that time and their descendants likewise.'

'Do they attack people outside of the village, as Robbie said?'

'There have never been any reports of Woeful killing human beings. They have, however, been known to stalk from the trees for long periods of time, hours, sometimes, before leaping down with the apparent intention only of stealing what they can. And, as your brother so helpfully informed you, when the Woeful do kill for food, their preferred method is to slash at the throats of their victims with their talons. Their usual prey is deer, wild cats, dogs, pigs, cows and,' she paused for a second, before saying in an apologetic voice, 'horses.'

The world stood still. My heart thumped wildly and my breathing became erratic. Nerys took hold of my hands firmly and said, 'Amarilla, breathe. Breathe, slowly and deeply. Listen to me, focus on my voice, and breathe.'

I matched my breathing to the deep, slow breaths she was taking. 'How often have horses been killed?' I whispered.

'We don't know. Every now and then, remains have been found, but we don't know.'

'If they're killing horses, why are the Woeful not hunted down?'

Nerys sat back into her chair. 'And there we have it. You have just felt fear such as you've never before felt in your life and your immediate reaction was to want to lash out at what you perceive to be the cause of it – the Woeful, the potential threat to your horse. You will need to find the courage to avoid falling into the same trap that the people of The Old did.'

'But what about the horses? How do we help them to stay safe?'

'We don't. Amarilla, let me speak,' she said, raising her voice slightly as I opened my mouth to protest. 'The same thought has occurred to others over the years, believe me, but The New communities have always been advised to leave the horses to take their own chances.'

'Who by? Who thinks we should just leave the horses to be slaughtered?'

'They do. Amarilla, it is the horses who have always counselled us not to interfere, to live our lives and to allow them to live theirs with no interference. The horses know everything we think. They know everything we feel. If there is even the beginning of an idea in any of our communities to hunt the Woeful, one of the Horse-Bonded always appears and advises that the horses ask the humans not to proceed. They council that to hunt the Woeful would do untold damage, not only to those poor creatures themselves, but to us as human beings. They applaud the huge leaps we have made to evolve and live a different way from those of The Old and they are adamant that all would be put at risk were we to harm the Woeful. I'm sure you of all people will respect the advice of the horses.'

'Of course, it's just that...' I didn't know what I wanted to say.

Nerys said, 'You fear for your horse, I know. But trust her. Horses have a highly evolved flight instinct and are extremely fast when they need to be. The Woeful may be strong and able climbers, but once on the ground, they aren't much faster than you or I. The odds are in the favour of the horses. Try and remember that. Amarilla?'

I sighed. 'Okay. What do I need to know in order to be allowed out of the village on my own?'

'You will need to learn to be aware when you are being watched. If a

Woeful comes across you, it will stalk you for a while before leaving the safety of the branches. The Woeful will not accost you unless they are sure you have something they want, and to this end, they tend to observe for some time. They stare, much as a cat does when stalking its prey. We all have the ability to sense when someone or something is directing its energy in a focused way towards us; we experience an uncomfortable, vulnerable feeling and very often the hairs on the back of the neck will stand up.

'I will ask certain members of the village to stalk you over the days to come. If you become aware at any time of someone focusing on you, you are to treat it as if one of the Woeful is actually stalking you. You will put down on the ground anything you are carrying and leave it there, and you will run to the nearest building and tell an adult what has happened. Do you understand?'

'Yes, but why do I need to put my things on the ground?'

'From all our experience, we can be reasonably sure that the Woeful will not attack your person to cause you harm intentionally. That is not to say that you would be sure to escape injury should you try to hold on to something they want, however, as those talons of theirs are extremely sharp. Your first thought once you realise you are being watched MUST be to release anything in your possession. Until you have proved you will do this, you won't pass the test.'

When I arrived home later that day, I was still feeling shaken. My mother immediately rushed up to me to tell me how pale I was and ask if I was sickening for a cold.

'I know about the Woeful, Mum,' I told her. She gave me a long hug and sat me down with a mug of warm milk as she used to when I was little, then for once, she let me be.

As I lay down to rest for the night, I pictured my horse easily and my weariness from the emotion of the day started to recede. In my mind I saw her lying down, surrounded by the first fallen leaves of early autumn. The rest of her herd lay around her, but one who kept watch. She rested her soft, pink muzzle in the grass and each time she breathed out, the surrounding blades of grass flattened slightly as her warm breath passed over them. Her eyelids rested but weren't completely closed and from time to time, she would twitch and lift her head slightly before sinking her nose back down into the grass and the leaves. Peace. It oozed from her, surrounded her, was her. I found it too.

FIVE

Tugged

Over the following week, three people, including my sister Katonia, told me that they'd stalked me, to no avail. One of my stalkers reported seeing me rub the back of my neck a few times and Katonia said that when she saw me hesitate in my tracks for a few seconds, she was sure I had sensed her, but clearly, I hadn't been aware enough of their focus on me for me to consciously register what was happening.

The next stalking was more successful, however, and this time Uncle Jodral was the perpetrator. I left my house after dinner one evening to go to see Cherrie, a friend who lived at the far end of the village, and as soon as I left the house I felt uncomfortable. I couldn't stop myself looking down to check that I was wearing clothes, as curiously, I felt naked. Seeing that my shirt, leggings and boots were still in place, I shivered and started my walk to Cherrie's house. The feeling didn't leave and I felt more and more uncomfortable. A few minutes later, the hairs on the back of my neck stood up and realisation dawned. Remembering Nerys's instructions, I put the cake I was carrying for Cherrie's mother on the ground and ran to the nearest cottage, which happened to be the chandlery. I banged on the door.

'Amarilla, what a lovely surprise, are you alright? You look rather unnerved,' said the Chandler on opening the door.

'Miss Matti, sorry to bother you, but I know someone is stalking me and yours was the nearest door to knock on.'

Miss Matti stepped out on to the door step and called out, 'Jodral, you can come out, your work here is done.' She said to me, 'That saves me a job in the morning, I was going to stalk you as you left for your studies. I'm relieved I won't be needed, I've never been good at moving around quietly, all that hopping from house to house while staying focused on the subject, it's really not very easy.'

Uncle Jodral reached my side. 'Well done, Am, that was less than five minutes. I bet next time you'll know straight away and then you'll be up to the level of awareness needed to pass the test. Miss Matti, what's wrong?'

Miss Matti had put both hands up to cover her face. 'Oh, me and my mouth, I've just revealed to Amarilla that I was meant to be the next to stalk her, in the morning. What now? Nerys will think I did it on purpose, she knows I hate doing it, last time I walked into the corner of the Miller's cottage and gave myself a nose bleed.'

'No one is going to tell Nerys, are we, Am? You'll just have a headache in the morning and be unable to do your stint, and Amarilla will pass her test once the next person stalks her. Now don't think on it again, okay?' he said.

Miss Matti nodded and retreated back into her cottage, closing the door softly behind her. My uncle and I walked back to the cobbled road and I retrieved my cake. We allowed ourselves to laugh.

'Well at least you know you're safe in the morning, Am,' said Uncle Jodral, 'but you will be stalked again at some point. Remember how you felt when it was me stalking you, and next time you should pass.'

I left Cherrie's house just as it was getting dark, this time carrying a bottle of home-brewed cider for my parents from Cherrie's father. Seconds after

I had started my walk up the road, I felt it – that naked, vulnerable feeling. Immediately, I put the bottle on the ground and ran back to Cherrie's house. Her mother answered the door and after I had explained why I was back, she called out to whoever was stalking me. No one answered. The night was still. Cherrie's father joined her and loudly repeated her request for the stalker to show himself. Still no one answered. I saw Cherrie's parents look at each other questioningly as the darkness fell.

'Amarilla, I think you'd better come back inside,' Cherrie's father said.

Just as I made to step into the house, I heard a rustle behind me and then someone grabbed my shoulder and shouted, 'BOO!'

I screamed, my heart pounding as Robbie's laughter rang out behind me.

Cherrie's mother said, 'Robbie Nixon, really. At some point you will have to grow up and realise that your childish pranks are no longer funny. What are you now, twenty-one? You nearly frightened your sister to death, not to mention me and Gray. And you an Earth-Singer too, the sooner you find a nice girl to settle you down, the better for all of us.'

'Mrs Blake, does this mean I've passed the test?' I said.

Cherrie's mother asked Robbie, 'Well? How soon did she sense you?'

'Wait until I tell Con,' he gasped. 'Straight away, Mrs Blake, she's definitely got it. So, Am, how lucky are you that I was able to fill in tonight? Uncle Jod came round and told us of Miss Matti's slip up, so I volunteered to stalk you tonight so you could pass the test and she wouldn't be in hot water with Nerys tomorrow for missing her stint. And of course you passed once I took a turn, how could you not.'

'I can't believe my luck, Rob,' I said drily.

The next couple of years saw me happily immersed in my studies, although a part of me was always on alert in case my horse tugged me. My herb journal was slowly filled with the names of herbs which would ease many of the ailments listed, and I kept detailed notes regarding which part of the herb I felt would be most potent to use, dosage and methods of storage.

I thoroughly enjoyed being present during Nerys's consultations with patients. To begin with, I merely observed how she proceeded during a consultation, and used my senses to practise tuning in with the different complaints. Then, when I left the room so that Nerys could prescribe the necessary herbs without me being able to hear, I would leaf through my herb journal and mark a page to remind myself of yet another ailment I would be able to create with my mind and on which I could work.

As time went on, Nerys allowed me to consult with the patient while she stayed in the background and observed. By then, I was easily able to sense the condition that was causing a problem and increasingly, I knew which herb or herbs I could prescribe. Dosage wasn't difficult, but needed to be overseen by Nerys to ensure that the patient's treatment was sound and of maximum benefit.

Much as I enjoyed being able to work with patients to help them feel more comfortable, the part I loved most about my apprenticeship was venturing out by myself in search of new herbs with which to work. I loved the anticipation of tuning into a herb that was new to my senses, feeling around with my mind until I was sure I had a grasp of its vibration, then deciding on which ailments I would test it first. And the thrill I felt when I knew I had matched a herb with the condition it would ease, was addictive.

It was to this end that I found myself out in the woods on one of my herb-collecting forays, one early autumn morning. The chill of the season crept insidiously through the dense woodland but I was dressed for it in warm, brown leggings over woollen tights, wool-lined leather boots, a green shirt and a thick, green woollen pullover. I carried my basket, which contained my herb dictionary, my lunch and my waxed cloak in case it should rain.

I cursed as I fought my way through dense undergrowth, but I felt my excitement rising as I spotted a plant that I hadn't seen before. I felt slightly guilty as I trampled the plants around the one that had captured my interest, then spread my cloak, waxed side down and knelt on it, ready to tune in to the new herb.

I cleared my mind and allowed my senses and then my awareness to penetrate the tiny-leafed plant. I easily sensed its vibration and was just considering on which ailment to test it first, when I felt something else. Something was pulling my mind away from the herb and in a different direction entirely. Strange. I tried to pull my awareness back to myself with the intent of redirecting it wholly back to the herb, but found that I couldn't, completely. Whatever had caught at me had no intention of letting go. I relaxed my attention from the herb. Immediately, my mind was pulled so strongly that I felt it was being pulled loose from my body. I was so shocked that I rolled off my heels and sat down firmly on my bottom, trembling.

It was as I tried in vain to get control over my mind, to pull it all back to join the part of it that was anchored in my body, that I registered the gentle warmth, the love, peace and wisdom that was my mare. The sense of her that had always been at the edge of my mind, untouchable, unreachable, but always there, was now in my mind with me. She filled all my senses as she touched, no, melded my mind with hers and pulled it towards herself.

A vague part of me registered that I was being tugged; my mare was calling for me as I had waited so long for her to do! I stood up and began to run to catch up with my mind as I felt it stretch out, ever thinner, between my body and hers. The undergrowth snagged at me, but I paid it no heed and blundered on until eventually, I emerged from it into the more densely growing trees. Here, there was less undergrowth and my path was easier. I ran for all I was worth.

It was a strange sensation, to be running full pelt through the woodland with only a tiny part of my mind belonging to my body and registering what was happening. The rest of my mind was with her. Nothing had any relevance in my life any more except finding her. I ran until my lungs heaved and I had to lean on a tree to regain my breath. Then I was off again, running towards her, running, running, running.

At some point, the tiny part of my mind that still looked after my body realised that it was getting dark and that hunger pains gnawed at my stomach. I was exhausted, but still I wanted to carry on; my body could recover once I had found her. Everything would be alright once I had found her. By now, I had reached open countryside and the moon was bright in the night sky. I continued, but slowed to a walk as my body began to protest more strongly. At some point, I must have dropped down, exhausted, and fallen asleep.

I woke up the following day with the sun high in the sky. I was as cold and damp as the scrub in which I was lying and I cursed myself for sleeping so long. I had no idea where I was and I didn't care. Within minutes, I was up and running again, following my mind to my horse. Every now and then, I thought I felt her pushing at me slightly and my mind seemed to contract as it bounced back to me. But I flung myself straight back to her and forced my body to try to keep up.

I was vaguely aware that my body was now extremely hungry and thirsty. I was stumbling a lot and twice I fell headlong, landing once on my hands and knees and once on my chin. The blood from my chin dribbled down my neck and dried to a crust, but still I pushed my body to carry on. At one point, I reached a stream and fell down on my knees to drink until my thirst was slaked. Then I carried on.

As luck would have it, I collapsed next to some brambles that night and ate my fill of their ripe, bursting berries, my mind still full of my horse. I could feel that she, too, crossed open country and for the first time in her life, she was alone. She missed her mother and her herd, but she was intent on finding me. Her body wasn't hungry or thirsty, so I immersed myself even more fully in her as I tried harder and harder to ignore the protests of my own body. She was concerned about something and again, I thought I felt her push at my mind. I fell asleep and dreamt of her resting peacefully under some trees.

I don't remember much about the next few days, apart from feeling an urge to run, but being mostly reduced to a stumbling walk. I must have come across more streams from time to time, as I remember drinking. I pulled fruit from trees and ate as I lurched my way towards where I knew my mare was, but it wasn't enough. As the sun made its way down behind the hills in front of me one evening, my legs gave in. I landed in a heap in some long, reedy grass and was unable to make my body get back up. My head was spinning and my vision kept coming in and out of focus. My hunger pains were intolerable, my chin throbbed and the skin on my knees and on the palms of my hands was shredded. And still I was desperate to continue.

I had felt my mare's concern increase over the past few days and she had kept pushing at me with what felt like increasing determination, which I found hurtful and confusing. I was sure that if I could just reach her, everything would be explained and it would be alright. At the present moment she was frantic. What was wrong? Was she ill? Was she lost? No, she couldn't be lost, she just had to keep heading towards me. What could it be? I howled and cried with worry and frustration. This wasn't anything like how I had imagined going to find my horse. I must have passed out.

My next memory was of waking and being aware how cold I was. I couldn't feel my arms and legs and when I tried to lick my lips, they cracked. Immediately in front of my eyes there were long stalks of grass and... legs. Six of them. How strange. Did I know of any six-legged animals? No, I didn't think so. Two of the legs wore black leather boots with buckles at the ankle and four of them were black and hairy. I came to a little more. My mare. I had to get to my mare. I tried to move my mouth to tell the legs how important it was that I get up and start walking again, but nothing came out. Just as I was losing consciousness again, I felt arms underneath my body and then I was lifted, carried and put down heavily on my front, across something warm and hairy. I sank down into the warmth, my arms and legs dangling, and let the blackness take me.

The next time I regained consciousness, I was still draped across the back of what I decided had to be an animal. I had black hair brushing against my mouth and I could see a black, hairy belly hanging down in front of my eyes and my feet were on the other side of it. We were moving, I decided, as my hanging arms and legs swayed from side to side. Something warm and heavy covered my back. Most of my mind was now anchored back in my body and it felt as if my mare were leaning against it somehow, holding it there. She felt calmer now but her concern remained. I was being carried towards her and I was warm. As that thought took hold and comforted me, I once again let go of conscious thought and sank into oblivion.

Some time later, I found that I was stationary and lying on my back.

My vision wouldn't focus properly but I thought I could make out branches above my head and I definitely smelt the moist, earthy smell of the forest, combined with the smell of smoke from a fire that crackled near my feet. Someone cupped my head in a hand and lifted it, and warm soup touched my lips. I opened my mouth and savoured the taste of onion soup.

'That's it, slowly,' a female voice said kindly. 'You don't want to burn your mouth, you're in enough of a state as it is.'

I sipped slowly, although my every fibre wanted to gulp it down. Once I had finished, my head was gently lowered back down to the ground and I slept once more. I dreamt of my piebald mare cantering along the side of a grassy hill in the moonlight. Her long, white, wavy mane lifted and dropped as she flew gracefully through the night, and every hair on her body reflected the silvery light of the moon. She was calm, focused and very determined.

I stirred as one particular member of the dawn chorus, a crow I think, cawed from the branches above my head. As I drifted back to sleep, I dreamt that my mare was drinking thirstily from a fast-flowing, shallow river. She was aware of me and lifted her head, ears pricked as water dripped from her muzzle. I reached towards her with all of my being, but she blocked me and pushed me back, allowing only the smallest thread of my mind to stay with her. Hurt and confused, I nevertheless relished my contact with her. I felt as if everything would always be alright if I were with her. I needed to be with her, that was it, I needed to travel to where she was, without delay. I came awake with a start and sat up, feeling dizzy.

'Want some more soup?'

I looked up and my eyes almost focused on a figure sitting across the fire from me. She was stirring a pot of what smelt like the same soup that I had been fed the day before.

'Yes please. Thank you for helping me. More soup and then I have to go and find my horse, I'm being tugged,' I said.

'First things first, get some of this down you.' She handed me a bowl of steaming soup. I tried to look up at her to smile my thanks, but found that all of my effort was needed to take the bowl and spoon from her. I recognised her black boots with the buckles at the ankles and my mind returned to the day before.

'There were six legs,' I said, 'and only two of them were yours. Who do the other four legs belong to?'

'They belong to Oak. And magnificent legs they are too, don't you think?'

I nodded dimly, not really taking in what she had said. I decided to concentrate on getting each spoonful of soup to my mouth without spilling any. After I had finished the last spoonful, a hand with some bread appeared in front of me. I took the bread and began to eat, wondering if I was really awake and eating, or whether I had passed out again. It wasn't long before I found out, as I was briefly aware of the bread falling from my hand before I fell out of the conscious world yet again.

I don't know how long I was left to sleep before I was gently shaken awake.

'Do you think you could sit up and ride in front of me if I hold you?' asked my rescuer.

'Ride? Um, I can try,' I said, fighting to keep my eyes open as they tried to close.

'Oak will lie down to make it easier for you to get on his back.' Hands appeared under my arms and heaved me up onto my feet. 'Right, step astride him and then sit down slowly and gently onto his back. That's it, now Oak is going to stand up. Hold onto his mane and lean forward, I've got you.' One arm appeared around my waist and held on tightly and another reached past me and held on to a chunk of mane. There was a lurching sensation. 'Well done, Oak. Are you ready?' she said into my left ear.

How long we rode I have no idea, I just focused on trying to stay upright and awake whilst sensing what my mare was doing. She had lain down to rest for a while and had then spent some considerable time grazing. Now she was on the move again at a steady trot along a muddy track. The same calm determination drove her onwards and the comfort I felt at knowing that we steadily approached one another was immeasurable.

We stopped for lunch at the edge of a stream and I was helped down from Oak's back to sit at the water's edge. I leant forward and cupped water in my hands, splashing it onto my face and rubbing it into my eyes in an effort to fully open them. The palms of my hands felt as if they were on fire and I was shocked at the sight of the red water that ran back to the stream.

'It's just from your hands and your chin, nothing serious,' I was informed. 'I bet it hurts like mad though, you'll have to wait until we get to Coolridge to get cleaned up properly.'

Some bread and a large chunk of cheese appeared in front of me. 'Thank you,' I said. 'Where's Coolridge?'

'About five miles north from here. We'll be there later today. Oak is having to go more slowly than usual with two of us to carry.'

Once I'd eaten, I was again hauled to my feet and led to where Oak lay down to enable me to mount. As he lurched once more to his feet with me on board, I had my first proper look at my rescuer as she held firm to my leg to support me. Taller than I, she was dressed all in black, complete with a hooded black cloak. She had her hood up but I caught sight of black hair around her pale face, before she swung herself up behind me.

I was lulled into a doze by Oak's movement and the warmth emanating from his broad back beneath me. My mare also rested, although not as peacefully as did I. She felt vulnerable and came to full alert at every sound, and I worried for her. Once more, I tried to reach to her with more of myself and once more I was pushed back.

I was prodded to wakefulness by a finger in the ribs. 'Wake up now, we're here,' said my rescuer, and she disappeared from behind me. I was helped down from Oak's back and managed to land on my feet. I put my hand to his side.

'Thank you, Oak.' I rubbed my hand over his fur and put my heart into my words. 'Thank you.'

'He says you and your horse are very welcome and he hopes you find a way to control your mind. Your horse has been struggling to keep you in one piece,' the woman said from behind me.

Shocked, I spun around to face her and then staggered back to lean against the ever tolerant Oak. 'What does Oak know about my horse?'

'He knows that she's okay, she's on her way to find you and is taking good care of herself. Unlike you. She felt you lose your mind soon after she tugged you and she's been frantic. She asked Oak to help you as she was still some distance away and Oak was the closest bonded horse. He told me we were needed, so we came to find you. The rest, I'm hoping you'll tell me once you've had a decent meal and a good night's sleep.'

With a snap, my world came back into focus. 'You're Horse-Bonded and Oak is your horse,' I said solemnly.

The black eyes in the pale face smiled along with her mouth. 'Thanks for telling me, I'd never have known. Welcome back to the land of the living, I'm Rowena.'

SIX

Meetings

*R*owena left Oak standing in the road and helped me through a wooden front gate and up a neatly cobbled path to a stone cottage, very similar to those of my own village.

As we approached the front door, it was flung open and an elderly man beckoned us in to a small living room. On one of the walls there was a mural, depicting a man of middle years sitting down in a summer meadow with his legs crossed out in front of him. He leant back against the brown and white horse lying down behind him. The mural was so infused with emotion that I could feel the depth of feeling that existed between its subjects as if I were one of them.

'Come in, come in,' said the man. 'Rowena, sit her down over there by the fire, that's it, you rest there, my dear, while I prepare a nice hot bath for you and then you can get yourself cleaned up.'

The man left the room and Rowena went back out to Oak, telling me over her shoulder that she would see him to his paddock and then be back.

I relaxed into my chair and for the first time registered my appearance. I was mortified. My leggings had large holes at both knees, and they were covered in slits and pulls, almost to the point of indecency. My pullover was likewise hanging on me in shreds and was filthy. A wide streak of dried brown blood ran down the centre, presumably having originated from my chin. I still had both boots on, which I considered a miracle, but there were deep gashes in the leather through which the wool lining was hanging. My hands had brown dirt ingrained into them and the palms were covered in lacerations which were trying to heal, and were at present expelling a nasty-smelling pus. It dawned on me that was likely not the only part of me that smelt; after days of running, sleeping rough and not washing, I must really pong. My embarrassment grew. What had I been thinking? My horse. I had been trying to get to my horse.

I knew that she was getting closer all the time and I felt her weariness. I didn't try to push myself towards her again as I knew she'd push me back, but as I sat and thought of her and sensed how she felt, I realised I didn't need to push towards her anyway; the edge of my mind now seemed to be melded with hers and I could know everything I needed to just from being aware of that part of our minds that we shared.

The man re-entered the room and handed me a towel. 'Right, my dear, up you get, there's a nice hot bath waiting for you upstairs and I've a stew on that should be ready by the time you've finished. I'm Adam, by the way.'

I got to my feet, holding the towel in front of me in an attempt to preserve my modesty. I shook his gnarled hand gingerly, trying to keep my palm cupped so I wouldn't have to press my sore palm against his. 'Thank you, you're really kind,' I said. 'I'm Amarilla and I'm on my way to find my horse.'

'I know you are and it sounds as if you got yourself in a bit of a pickle, but never mind that now, you go and get cleaned up and then I'll get Ro to bring you up some of my special stew before you get your head down. Have a good night's rest and then you can tell us all about it in the morning. Come with me, just this way.'

He led me along a short, narrow hallway to some stairs. I could smell what had to be his special stew and my stomach gurgled noisily.

'Up the stairs there, first door on the left. That's it, up you go,' he said and went into the kitchen.

The bath was indeed hot and all my cuts and bruises announced themselves painfully anew as I lowered myself into the water. When I had finally managed to sink down into the warmth, I set about cleaning off days of accumulated grime. The water was brown by the time I had finished and the thought of donning my rags was repulsive to me now that I was clean. I didn't have the courage to call down to Adam or Rowena to ask them to provide me with any clean clothes, so I sat down on the bathroom floor wrapped in my towel, and leant back against the bath.

The next thing I knew, Rowena was kneeling beside me. 'Come on, sleepy,' she said, 'come and have something to eat and then you can sleep as long as you need to. Up you get.' She offered a hand and hauled me to my feet.

'I don't have any clothes, I'm really sorry, you came and found me and looked after me and you're forever having to lift me up because I'm always asleep, and now I don't have any clothes,' I told her in a shaky voice and then dissolved into tears.

Rowena put an arm around my shoulders and gave me a brief hug. 'Let's get you into your bed. Adam's left one of his old shirts there for you to wear and I'll sort out some proper clothes for you in the morning. What did happen to your stuff by the way? It's a shame you've lost all the gifts from your Quest Ceremony.'

'I didn't h-have a Quest Ceremony, I didn't br-bring any stuff,' I mumbled as I followed Rowena into a small bedroom and sat down on the bed. A large bowl of the promised stew steamed tantalisingly on the bedside table.

'Well that makes two of us, I didn't have one either, but at least I made sure I packed enough gear so I could look after myself. Why didn't you bring anything with you? Spare clothes and food, at least?'

The full implications of what I had done swamped me. The second I had been aware that my mare was tugging me, I had just left and followed my mind. I hadn't told my family and friends what had happened and where I was going – for all they knew, I was trapped somewhere and hurt, maybe even dead. I hadn't even remembered that they existed until a few moments ago. My tears flowed anew. 'I was in the w-w-w-woods looking for new h-herbs, when I was t-t-tugged, and I just g-got up and r-r-r-ran.'

Rowena was incredulous. 'You mean you didn't even tell anyone you were leaving? Oh, are you an orphan? Do you not have family? But even then, surely your friends would have wanted to know so they could give you a proper ceremony and everything, surely you have friends?'

I nodded and took a deep breath before answering. 'And family. I have parents, a sister and two brothers. I didn't think. I couldn't think. When my horse tugged me, most of my mind went to her and I just got up and ran after it, I felt as if I would lose it if I didn't, so I just ran and ran and I was hardly even aware of how cold and hungry and tired I was until I collapsed. And then you found me.' I looked down at my feet in shame.

'Phewee. That's not what normally happens when a horse tugs a human and it's not supposed to. No wonder your horse was beside herself. Eat your stew and then get into bed and when you come downstairs tomorrow, Adam and I will have figured out what to do. There's some salve on the bedside table to ease your cuts and stop them becoming infected. Amarilla,' she said and waited until I looked up to meet her dark eyes before continuing, 'it will be okay. Do you trust me?'

'Yes.'

'Then believe me when I tell you that it will be alright. Nothing has happened that can't be fixed, and you are among friends who will help you to fix it. Okay?'

I managed a weak smile. 'Thank you, Rowena.'

'See you in the morning.' She backed out of the room, pulling the door shut behind her.

The stew was delicious and as I lay down, clean and warm and with a comfortably full stomach, I let my awareness go to my horse. She too had grazed plentifully and was now sleeping standing up under a large oak tree with one hind leg resting. She was weary and had sore hands. No that was me. She was weary and had lacerated knees. Or was that me too? I twitched and flicked my tail as an owl hooted in the tree overhead. That was definitely her. I allowed her peace and contentment to fill me, and drifted off to sleep.

The sun had long been up when I woke the next morning. As I sat up in bed and rubbed my eyes, I realised that I was feeling completely normal again. There was a pile of clothes on the end of my bed and I leant forward to rifle through them. There was winter underwear, woollen tights, two pairs of leggings, both black, two undershirts, two white overshirts, a thick green pullover, a black wool-lined cloak and a pair of black leather boots with buckles at the ankles like Rowena's.

I dressed quickly in a pair of leggings, an overshirt and the pullover, all of which fitted me reasonably well and appeared to be brand new, I noticed with a grimace. How would I repay Rowena? I opened my bedroom door and stuck my head out. I could hear voices coming from downstairs and followed them to the kitchen, where I found Adam and Rowena sitting at the kitchen table, sipping greenmint tea.

'Good morning,' said Adam, 'you look better this morning, would you like some porridge?' He was already making his way to the stove where a pan sat half on and half off of the heat plate, keeping warm.

'Yes please, thank you, I slept really well. Thank you for everything, I'm so grateful.'

Rowena pushed a chair away from the table with a booted foot and beckoned me to sit on it. 'Come and have your breakfast. How's your horse this morning?'

I shifted my awareness from my immediate surroundings to the part of my mind I now shared with my horse. 'She's alright, she's walking through a forest and she's concentrating in case she senses anything amiss. She wishes she were out in the open. She doesn't want to have to try to move at speed because it won't be easy through the trees, but at least they're not too close. They're really big trees.'

'Big trees, hmmm, can she smell smoke?' asked Adam, putting a bowl of porridge with slices of apple on top in front of me.

I paused for a second. 'Yes, now you mention it, but it's very faint. I doubt I'd be able to smell it with my own nose but what she senses from her nose is different from what I sense with mine. I know its smoke she can smell but it's not how I would smell smoke.' I looked from Adam to Rowena. 'I'm not making much sense, am I?'

They both laughed. 'You're making complete sense,' said Rowena.

'The smoke smells more as if it's made up of lots of smells when you sense it from your mare doesn't it?'

'You know it's smoke, even though it's not how you smell smoke, and you have no idea how you know that it's smoke anyway,' said Adam and laughed. 'Now we're all talking nonsense together and yet we all know what we're talking about.'

'You're Horse-Bonded too, aren't you?' I asked Adam. His laughter died down and Rowena sat up straighter in her chair.

'I was,' he said. 'Peace died a few years back. Bonded for forty-one years we were, he tugged me when I was twenty-nine. I'll never stop missing him as long as I live, but I try not to think too hard about him, I don't want to disturb him where he is now.'

The mural in the living room came into my mind and I remembered the strength of feeling that emanated from it. 'That's you and Peace in the mural. I'm so sorry for your loss.'

'Don't be, there's no need. I count my blessings that he chose me to share his life. All he taught me, all he was, all we shared, is still with me constantly. I know he's fine where he is now, because he stayed with me for a bit after he left his body and he told me so. Once he knew I'd come to terms with it all and would be alright, he moved on. What's there to be sorry about?'

'He was beautiful,' I said.

'Yes, he was,' replied Adam. 'Now, back to your horse. Can she smell water at all?'

'Yes, she's aware of a large body of water. She's between it and where the smoke is coming from.'

'She's a day's ride away from here,' said Adam and looked at Rowena. 'She's in Tall Wood, the charcoal burners are at work there and Lake Charlton is at the far end.'

Rowena nodded and then said, 'Adam and I have been discussing your situation and we have a plan. But first I need to ask, are you able to keep your mind with you, or is your horse still having to hold you together? Oak let her know when we had found you and she told him that she'd managed to push you back to yourself while you were unconscious, but she didn't know if she'd be able to hold you together once you were awake again. It's an unnecessary burden you're placing on her if you're relying on her to keep your mind intact.'

'It's okay, I realised yesterday that there's part of my mind that is joined with part of hers and I just have to be aware of that part of my mind to know how she is, I don't have to try and reach her with all of myself. Not that that was what I did anyway when she tugged me, it just happened,' I replied.

'How do you know your horse is a mare?' asked Rowena. 'I didn't know anything about Oak until I met him, did you with Peace?' she asked Adam, at which he shook his head.

'I've known what she looked like and that she was female since I was seven,' I told them, 'and then four years ago I started to sense her as a sort of whisper that kept passing by my mind. A couple of years ago, I felt her change and realised I had a definite sense of her at the edge of my mind, but if I reached for her she moved further away. She wouldn't allow any contact. I dreamt of her though and I think I was seeing what she was actually doing. And then when she tugged me, I recognised it was her and my mind just flew to her, I couldn't stop it and I wouldn't have known how to try. So, I just followed it.'

There was a stunned silence. Adam had raised his mug to his mouth to take a sip of tea and then lowered it back down slowly as I spoke, staring at me all the while. Rowena was frowning slightly.

Eventually Adam said, 'I think you'd better tell us everything, from the beginning.'

Several hours, a bowl of porridge and numerous mugs of tea later, I finished my tale. Adam and Rowena were encouraging listeners and I felt completely at ease as I told them the story of my life so far. They asked the occasional question, but otherwise let me talk at my own pace until I was hoarse and had no more to tell.

'Well, it sounds to me as if you've spent a long time throwing as much of your attention and awareness after your horse as you could, but she managed to hold herself apart from you. When she tugged you, your mind flew down the path it had been trying to find for so long and you lost yourself. She must have wondered what on earth was happening,' said Adam.

'That's what she told Oak, she said you had lost your mind,' said Rowena. 'I didn't realise she meant literally. Bloody Nora what a tale, nothing's ever happened like this before, I wonder what it means?'

Adam said, 'I don't know, but I think Amarilla here's one to keep an eye on, she and that mare of hers. How old are you?' he asked me.

'Sixteen,' I said.

Rowena sat up straight in her chair. 'Sixteen? Honestly?'

'Yes, I know I'm young, it's why hardly anyone believed me when I told them my mare would tug me soon, but when I felt her change a few years ago I knew she wouldn't leave it very long, I don't know how I knew but I just did. How old are you?' I asked her.

'Twenty-three. Oak tugged me nearly three years ago and I was considered young,' she said.

'Well things are definitely changing. I sense interesting times ahead, but the horses will know what they're doing. I'm grateful to you both that somehow, I seem to be involved in it,' Adam said with a smile. 'Now, Amarilla, if you're in agreement, this is what Rowena and I think should happen. We, and the villagers that Rowena spoke to while you were asleep, would like to give you your Quest Ceremony this morning. After that, you will go to find your mare and with any luck you'll bump into her before the day is out.'

I opened my mouth to speak but Rowena held up her hand. 'Let Adam finish.'

'Rowena and Oak will leave when you do, and will travel to Rockwood to let your family know what has happened and that you are alright, then they will meet you at The Gathering. I, too, will travel to The Gathering so that when you and your horse arrive, I can continue your apprenticeship with you until I deem you qualified. If you have repeated the words you spoke at your Apprenticeship Ceremony accurately, and I have every reason to believe that you have, then you aren't breaking any of your promises to your Master. I'm sure Master Hicks will be relieved to learn that you will be taken on by another Master, that's me,' he put his hand to his heart, 'rather than waste all of your training. Being a qualified Herbalist will be of immense use to you and everyone else, as you'll discover once you reach The Gathering.'

I didn't know what to say. I looked from one to the other of them as they grinned at my confusion. I finally said, 'But none of the villagers here know me, I can't accept gifts from them, I feel bad enough that you've given me clothes that I can't pay you for. And what's The Gathering?'

Rowena grinned and rose to her feet. 'We'll leave your mare to fill you in on that, you may as well do one thing the way it's normally done, now here is a back-sack. You need to go and pack your clothes into it before your Quest Ceremony. The weather will hold for the next few weeks, according to the Weather-Singer I asked this morning, so you can pack your cloak, put it near the top though, you'll need it at night time. I'm just off to let everyone know your ceremony will start in an hour.'

I already liked Rowena a lot. She was a strange mix of older sister and mother; there was something about her that spoke of being used to organising and thinking for other people less capable than herself. She carried with her an air of melancholy though and I had a feeling that she probably had a temper. Her black clothing, her height, her black hair and eyes combined with her pale skin to give her an appearance of someone not to be trifled with and yet she had shown me nothing but kindness, and Adam clearly thought of her very fondly.

He was little taller than I, but of stocky build and had a ruddy complexion, telling of a life lived mostly outdoors. His white hair was thick, wavy and cut to his shoulders, and he had deep green eyes that spoke of an inner calm and self-assurance. He moved lithely for his age and the decor of his home spoke of a much younger person. I wondered if his youthful energy and outlook were as a result of having been Horse-Bonded.

I had known Adam for less than a day and Rowena for just a little longer, but I felt affection for both of them and looked forward to seeing them again once I had found my horse. My horse. She was so close now and I would meet her today. A tingle went down my spine and I found a new energy as I bounded up the stairs to pack my new belongings.

Over the next hour, the noise of people chattering excitedly below my bedroom window slowly increased in volume as a crowd gathered. I grew more and more nervous. By the time Rowena called up the stairs that it was time, I was pacing back and forth across my room. Was that a touch of concern I could feel from my mare? I tried to calm down so she wouldn't think anything was amiss. I took a deep breath, lifted my back-sack and went down the stairs. Rowena was nowhere to be seen, so I made my way along the hall to the front room and took one last glance at Adam and Peace in the mural on the wall.

As soon as I stepped out through the front door and onto the doorstep, cheering erupted. Rowena and Adam stood in front of me, smiling, and Rowena gestured to a pile of things laid out on a small table beside her. I could see a bow and some arrows for hunting, some blankets, a cooking pan with another, smaller one nestled inside it, and a plate, beaker, flask of water, cutlery and several knives. There was also an open bag of food which appeared to contain several loaves of bread, a large cheese, fruit and vegetables, and sealed packets of all different sizes.

'Adam and I are representing your family today, and we would like to give you your quest gifts,' Rowena said warmly, and then helped me to pack each item into my back-sack. I paused at a strange-looking blanket and she said, 'That's for your horse, I made it last night. It's to keep her warm and dry at night time. See, these buckles do up at her chest, these straps cross under her belly and do up at the side, and this layer makes it waterproof. I made one for Oak last winter as he hates the rain, absolutely hates it. I thought your mare might appreciate it. I had to guess size-wise, but from the sense of her that Oak gave me, I think it should fit.'

I couldn't find the words to express my gratitude to her, so I didn't try. I flung my arms around her and hugged her and hoped she understood. When I eventually let her go, she grinned at me and said, 'You're welcome. Go and find that mare of yours and I'll see you in a week or so.'

Adam opened his arms out to me and enveloped me in a warm hug. 'Good luck, Amarilla, find your horse, bond with her and cherish her. I'll be waiting for you at The Gathering.'

'Thank you both, so much, for everything,' I said. They nodded and smiled in unison, and Adam gestured for me to go and walk down the corridor the villagers had formed, leading out of the village.

Hundreds of smiling faces drew me away from Adam's cottage and I was overwhelmed as small coloured pieces of paper were thrown up in the air to land on me, along with small dried flowers.

'Good luck, Amarilla, take care,' 'All the best, dear,' 'Congratulations, Amarilla, find your horse soon,' and 'Stay safe, come back and see us with your horse some time,' were just some of the words of encouragement that I could make out from the calling strangers as I walked past them.

I heard a droning noise behind me and felt the pain recede from the gashes on my hands and knees. I looked down at my palms and saw that the lacerations had knitted together and now looked weeks old. I turned and saw a middle-aged, blond-haired woman walking behind me as she hummed. She smiled and indicated for me to carry on walking.

Little tiny horseshoes were hung on my clothes, my hair and my back-sack, so that by the time I reached the end of the human corridor, I was covered from head to toe in them. I turned and waved my thanks. 'Thank you, thank you! I hope to see you again.' I walked out of the village and was alone.

The warmth which the villagers had lavished on me persisted and I realised that all their good wishes had been captured by the charms that they had hung on me, and I really did take them all with me.

The cobbled street petered out soon after I passed the last houses and I found myself walking along a beaten track that wound its way up into the hills in front of me. I was following the sense of my mare in my mind and I shifted more of my awareness to her. She had left the woodland and she, too, was approaching hills. My excitement steadily grew. I had dreamt of her for nine years and in the next few hours, I would finally meet her!

When the sun reached its peak, I realised that I was hungry. I was walking alongside a stream that meandered down from the hills, and I decided to sit and eat some lunch whilst I had fresh water to drink. This was an improvement, I thought to myself as I sat on a boulder and munched a cheese sandwich; I was on the way to find my mare and, excited as I was, I was aware of my body's needs and I was looking after myself. At that, a feeling appeared in my mind that definitely didn't originate with me. Approval, that was it – my horse approved! I couldn't sit still any longer. I drank as much water from the stream as I could and then shouldered my back-sack and carried on my way, munching the remainder of my sandwich.

I'm coming, I thought to her and sensed her register my thought.

The afternoon was spent climbing and descending countless hills, some grassy, some forested and yet others that were covered in rocks and heather. By the time the sun was low on the horizon and I reached the top of yet another hill, my thigh and calf muscles were screaming. As I walked across the flat top of the hill and braced myself for yet another descent, I was aware that my mare was hungry and had stopped to graze.

Then I saw her. Not fifty metres down the slope grazed a piebald mare with a white mane and tail. She lifted her head to look at me with beautiful blue eyes.

You are here. The words appeared in my head and sounded like my own thoughts, except I knew I hadn't formed them.

She lowered her head and continued grazing. I stood and watched her for a few minutes, not really knowing what I should do. I sensed her contentment.

You're still grazing, I thought to her.

No reaction, other than a feeling of assent from her.

I've arrived, I've found you, why are you still grazing?

I am hungry.

Oh.

I didn't know what to do. This wasn't how I had imagined meeting my horse. I had dreamt that we would be thrilled to find each other, that we would share details of our lives, that she would tell me why she had chosen me, why I had been aware of her for so long, why she had tugged me when I was so young, what she planned to teach me, everything. Instead, she grazed on and ignored me.

I waited and I waited. I sat down, I stood back up. I unhooked all of the horseshoes from my clothes and my person, and stowed them carefully away in my back-sack. I took my pullover off. I put it back on again. I sat back down and still she grazed, still with that feeling of contentment.

The sun had gone down and it was nearly dark when my temper flared. My horse had filled my world for nine long years and I had lived my life preparing for the time when she would tug me. I had nearly killed myself trying to get to her and I had left all of my family and friends behind without so much as a word, all for her. And now she was ignoring me.

I got up, ready to explode. She lifted her head, still chewing, and watched me. I drew myself up to my full height and managed no more than two steps towards her before she spun around on her heels and sped off along the side of the hill for a short distance before spinning back around to face me, her neck arched, tail held high and nostrils flaring. I stood still and watched her, stunned. I sensed her fleeting feeling of fear, which turned to confusion and then, what was that, amusement? She found this funny?

'WHY ARE YOU IGNORING ME?' I yelled at her. 'DON'T YOU KNOW HOW FAR I HAVE COME, WHAT I'VE BEEN THROUGH, TO FIND YOU? AND THEN YOU JUST CARRY ON GRAZING AS IF I WASN'T HERE?'

She relaxed and lowered her head to graze once more.

You are here. I am here. Everything is as it should be, were the words I heard in my head. With them came a surge of love that wrapped itself around me. My anger disappeared instantly and try as I might, I couldn't find a reason to summon it back. She was right – I could feel it in the depths of my soul. Everything was as it should be.

SEVEN

Bonding

I woke the next morning with the dawn chorus. For the first few minutes, when the boundary between sleep and wakefulness was still hazy, I had no idea where I was. I was curled up on my right side, wrapped up tightly in my waxed cloak and my shoulder and head leant against something warm.

As I came to properly, I realised I was curled up next to my mare as she lay in the damp grass; I lay between her front and hind legs and my head and shoulder rested against her belly. She dozed still and I didn't want to disturb her, so I remained where I was and revelled in the warmth of her companionship.

Since her statement the previous evening, we had shared no more thoughts. I'd felt myself drawn into her way of seeing things and had realised that we were both hungry and weary, we had found each other and for now that was enough. I ate a simple meal whilst I could still just about see what I was doing, and then donned my spare leggings over the top of those that I was already wearing, put on an extra shirt and my pullover and wrapped myself up in my cloak before settling down to watch the dark mound that was my mare, as she grazed.

She grazed well into the night but eventually wandered over to where I sat, sniffed the top of my head and then rested her muzzle there gently, her warm breath creating clouds of mist that hung around my face. I raised a hand gingerly and stroked the side of her soft nose as she breathed the long, slow breaths of a horse at rest. After a short while she lay down with a grunt behind me. I shuffled back towards her and then as I grew sleepy, nestled down to sleep, feeling just about as content as I could remember.

As the dawn chorus now dispersed, my mare moved her head and let out a deep, long sigh. *Getting up,* she warned me and gave me time to stand before heaving herself to her feet. As she turned away from me to graze, I noticed her right side was damp from lying in the grass.

I have a blanket to keep you dry at night, it's in my sack. I'm sorry I didn't think to offer it to you last night, I told her.

She continued to graze but a feeling of *?????????* appeared in my mind.

It covers your body and will keep you warm and dry. Oak has one because he hates the rain. He is the horse you asked to help me.

I too dislike the rain. I like it even less when the wind blows, she told me.

I would have liked some porridge, but I couldn't see any wood around for a fire and I remembered that I'd used up all my water, so I settled on some fruit. I ate a generous helping of blackberries, raspberries and cherries, and three small red apples. I offered my horse the apple cores and she sniffed them and then took them appreciatively.

I removed the extra layers of clothing that I'd donned for the night and repacked my back-sack. That done, I was ready to move on, but I sensed my horse's need to graze for longer, so I moved nearer to where she now picked at the grass, and perched on a conveniently placed boulder. A few hours later, she had grazed her way across the length of the hill with me shadowing her, and her immediate hunger was abating.

We should move on, she informed me.

Where will we go?

The other bonded horses call it The Gathering. That is what their humans call it.

What's The Gathering? Rowena said you would tell me, Rowena is the person bonded to Oak.

It is a place where humans who are bonded to horses go to meet and learn from each other.

What will I learn there that you can't teach me?

There was a pause. *Oak says you will learn how to fit my saddle so I am comfortable when you ride me. You will learn how to look after it as well as how to take care of all my other needs. Though I can tell you that.* There was an air of haughtiness as those words came into my mind and she wrinkled the skin to the side of her nostrils. *You will learn to ride me as well. I will learn to carry you. Oak found that very strange to begin with.*

Why can't I hear you and Oak when you are communicating?

You can. You just do not.

Oh. I frowned to myself. *How will we find The Gathering? Can Oak tell you?*

He has no need. I can sense where there are a lot of bonded horses in one place.

Did you know Oak before you asked him to help me?

Not in the way humans talk of knowing each other. He was the closest bonded horse to where you were.

How did you know that?

I could feel where he was. I could feel where you were.

No, I meant how did you know he was the closest bonded horse? How can you tell a bonded horse from one who isn't?

We are all part of the whole and horses can be aware of each other any time we choose. Those of us who bond to humans stand out from the others. The joining of minds with a human changes our essence enough that we can easily be sensed by each other as being different from an unbonded horse, her words spoke in my mind.

Not that they were her words though, were they? I thought to myself. They were my words in my head. I was picking up the essence of her thoughts and my mind was putting words to them, so that they became thoughts in a form that I could understand. I felt her agree with my conclusion.

And I do not understand your words but I understand the energy behind them. I know what you mean and how you feel. She started to walk purposefully and I walked alongside her, trying to keep up.

Why is Rowena's horse called Oak? Do you have a name?

It is up to Oak and his Bond-Partner whether they reveal why that name was chosen. We understand the human need for names. The tradition since the first bonded pair has been for the human to look into the essence of their horse and then choose the word or words that they think fit it best.

Can I do that for you? How would I do that?

We will stop a moment. You should sit down.

I did as I was told and immediately, a rush of awareness swamped me as she showed me herself, her very soul. She held nothing back. She was vast, a never-ending abundance of energy and consciousness. There was a sense of age and youth, wisdom and innocence, enormous knowledge and experience, and a sense of nurturing, limitless unconditional love. She filled the whole universe and more, she was infinite. Infinite. Infinity. That was who she was. Infinity.

She knew. As soon as the word entered my mind she was aware of it, or at least she was aware of what it meant to me as a human. I felt her approval.

I said out loud, 'Infinity. That's who you are.' I got back up to my feet and we began to walk once more. *What will you call me? Will you use the name my parents chose for me, or is it also customary for a horse to choose a name for her Bond-Partner?*

Walks A Straight Path.

What? We were twisting between trees.

Walks A Straight Path. That is who you are.

'WHAT?' I stopped, dropped my back-sack and put my hands on my hips. Infinity glanced back at me briefly but carried on walking. 'WHAT?' I yelled again as her white tail swung from side to side and moved steadily away from me. 'I CHOOSE "INFINITY" FOR YOU AND I GET "WALKS A STRAIGHT PATH"? YOU CAN'T BE SERIOUS.'

It seemed that she was and furthermore, she had no intention of stopping to wait while I yelled at her. I was forced to pick up my sack, swing it hastily over my shoulder and run awkwardly after her. 'Isn't there anything else that describes me better?' I asked as I caught up and slowed to walk next to her again.

No answer. I could feel that a small part of her was aware of keeping us moving towards The Gathering, a larger part was alert for the smell of water or anything that could spell danger, and the rest was the same feeling of contentment that I had first sensed in her as she had grazed the evening before. My outburst had affected her not at all.

'Walks A Straight Path,' I grumbled to myself, 'what's that supposed to mean, anyway.' I pictured a narrow, straight path leading away in front of me and realised that I'd far rather be walking on that than weaving in and out of trees, tripping on tree roots and brambles and having to be diverted by the dense, prickly bushes that occasionally blocked our way. I wanted to know where my destination was and then reach it with the minimum of interference, just as I'd lived the past nine years of my life; my goal had been to find my horse and be one of the Horse-Bonded and I had ignored anything that didn't aid me in achieving just that. I sighed. Her words described me exactly. It was how she thought of me and as I realised that, I decided I loved it. *Walks A Straight Path. Thank you, Infinity.*

Warm, nurturing energy emanated from her and wrapped itself around me.

We walked on for the next hour or so, with me mulling over our conversation and Infinity concentrating on her now more urgent quest to find water. She finally scented some as we left the woodland and began to walk across flat meadowland. It was directly in front of us, her nose told us, and we were both relieved when we finally reached a narrow stream. I stood back while she sniffed it and wrinkled her nose.

Sheep. They drink it and then they add to it. She waited until whatever it was that the sheep had added had flowed past her and then lowered her muzzle to drink. When she had finished, I approached with my flask. She sniffed the water again. *Clean,* she told me and then stepped over the stream and began to graze on the other side.

Thank you.

??????????

For checking the water for me.

?????

I was beginning to realise how different horses and humans were. My human manners and social customs mattered little to Infinity and my tantrums even less. I had an insatiable appetite for learning and conversation, whereas she apparently had the knowledge of ages and showed no immediate desire to add to it. Maybe she had all the answers she would ever need.

Not all the answers.

Is there anything you want to know about me?

I know you as I know myself. I knew you before you were yourself and you knew me. You forget now that you are in your human body. I do not.

I was confused. She knew me before I was myself? I knew her? But I had known her. As soon as I had understood the idea of the Horse-Bonded as a seven-year-old child, her image had flashed into my mind.

How old are you? I asked her.

By way of an answer, Infinity showed me herself trying to stand on wobbly legs as her mother cleaned her glistening, newly-born body. They were near a river which ran low in its banks and they were surrounded by lush grass, dotted plentifully with flowering meadow herbs. The sun was hot and high in the sky. She was born in the middle of summer. She showed me four more summers and then herself with me in the early Autumn. She had seen four more summers since her birth. I had first begun to sense her as a fleeting whisper beyond the edges of my mind when I was twelve. Four years ago.

I began to sense you once you were born, I affirmed to myself as much as to Infinity. But why had I known what she would look like before that and what had changed two years ago, when I had begun to be aware of her in such a more definite way? I wondered.

You were more aware of me once I reached the age where my concerns passed beyond merely how to use my body and be a horse. My attention began to turn towards my purpose in this life. Towards you. You sensed me as I sought for you but the time was not right for either of us then.

But I knew what you would look like even before you were born. How is that possible?

When your mind was awakened to the idea of a human bonding to a horse your soul spoke to you of our agreement. Of me.

Our agreement? What agreement? When did we make an agreement?

The last time we were here together.

I don't understand.

I know. I will show you. She showed me a tall, dapple-grey mare being ridden by a thin man of about forty, brown-haired with blue eyes and pale, blotchy skin. It was Infinity and me. I was seeing two beings who bore no physical resemblance to either of us, but I knew who they were as surely as I recognised my own face in the mirror.

The man was dressed in cream-coloured leggings with black, knee-length boots and a green jacket with a matching peaked hat. He had a sword hanging from the left side of his belt. There were other horses, all ridden by men dressed in an identical fashion. They were walking next to each other in a long line. The mare was as underweight as the man was thin, and there was an air of incredible sadness about them both.

The man on the horse next to them had three stripes on the arm of his jacket. He shouted, and all of the men drew their swords and raised them, points in the air, before urging their horses forward to a gallop. I could hear the bangs that subsequently erupted, as if I were actually there. Horses and men went down screaming, Infinity and I among them. The brown-haired man and his grey horse were both shot in the chest and lay dying together. As they died, they relaxed, relieved to be going. The horse left her body first and waited for the man to join her. It wasn't long before he did.

Next time, he told her.

Next time, she agreed and they left it all behind.

I blinked as my present surroundings came back into focus. I shook my head from side to side slowly, frowning as I tried to grasp what it all meant. I had recognised Infinity and myself even though we didn't look anything like our present selves, I wasn't even the same gender for goodness' sake. We had lived different lives and had died together, yet here we both were, alive, together again. How was that possible? Infinity stopped grazing and looked at me. And I remembered.

I had been a government advisor when war threatened to break out. I knew a way to reach a peaceful solution to the troubles my government was facing, without the need for any fighting, but those I advised were driven by fear and I couldn't get them to listen to me. When I refused to obey orders to remain silent about my ideas once war broke out, I was sent to the front line. I was sensitive and the avalanche of human terror and pain there overwhelmed me. I was close to insanity by the time I was led to the stall of a tall grey mare one morning and told that I was to ride in the cavalry. I was handed a brush and told to groom my new charge. As soon as I entered her stall, I was enveloped by a nurturing, limitless love that I now recognised as Infinity. The noise of the other men and horses disappeared, blocked out by the love of my horse. For the first time since arriving at the front, I felt safe and calm.

The emotions I felt in that lifetime were real to me again and tears poured down my cheeks. Infinity sent her energy to twine itself around me, comforting me as she felt my pain.

You told me that as long as I kept my mind with yours, I would be alright. You said I was before my time and you asked if I would help you to help humans and horses to evolve further in the future, when the time was right. You said that humans wouldn't be ready for a long time to come. We would need to agree to find each other again when the time was right, in different bodies, different lives. I didn't even need to think about it before I agreed. It was the thought of our agreement and the delight of my bond with you that made the last few months of my life bearable, as we trained together to fight in the cavalry. We died in our first charge, thank goodness. I couldn't have killed anybody and neither could you.

I felt her brief agreement.

It still doesn't explain how I knew what you'd look like this time though, you were a dapple-grey last time, and taller.

I am aware of all of my incarnations. I knew what my appearance would be in this one and I showed you in the same way I showed you our last incarnations together just now. It was one of the things on which I taught you to focus so that you could block out everything you could feel from the other men. Your soul remembered it well.

You know what your future lives will be? How can you when they haven't happened yet?

Time in a linear form is a fabrication of the human mind. You think of events happening one after the other. Accept that they are amassed on top of one another and occur simultaneously. When your mind is less restricted you will be aware of this.

Why is my mind restricted?

A good question.

Is it because I'm human?

That has always been the excuse thus far.

I sensed that Infinity wanted to be left to graze in peace now. I had collected some dry twigs and sticks during our walk through the forest, storing them in an improvised sack made by knotting my cloak together at the corners, so I decided to get a fire going and make myself some porridge and some tea while I attempted to make sense of everything I had just learnt.

Hours later, Infinity finished grazing and was ready to move on. It was going to take a while to get to The Gathering at this pace, I thought to myself as I scattered the remains of my fire and shouldered my back-sack; Infinity wasn't able to move at the speed that she would have done alone due to my relatively slow walking pace and I was restricted from walking for as long as I would have done by myself, due to her need to graze for hours on end.

All is as it should be. Her contentment eased my concern. We were spending time on our own, I realised, getting to know each other's thoughts and habits, and, well, bonding.

All is as it should be, I confirmed to her and put my hand to rest on her shoulder as we continued on our journey.

As we passed through an area of sparse woodland, an injured rabbit stumbled across our path. I quickly caught and dispatched it, and I wanted to stop and cook it while sticks were in abundance to make a fire. Infinity expressed a strong reluctance to stop and rest among so many trees, however, and I realised that whenever we passed through woodland, I felt an increased sense of alertness from her. Of course. The Woeful. I collected sticks into my cloak without complaint and we walked on until we reached the banks of a large lake, where Infinity was comfortable to stop for the night.

I set about making a fire and skinning my rabbit while Infinity grazed nearby. I blessed the rabbit as I worked, thanking it for providing me with sustenance at such cost to itself, as my parents had taught me.

No need, Infinity interrupted my ritual.

????????

The rabbit was injured. He had lived his life and it was his time to go. He chose you to help him and you did.

He chose me?

Did you think it luck that he appeared in front of you when he could easily have hidden?

Does that mean he was actually happy for me to eat him?

You will not be eating him. You will be eating the body he left behind. He moved on quickly and now considers whether he will take the form of a rabbit in his next existence here.

I dropped the stick I had just been about to add to the fire. *You mean rabbits can live more than one life too?*

My clear assumption that only humans and horses – the more advanced animals as I saw it – could reincarnate, was so ridiculous to Infinity and so, I sensed from her, typical of a human, that she had nothing to offer me by way of a reply.

I could feel my temper beginning to rise and tried to swallow it back down. I wasn't used to feeling so constantly stupid. At school I had excelled in the few subjects that had captured my interest and had been totally unconcerned by my failure in those that didn't. As an Apprentice Herbalist I had grown used to frequent approval of my natural ability. Feeling as if I knew nothing about anything was a new experience for me and I didn't like it one bit.

Infinity grazed peacefully, her attention now taken up fully by a sweet-smelling herb that she didn't come across very often, but liked very much. My hands were shaking with anger as I tried to skewer the skinned rabbit with a stick that I had cleaned and sharpened to a point.

The stick exited the carcass at the wrong place and went into my hand, which was the last straw. I flung it to the ground by the fire and stood up, hands on hips.

'LOOK, I KNOW I HAVE A LOT TO LEARN, THAT'S WHY I ASK YOU QUESTIONS,' I yelled.

Infinity flinched and then returned to her grazing, unaffected. Her lack of reaction gave me pause to think. I had always thought of myself as even-tempered and polite, and yet here I was, shouting at my horse for the third time since I first met her only the previous afternoon. What was happening to me? My mother flicked into my mind and suddenly I understood how infuriating I must have been for her to deal with. I had now come across someone who mattered very deeply to me and yet thought and behaved in a way that I didn't understand, and I responded by being overly emotional, in exactly the same way as had my mother with me. I wasn't going to carry on like this, I decided.

Infinity was with me every step of the way as I thought through my behaviour, but she stayed quiet, giving me space to think. How would I have wanted my mother to respond to me? I pondered. I would have liked her to just listen to me and accept what I said, even if she didn't understand me or agree with me, I realised, finally. Acceptance. Was that it? I just needed to be able to accept new ways of thinking, of being, new ways of another being responding to me. Would that be enough?

We will do well together you and I, Infinity informed me.

I agreed happily and sat back down to cook my dinner.

EIGHT

Fear

$\mathcal{I}$ slept deeply that night. I dreamt that I rode Infinity in a cavalry charge while my mother stood on the sidelines, yelling that I should have listened to her and stayed at home. We pulled up sharply as a rabbit stepped calmly into our path. He told me that in his next life, he would take the form of a fish and he needed me to agree that it would be I who would catch and eat him. Then his head turned into that of Robbie, who yelled, 'GOTCHA,' before hopping back into his burrow, giggling.

When I woke the next morning, curled up once more in the safety and warmth afforded by Infinity's body, I felt refreshed and calm. I grinned as I remembered my dream and then felt a pang of remorse as Robbie and my mother came into my thoughts. I hoped Rowena had reached my family by now to let them know I was alright.

She has. She and Oak travel now towards The Gathering.

When will they be there? When will we be there?

I could feel Infinity trying to get a sense of time in the way I thought of it. She knew where she was going and she had a sense of how far away we were, but she didn't know how to fit that into my concept of hours and days; she lived entirely in the present. *They will get there when they get there as will we,* was the best she could offer me.

I yawned and then stood up. Infinity got to her feet shortly afterwards and flung each of her hind legs out behind her in turn, stretching her muscles. She wore the waterproof blanket Rowena had made for her and was very taken with it. I went to remove it, but was halted by her thoughts. *Not yet. I will wear it until the sun warms me.*

I smiled. My mare was quickly learning to enjoy having a human caring for her. *Is there anything else I can do for you?* I asked her.

I am uncomfortable and I itch. She had complete confidence that these issues would be addressed immediately. I had a sense of skin irritation behind both of her elbows, and found encrusted mud there, which I scraped off with my fingernails. I was drawn to her left hind leg, and scratched the exact spot where I could sense she would appreciate it. She lifted her head from the grass and her upper lip wiggled from side to side.

I cannot reach you, she told me.

I'm alright, I can scratch myself, I thought I reassured her. Immediately I felt her affront. She showed me images of herself with various members of her herd, engaging in mutual grooming. As the horses groomed each other by wiggling their top lips and biting gently on different parts of their partner's body, they solidified their bonds with each other, as well as reaffirming their relative positions in the pecking order.

When Infinity groomed with her dam, she was manoeuvred into the position which suited her mother's needs best, which was usually to work on the left side of her withers and then down the left side of her back. In return, her mother oozed with maternal affection, giving security and peace to Infinity as she was groomed down her own left side. A similar situation arose when she groomed with other older mares of her herd, in that she would go along with their preferred grooming patterns. When she groomed with other youngsters however, it was an opportunity to jockey for position in the herd as much as it was for mutual pleasure. With other fillies, Infinity was bossy and insistent and usually got her grooming partner to follow her lead in terms of where on each other's bodies they groomed, and for how long. With the colts, however, grooming sessions tended to be short and typically ended with squealing and kicking from Infinity as she found them slow to submit to her instructions.

I began to understand that grooming Infinity was going to be much more than just making sure her body was in good condition; it would help her bond to me as horse to human. *How about if I scratch your front leg?* I asked, anxious to make good my error. The sense of affront eased away and was replaced by contentment.

I moved to one of her front legs, knelt down and began to scratch with my nails. Immediately, Infinity's top lip started to wiggle on the top of my head. The harder I scratched, the harder she wiggled, and I began to giggle. I worked my way around her leg and then moved to kneel in front of her as I started on the other front leg.

My legs itch when my coat changes, she told me. Of course, I realised, she would be growing her winter coat.

Is there anywhere else that itches when your coat is changing? I asked her, noting that she didn't seem to be directing me to scratch various parts of her body in the physical, pushy way that she had done with the other young horses she had shown me.

You are not a horse. There is no need to treat you as one. She performed an inventory of her entire body and then gave me a sense that she would appreciate being scratched around the neckline of her rug. I stood up and began to scratch where Infinity had indicated and she started to wiggle her lip on my back and shoulders and then, as I scratched harder, she used her teeth.

'OUCH!' I yelled, rubbing my shoulder furiously. 'No teeth Infinity, my skin isn't tough like yours, you hurt me.'

Her shock at my shout was replaced immediately by understanding. She touched her muzzle to the place where she had bitten me, and pushed my hand aside, wiggling gently on the sore area. No apology was forthcoming and I realised that none was needed. I resumed my scratching of her neck and then gradually worked my way around to her other side until Infinity was satisfied. Neither of us needed to signal that the grooming session was over, we both merely ceased and then Infinity went back to grazing while I assembled another fruit breakfast from my rapidly dwindling supplies.

I breakfasted, had an extremely cold bath in the lake and found some starflower, whose petals I ground to a paste with some water and then smeared onto my shoulder to bring out the bruise more quickly and ease the pain. I also found some other herbs that I had grown used to having in supply during my apprenticeship, and prepared them for storage in one of my empty food packets in case of need.

The day was nearly half gone when Infinity let me know that she was ready to move on. I removed Infinity's blanket from her and tied it to my back-sack, before resuming my place at her side. We walked along the length of the lake and then up a steep, scrub-covered hill. As we reached the top of the hill, all we could see in front of us were trees. Deciduous woodland stretched away from the foot of the hill as far as the eye could see and I felt the tiniest flutter of nervousness from Infinity. I drew in a deep breath and tried to release my own anxiety as I let it back out. I put my hand to Infinity's shoulder.

Can we go around it? I asked her.

Why?

I know you feel uncomfortable in the forest.

I am prey. If it is my time to go then a predator will catch me and I will leave my body for it to eat. If it is not my time then I will escape any predator that hunts me.

I couldn't believe that she could be so accepting of her possible fate.

It is something humans would do well to learn, I was informed.

So why don't we all just lie down and die then? Why would you even bother to try and escape a predator if you can accept your death so easily?

Being able to accept that my body will die when the time is right does not mean I cannot live a full life up until that point. As a horse I feel fear and flee when I sense danger. If it is time for me to go then I will not escape that danger. If I am to stay here for longer then I will. I accept either outcome. It is only my body that will die. You know this is true.

I took another deep breath. Okay, I told myself, so we would enter the woods and be in there for goodness knows how long. No matter if a Woeful found us, because if it was Infinity's time to die they would catch her and if it wasn't then she would escape. Hang on though, Infinity had known what she would look like in this lifetime. She would know, then, wouldn't she, when she was due to die?

If I so chose.

And do you choose?

No.

Couldn't you just look and see if it will be in the next few days?

I could. But I will not.

Why?

I chose to give you information from this lifetime so that your time as a soldier would be possible to bear. I choose not to know what will happen now that we are living the life we agreed because it would distract us both. You and I have much to do.

But we won't get to do it if you don't live past the next couple of days, will we?

If you look into your soul do you think our time together will be over soon?

I allowed my mind to quieten, much as I used to when hoping to get a sense of Infinity when I was back at home in Rockwood. All I could feel was a sense of anticipation, of a purpose as yet unfulfilled.

It's not over, not yet, I affirmed to us both. We made our way down the hill and into the forest.

Doubt crept in and grew steadily over the following couple of days. What if it were wishful thinking that I had felt it wasn't Infinity's time to die? If a Woeful found us, would she die quickly? Would I be injured and forced to watch Infinity's body being eaten in front of me? I became less and less aware of Infinity in my mind as it filled with fear. My body ached with tension and my heart hammered continuously in my chest. No matter how often I took a swig of water from my flask, my mouth remained dry. I barely ate and slept not at all.

Infinity was forced to graze the leaves from the lowest branches of selected trees, as the patches of grass that we came across were small, few and far between. I couldn't keep still as I waited for her to eat to her satisfaction in each grazing session; I wanted to be moving and leaving these woods behind as soon as possible. I paced backwards and forwards, around trees, around Infinity. My frustration and irritation grew in proportion with my fear.

It was on the afternoon of day three of our journey through the forest, when Infinity insisted on a particularly slow perusal of the surrounding trees for any morsels she might have missed during her several hours of grazing from them, that my fear became all-encompassing and I stopped having any awareness of her in my mind at all. I lost control of myself.

'Infinity... come... on,' I whispered as fiercely as I could. 'We... can't... stay... here... another... second.'

Infinity ignored me and continued her slow meanderings.

'INFINITY, STOP IT, WE'RE LEAVING RIGHT NOW,' I yelled. 'I CAN'T... DO THIS ANYMORE, I JUST... CAN'T.' I ran up to Infinity, flung my arms around her neck and tried to pull her away from the tree whose leaves she was currently munching. She snorted and pulled away from me.

'INFINITY, MOVE,' I yelled at her again and began to pace up to her aggressively, waving my arms, trying desperately to get her away from the tree. She spun around so that her hind end was in my face, and backed up, pushing me until I fell back against another tree. She then stood there with one hind leg lifted, threateningly. She wouldn't kick me, would she?

It was too much. Sobs broke out from deep down inside of me and I sank down onto the forest floor, leaning back against the knobbly tree trunk. As I cried, I felt the tension begin to leave me. Infinity lowered her leg to the ground, turned to face me and then came and stood over me, her muzzle gently resting on the top of my head. Her warm breath soothed me and I felt her nurturing love surround me, wrapping me up and keeping me safe. As my fear receded, Infinity flooded my mind.

I have not been able to reach you.

Why not? I've been so afraid, I told her.

You made your fear your sole focus and allowed it to overwhelm you. I could not penetrate it.

But surely you feel fear too?

Not at present. There is nothing of which to be fearful.

But the Woeful, they are to be feared.

Are there any Woeful here now?

My senses hadn't been alerted. The hairs on the back of my neck were at peace. *No, but one could begin stalking us at any time.*

And that will be the time when fear will have its use. Until then you would be better served looking after your body and mind as normal. That way you will be better able to respond should your fear be warranted. You are underfed and exhausted.

Her calm logic hit its mark. *I need to eat, rest and calm down.*

I felt her assent. *We will stay here until first light tomorrow.*

I fought down the panic that tried to rise once more, and nodded. As Infinity resumed her browsing, I retrieved my sack from where I had left it and searched through the remainder of my food stores. Dwindling as they were, there was still more than there should have been; I realised fully just how little I had eaten over the past few days. I gathered sticks, lit a fire and made a double quantity of porridge. I ate the lot, followed by the remainder of my fruit. I washed it down with several mugs of tea and realised that I felt a whole lot better. Infinity's relief and approval washed over me.

The light that reached the forest floor was waning and a chill was beginning to announce itself. I put extra sticks on my fire, donned extra clothing, wrapped myself in my cloak and leant back against the tree. However much calmer I was, I wasn't convinced that I would be able to sleep. Infinity made her way over to me and stood with her head above mine.

Rest easily. I will keep watch for both of us.

But what about you? Don't you need to sleep?

Not as much as you. Sleep. She wrapped me up with her nurturing warmth. My sense of everything else receded – the last few bird calls, the crackling of the fire, the leaves swirling down to land on us – as Infinity filled my awareness with her calm assurance. I slept deeply and peacefully until the dawn chorus roused me the following morning. I opened my eyes and saw that Infinity still stood over me, dozing but alert with the part of her mind that needed to be. I sat up and realised that I hadn't even put her blanket on for her.

It is less cold under the trees than out in the open. Nevertheless I missed it, I was informed. There was no hint of displeasure.

I knew she wouldn't comprehend my gratitude to her for keeping watch, so I tried to send her the warmth of my feeling in the way she so often did to me. She responded likewise and then moved off to browse the branches. I stoked the embers of my fire until there was potential for a flame, blew on them until the fire found its will and then gradually added sticks until it was hot enough for me to cook the remainder of my porridge.

Infinity moved slowly on through the forest during the morning, browsing as she went. Every now and then I could feel fear threatening to take hold of me again and I had to take a long, slow breath and remember Infinity's instruction from the night before. I decided to collect herbs to add to my stores, in order to give myself something else to think about. In the process, I lost sight of Infinity. My panic rose unhindered. *INFINITY!*

There was a crashing through the undergrowth and Infinity burst between a sapling and a tree, skidding to a halt in front me, her eyes wide and her sides heaving. *???????????*

I flung my arms around her, pressing my face into her warm neck. 'I'm sorry, I couldn't see you and I panicked.'

More work is needed on the appropriate use of your fear, she observed. I couldn't help but agree.

It was during the afternoon of our fourth day under the trees, as I walked beside Infinity, that I remembered something about which I wanted to ask her. *When I asked why I can't hear you and Oak when you communicate and you told me that I can, but I don't, what did you mean?*

You have the ability to hear us but you do not use it. All humans do. Some horses try for many years to make their chosen humans aware of them before they finally penetrate the barriers of the human mind and their person recognises that their horse calls for them. You were aware of me so early because of our history together. Your mind yet blocks out all other horses.

You mean any human can communicate with any... I stopped in mid thought. I felt acutely uncomfortable and the hairs on the back of my neck stood bolt upright. My skin crawled as if small insects were groping their way over my entire body.

I feel it too. We are hunted. Infinity's thought was edged with panic.

As the Woeful stared at us from behind, above and to the left slightly, she revealed something of herself to us. She was only moderately hungry but the scent of horse drew her like a moth to a flame.

My heart hammered in my chest. *Go, Infinity, leave me. Alone, you can escape her. I'll drop my back-sack, maybe she'll go for that and you can get as far away as possible. I'll find you once we are both clear of the woods. Please, Infinity, go now. GO.* I tried to push her to go with my mind.

You carry my scent, she will hunt you now as readily as she hunts me. You are slower than I. I was aware of how hard she strained against the flight response that her every instinct tried to initiate. I was terrified for her.

Please go, Infinity, please, she might still go for my back-sack and leave me alone, please just go, I begged her.

We both live or we both die. We have work to do together. So we will live. Leave your possessions on the ground and sit on my back.

But I can't ride, I don't know how to, what if I hurt you? We still walked side by side in our usual unhurried pace, but it was becoming nearly as hard for me not to lose control and run as it was for Infinity.

Hurry.

I let go of my sack, stepped onto the trunk of a fallen tree to my left and flung my right leg over her back. I grabbed hold of huge chunks of her mane in each hand, feeling extremely precarious astride her wide, warm back.

Hold tightly to me, was all the warning I had to close my legs around her sides as firmly as I could, before she leapt forward into a fast canter. My upper body was left behind and I almost lay down flat with my back to hers, which proved fortunate as a low growing branch flew past just above my face. I managed to pull myself upright and then duck low over her neck just in time to miss another low branch, which snagged at the back of my jumper. My legs gripped hard, but I couldn't seem to help bouncing around on Infinity's back as she raced between the trees.

The woodland was ancient deciduous, its huge trees spaced far enough apart that we were able to move at breakneck speed, but Infinity had to weave from left to right to avoid trees in her path. I stayed low with my arms wrapped around her neck in an attempt to avoid being flung from her back. At one point, Infinity darted to the right and I found myself hanging from her left side, desperately trying to grip on with my right calf. She slowed and darted left towards a tree, where she halted momentarily, just long enough for me to push against the tree trunk and centre myself on her back once more. Then we were off again. All the while, a crashing accompanied us from above and behind as the Woeful pursued us through the trees. On the ground she would be no match for Infinity's speed, but in the trees, she was in her element as she leapt and swung powerfully from tree to tree.

Was it wishful thinking, or was the crashing behind us subsiding?

You're winning, Infinity, we're leaving her behind. Just a bit further now, keep going, my beautiful girl, keep going, come on, just a bit further, you can do it. I willed her on with as much energy as I could muster.

I felt her take heart from me and find yet more strength and endurance. She sped on, but she was getting lower and lower in front of me all the time. She stumbled but used her momentum to keep herself up and moving forward. The noise behind us was definitely waning, and Infinity began to slow her pace, sweating and breathing heavily. I tried to sit up and balance myself by holding her mane, anxious to get off her neck as she laboured. There was silence from behind us now. I realised I felt comfortable in my own skin again and noted the singing of the birds in the trees above us. And was it my imagination, or was it much brighter in front of us?

I was just allowing myself to hope that maybe, possibly, we had found the edge of the forest, when Infinity stumbled again. This time she had neither the momentum nor the strength to right herself and she pitched forward and down onto her knees. I flew over her head and stuck my left arm out in front of me in a reflexive attempt to break my fall. There was a sickening crunch and pain shot up my arm as I landed on top of it. I fought down a scream, conscious that somewhere behind us was a frustrated Woeful, and managed a strangled yelp instead.

I sat up and gritted my teeth as I lifted my arm into my lap with my other hand, trying to ignore the odd angle between my elbow and wrist. Sweat broke out on my forehead and my breathing became a pant as a fresh wave of pain washed over me. I felt dizzy and feared I would faint. *NO*, I told myself, *STAY AWAKE.* We weren't out of danger and on no account could I afford to lose consciousness. I made a determined effort to slow my breathing and eventually managed slow, deep breaths.

I looked up to see Infinity standing a short distance away, dripping with sweat, her sides heaving. She stood with her front legs out in front of her slightly and her head low, almost touching her front feet. Her front end was lower than her hind end and her back legs quivered. I needed to get her moving. I could feel her exhaustion as easily as my own pain and I was aware of her muscles starting to stiffen as the chill autumn air cooled her sweating body. I cradled my broken left arm with my right, got to my knees and stood up, my worry for Infinity now acting as well as any painkiller would have.

Infinity, we have to move on, I told her. *The air is chilly and you're getting cold. We have to move on so your muscles don't seize up.*

She didn't respond. I nudged her leg with my knee.

Infinity, please, you have to move. You have to walk with me. The Woeful is behind us somewhere and she might not have given up completely, we have to get out of the forest.

Still no response. Was she hurt? I wondered and began to search her perception of her body for any awareness of pain.

No but you are. Her thought was very faint.

We have to move on now, please try and walk with me, Infinity, please try, I begged her. In response, she lifted her head slightly and took one halting step with her left hind leg.

And another, come on, Infinity. I could feel her awareness slipping away again. *Infinity, move, please move. Infinity, INFINITY, INFINITY, FIN!* She was back with me. *Move now, come on, I'm with you. Please try another step, please, Fin.*

She lifted her head further with great effort, and moved her left foreleg.

That's good, that's my girl and the next one, come on, Fin, move the next one, I pleaded with her and was rewarded by her right hind leg taking a step, followed haltingly by the right fore. I nudged her again with my knee. *Come on now, keep going, that's it, that's my beautiful girl, keep going, Fin, come on you can do it, I know you can, that's it, well done.* I kept up constant encouragement as she slowly, stiffly, moved one leg after the other.

I could see sunlight streaming in past the last trees in the distance as Infinity began to walk more fluidly. The sweat was beginning to dry on her and her breathing was returning to normal. We needed water urgently, I realised.

I smell water not far away. Her thought was stronger now.

How are you feeling? I asked.

My front legs ache and I feel strange but I do not have pain in the way you do.

Why did you become lower in front as you galloped? Surely you wouldn't have stumbled if you'd carried yourself as you normally do?

It is different with weight on my back. There was too much weight on my front legs. As I tired I was unable to hold myself up and avoid tripping.

It was my fault. It was my weight that had unbalanced her to the point where she fell, and my leaning forward on her neck would have made it even worse. Guilt overwhelmed me. She should have gone on without me.

Why do you suffer?

I feel terrible that your body was put under so much stress because of me.

??????????

It was because of my weight on your back and neck that you fell, you have sore legs and you exhausted yourself because of me.

Yes.

That is why I suffer.

??????????

I could feel Infinity trying to recognise the emotion that I felt in terms of those with which she was familiar, but she just couldn't. As far as she was concerned, we both did what was necessary and that was all there was to it. I found her attitude as confusing as she found mine.

We exited the forest and as my acute concern for Infinity began to recede and my adrenaline levels fell, I was shocked by the intense, shooting pain in my arm. I felt my body preparing to vomit and decided that I needed to concentrate on its immediate needs.

That I understand, my mare told me approvingly.

NINE

Special

We came across a stream an hour or so after exiting the trees. I waited while Infinity sniffed the water and then drank her fill. I could feel her body begin its recovery as it was gradually rehydrated. When she'd had enough, she once more sniffed the water and then began to graze beside it, knowing that I had registered her judgment that it was safe for me to drink. I bit back my thanks, knowing they were unnecessary.

I knelt down at the edge of the stream and slowly, painfully, lowered my broken arm onto my knees. Sweat poured down my face and I gritted my teeth hard to avoid shouting out with the pain, but finally my right hand was free to cup water. I drank for what seemed an eternity and when I'd finished, I washed the sweat from my face. As I stood back up and re-cradled my left arm with my right, I surveyed the horizon in all directions and realised that I could still see the forest clearly.

We need to move on, I told Infinity.

No answer.

Fin, please, we need to move on. I know you're hungry, but we're too close to the woods.

Her hunger was not great enough for her to follow us this far from the trees.

There's grass as far as I can see in the direction we were heading, could we just move on for maybe a few hours and then stop?

Be calm. I will graze and you will come to terms with your fear.

Infinity's way of living entirely in the present, with no thoughts of the past or future, seemed to give her freedom from the fear that affected me and clearly served her well, I decided. Infinity was quiet and still at the back of my mind but taking notice of my thoughts. I resolved to attempt to live solely in the present as did my horse. A faint flicker of approval. I breathed deeply and brought my focus entirely into the present. The pain in my arm intensified as it became the sole object of my attention. I needed to focus on my arm. Distinct approval now from Infinity.

What to do with my useless, painful, broken arm? I could cast about for some arnollia to ease the pain, but then I would have to let go of my broken arm in order to pick it and that thought left me feeling faint. If only there was a Bone-Singer around nearby, I thought wistfully.

You can heal it.

No, I can't. Even if I could find and pick the herbs that I know would help, none of them would heal the bone, only relieve the pain and help the surrounding tissue to heal, and that isn't going to be much help until the bone is in one piece again.

I am familiar with the function of herbs. I select herbs to assist my body in the same way that you do. You can heal the bone. You know how it is done.

You select herbs to heal your body?

Of course. Concentrate on healing your bone.

But I'm not a Bone-Singer.

You do not see yourself as one. There is a difference.

I pondered over her words. Did she mean that if I saw myself as a Bone-Singer then I could be one? I felt her assent. I could be a Bone-Singer. But how? I didn't have any training, I was a Herbalist, I had practised tuning into herbs, not bones, how could I possibly...

It is the same.

??????????

You can tune into herbs. Your Bone-Singers can tune into bones. That is what you believe. In truth any human can tune into anything if they believe they can.

But we are tested, different people show aptitude for different Skills and that is what they train to do, that's how it's been since the first humans discovered the Skills, I protested.

Humans show aptitude for what they believe they will. All humans have the ability to do any of the things that you call the Skills. They are all the same. You perceive them all as being different and so that is how you experience them.

But Bone-Singers don't just tune into the bones, they have to find the right tone to resonate with the injured bone, they have to use their intention to cause it to knit together and they have to adjust the sound they make as the bone heals, I argued. *It's very difficult and I have no training.*

You explain why you do not heal bones. You do not explain why you cannot.

So, you are actually telling me I should try to heal my bone by bone-singing?

No.

Well phew because…

Do not try to heal it. Heal it.

Could she be right? Maybe I would have had an aptitude for bone-singing anyway, I never found out as I didn't test for it… I could feel Infinity's irritation at my thoughts. Could it really be true that anyone could do any of the Skills? Why didn't everyone show aptitude at testing then?

You underestimate the power of belief. The humans who perform these 'Skills' are those who believe they can.

Right, so I just need to believe I can sing my bone back to normal and I'll be able to do it. I tried to convince myself.

Do you have trust in me?

Of course I do, completely, absolutely, how can you doubt…

Then know that I am right. And go further than merely believing you can do it. Know you can. It will make a difference.

I took a deep breath. Of course I trusted her. With my life and with my soul. So then, if she said I could do it then I must be able to. I can do it. I can do it. I repeated it over and over to myself until I thought I had enough conviction.

If you do not know for certain then you do not know, I was informed.

Trying to convince myself wasn't going to work, I realised. Infinity had told me with utmost sincerity that I could bone-sing. I felt her total conviction and allowed it to fill me. And I knew that I could do it. I would heal myself. I sat down on the bank of the stream and slowed my breathing, taking long, deep breaths as I allowed my attention to wander around my body.

It was easy. I quickly sorted through the different tissues, getting a feel for them. I then turned my awareness to focus solely on my bones. Once I had tuned into one of them, it was effortless to tune into any of the others and when I came across the one that was broken, the discord that emanated from it shook me. Infinity was with me instantly, steadying me until the shock passed. Then she faded into the background, leaving me to carry on by myself. I was still tuned into the broken bone and I had to clamp my jaws together to stop my teeth from chattering at the discord that it was broadcasting. I suddenly noticed that without trying, I was making a low, harsh tone that resonated exactly with the broken bone. Instinct took over and I immediately sent my intention for the bone to heal along the pathway travelled by the sound to the bone. I felt the attraction between the broken ends of the bone, and my intention caused them to begin to fuse back together. I needed to change the sound I was making, I realised, as the noise that I was currently producing no longer resonated with the bone as it began to heal. I softened the tone and the pain in my arm lessened significantly as my continued intention encouraged the bone to knit together more firmly and become whole once more. I'd done it.

My concentration wavered as I realised how tired I was. I hadn't yet healed the bone back to the full strength of my healthy bones and I just couldn't find the concentration to be able to do it. My bone was whole once more, albeit not nearly as strong as it should be, and the pain would be manageable once I had found the right herbs. That would do, wouldn't it?

It will be enough for now, agreed Infinity.

I sank back into the grass and lay on my back, resting. I felt completely exhausted and as the sun made its way down behind the hills in front of us, I realised that I was getting cold too. A slight breeze was getting up and the thought of spending the night out in the open with only my shirt and pullover to keep me warm was extremely unappealing.

Infinity, we need to move on now, we need to find some shelter, I told her, hoping upon hope that this time she would agree to go. By way of an answer, she stopped grazing and began to move on towards the hills. I fell in beside her, keeping my eyes on the ground, searching for the herbs that I needed to hasten the recovery of my arm.

We reached the foot of the hills just as night fell. Boulders littered the ground and I found one that was large enough to shelter both of us from the breeze. I knew Infinity would want to graze more before she slept, so I leant back against the boulder, my knees pulled in to my stomach, and munched on some arnollia leaves that I had gathered for pain relief, along with the root of mennawort, which would act as an anti-inflammatory for the soft tissue that had been damaged by the broken bone. I would normally have ground the mennawort root before adding it to the arnollia leaves and making a hot tea with them, sweetened with honey, but this would have to do. I tried not to gag as the bitter mennawort root churned around in my mouth.

It had been an exhausting day and hunger gnawed at my stomach, but I couldn't help feeling buoyant. I had healed my own bone! With no training, just an absolute certainty that I could do it, I had managed to bone-sing. Infinity was turning on its head my idea of what was possible in life. Any human could perform any of the Skills. And, I suddenly remembered, before the Woeful had distracted us, Infinity had been in the process of telling me that any human is capable of communicating with horses! It seemed that the idea I had grown up with, that only certain people could do certain things, was completely false. Why was no one else aware of this? I wondered to myself as I shivered against the cold, hard boulder.

Some humans are aware of it. Infinity was making her way over to where I sat. *The human urge to feel special is very strong. Strong enough to prevent the sharing of truth.*

?????????

When Mettle and Jonus helped humans to remember their latent abilities they always told that EVERYONE had the memories that needed waking. But it was always only the first few to remember that were celebrated as being the gifted ones. As soon as a few could perform the 'Skills' no one else continued to try. The original message was forgotten. The belief arose that only a few individuals could do the different tasks. Special individuals. That belief has limited humans ever since.

But you said some humans do know the truth?

Yes.

Why don't they say?

They would no longer be seen by others as special if everyone could do what they do. If others do not see them as special they cannot see themselves as having worth. This is at the root of many human mistakes.

I remembered back to how I felt when I was accepted to train as a Herbalist. The approval from my family and friends both then and later, when I had proved to be such an able student, had left me feeling happy, accepted and, I hesitated now to admit it, special. I thought about all the attention lavished on the Horse-Bonded when they had their Quest Ceremonies and then later visited the villages. How would people feel about the Horse-Bonded if they knew that they weren't special at all? But then we are in one sense, I decided; maybe everyone is capable of communicating with horses, but not everyone gets chosen by a horse, do they?

Not everybody needs to be.

What?

Most humans will achieve their life purpose without a bond with a horse.

So those of us who are chosen by horses are chosen because we are lacking in some way?

That is the reason some humans are chosen. Others are chosen because there is an opportunity for rapid progression in their evolution that will not happen without the aid of a horse. And some are chosen because they have the potential to make a difference to others. A horse can help them to achieve that potential.

I knew she meant me. I felt extremely pleased with myself and relieved that I wasn't one of those chosen because they needed help so desperately. Infinity lay down in front of me so that as I turned around to settle against her, I was nestled between her and the boulder. I felt her amusement and realised the trap I had fallen into. I was feeling special again. Well, what was wrong with that? I couldn't help it if I were relieved to have been chosen for a good reason and not because I needed help, could I?

Why do you assume you do not need help?

Because we agreed to help horses and humans evolve further, that's why we're together.

You cling to that idea alone because it boosts your idea of yourself. Do you think you are in a position to perform our task in your current state?

I thought back to the events of the past years of my life and realised how little I had known about the true order of things, and how much I had learnt already in the short time that I had been under Infinity's instruction. I sighed. From what little she had already taught me, I could guess how much more there would be to come. I felt very small and insignificant.

No need, Infinity told me.

??????

No need to feel as you do now. No need to feel special. No need for any of it.

Then how should I feel?

You will learn.

I snuggled down against her, wrapping my arms around my body as my stomach grumbled loudly. I must have fallen asleep.

Someone was shaking me and they wouldn't stop. My bed was wet and cold.

'Leave me alone, I need to sleep,' I murmured.

Walks A Straight Path. I need to rise.

I woke fully and realised that Infinity was quivering from side to side in her attempt to wake me. I sat up in the dewy grass, shivering, and moved away from Infinity on my hands and knees. Infinity heaved herself to her feet and immediately began to graze next to me. She was hungry. She hadn't grazed for as long into the night as she usually did, I realised.

You were cold. You needed my body heat.

I mustered as much love and warmth as I could and sent it to her, attempting to envelop her with it as she did to me. She might not need gratitude but I could love her as much as I wanted to.

She would be a while grazing now, I thought to myself, what to do while I waited? Going back to sleep wasn't an option, I was too cold. I couldn't hear water nearby and Infinity couldn't smell any either. I had lost all means of catching or cooking food when I abandoned my back-sack. I decided that my best chance of sustenance was blackberries. I searched around the boulders for brambles whilst jumping up and down and rubbing my arms in an attempt to warm up, but I couldn't find anything to eat.

We are not far from The Gathering. You will survive, Infinity observed. I noticed it didn't stop her eating her fill though. I stomped round and round the same boulder, beating an angry, muddy path in the grass. Infinity grazed on.

When the sun was high enough to spread a little warmth on the landscape, Infinity was finally ready to leave. I was feeling weak and light-headed from hunger, so I put my hand on Infinity's side to steady myself as I took up my place next to her. She stopped. *I will carry you. Climb onto my back.*

No, I'm alright, I just need to put my hand against you in case I trip.

You are weak. I can carry you.

I had no intention of sitting on her again until someone was there to teach me to ride properly.

Last time we moved at speed. This time I will walk. I will not fall.

As long as I can lean against you if I need to, I'll manage. I might find some berries on the way and I'll need to be on the ground to pick them. It was a weak argument and Infinity wasn't fooled, but she didn't press me further.

I eventually found a dense bramble patch at the foot of some pear trees. The blackberries were beginning to ripen past their best and I tried to ignore the little white maggots crawling out of a large proportion of them as I picked the best ones and gobbled them down. They were juicy and I was grateful for the sweet fluid that trickled down my throat. I picked some pears and ate them as we walked.

The sun was reaching its zenith when we came across a dirt track. I could see something moving along it, away from us, in the distance.

We are close to The Gathering now, Infinity informed me.

My heart lifted, but then sank as I realised that before too long, Infinity and I would no longer be alone together. Strange as the last days had been, they had also been wonderful and I wasn't sure if I was ready to re-enter the world of humans just yet. I felt nervous. I wondered how many people and horses would be there and what they would think of Infinity and me. What would I do when we got there? Was there a particular person I should go and see to announce my arrival? What if they turned me away because I was too young?

You are absent from the present again.

I resolved once more to keep my attention in the present and allow events to unfold as they would. Instantly I felt better.

We turned to follow whatever it was that I had seen moving along the track. It wasn't long before we came across a fresh pile of dung that I recognised as that of a donkey, and as we rounded a sharp bend half an hour later, we came across its source. Halted on the track in front of us was a wooden cart piled high and covered with a tarpaulin. I could hear voices coming from around the front of it.

'Um, hello?' I called out as Infinity and I came to a halt behind the cart. A man and a woman appeared. The woman was taller than I and much more heavily set. She wore bright yellow leggings and appeared to be wearing three or four shirts layered on top of each other, so that she had multiple collars at her neck, all in equally garish hues. Her black, knee-length boots seemed very dull by comparison with the rest of her attire. Her face showed her to be in her mid-thirties, I guessed. The man was dressed in brown, from his shirt and pullover down to his boots. He had a ruddy complexion and the lines on his forehead and at the corner of his watery blue eyes put him at a good few years older than his companion.

They both wore bandannas on their heads, knotted at the nape of the neck, which kept their long hair away from their faces as well as announcing their Trades to all; the woman wore the yellow bandanna of a Herald, and the man wore the red of a Pedlar.

Pedlars travelled far and wide, and made regular journeys to the ruined cities of The Old. They scavenged objects that could be useful to those of The New both from ruined buildings and from the old rubbish landfill sites that were always located on the outskirts of the cities. They then visited the villages of The New, trading their finds for food and lodging, as well as for goods that they could trade on elsewhere. They were vital suppliers of metal for the Metal-Singers, and many Glass-Singers bought the glass bottles and jars that pedlars carried, finding it quicker to sing them into new shapes than to sing fresh glass from sand.

Heralds took news and messages between villages in the form of verbal announcements, private messages and written letters between individuals. It was customary for the receivers of the messages and news, whether individual households or villages as a whole, to provide for the Herald's needs during their visit and they generally seemed to live well by their chosen Trade. For many people of The New, Heralds were their only link to family and friends who had moved away to marry or to find work, and their arrival in the villages was generally the cause of much excitement.

Working as a Pedlar or a Herald involved long periods of time on the road and it was thus very common for members of the Travelling Trades, as they were known, to team up and travel together.

The couple smiled at Infinity and me. 'Hello,' the woman said in a hearty voice. 'We seem to be blocking your way, our apologies. I'm Salom and this is Pete.'

'I'm Amarilla and this is Infinity.' I shook their proffered hands.

Pete whistled as his gaze wandered over Infinity. 'An' ain' she jus' the beau'y.'

I felt a flush of something from Infinity and recognised it as satisfaction. I watched her turn her head to the side slightly and blink very slowly, accentuating her white eyelashes against the blue of her eyes as she did so. Her performance had the desired effect, and both of her admiring humans drew a sharp intake of breath. She revelled in their admiration.

Feeling special, are we? I teased her.

Always. Not in the sense you mean.

Well why is it that if I feel special, it's undesirable?

You feel special only when others tell you that you are. You have little sense of your own value. I know my worth and how others feel about me affects it not. I can enjoy the admiration of others because I do not need it.

Oh. I frowned as I tried to understand the difference. Salom and Pete continued to admire Infinity. She batted her eyelashes at them unashamedly and I couldn't decide whether I was amused or irritated.

'How long have you been bonded?' asked Salom.

'Not long, we're on our way to The Gathering for the first time,' I replied.

'Oh, how exciting for you and here we are, slap bang in the way.'

'Don't worry, we can squeeze around,' I replied. 'Is there a problem with your cart?'

'No' the car', nah,' said Pete, 'i's one o' the donkeys.'

'Can we help at all?'

'Thank you, we're not really sure what's wrong yet, she just started limping. We were just having a look at her when we heard you calling,' replied Salom, as she led the way around the cart to one of the four donkeys that pulled it. 'This is Salsh.' She patted the donkey at front right of the traces. 'I've felt down her leg and can't find any heat, I was wondering if she's strained her shoulder.'

She has a sore foot. She trod on a sharp stone. Some of your herb will help. She is very thirsty, Infinity told me.

'Infinity says that Salsh has a bruised sole from a sharp stone. I have some arnollia here for her to ease the pain,' I said, pulling the limp remains of the herb that I had gathered the day before from the pocket of my leggings, 'and if I can find some starflower, you can grind the petals with some water and smear it on her sole to bring out the bruising more quickly.'

Salom took the arnollia from me and held it out to Salsh, who took it and began to chew. 'Thank you, thank you both so much, is there anything we can give you in return?'

'Do you have any water I could drink? I lost my flask,' I said.

'Of course, of course, Pete, Amarilla needs a beaker of water,' she called over to where Pete was stroking Infinity's neck as he chattered to her.

'Infinity said Salsh is very thirsty too,' I said, hoping they didn't think I was criticising them.

No need.

What?

No need to concern yourself with what others think of you.

But I want them to like me. What's wrong with that?

No need.

I felt a bit irritated. Being tutored when we were alone was one thing, but we had company and it was difficult to concentrate on behaving in a normal fashion when I had the fountain of knowledge picking me up on everything I said and did.

No need.

What now?

No need to behave in the way in which you are expected.

Then how do I behave?

As yourself.

Pete appeared in front of me with a large beaker of water. 'T'ain' very fresh bu' i'll do,' he said. He carried a wooden bucket in his other hand with water slopping over the edge, which he offered to Salsh. 'Should o' bin a' The Gatherin' ba na, she's thisty cas we bin longer un we thau.'

'How much further is it?' I asked.

'Bou' 'alf an 'ar,' he replied. My heart leapt and sank again.

I cast about, looking for starflower among the many grasses and herbs on either side of the track. It wasn't too long before I found some. I took it over to where Pete and Salom sat on the verge, eating their lunch. They had unharnessed the donkeys and tethered them to graze, and I noticed that they had set out a place on their blanket for me. My mouth watered. There were cheese, bread, slices of ham, some kind of chutney, and a large fruitcake.

I held some starflower petals out to Salom. 'Here you are, grind these with a small amount of water and rub the paste on to her sole. If you have something to bind it in place, she should be comfortable enough to carry on to The Gathering.'

'Bless you,' she said, 'now come and sit down and eat with us, you look like you could use a good meal. You don't appear to have any belongings with you?'

I sank down gratefully onto the blanket and told them of our encounter with the Woeful as I made myself a sandwich. They listened avidly and were such an encouraging audience, Salom in particular, that I ended up outlining everything that had happened since I had been tugged.

'We know Adam,' Salom said when I had finished. 'So, he and your other friend are waiting for you, are they?'

'They should be there by now,' I replied. 'If you don't need any help, Infinity and I had better be on our way. We'll see you there?'

Pete waved his piece of cake at me. 'Ta ma luv, wizl see ya bith tha'.'

Salom stood up and hugged me. 'You'll be fine, there's always a nice crowd at The Gathering.'

I hugged her back. 'I'm glad we met you. How long will you be staying?'

'A few days. I'll search you out before we leave, don't worry. If you have any messages for your family, write them down and I'll take them.'

I held my hand up in farewell to them both and continued on to The Gathering with Infinity.

TEN

Arrival

We reached The Gathering all too soon. I think I'd expected nothing more than some tents arranged at random around a campfire with horses grazing nearby, so when we had our first glimpse of our destination, my jaw dropped. We had just passed between some steep-sided hills and then the track dropped sharply away down from us, leaving The Gathering in plain view below.

There were huge, grey stone buildings, larger by far than anything I had ever seen before, arranged around a vast cobbled square with an enormous statue in the middle, of a person standing with a horse. Stretching away from the buildings, as far as I could see, were fenced paddocks containing horses, sheep, goats, cattle and crops. Some of the paddocks were larger and people rode horses within them. I could see people tending to the livestock and some Earth-Singers were at work, lifting the surface soil away in a couple of the enclosures, so that whatever they were harvesting could be lifted without the need for digging. People milled about in the square, some stopping to chat, others hurrying about their business. It was an amazing sight. I felt extremely daunted, and embarrassed by my ragged appearance and lack of belongings. My feet slowed to a halt and I couldn't seem to make them move again. Infinity stood next to me, waiting patiently.

My attention was drawn suddenly to the nearest building. It was four storeys high, and someone had opened a window on the top floor and was hanging out of it, waving both arms. I squinted, trying to see who it was and a pale face surrounded by long black hair came into focus. Rowena. The sight of her lifted me and gave me the courage to walk down to The Gathering, my hand resting on Infinity's neck as she walked by my side. Rowena disappeared from the window and as we reached the building, she exited it at a run. Her face changed quickly from one of smiling welcome to one of concern as she took stock of Infinity and me.

'What happened to you?' she said. 'Can't Oak and I leave you alone for five minutes without you getting yourself into a scrape? Oh, never mind that now, you must introduce me to your mare. I've been dying to meet her.'

'Rowena, this is Infinity.'

Rowena held the back of her hand out for Infinity to sniff and said, 'Blimey, Infinity eh… interesting.'

'Er, what's interesting?' I asked.

'You, her, the whole caboodle, but anyway, I can see you need a bath, food and some fresh clothes, much like the last time we met,' she winked at me, 'and I imagine Infinity could do with some grazing time and a rest?'

That would be welcome.

'Yes please to everything,' I replied. 'Where will Infinity be staying?' I hoped it wouldn't be too far from where I would be.

'Newly bonded horses usually go in the paddocks closest to the buildings,' she said. 'Don't worry, we've all felt as you are feeling now, it's weird to suddenly be back with humans when you've grown used to being alone with your horse. She'll be close enough for you to get to in an instant if you feel strange without her at any time. You'll get used to being around other people and horses soon enough, and then you'll cope with being further away from her. Will Infinity be comfortable in a paddock by herself, or shall I ask Oak to join her?'

I would welcome a grooming partner.

I felt my cheeks redden as I passed Infinity's reply on to Rowena. With all the drama surrounding my arm, I had failed to take care of my horse properly. She had shown me the importance to her of mutual grooming and I had neglected her.

You suffer your strange emotion again. No need, Infinity informed me.

Rowena sensed my discomfort. 'Everything okay?'

I sighed. 'I don't even know where to begin.'

She laughed. 'You too, eh? It took me and Oak nearly three weeks to travel here after we first bonded and by the time I got here, I was struggling to remember my own name. The first few months of being bonded to a horse are a bit like being blindfolded and spun around until you don't know which way is up and which is down, but as time goes on you'll get used to the fact that nothing is as you thought it was, believe me. Let's show Infinity to her paddock and I'll ask Oak to join her. Then I'll let Adam know you're here while you have a bath.'

'That would be great, thanks,' I replied, feeling strange to be offering gratitude.

'This way.' She turned and walked past the building from which she had exited, into the square. 'At the moment, you'll be feeling weird that you're back in the world of human conversation and social customs, but don't forget, this isn't a normal community. You are among people who understand how you're feeling and what you're experiencing, we've all been there. Although possibly not in quite such a dramatic way as you've managed so far – care to summarise your latest mishap for me?'

'We were hunted by a Woeful. I had to leave all my stuff behind and ride Infinity, she fell, I broke my arm and I had to heal it. I'm so sorry, she loved the blanket you made for her, and we had to leave it behind with everything else.'

'Never mind the blanket, you were chased by a Woeful? Bloody hell,' said Rowena.

Infinity and I were attracting attention as we crossed the cobbled square. Many people were watching us and some were making their way over to intercept our path. Rowena came to our rescue, calling out, 'Not now, folks, sorry, Amarilla and Infinity need to rest and recover, they've had a bit of a time of it. There'll be plenty of chance for you to meet them tomorrow.'

At Infinity's name, everyone within hearing distance reacted. Some gasped, others raised their eyebrows, and a few frowned thoughtfully. A man to our left started to speak, but was cut off by Rowena saying, 'Seriously, Shann, not now.'

'Thanks, Rowena, I'm glad you're here,' I whispered.

She put an arm around my shoulders and hugged me. 'We're glad you're here too, me and Oak.'

It was a relief when we left the buildings behind us and approached the paddocks. I could see that those closest to us were empty. There were full water barrels by each gate and the grass was still plentiful.

Rowena addressed Infinity. 'Oak prefers that one,' she pointed to the one on our right, 'as he likes to rest under that big beech tree, but you choose whichever you prefer.'

Infinity walked towards the paddock Rowena had indicated and I opened the gate to let her in. Once inside, she immediately began to graze.

Rowena called out, 'Infinity, we're shutting the gate to keep the livestock out, not to keep you in, if you want to move somewhere else, let Amarilla know and one of us will come and open it.' She turned to me and explained, 'We need to keep the gates closed, otherwise you find you're moving sheep or goats from one paddock to another and they keep disappearing into all the paddocks they pass on the way. All the horses know they are free to change paddocks whenever they want, they either let us know and we open the gates to let them in or out, or they jump the gates and help themselves.'

I nodded. *Infinity, is there anything you need before I leave you for a while?*

I am content.

Rowena and I turned back towards the buildings. 'Who looks after the livestock?' I asked her, feeling a pang at leaving my horse but allowing her contentment to comfort me.

'We all do. Everyone is on a rota while they're here. We all take a turn at cooking, cleaning, fetching dung and firewood, tending the crops and animals, all the usual chores, and we all give freely of our specialist knowledge in the Skills or Trades to anyone who needs it. I'm a Tailor.'

We walked back across the square to yet more staring, and into the building from whose window Rowena had been hanging when Infinity and I had arrived. She told me that she and Oak had arrived a few days earlier. She had found two empty rooms next to each other and bagged them for us both.

My room was bare stone walled with a bed, bedside table, wardrobe, high backed comfy chair and a small fireplace with a prancing horse expertly carved into the mantelpiece. A huge sack of my clothes and other personal belongings sat on the bed, brought by Rowena from my house in Rockwood. She told me that there were two bathrooms on each floor and a main dining room in a separate building, where everyone ate together. She showed me to one of the bathrooms on our floor, pointed me to a cupboard containing fresh towels and told me that she would be back later with some tea and with Adam. I started to ask her about her trip to see my family but she held her hand up to me and told me it would keep until I smelt better. It was impossible to take offence at her words because of the grin that accompanied her teasing and also, I realised, because I found her bluntness very easy to be around since my time spent with Infinity.

An hour later, I sat cross-legged on my bed, wet-haired and clean, and wearing my own clothes from the sack that Rowena had brought for me. I unpacked the remainder of my belongings and my heart wrenched with each item. There were all my clothes, carefully folded and packed, including the cloak that I had left behind in the woods when I was tugged. My family must have searched for me until they found it, I realised. What must they have thought when they found it but not me? There were my herb journal and dictionary, with a note attached from Nerys wishing me well, itself attached to a sealed letter addressed to "Amarilla's new Master of Herbalism". A new hairbrush was wrapped in a thin, delicate scarf that I recognised as Katonia's. A note attached to it from my sister sent all her love and hopes that I would visit home soon. A small box contained my one piece of jewellery – a silver necklace that I had received from my parents when I began my apprenticeship. There was a bundle of what appeared to be tail hair from one of our donkeys with a note attached to it from Robbie and Con, saying they thought I might like to know that if things didn't work out with my horse, there were always the donkeys back home to play with. I smiled. Some things would never change. There was a delicate little bag containing dozens of the tiny metal, glass and grass horseshoes normally gifted to someone at their Quest Ceremony, with a note from my aunt and uncle saying they were sorry not to have been able to give them to me in person and to keep them for luck. Last but not least, there was a letter from my parents, attached to a bulky canvas bag. I bit my lip and opened the letter, taking a deep breath as I recognised my father's writing.

Dear Amarilla,

Your mother and I are so relieved to hear that you are safe and well. Rowena has explained what happened to you when you were tugged and although I can't say I completely understand what happened, it sounds as though you have had a difficult time. By the time you read this, you will be with your horse and I know what that will mean to you. You were right, my Amarilla, all this time you were right, about your horse, about everything. I am so proud of you. Your mother and I managed to purchase the enclosed for you before Rowena left to meet you and we hope they will be useful in caring for your horse. I understand that you have much to learn from the other Horse-Bonded, but please come home to us as soon as you possibly can, we are all so keen to meet your horse and to see you again, we miss you terribly. Take care of yourself my darling, with love from us all,

Dad

A large teardrop fell from my cheek and smudged his name. With trembling hands, I opened the canvas bag and shook the contents onto my bed. There was a metal hoof pick with A.N. engraved on the handle, and an assortment of brushes similar to those we had for our donkeys only larger, all with my initials carved onto their wooden backs. A sheepskin hand mitt completed the grooming kit and as I inserted my hand I could imagine how much Infinity would appreciate the soft feel of it on her face.

?????????

My parents have sent me some equipment so I can groom you properly. There is a soft sheepskin I can rub your face with.

I felt her brief approval before she turned her full attention back to grooming with Oak. I was aware that her neck ached. She was having to stretch up high to reach his withers as he towered over her but she didn't mind, she was finding him a very agreeable grooming partner. I smiled and felt slightly sorry for him.

'What gives?' Rowena entered the room carrying a tray.

I hastily wiped my face with the cuff of my pullover. 'I was just pitying Oak. Infinity's finding him a good grooming partner and that can only mean that she's being bossy.'

'Have no fear where my boy is concerned, he won't do anything he doesn't want to.' She put the tray on my bedside table and noticed the grooming kit strewn across the bed. 'Your mother sent your father all over the place to get that kit together and engraved before I left, poor man, I'm not sure she even let him eat until it was sorted. She's some woman, isn't she?'

'My mother?'

'Oh, she was in a dreadful state when I arrived, she'd taken to her bed and was refusing to leave it again until she had some news of you. Your sister has had a hard time looking after her. When I told her you were alright, she fainted and then when she came round, she hugged me so hard I thought my eyes would pop out. Your father had to prise her off of me in the end. He's nice, I liked him.'

'But it was my mother who wanted me to have a grooming kit?'

'Oh yeah, once she finally calmed down, she set your sister to washing all of your clothes so you would have all your own stuff clean and fresh, and she told, no, more ordered, your father to go and not only find everything you would need to groom your horse properly, but to have everything engraved as well. Apparently, no horse who is bonded to a daughter of hers will be allowed to appear unkempt.' She grinned.

'She wasn't angry with me?'

'Angry, no. Emotional, definitely.'

'But she didn't write to me, my father wrote me a letter and just said they were both relieved I'm okay. I can't believe she's not angry.'

'Well, obviously I don't know her as well as you do, but no, she was definitely very relieved, anxious that you would have everything you need, and proud, I would say. I have a feeling your sister and brothers may get very sick of hearing about you being one of the Horse-Bonded before long. Your brothers don't say much, do they?'

'Robbie and Con? You must be joking, they never shut up!'

'Well the Robbie and Con I saw hardly said a word the first day I was there and I have to say, for Earth-Singers, they were very pale-faced.' She looked at me as I sat with my mouth open. 'I think your disappearance might have affected your family in more ways than you thought.'

'Didn't my brothers even attempt to play a joke on you while you were there?'

'Well I was only there for two days but no, not that I noticed. Hang on though, I did notice Con undo your mother's apron string while she was stirring the soup for lunch just before I left, is that the sort of thing you mean?'

I grinned with relief. 'Exactly the sort of thing. And they sent me some donkey tail hair. Hopefully things will be returning to normal now.'

'They were all happy enough when I left. Your brothers and father were going to go back to work the following day and your sister was going to spend another couple of days with your mother and then do the same. She's a nice person, I liked her a lot.'

'Katonia?'

'Yeah, very different from you from what little I know of either of you, very friendly and welcoming.'

'Are you saying you don't think I'm friendly and welcoming?'

She laughed. 'You know what I mean.'

'Katonia is always clean, tidy and in control of herself?'

'Exactly.'

There was a knock on the open door, followed by Adam's voice. 'Okay to come in?'

'Adam!' I rushed to where he stood in the doorway, and gave him a hug. 'It's so good to see you again.'

His smile lit up his face. 'And it's good to see you too, Amarilla, and your beautiful mare – I saw her in her paddock. I stayed well back so as not to disturb her but I had to see the horse everyone's talking about.'

'Everyone? Why is everyone talking about her?'

'Now let me see,' he said. 'Number one, any new horse always creates a stir. Number two, her name is Infinity, and number three, there is a Herald by the name of Salom in the square right now in the process of telling your entire story to all who are interested, and that's pretty much everyone staying here.'

'You told your story to a Herald?' Rowena asked incredulously.

'Infinity and I overtook her and a Pedlar called Pete, just before we got here. One of their donkeys was lame and we stopped to help, and they gave me food and water. They were so nice. Salom didn't question me for my story, she just noticed I didn't have any belongings and I kind of ended up telling her everything.'

Rowena rolled her eyes. 'Well of course she didn't come right out and ask you for something to gossip about, she's a professional. Heralds have a way of wheedling information out of people, that's how they make a living, and now she'll tell anyone who'll listen anything they want to know about you. Honestly, Amarilla, you're going to need to grow some common sense.'

'Rowena, why don't you pour us all some tea,' Adam said.

Rowena glared at him but then sighed. 'Amarilla, I'm sorry. I've had experience of Heralds spouting off about things that would have been better left alone, but that's no reason to go off at you. Forgive me?'

I nodded and smiled at her. I asked Adam, 'Why should Infinity's name cause so much interest?'

His green eyes twinkled. 'Amarilla, your horse will have told you that the way we name our horses has been a tradition since Jonus first told Mettle that he wanted a name to call him by.'

I nodded.

'And you know from when you chose Infinity's name, that a horse's name is an indication of what their bonded partner sees in their essence.'

I nodded again.

'Well it's more than that. It's probably easiest to explain by telling you about Peace and me. What seems an age ago now, I married the woman of my dreams and I thought I would burst with happiness. I was doing well as a Herbalist, she was a gifted Weather-Singer and we had plans to live happily ever after. Sadly, within two years she was dead. She died giving birth to my daughter and my daughter died a few hours later. I'm afraid I rather lost my way. I was angry. Furious, as I never knew I could be. I had no interest in my work, my home, my family, nothing. Everyone told me that with time I would get over it and live my life, albeit a different one from that which I had planned, but I didn't allow myself to get over it. I indulged myself in my anger and pushed away everyone who cared for me. In the end, I packed my back-sack and left my village. I lived rough in the woods for three years until Peace tugged me.

'It was a dark time, I won't pretend otherwise. When I first felt Peace tugging at me, I fought him, just as I had fought everything else since Bronwyn and Alita died. I just wanted to be left alone to wallow in my own self-pity, to continue being angry at the world. Luckily for me, Peace persisted until I had no choice but to go to him. I'm not proud of how I behaved in the first few months after he and I found each other and it doesn't need speaking about, but the point of my story is this. When I was having one of my more rational moments, I asked his name and he told me how to choose it myself, as you and all the other Horse-Bonded have done. When he revealed his essence to me, I saw many aspects to him but the main sense I got from him was immense peace, as you will already have surmised. It was many years before I realised, and he confirmed to me, what every Horse-Bonded eventually learns. Considering my history up until that point, can you speculate as to what that should have been?'

I looked at Rowena, hoping for inspiration but she merely munched on a piece of apple cake and smiled at me. Adam began to tuck into his own piece of cake, clearly content to wait until I had an answer for him. Infinity monitored my thoughts closely. Eventually, I had an inkling. 'You saw in Peace what you needed yourself?'

'Yes, well done,' Adam said, 'but it goes further. I saw in him not only what I needed, but what I had the potential to be. I recognised peace most strongly in his essence because, hidden as it was, it was present and ripe for development in myself. By choosing to spend his life with me, Peace enabled me to find and develop that part of myself which I so desperately needed and wanted to flourish, but wouldn't have had even the faintest chance of finding without him.' He stopped speaking then and looked at me expectantly. I could feel Infinity waiting too and I thought through everything Adam had said. Adam saw in Peace what he himself had the potential to be.

'Infinity is what I have the potential to be,' I said faintly and felt a sense of triumph from Infinity before she reverted her attention to grooming with Oak once more. 'But how? What does it mean?'

'That's what everyone else is wondering,' said Rowena. 'Now you see why you're the talk of the town. The other horses have perfectly respectable names like "Tranquil", "Noble", "Verity", "Temerity", as well as the more obscure ones like my "Oak", Shann's "Spider" and Justin's "Gas", but then you arrive with your own Herald to tell everyone just how young and accident prone you are, and your horse is called no less than "Infinity"!'

I looked from Adam to Rowena and we all burst into laughter. It was Adam who recovered first. 'It's good to see you have a sense of humour, my dear, I've a feeling you're going to need one,' he said, still chuckling.

Adam and Rowena insisted on hearing everything that had happened to me since I left them in Coolridge. While Rowena wanted exact details of Infinity's and my encounter with the Woeful, Adam was more interested in how I'd healed my broken bone with no training, and in Infinity's assertion that anybody could perform any of the Skills. When dinnertime arrived, they said their goodbyes, leaving me with the food tray Rowena had thoughtfully brought so that I could eat in my room in peace.

After they had left, I thought over everything Adam had said. Infinity. I thought back to when she had revealed her essence to me, and felt again that sense of how vast she was, part of everything that existed and more, so much more. How could I be that?

I missed Infinity's physical presence keenly all of a sudden. I could hear people moving around in the building, no doubt preparing to go to eat, so I ate my fill while waiting for the building to fall silent and then made my way to Infinity's paddock. The square was illuminated by light spilling from the numerous windows of the surrounding buildings. Once I left it, I followed my sense of Infinity through the dark to the paddock where I had left her. She was waiting for me at the gate.

Walks A Straight Path. All is well. She enfolded me in her energy. I stroked her face and she rested her chin on my shoulder. Each of her slow, deep breaths blasted warm air into my ear. Just as my shoulder was beginning to ache with the weight of her head, she removed it. I stroked her neck, feeling much better.

Rest well, Fin, I told her, *I'll be down to see you in the morning.* She wandered off and I made my way back to my room, looking forward to spending the night in a warm bed.

I woke the following morning to a loud thumping on my bedroom door. 'Amarilla, for the love of autumn, wake up, or decent or not, I'm going to come in and drag you out of bed,' groaned Rowena's muffled voice.

I threw back my heavy, warm covers and stumbled to the door in my nightshirt. 'Are you alright? Have I overslept?'

'Yes to both questions. Bloody hell, I nearly thumped a hole in the door,' she said, striding past me into my room and flinging back the curtains. Light streamed in. It was long past dawn, the time I had become accustomed to waking alongside Infinity. Infinity!

Are you alright? I sent her the thought in a panic, but immediately knew that she was. She grazed alongside Oak and had been doing so for hours. She was well rested and content. It had been a cold night though and she had missed her blanket.

'You'd better get dressed,' said Rowena. 'I left you to sleep as long as I could, but if we don't go down now, we'll miss breakfast.'

'But I need to go to Infinity first,' I protested as I began pulling on a pair of woollen tights.

'She's fine, you know she is. I've already been to see her and Oak, I've mucked out their field shelter and checked the water in their paddock. You need to eat, you're in for a busy day today. You'll need to go and register with the Overseer so he can put you on the duty rota, Adam wants to see you about your apprenticeship, Infinity will need to be measured for a saddle and I've no doubt Feryl will find one that you can both make do with for now so he can get you on board today and begin your riding instruction.' Anxiety must have shown on my face. 'Don't worry, Shann's going to do my chores so I can accompany you today. I'm not leaving you on your own on your first day now that Salom's opened her gob,' my friend told me and I could have hugged her. 'Get dressed, I'm going to the loo. I'll meet you in the corridor.'

We made our way across the square, heading for an imposing five-storey building with numerous chimneys and huge windows spaced evenly along its length. There was an enormous doorway at one end of it and on reaching it, Rowena leant against the oak door and waited for me to enter in front of her. Every part of me wanted to run to my mare.

Merely be yourself. Her thought calmed me and gave me courage.

I stepped through the door into an entrance lobby and then through another, smaller, door into the dining hall. Long wooden tables stretched away from where we stood to the far end of the hall, where I could see another table laden with what looked to be the remainder of the breakfast food. Huge fireplaces dominated three of the plain stone walls at regular intervals and some of them had fires burning within. The windows of the fourth wall allowed the morning sunlight to flood in, giving the hall a warm, even cosy, feeling despite its size. The floor was made of enormous stone slabs, each easily the size of our kitchen table at home.

There were still some people eating at the tables, but judging by the empty bowls and plates left strewn about, most had been and gone, about which I was relieved. The man Rowena had spoken to in the square the previous day was just wiping his mouth and getting to his feet as we approached him on our way to the food table. He was tall with wide shoulders and had brown, shoulder length hair and hazel, laughing eyes.

He held a hand in front of Rowena's face. 'Don't say it, Ro, I know

I'm late, I'm on my way now. It's the sheep in the furthest paddock whose feet I'm helping to trim and I have to pick up the worming paste from Adam on my way. See, I was listening. Morning, Amarilla, I'm Shann. My horse is Spider, he's the amazingly handsome bay in the paddock a couple down from your mare, you'll have to meet him later because... I'm... late.' He tried to dodge Rowena's fingers, which were flicking at his ear, and left us at a run, laughing.

As we made our way to the food table, I was awarded nods and smiles by most of those we passed and several stood and introduced themselves. I learnt that a tiny, middle-aged woman with a black and grey ponytail was called Quinta, and that her equally small horse was called Noble. They had just returned from a year long trip visiting villages, helping where they could. I met an elderly lady called Turi whose horse had sadly passed away, but who couldn't think of living anywhere but The Gathering and was now the resident head cook. A thin man, whom I judged to be in his fifties by his lined face but not yet completely grey hair, introduced himself as Newson and assured me that I would meet Integrity, his grey mare, very soon. The last person to stand up and greet me was none other than Holly, whose Quest Ceremony I had attended as a child.

'Amarilla, it IS you,' she said. 'I couldn't believe it when I heard your name flying around yesterday, and for your mother's sake, I hoped it wasn't the Amarilla from home, but it's good to see you here. How is your mother coping?'

'I think she's doing okay, thank goodness.'

'Well that's a relief for your father. We'll have to catch up properly sometime soon, I'm late meeting someone, but it's good to see you Amarilla,' she said and hurried off towards the door.

As I piled my plate with fried eggs, tomatoes and bread, I relaxed and began to look forward to my day and all of those that would follow. I was Horse-Bonded and I was at The Gathering with Infinity. I smiled.

ELEVEN

Settling

$\mathcal{M}$y first morning at The Gathering passed so quickly, I hardly had time to blink. First of all, and despite Rowena's protestations that we didn't have enough time, I insisted on fetching my new grooming kit and taking proper care of my horse. Infinity was aware that my actions were governed by the "strange emotion" I felt for not tending to her as I should have after breaking my arm and I was aware of her exasperation, which was exacerbated as she became aware of my intention to visit a Bone-Singer after I had finished tending to her.

I know I can finish healing it, I trusted you enough to heal it in the first place, but I need my bone back to full strength before I can damage it again and I can't afford the energy or the time to do it now, I told her.

There will always be an excuse to avoid that which is difficult.

Please, Fin, don't give me a hard time, not this morning.

She withdrew her disapproval from my mind and directed all of her attention towards grazing. I sighed as I returned the various components of my grooming kit to their bag.

'Wha's up?' asked Rowena. She sat on the top rail of the fence, swinging her legs back and forth as she waited for me.

'Infinity disapproves of me wanting to go to a Bone-Singer to finish healing my arm. She thinks I should do it myself.'

'Well if it was me, I'd think carefully before ignoring her advice, but first things first, we need to go to the healing rooms to see Adam. Then we'll go and see Norieva – he's just taken on the Overseer's role for a while – and then I said we'd be at the Saddler's workshop with Infinity just before lunch.'

The healing rooms were on the ground floor of the building next to the one in which I had my room. Rowena told me that there were usually three or four practitioners of each Skill present at any one time, along with a number of Apprentices, so any injuries or illnesses tended to be dealt with swiftly. She couldn't resist commenting on how lucky that was for me.

As we walked along the corridor, many of the doors were ajar and I could hear the murmur of voices within several of the rooms. I wondered whether to ignore Infinity and knock on the door of one of the Bone-Singers. I decided against it for now.

Adam opened his door at Rowena's knock and welcomed us warmly. The stone walls of his consulting room were decorated with large, coloured drawings of different herbs with their names written underneath in stylised lettering. One wall was lined with shelves, upon which sat jar upon jar of dried herbs. On the windowsill were small troughs with live herbs growing in them. Three large comfy chairs were arranged in a small circle and a tall cabinet stood in the corner next to the window. I guessed that it contained his notes and patient records. A door stood ajar and I could see that it led to Adam's bedroom, a room similar in size and contents to my own.

It was quickly arranged that I would be at Adam's disposal for the two hours after breakfast each day. He showed me some small rooms at the end of the corridor that I could use for preparing herbs or writing up notes in peace and quiet, and then he bid us farewell as a patient arrived for a consultation with him.

Next, we entered our own building and Rowena knocked loudly on the first door that we came to. A loud, high-pitched and harassed voice bade us enter. On complying, I saw a man of slight build with grey, wiry hair and the most enormous hooked nose, sitting behind a huge wooden desk. He paid neither of us any attention. He muttered to himself constantly as he scribbled on pieces of paper before stacking them into tall, teetering piles with his knobbly fingers. Occasionally, he would shake his head violently and the muttering would get louder as he crossed out whatever offended him and wrote his correction in its place.

'Norieva, this is Amarilla Nixon. She's come to register for the duty rota. Norrie?' said Rowena. The muttering and scribbling continued. 'Norrie?' she said louder and then finally shouted, 'THUNDER AND LIGHTNING, NORRIE, WE HAVEN'T GOT ALL DAY.'

Norieva jumped and knocked a pile of papers to the floor. He glared up at us both with black eyes. 'What is the meaning of this, Rowena and... nameless person?' he squeaked. 'Can't you see I'm hopelessly busy? And now look, papers all over the floor, more work for me, always more work for good old Norrie and always interruptions...'

'We knocked and you told us to come in, and I told you at dinner last night that I'd be bringing Amarilla to register with you. If being the Overseer stresses you so much, why don't you just say you don't want to do it anymore, or at least have an assistant? All the others do when it's their turn,' said Rowena.

Norieva glared at her and she returned his glare defiantly. He transferred his gaze to me.

'Um hello, n-nice to meet you,' I said.

Norieva took a form from a tray and then asked for my name, my horse's name, any Skills for which I was training or qualified, and any chores for which I had a particular liking. He told me to check the rota on the dining room noticeboard on Sunday evening, to see my duties for the following week. Since today was Wednesday, I should apparently think myself lucky to be having four days grace before I would muck in with everyone else. Unlike him, who toiled constantly, day in, day out when there were so many other things he could be doing instead...

'Yes, thanks, Norrie, we'll leave you to your martyrdom,' Rowena interrupted cheerfully and prodded me towards the door.

'Thanks, Norrie,' I said. Once the door was closed behind us, I breathed a sigh of relief.

'He's a sweetheart really,' said Rowena, 'he just doesn't handle stress very well. It's a shame he doesn't seem to allow Dragonfly to help him much when he's apart from her, maybe it's because he bonded late in life, who knows. I'll make sure you have a chance to sit with him at dinner some time, he tells the best jokes, no, really, he does,' she said as I looked at her disbelievingly.

We headed back towards Infinity's paddock. It took an age to get there, as people kept appearing in front of us, wanting to introduce themselves and to know if all that Salom had said about Infinity and me were true. When we finally reached our destination, we found a group of people talking near the paddock gate and every now and then, one of them would glance at Infinity. She was well aware of their interest, and it pleased her. They each introduced themselves to me, commenting on how beautiful Infinity was, before continuing on their way. I felt her pleasure intensify and couldn't help but smile.

Come on, you vain horse you, it's time for us to visit the Saddler, I told her.

As I held the gate open for Infinity, I felt something flit past the edge of my mind towards Rowena, very much like when I used to get a sense of Infinity before she tugged me. Strange. Did I imagine that?

You did not.

What was it?

Oak communicated with his human. Your mind opens further.

'Come on, we'll miss lunch at this rate,' said Rowena. I hurried after her with Infinity at my side.

Instead of entering the square, we turned left to go behind the building that housed the dining hall. It was soon apparent that, large as it was, the dining room didn't go back the full depth of the building. Along the back of it was a row of large rooms with windows that ran from the ceiling to the floor, admitting as much light as possible onto the people who worked within; the workshops.

Rowena led us to a room about halfway along the building, knocked lightly on the door and entered without waiting for an answer. There was an enormous workbench directly in front of the windows, which was littered with tools and pieces of leather of varying sizes. Along the length of the far wall ran an open-fronted cabinet with large cubby holes, containing leather, tools and saddles.

'Come on in, both of you,' Rowena said over her shoulder and then yelled, 'MASON, WE'RE HERE.'

A door to the back of the room opened and a bear of a man with a head and beard of thick, black hair entered, carrying a steaming mug in his hand. 'For the love of autumn, Rowena, there's no need to shout, I'm right here. Oh, my lovely, you must be Infinity,' he said as my mare stood with her head over my shoulder.

'Um, I'm Amarilla,' I said as Mason held his hand up to my shoulder for Infinity to sniff.

'And so you are, my sweet, so you are.' He smelt of leather and sweat and had a gentle manner about him that was at odds with his brawny appearance. Infinity and I both instantly liked him.

Mason walked slowly around Infinity, looking at her back from all angles. 'Now, what have we here then, my lovely, quite wide here, but not so much there, saddle'll need to sit back away from you a bit just there, won't it? Can't have anythin' restrictin' those magnificent shoulders of yours, hmmm, don't you worry, Infinity my lovely, I'll have you in a saddle so comfy you'll be wantin' to sleep in it, you just ask my Dili, she'll tell you...'

'Dili's his horse,' whispered Rowena. 'You can't miss her, she's enormous, makes Oak look small. Dili is short for Diligence by the way,' she added.

Infinity loved Mason's quiet chatter and the close attention he paid to her, and I saw her batting her eyelids at him more than once. She allowed him to put several of his saddles on her back and bent around to sniff each one with deep consideration whilst he adjusted the way that it sat on her using different pads and straps. She liked the feel of the second of the four that he tried the best and I was just about to tell him so, when he announced that he would be making a saddle very similar to the second one that he had tried on her, with a few minor adjustments. I smiled and thanked him, and was rewarded with a big beaming smile in return. I shook his hand and promised to be back in two days to collect Infinity's saddle.

'Look forward to it, look forward to it. Ro, make sure Dili has enough water on your way past her this evenin' will you? I may be workin' late on this, can't have Infinity waitin' for her saddle, can we, my beautiful?' He was rewarded with yet another bat of Infinity's eyelashes, before we left him scurrying around his workshop.

'How long before lunch?' I asked Rowena.

A bell rang loudly. 'Right now. I'll go on ahead and pile our plates, shall I, while you go and let Infinity back in with Oak?'

'Could you just save me some? I need to be with Infinity for a bit,' I said.

'Sure. I'll eat mine and then bring yours out to you. That okay?'

'Thanks a lot, see you later.'

Infinity knew what I had in mind and her approval washed over me. We meandered back to her paddock, meeting more people on the way. One man was accompanied by his horse, a tall, chestnut stallion who pranced, rather than walked next to him. The man also had a spring in his step and as the two of them approached us, I realised that I seemed to be having trouble seeing where the boundary between them was; it was as if the man's side blurred into his horse's shoulder. I blinked frantically, thinking that I must have something in my eye. Infinity's interest in the handsome stallion was overshadowed by her interest in what was happening to me.

You see true, she informed me as the twosome reached us.

The man asked, 'Are you alright?'

I continued to blink as man and horse stood directly in front of me, but it had no effect on what I was seeing. 'Um, sorry, I'm not sure. My horse says I am though,' I said, feeling a bit stupid. 'I'm Amarilla and this is Infinity.'

The man shook my hand. 'I thought you might be. I'm Justin and this is Gas. Do you want to sit down?'

I gave up trying to clear my eyes and decided to accept what they were telling me. 'No thanks, I think I just have something in my eye. Gas?' I held out the back of my hand to the chestnut horse, as I had seen everyone else do when they met Infinity. He sniffed it politely.

Justin laughed. 'I have a warped mind, but yes, Gas is his name and

judging by his antics this morning, he's a bit too full of it. Look at this.'
He pointed to a gash on Gas's knee. 'He's been tearing around with
Spider and didn't see the stone flying from Spider's hoof until it cut him.
I was just about to go for lunch, but never mind, soon get this cleared up,
I just need to catch Adam. See you both around, if you're sure you're
okay?'

I nodded.

'Come on, Gas,' he said to his horse and lifted a hand in farewell to
me as the two of them sprang off towards the square. I looked over my
shoulder at them and they still appeared to be joined somehow, as if they
were one.

You see true. Worry not.

I needed energy and focus for what I was about to do, so I decided to
accept Infinity's advice. Oak whickered his welcome as Infinity and I
entered her paddock and headed for the beech tree. He kept a respectful
distance as I sat at the base of the tree and leant back against it, whilst
Infinity began to graze near my feet.

Knowing that Infinity was right there next to me gave me the
confidence to simply sing my bone back to full strength. It was as simple
as that, as easy as tuning into herbs and testing to see what they could
help with. Infinity was right – it was all the same. I smiled to myself
while Infinity grazed on. I was so happy to be with her.

And I with you, she told me before walking over to a muddy patch
near the water trough and rolling.

I was still smiling when Rowena appeared with a dark look on her
face and Salom at her side. Rowena was carrying my lunch, so Salom
opened the gate for her to come through, which she did grudgingly.

'Salom wants to talk to you,' she said, rolling her eyes, 'can't wait
apparently.'

'Settling in well, Amarilla?' Salom asked me, jovially.

'Yes, thank you, how is Salsh?'

'Fit as a fiddle, thanks to you. We're off in the morning, so I just
wanted to check if you had any letters or messages for me to take to your
family.'

'So you can have more gossip to spread around? Amarilla's not that stupid,' muttered Rowena.

'Gossip? How dare you, I am no gossip, I am a Herald and a very good one,' retorted Salom.

'And how do you expect Amarilla to trust you after you announced everything she told you to everyone in the square? Do you have any idea how upsetting it is to hear people talking about you?' Rowena stormed. I had a feeling this wasn't just about me anymore.

'Amarilla told me what happened to her whilst I was wearing my bandanna, just as I am now. Any information given to me whilst I am advertising to all that I am on duty, is for me to part with as I see fit, whereas any letters or private messages I carry remain private between the sender and the receiver. Rowena, you know all this, why must I justify myself to you?'

Rowena didn't answer, but looked away towards Oak. I felt his thoughts flutter past my mind to her.

'Um, Salom? I would like you to take letters to my family please, can I bring them to you this evening? I'll write them after dinner,' I said.

Salom told me where her room was and then with a last glance at Rowena, who pointedly ignored her, she left us and made off in the direction of the fields.

'Are you alright?' I asked Rowena as she sat down beside me and handed me my lunch.

'Fine, just can't stand Heralds. Gossips, the lot of them, whatever Miss High and Mighty says. Eat your lunch.'

I was ravenous and more than happy to eat in the silence that ensued whilst Oak's thoughts flew past me. Rowena gradually calmed down and eventually took a deep breath and leant back against the tree. 'Sorry, Am, I shouldn't take my anger out on you,' she said.

'It's okay, do you want to talk about it? It'd be a refreshing change to talk about someone else's stuff.'

'There's not much to tell. My dad left my mum when she was pregnant with me, after she broke her agreement with him never to conceive. My mum was heartbroken and could never love me as a result. She remarried and had eight more children, all of whom she loved to bits.

I used to escape to the woods whenever I could, and there was one tree that I used to climb and sit in for hours. It had big strong branches and I used to feel safe and protected up there, almost as if I was loved. You can guess what type of tree it was.

'Anyway, when I was tugged, I knew my mum wouldn't give me a Quest Ceremony, so I waited until everyone was asleep, gathered what I needed, kissed my brothers and sisters as they slept and left something on each of their pillows that they would know was from me, and left. By the time I'd found Oak and arrived here, a Herald had arrived ahead of me, warning that a thief of my description was at large. I'm not proud that I stole from my family, but it was only the minimum that I'd need to survive. Bloody Herald.'

'That's awful. Surely everyone here accepted you once they knew what happened though? And they're all Horse-Bonded and Oak had chosen you to bond with, that must have counted for a lot?'

'It was horrible to begin with, as I had no idea why everyone seemed to be so suspicious of me, but luckily, Adam was here. He listened to me and I don't know what he said to everyone, but things gradually got easier from then on, no thanks to that Herald. Anyway, I saw Feryl at lunch – he's Master of Riding here, I think I told you last night – and he's expecting you both mid-afternoon. I was thinking that would give you a bit more time to yourself first, but by the look of Infinity, there'll be no relaxing for you. Good job you left your grooming kit down here.'

It appeared that my horse had been intent on caking every inch of herself with mud when she rolled, and she had pretty much achieved her aim. I made to rise, but Rowena grabbed my arm. 'Come on, sit down and chill for a bit, you don't think I'm going to leave you to tackle that on your own do you? Let your lunch get down and then we'll take one side each.' I grinned at her gratefully.

At the appointed time, a more or less clean Infinity and I, with Rowena and Oak in tow for moral support, made our way to the larger paddocks that were set aside for riding. I felt extremely daunted when I saw the number of people sitting on the fence of the paddock to which Rowena directed me.

No need, Infinity informed me. Her calm confidence soothed me.

A man leant on the gate, watching us as we approached. He wore fitted, knee-length, brown leather boots and thick, brown leggings which had leather patches stitched to the inside of each leg. His short, black hair was speckled with grey and the blue of his pullover matched exactly that of his eyes; I had a distinct feeling it wasn't by chance.

'Amarilla and Infinity, right on time,' he said loudly. 'Come in, come in, I've got some saddles here, I'm sure there'll be one we can use until your own is ready.'

He offered his hand for Infinity to sniff only very briefly, before hauling the first saddle to be tried off the fence and straight on to her back. She stiffened, laid her ears flat back on her head and snorted. Feryl appeared not to notice. I moved in front of Infinity and put my hands either side of her neck.

Fin, it's alright. I know he's rude but he doesn't mean you any harm.

I am aware of what he means.

Feryl was busy explaining to those who sat on the fence, why the saddle he had put onto Infinity wouldn't be suitable. When he had finished, he removed it and then approached her with the next one to try. She sidestepped away from him, ears back and tail swishing.

'Just stand still, there's a girl,' said Feryl and approached her again. She sidestepped once more. He looked at me, still standing at her head, and frowned slightly. He propped the saddle on one hip and held the back of his spare hand out for her to sniff. To begin with, Infinity looked away, completely ignoring him. Some of the people on the fence began to whisper to each other and Feryl's cheeks flushed pink. After some minutes, Infinity finally deigned to sniff his hand and I saw his shoulders sink slightly with relief. 'Right, now, Infinity, I'm just going to put this saddle on your back to see if it fits. Stand still for me, there's a girl,' he said so that only my mare and I could hear him.

Come on, Fin, you've made him suffer, please let him put it on?

She let out a deep sigh. *I will allow it.*

'She'll allow it,' I told Feryl, hoping he would realise that at any moment she could choose to disallow it once more. Feryl appeared to have learnt his lesson, however and treated Infinity with the utmost courtesy from that point on. It was a relief when he found a saddle that he deemed would suffice, and announced that it was time for me to get on.

Feryl told me to climb the fence, ask Infinity to stand alongside it and then put a leg over the saddle and sit down on it. We managed that without incident and once I was on board, Feryl altered the length of my stirrup leathers so that my feet rested comfortably in the stirrups.

He raised his voice once more as he instructed me how to sit in the saddle, apparently keen that everyone within earshot should hear his words, and he kept it at the same level throughout the lesson that followed. He taught me how to use my body, rather than my mind, to ask Infinity to move forward, turn and halt, so that our minds could be free to communicate about other things whilst we moved around together. Infinity followed my body's suggestions easily and Feryl seemed satisfied.

As we continued to practise what we had been shown though, I couldn't help but notice that Infinity seemed to be getting lower in front of me than she had been when I had first mounted, just as had happened when I had ridden her in order to escape the Woeful.

Fin, are you alright? I asked.

Her reply was slightly fainter than usual. *I am enjoying learning how our bodies can move together but I am pressed down onto my front legs by your weight. I cannot seem to remedy the situation.*

I immediately relayed what she had told me to Feryl.

'Oh, don't worry about that, all horses find it strange to begin with,' he replied. 'As time goes on, Infinity will get stronger and better able to balance with you on board.'

I need help to transfer your weight away from my front legs now. This cannot wait.

I passed Infinity's request on to Feryl.

'All in good time, this is your first lesson and you have much to learn. Be patient,' he said and then to his onlookers he added, 'to be so young and innocent!' Some of them laughed, others looked slightly uncomfortable and Rowena had a face like thunder.

Infinity wasn't convinced by Feryl's assurances and I was disturbed by his dismissal of her concerns. I was relieved when he announced that our lesson had come to an end and showed me how to dismount and remove the saddle.

'Same time tomorrow, girls,' he said and I felt Infinity bristle slightly at the sound of his voice.

Rowena appeared at our side with Oak. 'Bloody man, he had no right to talk down to you like that, are you okay?'

I nodded. 'He probably just isn't used to teaching someone as young as me.'

'That's as maybe but however young you both are, Infinity is a horse and her thoughts and opinions should be heeded, as Feryl well knows. I don't know what's got into the man.'

'I'm not really looking forward to our lesson tomorrow,' I said as she vaulted onto Oak's bare back from a standstill. 'Did Oak struggle to carry you when you were learning to ride? Don't you ever bother with a saddle?' I added.

'Not always, no. I use one most of the time so Oak doesn't have to suffer my seat bones digging into his back on a regular basis, but we both like to go for a ride without, once in a while. Feryl doesn't approve of me riding bareback, so now seems like an ideal time to do it. We're going down to the river. Want to come?'

I looked around at Feryl and saw him watching Rowena with a scowl. 'We'd love to come with you if we won't hold you up?'

'Nope, we'll walk with you until we get there and then if you don't mind, we'll leave you for a bit and go for a blast.'

I walked alongside Oak with Infinity on my other side.

Rowena said, 'To answer your question, Oak did find it strange carrying me to begin with, but it got easier for him as my balance improved and he built up more muscle and got stronger in his back. Sometimes in our lessons though, I used to get the impression that Oak was waiting for Feryl to say more but whenever I asked him about it, he said that he felt there was more to be gained from the ridden interaction than we were being taught, but he either couldn't or wouldn't pinpoint for me exactly what was missing.'

It was not so pressing an issue to him but he felt it nevertheless, Infinity informed me.

What was?

All will become clear.

For the love of light, Infinity, can't you just tell me?

I could. Learning by experience will be more thorough.

'Aaaaagh!' I exclaimed. Rowena and Oak both jumped. 'Sorry, it's just that Infinity knows what Oak was missing, it's to do with the problems that she and I are having, I think, but apparently I will learn it more thoroughly by experience.'

Rowena sat up straighter and I felt the flutter of Oak's communication with her. 'We're going to have to watch all of your riding lessons, this is the start of something, Oak can feel it,' she said. Oak developed a very definite spring in his step and Rowena laughed at his exuberance.

I laughed along with her and we chatted excitedly until we reached the river. There, I sat down on a large boulder as Oak kicked up his heels and then thundered off along the riverbank. Rowena's black hair flowed behind her as she crouched low on Oak's back. I could feel Infinity fighting her instinct to follow them.

Go, Infinity, go, I urged her.

I felt her fleeting regret that she couldn't take me with her, then she launched into a flat-out gallop, following in Oak's enormous hoof prints. Her feet pounded the ground wildly and her tail streamed out behind her as she forced her way through the cool autumn air. It wasn't long before she caught up with Oak's heavier pace and then slowed to match his speed and gallop beside him as they tore off into the distance. How I longed to be with them. But what if I never learnt to ride well enough for her to be able to carry me? Now the following day's riding lesson couldn't come soon enough.

TWELVE

Difficulties

I rose the following morning with an air of determination; I wanted to ride well, I wanted my horse to be able to carry me without harm to herself and I wanted some answers as to how to achieve both of those things, today. My resolve faltered slightly when I found I couldn't walk properly as a result of the previous day's lesson, but as I moved around and my muscles stretched and eased, my focus returned.

During my first session with Adam, as he and I worked through my herb journal so that he could see the gaps in my knowledge, I was distracted. When my attention wandered for the third or fourth time, he banged my journal shut, chuckling as I jerked out of my reverie. He asked good-naturedly to know what was on my mind. I told him what had happened the previous day and what I had resolved to ensure in today's session with Feryl.

'I understand your distraction,' he said kindly, 'and I think in light of it, you may consider yourself excused from the rest of your morning's session with me.'

I felt awful. 'But we've barely started on my journal. I'm sorry, Adam, if I try really hard to concentrate, could we carry on?'

'You're a sweet girl, Amarilla, and your previous Master can't rate your abilities highly enough, but you must understand that as a Herbalist, people and animals will come to you for help and that puts you in a position of responsibility. When you're on duty, it is of paramount importance that you are able to concentrate your mind so that you can tune in to your patient's condition and the herbs that will help, to the best of your ability. I'm afraid there's a rule that I expect both my Apprentices and myself to follow most stringently; if it's not possible to leave personal problems at the door of the healing room, then for the sake of your craft, do not enter it.'

If anyone else had spoken his words to me, I might have considered myself rebuked, but from Adam, the message got through to me in the gentlest, nicest possible way. I promised both him and myself to adhere to his rule from the following day onwards and then donned my cloak and left the healing room, feeling guilty. Adam had left the home he had made for himself since Peace died, and returned to The Gathering to help me. True, he had told me that any of the other Herbalists in residence would have been happy to take me on and it was his curiosity over what Infinity had in store for me that had led him back here, but the fact remained that he had been extremely kind to me and in my first session with him, I had let him down.

You indulge yourself once more with the emotion that serves no purpose, Infinity informed me as I made my way to her paddock.

Indulge myself? I'm not enjoying feeling this way, I protested.

Then feel differently.

I can't just change how I feel because I decide to.

That is a falsehood and you have believed it for too long.

I don't understand.

You feel an emotion that has no purpose. You feel it when you have a realisation that you should have done something differently. Making a mistake is vital to learning. A young fox narrowly avoids being caught by a pack of dogs and he learns to avoid the area they patrol. A foal has a bitter taste in her mouth from chewing a particular herb and she learns to avoid it in future. A young human has her lesson ended prematurely because she is unable to concentrate and she learns to order her mind so that she can focus in subsequent lessons. Emotion such as you are feeling has no place in this process of learning.

But how do I choose to feel differently?

How did you choose what to eat for your last meal?

I selected things I have eaten before and liked.

It is the same.

I frowned to myself. How could it possibly be the same? Could I really just choose a feeling I liked and then feel it?

If you decide to.

But I might have upset Adam's feelings.

You are not responsible for looking after the feelings of anyone else. He Who Is Peace can also choose how he feels and this he knows. He has chosen to see things merely as they are and he suffers not.

Relief washed over me as I reached where Infinity waited for me at her paddock fence, and hopped up to sit on the top rail beside her; Adam wasn't cross with me. I didn't need to feel guilty.

There will never be a need.

But what if I cause someone to suffer and they don't realise that they can choose how they feel about it?

Then you will have been useful to them in highlighting that they yet have work to do on maturing as an individual.

I felt uncomfortable. Was it really true that I could just say and do whatever I wished and not care how anyone felt?

The only thing for which you are responsible is being the best version of yourself that you can be. You will make mistakes and there will be misunderstandings between you and those of both your and other species. Learn from your mistakes and allow others to learn from theirs but do not waste your life force worrying about how others perceive you, Infinity told me.

I just don't like the thought that someone is cross with me or doesn't like me.

And that is because you yet rely on the opinion of others as to whether or not you have worth. We have visited this subject before.

I remember. The human need to feel special.

When you can realise that every living being of every species has unconditional equal worth then you will be free of many of the restrictions that you place upon yourself.

Equal worth? A thought occurred to me. *Do you disapprove of us keeping livestock to kill and eat?*

Prey animals of several species are prepared to sustain humans with their flesh. This has nothing to do with their worth or lack of it. They require a standard of care that humans in present times adequately meet. They experience life in their chosen body and when their flesh is required they leave and then return at will in a different body at a time of their choosing.

But we kill them so that we can live. Isn't that making them of less worth than us?

Make no mistake. They enter into their roles willingly. They know their worth as equal to yours and if the care they receive is less than required they will allow their bodies to sicken and die. You eat their healthy flesh not because they are subservient to you but because they permit it.

Blimey – I recognised Rowena's influence on my vocabulary and grinned to myself – so I needed to know my worth and be the best I could be, then I would have no need for guilt. I was going to find that difficult, I knew, but at least I understood it. Try as I might though, I was still struggling with the idea that I could choose how to feel.

Halt yourself when you realise you are feeling something you would rather not and choose to feel something more pleasant, Infinity advised me. *Much may be learnt from observing the conduct of He Who Is Peace.*

Adam. *Is this what Peace taught him? To choose to feel peaceful instead of angry?*

That is for He Who Is Peace to tell you if he chooses.

The wind had got up and was blasting its way across the paddocks to where I sat with Infinity. I had wrapped my cloak around myself, but the wind kept catching the edges of it and billowing it out around me, and I was cold.

The weather changes, observed Infinity. As I rubbed my hands up and down her neck in an attempt to warm them, I noted how much thicker her coat was becoming. After hugging her and sending her a surge of warmth and affection, which was promptly returned, I left her and decided to go and sit with Rowena as she worked in the Tailors' workshop. I wondered whether I could find the nerve to ask her to make another blanket for Infinity.

When I got there, I was given a hot mug of nettle tea and offered a stool on which to perch next to Rowena's workbench. Rowena passed a waxed garment along the bench to me. 'Here you go, Am, the Weather-Singers have warned that some nasty weather is coming and I couldn't see Infinity go cold.'

I unfolded the garment, to find a waterproof rug. The material was a deep purple and she had used a lighter purple for the binding and the fastenings. This rug also had an additional blanket stitched inside it for added warmth.

'Thank you so much, Ro,' I said, at the same time as letting Infinity know what Rowena had done for her.

'Just one of the perks of being the friend of a Tailor,' she said.

We chatted the rest of the morning away while Rowena worked, then we dashed out to put rugs on our horses before lunch, as there was a feel of rain in the air. Infinity was delighted with hers and whilst I fiddled with the fastenings, ensuring they were adjusted just right for her, she bathed me in a feeling of warm contentment. Our timing couldn't have been better, as rain started to fall just as we were leaving the paddock, forcing us to run to the dining hall.

We were among the first to arrive for lunch. We hung our wet cloaks in the lobby area, before dashing into the dining hall and to the food table. Shortly after we had sat down with our soup, we were joined by Adam, Shann and Justin. Now that Justin was away from his horse, my eyes could focus on him properly. He was taller than Shann and had short, curly brown hair. He had a very defined brow over intense brown eyes and there was a sense of barely controlled energy about him. He constantly jigged his leg as he sat in discussion with Adam over the lack of progress of the healing of Gas's knee; it seemed that Gas was refusing to take things easy while his wound healed and it kept splitting back open and bleeding.

'If he would just consent to being in a paddock by himself for a few days instead of tearing around with Spider all the time,' complained

Justin, 'or even with a quieter horse who'll let him be so he can rest until it heals, but he won't hear of it.'

'I seem to remember having a similar conversation about you last winter when you had tonsillitis and refused to stay in bed,' smiled Adam and Justin grinned and looked abashed. 'Now I'm wondering about adding an extra herb to the unguent we've been applying to Gas's wound, to make it more elastic and stop it drying to the firm crust that seems to be the problem.'

I listened avidly to their conversation, keen to hear what Adam might come up with. Rowena and Shann began what I was coming to realise was one of their normal conversations, where Shann played the clown and Rowena was as rude to him as she could think how to be, so I shifted closer to Adam to better hear his ideas as he thought aloud. He finally settled on a couple of herbs that he wanted to try, and assured Justin that he would experiment with them after he had seen his last patient that afternoon. Fascinated, I asked Adam if I could watch him while he worked and he happily agreed just as Norieva sat down opposite him.

Rowena said, 'Wotcha, Norrie, tell Am that joke about the Weather-Singer who got stuck in the tree.'

A small piece of mustard-smeared ham slapped against her face and stuck there. Shann erupted into laughter at his prank and Justin's laughter was swift to follow. As Rowena removed the ham from her face while scolding Shann, I shrank back down into my seat as far as possible, waiting for Norieva's reaction to Shann's childish, albeit funny behaviour. To my astonishment, his girlish laughter joined Adam's chuckles and he did indeed then proceed to tell some of his jokes.

I couldn't remember ever having laughed so much. Rowena's description of Norieva was accurate; away from his office he was a sweetheart and he did tell absolutely the best jokes. The others laughed as much as I did, even though they'd heard his full repertoire many times before.

'Judging by the noise coming from over here, you're settling in well and that's always nice to see, Amarilla, but don't go spending too long in here, we don't want you late for your lesson, do we? Lots to learn, no time to waste,' Feryl said in a tone one might use to speak to a small child, as he made his way past our table to the exit.

Justin looked at me and rolled his eyes, and Rowena slammed the water jug down onto the table next to me. 'If that man patronises you one more time, Am, he's going to hear the sharp side of my tongue,' she said.

'You mean there's a soft side?' asked Shann.

'Um, Rowena, no don't, please,' I said. 'I don't mind how he talks to me if he can teach me to ride Infinity. Maybe he'll speak to me differently when he gets to know me better?'

'Don't count on it, Amarilla, the man's a pig-headed cretin,' said Justin.

'Oh, now look here, Justin,' said Norieva. 'Feryl had tremendous patience with me when I was learning to ride Dragonfly and you can't deny that he knows what he's talking about.'

'Gas doesn't think so,' muttered Justin. An uneasy churning began in my stomach; I needed to believe that Feryl could help me and Infinity.

'Oh, not this again, Jus,' moaned Shann. 'Let it go, can't you? It was ages ago now.'

'What was?' Rowena demanded.

Shann said, 'Justin and I arrived here within weeks of one another, so we were learning to ride at the same time. Feryl hadn't long risen to his post of Master of Riding and I think it's fair to say that Justin and Gas gave him a baptism of fire.'

'What happened?' I asked.

Justin answered. 'Not long into our first lesson, Gas began to get agitated. He began by grinding to a halt and refusing to move forward again when I asked him to. I asked him what was wrong and he couldn't seem to tell me. There was something about being ridden that unhinged him to the point where I could feel he was using all of his concentration to hold himself together, so that he wouldn't explode and throw me. I told Feryl and he told me to get off while we checked that the saddle was sitting properly, although I told him I didn't think that was what it was. Everything was fine, so I got back on and tried to keep Gas moving forward again, but it wasn't long before the same thing happened. Gas was in such a state that he couldn't order his thoughts at all and I told

Feryl I was getting off again. That was when Feryl and I had our first argument. The following day, the same thing happened and this time Feryl insisted on riding Gas to see if he could find the problem. Gas responded the same way with Feryl riding him, only Feryl wouldn't back off. He pushed and pushed Gas and got him moving again for a short time before Gas exploded, throwing Feryl and then galloping around the paddock, bucking like a mad beast. I could feel how stressed he was and I was furious with Feryl, and with myself for allowing it to happen.'

'You were a bit scary, mate,' said Shann.

Justin continued, 'That was the last time I trusted Feryl's opinion on what's best for my horse.'

'But you ride him now and he loves it, blimey you won the jumping at the last Friendly by miles,' said Rowena.

'Yes, well, Gas and I decided to go our own way for a while. Every day, I'd put his saddle on and just sit on him, and if he wanted to move he would, and if not, he didn't. Gradually, he found a way to move with me on him that he could cope with, but I left it to him to decide how far he moved. When he needed me to get off, I did, immediately. When he was happier to move for longer, we had another lesson with Feryl to learn how to move together better, everything you guys have learnt, but I took things really slowly with him, everything at his own pace. Feryl didn't like the fact that we did most of our riding sessions without him and he was a git to me in every lesson that Gas and I had with him. Eventually, Gas could do everything I asked him to, but I always felt he was having to compromise something in himself to do it. Still do, but he either won't or can't tell me what it is.'

'I never knew about that,' Rowena said thoughtfully, 'and I've always felt from Oak that he wanted more from our lessons, but like Gas, he doesn't seem to know what exactly. Amarilla and I were talking about it yesterday.'

I shook my head very slightly, hoping she would guess that I didn't want her to tell our friends that Infinity and I might be able to help. Not yet. She gave a hint of a nod by way of a reply and promptly changed the subject.

Soon after, Rowena and I donned our wet cloaks and ventured back outside to fetch our horses and get to Feryl's lesson on time. The rain had stopped, but a blustery wind flung wet leaves into our faces as we battled against it. As we made our way to the teaching paddock, I couldn't shake off the feeling of unease that I'd felt on hearing Justin's account of his and Gas's experience of being taught by Feryl. Infinity made no attempt to allay my anxiety, which concerned me even more.

As we reached the paddock, I was relieved to see that the group of onlookers was substantially smaller than on the previous day, a desirable effect of the deteriorating weather, I supposed. I removed Infinity's blanket and wrapped it around the top rail of the fence, glad to be left to saddle Infinity by myself while Feryl stood chatting animatedly with some of our spectators. I mounted as I had been instructed the previous day and then asked Infinity to move forward.

Feryl appeared not to have noticed that Infinity and I had begun the lesson without him, so I asked Infinity to move towards the centre of the paddock, where we practised our turning, stopping and then moving on again. We both enjoyed the feeling of moving together as a partnership.

We had weaved and circled our way over to the far side of the paddock by the time Feryl joined us, slightly out of breath. 'Good, very good,' he said enthusiastically, 'you're doing very well. I think we can move you both up to a trot now.'

Faster? asked Infinity. Her front legs were already under strain from the little we had done.

Yes. What do you think? Shall I tell Feryl that you can't?

When we escaped the Woeful there was more weight on my front legs as we went faster, she replied.

Right, time for answers, I decided. We halted and I told Feryl about how Infinity was feeling, the problem she'd had when we'd fled from the Woeful, and her concerns that if we went faster, the same thing would happen.

He nodded. 'She's not strong enough to carry you at speed yet, that will be why she lost her balance and fell, but she'll be alright carrying you in walk and trot.'

'She's worried about going any faster now though,' I said. 'If she's having trouble with too much weight on her front legs when we're going slowly, won't it just get worse when she increases pace?'

'Amarilla, you're going to have to trust me when I tell you that trotting will help increase Infinity's strength and fitness, and then she'll find it easier to carry you.'

We will try to do as he says, Infinity resolved.

'Okay, what do you want us to do?' I asked Feryl.

After a few minutes listening to Feryl's instructions, I asked Infinity to walk on and then move up to a trot. I was surprised and pleased to discover that I found Feryl's instructions very easy to carry out, and I absolutely loved the feeling of being able to move my body in harmony with Infinity's. I could hear Rowena cheering above the wind, which boosted me even more.

I switched my awareness from focusing purely on my body's movement, to Infinity. Shock jolted through me and caused me to lose my balance as I realised how much lower she was in front of me now – and where was she? Physically, she was beneath me, trotting around the paddock, but where was she in my mind? I had become used to an all-encompassing sense of her when I turned my awareness over to the part of my mind that we shared, but that sense was gone, except... there she was. Relief flooded me as I found her, but it was as if she and I were connected by merely the thinnest of threads, as if her mind were being confined somewhere that I couldn't access.

Infinity? What's happening? What shall I do?

This is not right, came Infinity's faint reply. The sense of desperation that accompanied it shook me to my core.

I relayed her response breathlessly to Feryl, who instructed us to stop. Infinity lurched back to a walk and then stumbled, before managing to halt. I pitched forward onto her neck, my bottom lip trembling.

Feryl was full of good cheer as he explained that Infinity had lost her balance merely because she had been trotting too fast. He then spent a good deal of time explaining how to use my body to help her to slow down in future, before declaring the lesson at an end. 'Don't worry, it will come, you just need to practise. We'll try again tomorrow, same time, alright?'

I nodded numbly, before sliding from Infinity's back. I felt tired and disheartened, but my discomfort was nothing compared with Infinity's. The whole front end of her body ached and her chest felt very strange. I focused all of my awareness to that area of her body and was horrified by what I discovered; her chest cavity had been compressed and it felt as if her very essence had become trapped inside. I rubbed Infinity's chest.

Fin, I'm so sorry. How do I help you? I asked her.

I would like my blanket and I need to rest, came the faint reply.

'That was a good effort, well done you both,' said Rowena, then saw my face. 'What's wrong?'

I described everything that had happened as Infinity and I walked to where I had left her rug.

I felt Oak's thoughts fly past my mind and Rowena said, 'Oak's concerned for Infinity too. Can we help?'

'Can you ask Oak what he thinks has happened?'

Oak's communication flowed past me as the four of us walked back to Infinity's paddock.

'Oak has confirmed what you're feeling from Infinity. It seems that in being pushed down onto her front end by your weight, her chest area has become compressed and that has shut down Infinity's ability to express herself fully.'

I opened the paddock gate and Infinity walked in slowly, with Oak close behind her. She drank deeply from the water trough and then wandered over to the beech tree.

Fin, what can I do for you? I asked her.

Nothing. Everything happens as it should. All is well. A muted wave of love and reassurance reached me.

How can all possibly be well? What if I've damaged you forever, what if you never recover back to yourself?

I will recover. We will use the experience to progress. She lay down at the foot of the tree. Wet leaves swirled all about as Oak stood protectively over her.

All of a sudden, there was a wild whinnying accompanied by a thunder of hooves. Oak drew himself up to his full height, ears pricked in the direction of the noise. Infinity's tired body language didn't change as she lay with her nose resting on one of her forelegs.

Rowena and I turned to see Gas galloping down from the fields towards us, with Justin on his back. My vision informed me, as it had the last time I saw them together, that I saw only one animal rather than two. Gas skidded to a halt in front of us and remained still just long enough for Justin to slide from his bare back, before turning and jumping the gate into Infinity's paddock from a standstill. He trotted majestically over to Infinity and Oak. Oak whickered to him, which he reciprocated and then both of them lowered their heads over Infinity's tired, sore body.

'What just happened?' I asked Justin.

'You tell me,' he replied. 'We were out for a ride with Shann and Spider and we were on the way home when Gas got all agitated. He said Infinity was in trouble and it was similar to what happened to him only worse, and he needed to be with her. He insisted on galloping all the way back and he knows I hate doing that when I haven't got his saddle on. Anyway, Shann and Spider kept up for a while and then got left behind, but we carried on, flat out, until we got here. And I bet he's opened his gash up again, we were only supposed to be walking until we have Adam's new unguent. So, what's happened to Infinity? I haven't felt Gas so beside himself since we had all our problems when I first rode him, and he was so intent on getting back that he wouldn't explain it to me.'

I told him what had happened, whilst the three of us stood leaning on the fence, watching our horses. He frowned thoughtfully and had just opened his mouth to speak, when all three of us started and then looked over to our three horses. Oak and Gas were helping Infinity, supporting and steadying her, but not in a way that was physical. I could feel that they were each sending energy to her, gently and not in such a way that she would feel invaded by it, indeed, I was aware that at any time she could hold it away from herself if she chose – but she did not. She allowed their energy to infuse and slowly revitalise her. I felt her chest cavity relax and open, and my sense of my mare instantly became stronger. Linked strongly as our three horses were at that moment, I realised suddenly that I was aware of Justin and Rowena through their bond with their horses, and that they were aware of me.

Rowena's emotions burned like a raging house fire. Anger and hurt were the overriding ones, but love was attempting to battle its way to predominance. Behind all the emotion was a quiet strength. Justin was a bundle of energy, barely contained and desperate for a direction in which to focus himself.

It was too much for all of us. I felt myself recoil from the intimacy we had shared just as my two friends did the same. All three of us sat down with a bump as our knees gave way simultaneously and, relieved for a diversion from our embarrassment at knowing each other's inner selves so intimately, we all collapsed into laughter. A steady thumping of hooves announced the arrival of Shann and Spider.

'Well this just gets weirder and weirder,' said Shann and pointed at Justin. 'You and Gas gallop off without a word of explanation, Spider knows what's happening but refuses to tell me – apparently you will tell me if you decide to – and when I finally catch up with you, I find you rolling around hysterically in the wet grass with two women! Anyone care to explain?'

We laughed even harder. When we finally stopped and allowed ourselves to be hauled to our feet by a now dismounted Shann, I was aware that Gas and Oak had ceased sending energy to Infinity and all three now rested. Infinity slept deeply and the two stallions dozed whilst continuing to stand over her, their noses almost touching above her back. It was a beautiful sight.

It occurred to me that our horses, linked as they had been, were completely at ease with being open to one another and had held nothing back. Unlike we humans. We had been exposed to one another for a fraction of a second and each of us had recoiled as if we'd been stung. As I half listened to Justin recounting to Shann what had happened, noting that he omitted the part where he, Rowena and I had been so intimately aware of one another, I had a fleeting insight into how humans must appear from the viewpoint of a horse. We didn't know our own worth and so we had a need to feel special. We were closed off in our own individual little worlds, which we protected fiercely from each other lest anyone realise just how little we each really thought of ourselves and how vulnerable we felt ourselves to be. I thought that we must seem ridiculous to the horses, since the horses know their place in the scheme of things and have no need for all of the complications with which humans insist on surrounding themselves.

Not ridiculous. My musings appeared to have penetrated Infinity's slumber. *Merely immature,* she added before dropping back into her deep sleep.

'I think we all need a cup of tea, and I happen to know that Adam is in possession of an extremely large fruit cake. Race you to his room, last one there's a loser,' said Rowena and dashed off in the direction of the healing rooms. There was a slightly hysterical tone to her voice and as I followed hot on her heels, I hoped that our friendship wouldn't suffer as a result of what she must have realised Justin and I had seen in her. As Justin overtook both of us, I could hear Shann's protests that he still had to see Spider back to his paddock. I ran on, leaving my beautiful piebald mare to rest.

THIRTEEN

Decision

*A*dam was busy with the last of the day's patients when we arrived at his rooms, so he deposited the four of us in one of the empty rooms at the end of the corridor, with tea and fruit cake, until he had finished. Justin, Rowena and I tried to look anywhere but at each other as we sipped our tea and nibbled from our respective slices of cake, and it wasn't long before Shann picked up on it and demanded to know what was wrong. Justin glared at Shann and shook his head. Shann looked at each of us in turn with a confused expression and I felt something dart past my mind to him. Spider was communicating with him, I decided. Shann shrugged, looked at each of us again and then asked if any of us would be assisting with raising the canopies the following day. I had no idea what he was talking about and was relieved when he broke the tension by explaining.

I learnt that when the weather changed for the worse each autumn, massive canopies were erected over the riding paddocks so that people could continue to work and learn with their horses throughout the cold and wet months. It required large work teams to erect the canopies, and sometimes some of the horses would volunteer to assist. I volunteered immediately. Justin did the same in an overly cheerful voice and after receiving thoughts from Oak, Rowena added in a slightly stiff voice that she and her horse would both be pleased to help. At that, Shann launched into a tale about the chaos Gas had caused when he helped to erect the canopies some years previously.

Adam entered the room to much laughter, courtesy of Gas and his antics. He asked us about our afternoon and I told him about Infinity's and my lesson, and what had happened to her. He said that Peace had helped a mare who'd had a difficult labour, in a similar way to that in which Infinity had been aided by Oak and Gas. We all agreed what a marvel it was and then Adam arose, saying he needed to work on the unguent for Gas's knee. I stood up to go with him as previously agreed, and Justin asked if he could watch also. My heart sank slightly; I had hoped for some space from both Justin and Rowena in which to gather my thoughts.

As it turned out, once Adam began his work, any concerns I had about Justin's presence were forgotten in an instant. Adam had sourced specimens of the two plants with which he wanted to experiment, and they sat in seemingly over-large pots on his workbench, along with a bowl containing some of the unguent that was usually so successful in healing cuts and abrasions, but on this occasion was being defied by Gas's personality.

Adam sat down at his bench and concentrated hard on one of the two plants. I thought I was imagining things to begin with, until I looked at Justin to find that his eyes had widened in disbelief; the plant was growing perceptibly larger in front of our very eyes. It grew steadily until it looked the right size for its pot, and then Adam turned his attention to the plant sitting next to it and repeated the procedure. When the second plant had reached a similar size to the first, he relaxed his concentration, looked at us both and grinned. 'Just a little something I've been working on. I'm going to need a fair bit of sap and I don't want to kill these beauties, so I decided to help them grow a bit so they won't miss what I need to take from them.'

'Flaming lanterns, Adam, how did you do that?' Justin asked breathlessly.

'Oh, I just took on board what Infinity told our Amarilla here, about the Skills all being the same. I decided that if it's all the same and Tree-

Singers can use their intention and song to help the trees grow faster and into the shapes we need, then surely I can do it with my little friends here.'

'But Adam, you didn't sing,' I said.

'Oh, I sang, just not out loud,' said Adam with a twinkle in his eye.

'You're going to have to explain what you mean by that,' said Justin. 'I have enough cryptic answers from Gas to deal with on a daily basis, without wondering what on earth you're talking about as well.'

Adam laughed. 'I sang to them with my mind. It's what the Tree-Singers do while they're singing out loud, whether they realise it or not. I have so many exciting ideas to work on, thanks to you and your wonderful little mare, Amarilla. There I was, living a quiet life in Coolridge, and then you appeared on my doorstep looking as if you'd been dragged behind an ox cart for days on end, and everything changed in an instant.'

'He Who Is Peace, you have nothing to thank us for,' I said. Adam looked searchingly into my eyes. I guessed he would realise that the honorific by which I had called him had come from my horse, but I couldn't have known what it would mean to him. Tears filled his eyes as he smiled, a faraway look on his face.

When he came to a few minutes later, he wiped his eyes and said, 'Well it just shows that one is never too old to be surprised. Now I think, Amarilla, that you would be the best person to perform this next stage, silly old man, look at me I'm quite overcome with emotion. You will need to tune in to the unguent and get a sense of the herbs that I have combined to assist in the healing of damaged flesh. Next, tune in to the herbs in front of you in turn, specifically the sap, and tell me which, if either, will be appropriate to try mixing with the unguent to make it more elastic. Any questions?'

I shook my head.

'Good, then if you will both excuse me, I will leave the room and return when I have pulled myself fully together.'

'What was all that about?' asked Justin once Adam had left.

I shook a hand at him to be quiet, as I had already begun tuning in to the unguent as I'd been instructed. I moved on to the potted herbs and it wasn't long before I decided that the sap of the second plant would suffice. After double-checking it, I allowed my concentration to lapse.

I looked towards the door, hoping Adam would soon return so I wouldn't be alone with Justin for too long now that I had finished my task. I had no idea how to deal with the fact that I knew more about him than he might want me to know. I stared at the workbench, feeling embarrassed.

'Amarilla, you have no need to feel awkward about what I saw in you, or what you saw in me. Shall we just say what we saw? I think if we both just talk about it, we can move past this horrible embarrassment,' said Justin.

I turned to face him. 'I felt you as raw energy, only just bound within your body and desperate for something to focus on.'

He looked at me thoughtfully. 'Well, that's interesting. What you saw in me is what I saw in Gas when we first bonded, apart from the bit about needing something to focus on. Now you know why I chose his name.'

Things began to come together in my mind. 'When I see you and Gas together, you blur together, and Infinity says I see true. I saw in you what you saw in him and Adam told me that when we name our horses, what we see in them is what we have the potential to be. I think you're nearly there.'

Justin frowned. 'Gas doesn't feel the need for something to focus his energy on though, he's just, well, Gas.'

I shrugged. 'Like I said, I think you're nearly there. You're close enough that I can't see you separately when you're together. And when you don't feel you have to have a focus anymore, who knows what will happen? What did you see in me?'

'I felt that you try and focus yourself in a single direction and find it difficult to make room for much else, but that direction is becoming a bit less defined, watered down somehow.'

My heart lifted. Did the fact that he'd seen my direction becoming less defined mean I was already changing, already on my way to reaching my own potential? I felt Infinity's calm confirmation of my suspicion.

Justin said, 'I don't know how Rowena carries all that pain and anger around with her every day and still manages to smile. Thank goodness she has Oak.'

Adam re-entered the room. I told him which plant I thought would work in his experiment and he thanked me and set to work. Justin and I left his room with a pot of the new concoction shortly afterwards and made our way back to Infinity's paddock. We found Infinity and Gas grazing peacefully, but Oak was missing and his rug was wrapped around the top rail of the fence. Justin went over to Gas with his pot of unguent and I walked over to my mare and put a hand under her rug at the neck, satisfying myself that she was warm and dry underneath.

I'm so relieved that you're alright, thank goodness Oak and Gas could help you, I told her.

Everything is as it should be.

So, you're saying it's okay, what happened to you?

Everything is as it should be.

I rubbed her neck thoughtfully. *Did you feel what happened to Rowena, Justin and me when you and their horses were linked like that?*

Of course.

I think I understand why I see Justin and Gas the way I do now. Will people see you and me that way as I get closer to being like you?

You are already like me. It is only awareness of that fact that you lack.

I smiled.

Justin called out to me that the unguent seemed to be staying in place, and raised his hand to signal his departure. I raised mine in return and wondered when Rowena would return from her ride with Oak. I hoped Oak could help her to be comfortable with the fact that Justin and I knew how she felt inside.

I groomed Infinity, passing a good amount of time in making sure she was clean and comfortable. I then mucked out the field shelter and picked up all the piles of dung that lay about the paddock, depositing all of the muck in a large bin by the gate. I had learnt from Rowena that the dung was collected, dried and compacted into logs that were then used to fuel the fires in the bedrooms. When I had finished in Infinity's paddock, I decided to be helpful and clear the neighbouring paddock as well. I introduced myself to the horses who grazed there – one of whom was Mason's horse, the enormous Dili – and then set about my work, doing a thorough job before making my way back to my room, sodden and cold.

When I knocked on Rowena's door the following morning, she was bleary eyed and still in her nightshirt. 'Sorry,' she said, yawning, 'I'm having trouble coming to.'

We agreed that I would fetch breakfast for both of us and we would eat in her room. I saw on my way out of the dining hall that Feryl had pinned a notice on the board for me. Apparently, the Weather-Singers had announced that they could sing the current strong wind down to a slight breeze by lunchtime, so that the canopies could be erected safely in the afternoon. He had therefore moved my lesson forward to just before lunch. As I carried on back to Rowena's room with a tray laden with toast, jam and tea, I had a sinking feeling in my stomach at the thought of another lesson and what it might do to my horse.

I found Rowena washed, dressed and in relatively good spirits. She made no mention of what had happened the previous day, so I let it lie. When we had eaten, we visited our horses to adjust rugs and check that they were comfortable. Gas was absent from the paddock when we arrived there, but we found Oak and Infinity warm and dry under their rugs despite the blustery wind and heavy showers. They needed little attention, so Rowena hurried off to her workshop where orders for rugs were piling up, promising to meet me for my and Infinity's lesson with Feryl later on.

I enjoyed my session with Adam that morning. He greeted me warmly and was thrilled to report that Justin had not long left him, having brought news that the experimental unguent was performing admirably. We spent two fruitful hours perusing my journal, discussing ailments for which I had already found treatments, and listing those for which I had yet to find a remedy. Our session came to an end all too quickly and I had to hurry to drop my things off in my room before meeting Rowena at the agreed time.

We once more trod the path to the riding paddock that Feryl favoured, tailed by our horses. I felt calm acceptance from Infinity. I had asked her several times during the morning if she would prefer not to have a lesson today – or any other day for that matter – after what had happened the day before, but she had insisted on participating.

Whilst Feryl chatted to a pupil whose lesson had just ended, I saddled Infinity and then mounted. I had tuned into her body before I sat on her back and I maintained my concentration so that I would feel any changes the second that my weight settled on top of her. My heart sank; the effect of my weight behind her shoulders was immediate, pushing her forward and down onto her front legs.

Feryl appeared at Infinity's head. 'Okay, we'll go into the middle of the paddock where we've got more room, warm up for a few minutes and then move up to trot, shall we?'

'No.'

'No?' Feryl narrowed his eyes. 'No to what?'

I leant forward, swung my right leg over the back of the saddle and slid to the ground. 'I can't put Infinity through another session like yesterday,' I said and felt a rush of approval from Infinity.

'I've been riding just a little longer than you have, Amarilla, and I can assure you that my practices are sound. There are further exercises and methods that we will use to encourage Infinity to balance better as we go along, but you need to learn to ride first. Come on now, hop back on and we'll just practise what we did yesterday, nothing more, okay?' said Feryl.

I looked at the ground and shook my head, biting my lip. Infinity shifted closer, until her shoulder touched mine. I tried to focus on her calm assurance.

Feryl sighed. 'Come on, you're just nervous. Would you like me to ask everyone to leave so you don't have to worry that people are watching you?'

I hesitated. Feryl was being kind to me, albeit in a condescending manner, and I didn't like feeling that I was being awkward. Infinity went very still beside me, both in body and mind. It was my decision. I thrashed around internally, trying to find a way to please Feryl. Then I remembered how Infinity's body had felt when I had sat on her back just minutes previously; my weight had immediately pushed her onto her front legs, and I knew it would only be a matter of time before her chest became compressed and she would shut down again.

'I'm s-s-sorry, Feryl, I c-can't,' I said. Infinity's love wrapped itself around me, comforting and reassuring me. And what was that? I felt a faint flicker of excitement and anticipation dart along our bond before I felt her take control of herself. Before I could ask her about it, Feryl turned to the people who had arrived to watch our lesson.

'Not to worry, Amarilla,' he said in a carrying voice, 'we all allow ourselves to be affected by nerves every now and again. What I'll do for you this session, I'll call Liberal and he and I will demonstrate the techniques for you and Infinity. Go on, over to the fence now, unsaddle your horse and make room for my boy.' He went quiet for a few seconds and then I felt the soft whisper that was his horse's reply. 'He's on his way,' said Feryl. 'Close the gate behind you, Amarilla, will you? My boy doesn't bother with gateways.' Several of his onlookers laughed appreciatively.

Infinity and I went over to where Oak and Rowena waited for us. I told Rowena what had happened, under my breath, and then turned to look behind me at the sound of pounding hooves. A very tall, black stallion was cantering majestically in our direction. As he approached the paddock fence, he gathered himself together and then soared over it before coming to a graceful halt beside Feryl.

He was stunning. His black coat was glossy and his four white socks gleamed a brilliant white. The fine, black hair of his mane and tail had a gentle wave to it and he had a narrow, elegant face with dark, soulful eyes. Was it my imagination though, or were the areas above his eyes more hollowed than they should have been?

Infinity monitored my musings closely and obviously. I continued to observe Liberal, hoping to notice something else that could help me to scratch the invisible itch that I was feeling. Feryl saddled his horse and then leapt on to his back from a standstill, landing gracefully in the saddle.

Rowena nudged me and said, 'Loves an audience, does our Feryl.'

I couldn't help but feel impressed by what I saw next; Liberal spun around on his hind legs and then powered off in trot. He glided majestically around the paddock before coming back to walk. He walked a large circle, which gradually became smaller, and then larger again. He moved up to a slow canter, then increased his pace to cover more ground before slowing again and dropping back down to a trot. Feryl must have been giving him all the signals he had been trying to teach me, yet he didn't appear to be doing anything other than moving with his horse.

Liberal proceeded to move easily through a set of increasingly difficult manoeuvres, holding his audience spellbound all the while. The muscles on his quarters and hind legs rippled as he used them to power his majestic body, however I noticed that the muscle on the underside of his neck appeared to be a little tight, as if straining. Infinity increased her presence in my mind once more.

Feryl ended his demonstration by cantering up to our little group and halting directly in front of us. I saw that I had not been mistaken earlier, there were definite hollows above Liberal's eyes, giving him a slightly drawn, weary look despite his majestic physique. He stared into my eyes and I felt as if he were willing me to understand something.

Fin, what does he want me to know? I asked my mare. She ignored my question and I felt a resistance against my mind from her; she had no intention of answering it.

'Any questions?' asked Feryl.

Rowena said loudly, 'I was just wondering, Feryl, whether Liberal struggles at all under the weight of that enormous ego of yours?'

Anger flashed across Feryl's face. He wheeled Liberal around and set him at a fast canter across the paddock, while shouting over his shoulder, 'I'll see you and Infinity here tomorrow afternoon at the normal time, Amarilla. I hope that you arrive in a better state of mind.' He and Liberal jumped the fence at the far side of the paddock and then galloped off down towards the river with Feryl's cloak billowing out behind them.

FOURTEEN

Observations

*O*ver lunch, I explained my refusal to ride Infinity to Adam, Justin, Shann and Quinta. They all agreed that I'd been right not to ride her when it didn't feel right, Justin more vehemently than all of the others combined. I was just about to relate what I'd sensed from Liberal when I felt Infinity resisting my thought pattern, making it difficult for me to order what I wanted to say. As my friends' conversation moved on to other things, I asked Infinity to explain herself.

I have given you time to consider fully whether any information you have about Liberal is yours to share, she told me.

But horses don't hide anything from each other the way we humans do, surely all of my friends' horses know about whatever it is that is bothering Liberal?

I felt Infinity's assent.

So, my friends could find out from their horses anyway, couldn't they?

Their horses will not impart that information to them.

But why not? If horses are completely open with each other, isn't that the way forward for all of us?

It is not so much that horses are open with one another as that we are not closed. We are parts of the same whole and this the horses know. Most humans have yet to grasp this truth. You believe you are all separate entities and there is much work each of you must do on your journey to releasing this falsehood. Bonded horses work within the current beliefs and limitations that you place upon yourselves. You have a strong need to work through your thoughts and issues privately and this we respect. Do you think it would help you if each and every horse told their person of your fears and limitations?

I recoiled at the very idea.

It would inhibit your progression, agreed Infinity. *If you were to speak of what you sense from Liberal you cannot help but impart information about his person and he has the same right to work through and release the things that hold him back as you or any other human.*

Okay, I understand, but why wouldn't you tell me what Liberal wants me to know? If he's decided it's alright for me to know something and I can't hear him, surely it's alright for you to just tell me?

You already know.

?????????

Liberal was not attempting to tell you something. He sensed that you already know what ails him and was attempting to assist in bringing it to the forefront of your mind.

And what do I know?

It is better that you come to the full realisation by yourself. That way it will better become part of you and of what you and I do here.

Oh, Fin, please just tell me?

I felt her move her attention from my mind to her grazing, and knew I would get no more from her. I sighed and moved my own attention to the friendly banter that was now being exchanged between my friends as they finished their lunch.

Later that day, Rowena and I added our weight to Oak's as he pulled on a guy rope attached to a tall pole at the corner of an enormous canopy. Shann was among four men pulling at another rope at right angles to ours, and slowly but surely the pole was rising.

'What am I going to do?' I said breathlessly.

'Flaming lanterns, Am, give it a rest now, can't you?' Rowena replied through gritted teeth. 'We've all told you, listen to your horse and stick to your guns. Why are you still churning it over?'

'Because Feryl is expecting Infinity and me for a lesson after lunch tomorrow and I don't know how to tell him that his way of teaching won't help us.'

'Just tell him Infinity doesn't want to do things his way and you're going it alone for a while,' she said.

'It's not really true though is it? It wasn't Fin's decision to stop this morning; it was mine. And what if he gets angry?'

'What if he does? What's the worst that could happen?'

'It's just that I've not even been here a week yet and I don't want to be upsetting people.'

Infinity let me know of her exasperation.

'If Feryl gets upset then that's up to him. You're doing what's right for you and your horse, and that's what you have to remember,' Rowena told me firmly. The pole came upright and a cheer went up from Shann's group. We all leant on our ropes as we waited for those with mallets and giant pegs to come along and secure them. Rowena put one hand out behind us and stroked Oak's huge rump as he waited patiently. 'Thanks, mate,' she said quietly and was answered by a low whicker.

Once Shann's rope had been pegged, he and his friends came to help Rowena and me to keep the tension on ours while Oak was released from the end of it. I breathed out a long sigh as a massive wooden peg was driven into the ground, securing our rope. Rowena was right. I would try to focus on the fact that what I was doing was right for me and my horse when I told Feryl we would no longer be accepting his help, and hope that would give me the strength to get the words out that I would need to say to him. And then what would I do? I could barely ride and here I was, about to refuse the help of a Master and go it alone.

You are not alone. I am with you. Infinity had confidence in me, I could feel it.

Once all three canopies were up and firmly secured over three of the riding paddocks, I hurried to fetch Infinity as we were due to visit Mason, who would hopefully have my horse's saddle ready for her. I was looking forward to seeing the big, kindly Saddler again, but was dreading having to tell him that I didn't know how much I would actually be able to use the saddle. I told Rowena as much as she walked with us on her way back to her workshop.

'Has Infinity told you she doesn't want you to ride her?' she asked.

'No, but I'm scared to. I don't know what I'm doing, where would I even start?'

'Well, why don't I, Oak, Justin and Gas try and help you? Justin and I know how to ride, and Oak and Gas were both unhappy to varying degrees with how Feryl taught us, so maybe between us we can work something out?'

My heart leapt. 'Do you think Justin and Gas would want to? I mean they got over their problems, they might not want to go back to the beginning with me and Fin.'

'Only one way to find out, ask Justin at dinner. See you there, hope the saddle's okay.' She disappeared through her workshop door.

Infinity and I received a heartfelt welcome from Mason. He brought out our new saddle and placed it carefully on my horse's back, clucking and chattering to her all the while. It was made of black leather that gleamed with the conditioner he had just finished wiping over it, and the stitching was white and stood out in stark contrast. He had stitched what looked like a number eight lying on its side into each saddle flap, just behind where my legs would rest. The symbol for infinity, I realised and felt a surge of affection for the burly man. He showed me exactly whereabouts on Infinity's back to put the saddle, and highlighted the sheepskin pad he had made especially to go underneath it.

'It looks fantastic, thank you so much, she loves it,' I said. 'I hope I can learn to ride well enough to make good use of it.'

'Of course you will, you'll pick it up in no time,' he replied. 'But you have a worry, I can see. If you want to share it, Amarilla, I'm a good listener.'

I told him all about the problems Infinity was having carrying me and about my intention to learn to ride without any input from Feryl. He listened intently and then asked, 'And how does my lovely Infinity feel about your plans?'

'She's happy about it,' I replied.

He smiled and put his arm over Infinity's back. 'If this beauty here is happy, then I see no reason for you not to be. I'm not much of a rider myself, never have been and I don't ask Dili to suffer my attempts at it now unless it's absolutely necessary, but I will give you one piece of advice, if you'll accept it?'

I nodded.

'Trust your horse in everythin', absolutely everythin', and one day that everythin' will make sense. And if there's ever anythin' I can do to help, you know where to find me. My Diligence's bones are far too old to be wanderin' far now, so I'm always here.'

I thanked him and then Infinity followed me out of his workshop, still wearing her new saddle with its stirrups shining and swinging on their leathers.

'You'll want to run those up so they don't bang her sides,' Feryl said from behind me. I turned to see him already sliding one of the stirrups up to the top of its leather, then winding the leather around it to keep it secure.

My heart began to beat faster. Now would be a good time to tell him we wouldn't be at our lesson the following day. My mouth and throat went dry and I just about managed to croak, 'Um, thanks,' at his retreating back as he hurried behind Infinity and off towards the workshops. I berated myself for being a coward.

I would feel your weight in the saddle, Infinity interrupted my thoughts.

Why? I have no idea how to help you balance yet.

From here to my paddock. She moved to the fence and looked at me expectantly.

I sighed. What harm could it do over such a short distance? I reasoned with myself and pulled back down the stirrup Feryl had run up, before climbing the fence and hopping onto her back.

The saddle was wonderful. The one I had been using was too large, I realised as I now sat cocooned and very comfortable. Infinity positively crooned over the feel of the sheepskin pad that cushioned her back and shoulders. She could feel exactly where I sat, as the saddle wrapped closer around her than the one we had borrowed, and she drew confidence from being able to feel more easily what I was doing with my weight. The issue of too much weight on her front legs remained, as expected, but we both felt heartened by the feeling of extra comfort and support.

I left her rugged and grazing happily as I carried her saddle to the tack room that was shared by all of the Horse-Bonded. It was the first door I came to in the building on my right as I entered the square and it was cavernous, I discovered on entering. Saddle racks lined the stone walls at three different heights and I passed hundreds of saddles before I reached an empty saddle rack that I could reach. I hoisted my saddle onto it, gratefully. I noticed as I did so that Mason had stitched the infinity symbol onto the back of the seat, and that each and every other saddle had a different symbol stitched into the same place. The one next to mine had a beautifully stitched dragonfly in many different colours of thread. I smiled to myself as I realised it must be Norieva's.

I wandered along the saddles, looking for any symbols I might recognise. I saw a spider on the saddle that had to belong to Shann, and eventually found one with an oak tree stitched in so much detail that even tiny acorns were visible. There was one with a shooting star, another with a horse and human stitched standing side by side, the human standing hands on hips and staring out of the image. I saw one with a horse standing with its neck arched as an infant sat astride. Was that Quinta's saddle for Noble? I wondered to myself. Other saddles had initials instead of symbols or pictures, but each and every one was decorated in the most intricate detail.

I noticed a saddle on its own, on a rack on the far wall. I was puzzled as to why someone would store their saddle where they would have so much further to carry it than was necessary. When I reached it, I saw that it had been made in a very different style from my own. It was much larger and looked old and worn, yet had clearly been recently cleaned and conditioned. The symbol on the back was a dove. The sign for peace. I reached out a hand and touched the saddle, as if by being in contact with it, I could somehow know the horse who had worn it and who had been so dear to my friend. My heart ached afresh for him, to see his saddle sitting alone but clearly not abandoned, still cherished by Adam as a link to his soul mate.

Give a human a chance to be overly emotional and they will surely take it, Infinity noted.

He loved his horse so much, I just feel for him, that's all. I know how I would feel if I lost you, and we've only been bonded a short time. Adam was with Peace for over forty years.

You do not know how you will feel when I decide to leave my body because you are not yet the person you will be when that happens.

Well that was me told, I thought to myself as I gave Peace's saddle one last stroke and made my way back to my room to have a bath before dinner.

I hardly slept that night. Justin had been enthusiastic when I asked if he and Gas would help Infinity and me in our efforts to form a riding partnership, and had agreed to meet us, along with Oak and Rowena, at the riding paddock furthest from Feryl's preferred one, before lunch the following day. That meant I had to find Feryl in the morning and tell him I wouldn't be having any more lessons with him. Dozens of different conversations roiled around in my mind, all of them ending with Feryl being angry with me. I tossed and turned and tried to picture myself not caring what he or anyone else thought, just thanking him for his efforts so far and then telling him what I had decided. Every time I tried, my stomach churned relentlessly.

'U 'ook rough,' Rowena told me through a mouthful of toast the following morning. 'Bad nigh'?'

I nodded and smiled weakly. 'Too hot, must have had too many covers on.'

She nodded and helped herself to the last piece of toast on Shann's plate while he was turned away from her. She winked at me and began to spread it with butter. Remembering Adam's rule, I knew I would need to find Feryl before my work on my apprenticeship that morning so that I would be able to concentrate fully on my studies. I forced my porridge down and hurried off to find him, with Shann's attempt at outrage over his missing toast ringing in my ears.

I knew that Feryl usually rode Liberal before he started teaching for the day, so I made my way to his riding paddock, taking strength from the sight of Infinity as I passed her. She was standing nose to nose with Oak, dozing peacefully despite the wind that buffeted them both.

As I neared my destination, I could see that Feryl was still riding. Liberal was cantering slowly and powerfully, and when he reached the far corner from where I approached, he cantered with his hind legs on the spot and his front legs on a circle around them, until he had turned to face back from whence he had come. He then launched into a much faster, but no less graceful canter along the fence line before collecting himself and then coming to a halt. Feryl stroked his neck, talking quietly to him, and then jumped off.

I looked around. I could see many people already at work, tending to livestock or harvesting in the crop paddocks, but there was nobody in our immediate vicinity. It had to be now. My heart thudded almost painfully in my chest as I climbed through the fence and walked over to where Feryl was loosening Liberal's girth.

'Come to pick up more tips, Amarilla? It will be a long while before you and Infinity are at this sort of level, but it never hurts to remind yourself what you're aspiring to I suppose,' he called out cheerfully.

'Um, I just came to say th-thank you for all your help, but I think Infinity and I need some time to practise on our own for a while, so we won't be c-coming for our lesson this afternoon,' I said.

'Nonsense, at this stage it's vital I'm there when you ride, to make sure you don't get into bad habits. We won't go too fast, don't worry, there'll be plenty of time for you to practise everything before we move on. You're not letting your nerves get the better of you again, are you?'

'It's not my n-nerves that are the problem,' I said. 'It's how Infinity is affected by being ridden. She's happy for us to experiment on our own and when I told Mason about it, he said that if she's happy about it then I have no need to worry. Everyone is telling me to trust my horse, except for you.'

'I can't imagine why you think Mason would have the faintest idea about anything,' Feryl said. 'Last time I looked he was a Saddler and I was the Master of Riding. Thunder and lightning, the man's all but given up on riding, he's so bad at it and I can't tell you who's more relieved, me or Diligence.'

'Well anyway, thanks, Feryl, but I won't be coming to any lessons for a while,' I said and then turned and ran.

'Amarilla, wait, you're being ridiculous! Oh, for light's sake, girl, have some sense, you'll ruin that horse of yours if you don't let me help you.' Feryl's words followed me. 'It's Justin isn't it? I've seen you with him, he's put you up to this, I shall have some harsh words to say to him.'

I hurried back towards my horse. I let myself into her paddock and then ran over to her. I slid my hands under her rug on either side of her neck, warming them as I hugged her. *I did it, Fin. It's just you and me now, and whatever help Rowena and Justin can give us. I have absolutely no idea where we are going to even start.*

She enveloped me in her warmth and reassurance. *We will start at the beginning.*

Adam sent me out to collect supplies of fresh herbs that morning, so I decided to go down to the river. The paddocks stretched as far as the eye could see and beyond from the buildings at The Gathering, then there was a short stretch of scrubland before the river. Turning right along the river, the wide expanse of water continued to wind through further scrubland before disappearing around some hills in the distance. Turning left, upriver, it wasn't long before the scrub gave way to a rocky hillside on our side of the wide, deep, slow-flowing river. On the other side, what looked like sparse, slightly boggy woodland dotted with springy heather led back into drier, mature forest. It was perfect for gathering a plethora of different herbs in a relatively small area.

I decided to stick to the open river bank for my morning's herb hunting, a decision approved enthusiastically by Infinity, who had decided to accompany me and had already found an area of grasses very much to her liking.

It was a relief to be away from people after facing up to Feryl that morning. I spent a thoroughly enjoyable few hours taking samples of herbs both new and foreign to me, even as they were passing what stores they could into their roots, ready to survive the coming winter.

The time flew and I had to rush to take my supplies back to my workroom, store them properly and then saddle Infinity, to be in time for our riding session with our friends. We had to pass the paddock where Feryl was teaching, and for once, I was glad of the spectators that lined the fence, as Infinity and I were able to pass unobtrusively behind them.

Rowena and Oak were trotting in a steady rhythm around the outside of the large paddock we had chosen for our session, but there was no sign of Justin and Gas. A couple of people I didn't know rode around side by side, chatting. Infinity and I entered the paddock, and Oak slowed to a halt in front of us with a soft whicker to Infinity, which she returned.

'Right, where shall we start?' asked Rowena.

There was a thunder of hooves from the direction of the river. I turned around just in time to see Gas and Justin sailing over the paddock fence, with Justin crouched low over his horse's back so as to fit under the canopy. They landed just behind the two horses whose riders were still chatting, and both horses spooked and shot forward, momentarily unseating one of the riders.

'Sorry, that wasn't my idea,' called Justin.

Gas slowed to a trot and then halted beside Oak, who gave him a reproachful look and turned his rear end slightly towards the gangly chestnut stallion, warning him to mind his manners.

'Sorry we're a bit late,' Justin said. 'Gas wanted to stretch his legs now his knee is healing, and I lost track of time. When I realised we were running late, he picked up from me what it was we were late for and just took off. He wouldn't listen to any of my requests to slow down, not even when Turi had to stand in the bushes to get out of his way. She's someone else I'll have to apologise to later, honestly, Gas, you don't make life easy for me sometimes. Anyway, what did we miss?'

'Nothing, we've only just got here,' I said.

Justin slid from Gas's back. 'Amarilla, you ride first. Gas, you'll just have to wait your turn.'

Rowena legged me up onto Infinity's back and a warm thrill shot through me as I sat down in my saddle. Unsuccessful as each of my attempts at riding had been so far, there was something exciting, exhilarating even, about this ridden relationship with my horse. I asked Infinity to move onto a circle, walking around Justin, Rowena and their horses. My friends watched us and immediately began to confer.

What do you need me to do, Fin? I asked her.

She pulled my awareness into her body with her.

There was weight on our back, pushing us forward and down. We had so much to be happy about and yet we couldn't find a way to express our joy. We wanted to gallop and leap around, tossing our head and kicking up our heels, but it was impossible with this weight. Everything was too hard. Our chest cavity was closing in on itself. There wasn't enough room now for happiness; not enough room for any emotion really, we were shutting down. What was it that we were happy about again? We couldn't seem to remember. Our thoughts were slow and heavy. Everything was heavy.

'Move it up to a trot, Amarilla.'

We flicked an ear. We understood Rowena's instruction, but we couldn't seem to respond straight away, even when the legs that curled around our sides began to nudge – my legs, I realised. My legs, asking Infinity's body to trot. Asking our body to trot. It took what seemed like an eternity for us to relay our intention to move faster to all of our muscles. Why was it all so slow, so heavy, so difficult? Our legs finally began to move quicker and we managed a trot. The weight on our back immediately seemed heavier and we were being pushed forward and down even more. We couldn't think straight now, it was too hard and required too much effort. We just focused on moving our legs and trying not to fall forward onto our nose.

Something was pushing at me. *Go... back...* Infinity was using what little force of personality she could still express, to push my awareness back to my own body. Suddenly, everything was free and light again; I was back fully in my own body. I was free to express myself again. But what about Infinity? I brought her back to a walk.

Fin?

You see now, came her muted reply.

I felt a gentle wave of love and support reach Infinity, and her body began to relax; Oak and Gas were once more helping her to recover. I could feel Rowena's concern and Justin's fascination through their bonds with their horses, and it was obvious from their faces that they could feel my devastation.

'I can't do this to her. I can't ever ride her again. It's not worth it,' I said shakily, dismounting.

'What happened? We were just about to start making suggestions when Oak and Gas told us to leave you alone,' said Rowena. 'Was it worse than last time?'

'Can you both stay open to me?' I asked, hoping they would be brave enough to allow me to use the link between our horses to show them what I didn't think I'd find the words to describe.

Rowena and Justin looked at one another and then back at me, and nodded, Rowena with a grimace. I relived what I'd just shared with Infinity. When I'd finished, Rowena staggered up to Oak and buried her face in his neck and Justin stood rooted to the spot, shaking his head slowly from side to side.

'Why didn't he tell me what the problem was?' said Justin. 'Why haven't any of the horses brought this up before?'

'Infinity told me before that it's a bigger issue for her than for most other horses, maybe that means it's easier for her to show me? But I'm not doing that again. I can't.'

You can. Infinity was much stronger already and she used the full extent of our bond to impress her next statement upon me. *It is the reason that we bonded.*

Rowena said, 'Now we can do something about it. We never would have realised what was happening if it wasn't for you and Infinity, but now we know we have to help them lift up in front and open their chests so they can express themselves fully. Oak is so excited about it all, he's buzzing and I've never felt that from him before.'

'It seems to be having the opposite effect on Gas,' said Justin. 'He's always buzzing about something and it's usually hard to get his full attention, but he actually feels as if he wants to concentrate on all of this. Very weird.'

'Infinity is feeling insufferably pleased with herself and I have to say I've felt that from her plenty of times,' I said and my friends laughed. 'So, where do we go from here?'

'On a fast road to disaster, I'd say.' Feryl was leaning on the paddock gate with a couple of other men, both of whom sniggered.

Justin stiffened. 'I don't think Amarilla was directing her question towards you, Feryl.'

Feryl ignored him and said, 'I can see how taking it in turns with your little friends to ride circles will help you learn to ride superbly, Amarilla. When will we be invited to view the display of your talents? Next week?'

I was shocked by his acid tone and felt myself shrink inside. Infinity appeared at my shoulder and I felt a flow of warm, supportive energy wrap itself around me.

Rowena glared at Feryl. 'Just who in the mother of storms do you think you are?' she asked him.

'Come on, let's just go,' I said quietly. 'Please don't argue, let's just go?'

'I, Rowena, am the one person around here who knows fully how to train someone to ride a horse,' Feryl said, 'and that is why I was made the Master of Riding. You three, on the other hand, are a group of arrogant children who are dangerously unequipped for what you are attempting. I will give you one more chance, Amarilla, to continue your lessons with me. Accept now or prepare to fail. Your choice.'

I felt thoughts fly past me from both Gas and Oak. Rowena was bright red with fury, but whatever Oak said to her appeared to be holding her in check. Justin's brow furrowed over his brown eyes, but he too held his tongue. They both looked at me.

My tongue was stuck to the roof of my mouth. I couldn't find the will to say anything, so I merely shook my head while looking at the ground in front of me.

'Then prepare to fail.' Feryl turned on his heel and stalked off with his friends in tow, both of whom made a show of shaking their heads.

I breathed out a long breath, relieved that the confrontation was over.

'Why didn't you say anything to him?' Rowena demanded. 'You don't have to be frightened of him, he may be Master of Riding but he's a pillock. He should be asking you what your horse thinks of all this rather than bullying you. Honestly, Am, you're going to have to learn to stand up for yourself.'

I nodded, knowing she was right. Infinity offered no counsel but I was grateful for her supportive energy that cocooned me still. We decided to call an end to our session for the day so that we would have time to try to come up with some ideas to try in our session the following day. I was dreading it already – what if Feryl decided to watch again?

Then maybe he will learn something, came Infinity's thought.

I managed a smile.

FIFTEEN

Discomfort

*R*owena questioned me again over lunch about my inability to stand up for myself with Feryl, but I had no explanation for her since I couldn't work it out myself.

'Well if you can't stand up to him, you'll just have to try and stay out of his way,' Rowena said, 'and that's not going to be easy.'

'What's not going to be easy?' asked Shann as he slid into the chair next to Rowena. 'Getting a word in when you're in the middle of one of your tirades?'

Rowena rolled her eyes. 'Shut up, Shann, we're having a serious conversation. Ser-i-ous, that's a word you need to learn someday, let me know when you do.'

I left them to their banter. As I passed between the tables, I exchanged smiles with a few people. Several others looked hastily away when my eyes met theirs. Feryl sat at the last table I passed and I heard the words "arrogant", "deluded" and "disaster" being emphasised, presumably for my benefit. I walked faster, anxious to be away from him and beginning to feel angry; angry that he hadn't listened to me, angry that he assumed he knew better than Infinity and angry with myself for being so pathetically unable to stand up for myself. To add to my discomfort, I realised that I also now had indigestion. I knew that greenmint tea would be the best thing for it but had no intention of walking back to the top end of the dining hall to get some, so I resolved to put up with it.

I spent a muddy afternoon digging up herbs from the verges of the furthest paddocks, placing them carefully in my basket, ready to be tested for their usefulness in easing two ailments – insomnia and stomach ulcers – whose remedies were proving elusive. Infinity munched nearby, emanating contentment. I, on the other hand, felt extremely irritable. I couldn't grasp the plants with gloves on, so worked barehanded and my hands grew numb with cold and crusted with mud. I couldn't shake the misery I was feeling at knowing that Feryl and surely countless others by now thought me arrogant and difficult, and the heartburn I'd had since lunchtime was nagging away at me. I kept trying to turn my thoughts over to how Infinity's body had felt when I rode her, in case an idea of what to do in our next session came to me but try as I might, my thoughts reverted back to what people would be thinking about me. At one point, I threw my trowel down in frustration as tears welled in my eyes.

It's no good, Fin, I can't help it that I care what people think of me.

You can.

But I was brought up to care that I didn't upset people, that's how people live together, how they get along with each other.

An excuse that will suffice as well as any other. You remain stuck in one mindset because you have not yet made the decision to change it.

What, so I just decide not to care and then everything will miraculously be alright? I asked.

Everything has always been and will always be alright. Choose to see it.

But how can I choose to see it if it doesn't feel that way? It feels as if everything is far from alright.

Where are you at this moment?

At The Gathering, kneeling in mud.

Is there somewhere else you should be?

No.

Someone you should be with?

No, I am with you.

Then everything is alright.

I suddenly saw things as they really were. I was worrying what Feryl and everyone else thought of me and would be saying about me – well who were these people? They were human beings, just as fallible as I, and as Infinity had told me before, they were all on their own journeys, working through and releasing the things that restricted them. It was what my horse thought that I needed to pay attention to and as far as she was concerned, I could choose to see that everything was alright. I could choose to see that it didn't matter what people thought about me. I felt a lot better. A thought occurred to me though.

What happens the next time someone doesn't like what I say or do? Will I be able to see things this way by myself or will you help me again? I asked Infinity.

I will help if necessary but I will not restrict your progress by helping when you are capable of resolving things for yourself. Choose to focus your attention on something other than where your mind wants to worry. At this moment you can choose to focus entirely on gathering your plants and thinking about our work session today. Each time your mind wanders make the choice to redirect your attention once more. As time goes by you will have to make the choice less and less. It will become part of a new way of being.

I was busy digging again as I pondered Infinity's advice. I resolved to try and do exactly as she suggested.

Do not merely try. Do.

I smiled. Okay, I would do as she suggested. A sense of satisfaction radiated from my horse.

When my basket was full, I brushed as much mud from my legs as I could and told Infinity it was time to head back. Indigestion still irritated me and I made a mental note to get myself some greenmint tea as soon as I got back to my workroom.

The following morning, I made my way down to breakfast feeling disgruntled. I had drunk several mugs of tea the previous afternoon, several more at dinnertime and another before I'd retired to bed and yet when I arose in the morning, I was still feeling unwell. I decided to drink plenty of water with my breakfast to see if that made any difference.

When I entered the dining hall, many faces turned in my direction and then turned quickly away again, and an undertone of whispers added to the usual hum of voices. As I stood trying to see if I could spot a friendly face, I caught whispered snatches of conversation from the tables nearest to me. "Infinity", "thinks she doesn't need Feryl", "that Justin" and "furious" were some of the words that reached my ears. I caught sight of Justin standing up near the food table, beckoning me to join him, which I did gratefully. I helped myself to some porridge and then followed him to a table nearby where Adam sat with Norieva. I sat down and breathed out a loud sigh, relieved to be less conspicuous.

'Don't worry,' Adam said to me, 'however much change is needed, it's human nature to resist it but we're very good at adapting once we get over ourselves and knuckle down. That's what will happen, you'll see.'

'And if there's one person who needs to get over himself, it's Feryl,' said Justin. 'He accosted me on the stairs as I was coming down to breakfast just now and told me in no uncertain terms how he holds me responsible for how Amarilla is behaving. Apparently, Gas and I are, what was it he said now? That's it – a corrupting influence.' He grinned. 'I quite like the idea.'

'Now now, you mustn't start on Feryl again, Justin, he's really very good at what he does, just look at what he's achieved with Liberal, and he wasn't made Master of Riding for nothing you know,' said Norieva.

'You always see the best in people, Norrie, I admire it in you I really do, but I listen to my horse over the likes of Feryl and so does Amarilla, and Feryl just can't get over the fact,' said Justin.

The breakfast sitting was nearly over when Rowena appeared at the food table with Shann close on her heels. They both scooped up what food was left and then came to join us. Justin raised an eyebrow. 'Sleep in, did we?' he asked them. Rowena's cheeks flushed red, but the ever brazen Shann did far better at keeping his composure.

'Ro may have done, I just decided to check on Spider before breakfast,' he said, stuffing half a cold fried egg in his mouth.

'That's very conscientious of you, a shame you didn't take as much care of yourself, did you know you have odd socks on?' asked Justin and then ducked his head under the table. 'Oh, and by a very strange coincidence, so does Rowena. What are the chances of that, each of you wearing one yellow and one brown sock on the same morning?' He grinned wickedly. Rowena ignored him completely and kept her face down as she ate her breakfast.

Shann grinned back at him and agreed, 'Just what are the chances?'

Norieva looked shocked and I didn't know what to say. Adam came to our rescue. 'Norrie, you've done a fine job with the rota as usual, but you must treat me the same as everyone else. I'm here taking up just as much space as the next person and I should be pulling my weight,' he said.

'Adam, my friend, I'm sure the other Herbalists won't mind me saying what is universally accepted. You are the most gifted Herbalist The Gathering has seen and your time is much better spent at your work than doing simple chores that anyone can do. Really, my treatment of you has absolutely nothing to do with your age,' replied Norieva.

'Whether that is truly the case, or whether you are still attempting to humour an old man, I would nevertheless like to be given a share of the chores along with everyone else. I need something to make me move this creaking body around now that Peace is gone, even if it is just sweeping floors.'

'What are you down for, Am?' Rowena said.

I shrugged. 'I don't know, I haven't looked yet.'

'I hope you've gone easy on her, Norrie, with it being her first full week here,' she said.

Norieva turned towards her with a dark stare. 'I treat everyone fairly, Rowena, you know that. I seem to remember that Amarilla has kitchen duty with you. I thought you might like to show her the ropes.'

Rowena groaned. 'Oh, not the breakfast shift? Just as it's getting darker in the mornings? Oh, Norrie, tell me you didn't?'

'I don't remember which shift I gave you, but if you have the early shift then you will just have to do it with the same good grace that everyone else does.'

It turned out that we had the afternoon shift, preparing the food for the evening meal. I was relieved, as it meant I could still attend to

Infinity after breakfast, fulfil my apprenticeship obligations and then carry on working with Rowena, Justin and the horses before lunch.

I left Rowena bolting down the remainder of her breakfast and went to see to my horse. I already knew she was warm and dry in her rug, but wanted to check it was still sitting on her straight and that all the straps were still adjusted correctly. I picked mud and stones out of her feet and brushed her behind her elbows and on her belly where dried mud stuck to her fur. When I'd finished, I stood and rubbed my chest with the heel of my palm. My heartburn still wasn't clearing.

You have discomfort in your heart. Do not fear. Everything is as it should be.

It's just indigestion, I've had it since yesterday. It'll clear soon, I told her resolutely.

She turned her head around and fixed her blue eyes on mine. As she held my stare, the pain lessened slightly. Then she put her muzzle to my shoulder and nuzzled me gently before wandering off to where Oak grazed. I didn't have a chance to question her about it as Rowena appeared, puffing, to attend to Oak. She climbed through the fence and I noticed that her socks, which she had pulled up past the tops of her boots to keep her knees warm, were now a matching pair, both yellow. I grinned to myself.

'Need any help with Oak before I go? I've got a few minutes if you're in a hurry?' I asked her.

'No, he's fine, I just don't feel right starting the day without coming to see him. Thanks though, I'll see you in a few hours?'

I nodded, waved and then hurried to my workroom through the light rain that, judging by the colour of the clouds, would shortly be turning much heavier. I buried Infinity's thoughts about my chest pain in my resolve to carry on drinking more water and tea. I helped myself to a huge mug of steaming tea from Adam's pot and then settled down at my workbench.

I pushed my body's discomfort to one side and cleared my head, ready to tune in to the first of my plant specimens from my gathering session the previous day. I spent a fruitless few hours taking one herb at a time and tuning in to it on its own and in combination with each of the others, trying to find something that would ease insomnia. I made sure I had noted down all of the herb combinations that I'd tried before finishing my stint for the day, and then donned my outer garments ready for my session with the horses.

'Any joy?' called Adam as I passed his open door.

I stuck my head around it and replied, 'Not yet, I'm pretty sure I need a combination of herbs, so I'm just ploughing through all the different combinations of the specimens I've got.'

He nodded. 'Your instinct is correct. The herb combinations you are looking for are those that are the least forthcoming, but will teach you the most.'

'In what way?'

He winked a sparkling green eye at me and grinned. 'In the way that will teach you the most.'

I shook my head. 'Between you and Infinity, it's a wonder I don't spend more time screaming.'

The rain was belting down and I ran hunched over my saddle, trying to protect it. Rowena was saddling Oak in the field shelter when I got to the paddock. She put his rug back over him once she had fastened the girth, in an attempt to keep both him and the saddle dry on the way to the riding paddock. After saddling and rugging Infinity in the same way, we ran to the riding paddock with the horses trotting behind us along the stony track.

We were relieved once we reached the shelter of the canopy. As we removed rugs and adjusted saddles it seemed strange to be standing on dry grass while rain lashed down just a short distance away. I looked around the paddock to see who else was there. There were three people, none of whom I recognised.

The sound of a trotting horse announced Gas's arrival and the fact that I needed to squint told me that Justin was on his back. The gate swung open and they shot under cover. Justin slid to the ground to shut the gate before coming to join us with Gas at his side. He saw me squinting and moved further away from his horse. 'Better?' he asked me and after I had nodded and grinned at him, he said, 'Right, anyone any ideas for today?'

I shook my head guiltily. I had thought and thought about everything, but still could not see a point to start from and Infinity was resolutely refusing to volunteer any ideas herself.

'Me neither. You, Ro?'

'The only thought I had was that seeing as Infinity struggles the most, maybe she would be the best at showing us if any ideas we have are any good?' She looked at me apologetically.

'So, shall I make an attempt at riding then?' I asked.

'Sounds like a good place to start,' said Justin.

I rubbed my chest with my fingers, trying in vain to ease the discomfort that persisted there.

'You okay?' asked Rowena.

I nodded. 'Just indigestion, I'll be fine.'

I led Infinity to the fence and mounted. The thrill I'd felt the previous day returned as I sat on my horse's back and I felt it magnified by Infinity. I leant forward and rubbed her neck.

'We'll just walk out onto a large circle around you again, shall we?' I asked my friends and both nodded their agreement.

Fin? I need to share your body again but I need to be a bit more aware of my own body than I was last time, can you help me to do that? I asked her.

Immediately, I felt my awareness being pulled, ever so lightly, into Infinity's body so that I was fully aware of both her and my bodies at the same time. It was like having double vision. I blinked in confusion as my brain tried to make sense of it.

As we walked around, I was vaguely aware of Justin and Rowena pointing out different parts of Infinity's body to each other and sharing ideas enthusiastically. At the same time, I could feel my weight pushing Infinity down onto her front legs as I sat comfortably in the saddle, waiting. I called out, 'Any ideas for me try?'

'Try leaning back, see if that helps,' called Rowena.

I did as she suggested. The pressure on Infinity's front legs eased a fraction, but not much. Her chest cavity was becoming compressed again.

'It's a tiny bit better, but it's not enough. She's shutting down again, please hurry,' I called back.

There was more discussion. Infinity's interest in what my friends were discussing was becoming more and more muted. Rowena raised her voice above the noise of the now torrential rain that was slamming down on the canopy. 'Can you squeeze your legs around her belly to try and help her lift up more?'

My hips screamed in protest but I squeezed as hard as I could. Infinity's body began to lift and the pressure on her chest cavity eased a little.

'It's helping, she's lifting and it's helping her chest,' I called. But then she toppled forward. Her chest closed down again and the hope that had begun to build inside her was compressed to nothing. A flare of panic broke briefly through the heavy nothingness and then winked out.

'STOP,' yelled Justin. I released the grip of my legs on Infinity's sides as she stumbled and then scrambled with her front legs before regaining her feet. Justin stood with his arms held out in front of him, apparently ready to try and catch me if I were thrown.

I hurled more of my awareness into Infinity's body desperately. Oak and Gas had beaten me to it. Her chest cavity was relaxing as their unwavering love and support worked to ease the effect my weight was having on her. Her muted feeling of excitement was becoming stronger.

I slid off Infinity rather than burden her with my weight any longer, and felt the acute awareness I'd had of her body recede.

Rowena came over and we stood discussing how I could help Infinity to move her weight back off of her front legs as she lifted, rather than leave her wobbling and in danger of falling forward again.

I would like a bridle such as I wore before, interrupted Infinity.

'Hang on, Infinity's asking for something,' I told my friends. *What do you mean?*

I would like a bridle with a bit in my mouth. With you holding the reins I would have some support. Something to lean on if I need to whilst we experiment.

I don't know what any of those things are.

Yes you do.

She transported us both back to the life in which she had been my cavalry horse. She showed me the leather straps that had buckled together to make her bridle, the metal bit that had sat in her mouth and the reins that had provided connection from the bit to the rider's hands. My hands.

'She wants a bridle,' I told Rowena and Justin.

'A what?' asked Rowena

I explained what it was and why Infinity wanted one, and Justin nodded slowly. 'Makes sense I guess, she'll have more confidence to try things if she knows you can help her stay upright if one of you gets it wrong.' I felt thoughts fly to him from Gas and he said, 'Gas wants to try one too. He's also impatient for me to get on and try what you just did with Infinity.' Gas was throwing his head around and fidgeting.

We watched first Justin and then Rowena try helping their horses to lift by squeezing with their legs. Gas lifted a small amount and then wasn't sure how to move with his body once it felt different from normal, and subsequently ground to a halt. 'Great, just like old times,' said Justin. Oak managed to lift himself a little more and the smile on Rowena's face told how they both felt about it.

Before we knew it, the lunch bell rang out, just loud enough for us to hear over the noise of the rain. We rugged our horses and took them to their respective paddocks, where they all made straight for their large, stone shelters. We ran on with our saddles, depositing them in the tack room before making the quick dash across the square to the dining room.

If I'd thought my entrance that morning had caused a stir, it was nothing compared with the reaction to the three of us arriving together. The hum of voices stilled to little more than a whisper as people sitting and eating marked our entrance. Those up at the food table turned around to see why everyone else had gone quiet.

Justin said, 'Come on, you two,' under his breath and made for the food table.

Rowena remained where she was and said loudly, 'Problem, is there?'

'Ro, leave it,' Justin said and beckoned her to follow us with a jerk of his head.

She ignored him and said, 'If anyone has a problem with me or my friends, let's hear it. No whispering, no nudging, no significant looks behind our backs once we've walked past, let's have it out in the open.' Her dark eyes flashed.

'Uh oh,' Justin breathed to me.

Part of me wanted to run and hide somewhere but the other part was fascinated by Rowena's confidence, her willingness to confront a whole room full of people. I felt Oak communicating with her and saw her shoulders drop down and relax from the fighting stance she had adopted, but she remained where she was. No one said a word and those at the tables nearest to her were suddenly very interested in their lunch.

'So, no one has the balls to come out and say it. You've all listened to Feryl back-biting about how Amarilla and Infinity don't want him to teach them, and you've had your minds made up for you that it's them with the problem, and presumably me and Justin for wanting to help them. You're no better than sheep, the lot of you,' Rowena railed.

The door opened behind her and Feryl walked in, wiping the rain from his eyes, with Adam just behind him.

Feryl's eyes narrowed. 'Back-biting? How dare you. I am the Master of Riding and if I have an opinion on the way a horse should be ridden then that is what it is, an opinion, and it is my duty to be honest and say what I think.'

'And what about what the horses think, Feryl, or doesn't that matter to you anymore? Amarilla is sixteen years old and as mild as they come, does she look like the type of person who would rebel against anything or anyone without good reason?'

All heads turned towards me and I shrank closer to Justin, but the focus on me was short-lived as Rowena continued, 'And as for Justin and me, our horses both want more out of how we ride them, much, much more and yet you've always refused to listen to either them or us, so now we are all working together, doing WHAT OUR HORSES WANT and if you, or any of the rest of you have a problem with that, then you don't deserve to call yourselves Horse-Bonded.'

The room was silent. Feryl looked at Rowena with fury in his eyes.

'You and I will discuss this another time, in private, where you won't have so many people to try and impress,' he spat venomously.

Rowena opened her mouth to retaliate but Adam stepped lithely between them and said in a calm voice, 'Well, that seems to have settled that. Feryl, Liberal's prescription is ready any time you want to collect it, no hurry though, just when you're ready. Rowena, Prista was telling me earlier about this idea you've had for waterproof saddle covers, won't you come and tell me about it over lunch?'

Rowena was drawn to walk with him. 'I know what you're doing, Adam,' she said, 'so don't try and convince me that you have even the remotest interest in saddle covers. Feryl had that coming, they all did. There were things that needed to be said.'

'I don't dispute what you say and I think we can all firmly agree that everything is now well and truly out in the open. I tend to find that's usually a good time to leave things to settle without adding any more fuel to the bonfire,' replied Adam cheerfully.

Thoughts flooded to Rowena from Oak and she slowly nodded her agreement. We all helped ourselves to food and sat down at a table together. I wasn't that hungry as my heartburn was worse than ever. I sipped at some more water.

Shann plopped himself down next to me, shaking his head so that water flew out of his hair and landed on me, Adam and the table. 'Good morning, everyone?' he asked and began to shovel jacket potato with cheese into his mouth. 'Wha've I missed?'

Rowena and I spent a companionable afternoon sitting at one of the long, wooden workbenches in the kitchen, peeling and chopping vegetables for the evening meal. We discussed what we had learnt from the morning's session with the horses and what we thought the next step should be. We finally agreed that I would go and speak to Mason about making bridles for our three horses and Rowena would approach Newson, a Metal-Singer, about making the bits for us. I quickly drew a picture of the bit that Infinity had been wearing in the vision she showed me, so that Rowena could take it with her.

There were twenty or so other people, most of whom I didn't know, working in the kitchen with us under Turi, the head cook. They all chatted and laughed together but largely ignored Rowena and me, apart from Holly. She approached us during our break and said, 'I just wanted you both to know that while I like and respect Feryl, I understand that you are guided by your horses and I wish you well.'

I thanked her, glad that maybe her words were an indication that not everyone was against what my friends and I were doing.

They are not against what we do. They are frightened of it, Infinity informed me.

Frightened? Why?

They fear what it means for them.

But why?

They will have to accept that what they have been doing is not as good as they thought. Their idea of themselves and what they think they have achieved with their horses is threatened.

But surely if someone can show them a way to ride that helps their horses more, they would be pleased? I mean we all want to do the best for our horses?

Walks A Straight Path you yet live up to your name. We have discussed the need most humans have to feel special. Humans who are chosen by us are not immune from that temptation. The Horse-Bonded are revered by your fellow humans. To a greater or lesser extent this gives them an idea of themselves that they are somehow significant. Important. They allow their bond with their horse to define them. Imagine how they feel when by your actions you tell them that their relationship with their horse is not all that they thought it was.

But how am I telling them that? I asked.

By revealing that your horse is illustrating the flaws in how people currently ride their horses. They wonder why their own horses have not done this. They ask themselves if maybe their link with their own horses is less strong than the one you and I share. They ponder whether they are less worthy of being given information than you. In questioning the bond they have with their horses they are forced to question the whole idea they have of themselves and their lives. They find this frightening.

Why haven't their horses questioned how they are ridden? Oak and Gas both did.

Horses choose to help their people for many different reasons. One horse may choose to help a person with a small change such as being able to balance evenly on both feet so that they are more even in temperament as a result. Another horse may choose to work with a person who has the ability to make huge changes to the human race. All changes a human makes are of equal importance to the human race however large or small they may seem because you are all connected. But even a small change can be an extreme challenge for a human. Until now there have been no humans with the mental and physical capacity necessary to help their horse make a change such as that which we attempt. The horses have always accepted this and been content to offer their aid regardless.

Do you mean that what you and I are doing when we're working on helping you to balance better, that's to do with our agreement? To do with us helping horses and humans to evolve further?

Infinity didn't reply and I remembered that she'd already hinted that this was the case.

'You've gone very quiet, everything okay?' said Rowena.

I nodded. 'Infinity's just given me a whole load to chew on and I just need to ask her something else.' *Fin, why did you tell me how the others are feeling? Isn't that meant to be kept private? Everyone having the right to work through their restrictions in their own way and all that?*

I gave no specific information about any individual. I have revealed nothing inappropriate, came Infinity's haughty reply. I sensed her grooming Oak's neck more fiercely, earning her a sharp nip in return. I grinned and told Rowena everything Infinity had told me.

'So, no pressure then,' Rowena said with raised eyebrows, 'we're only working on changing the world!'

SIXTEEN

Support

I asked Mason over dinner if he would make bridles for Infinity, Oak and Gas. He was only too happy to help, so we arranged that I would take Infinity to him to have her head measured after our riding session the following lunchtime. I spent the evening making drawings of all of the various components of the bridle just as Infinity had shown them to me, since Mason, like the rest of us, had never heard of a bridle before.

I had just sat down to breakfast the following morning when Mason's voice sounded in my ear. 'Close your eyes and hold out your hands.' I obliged and what felt like a leather strap was placed across my palms. 'And... open them.'

It was indeed a leather strap – it was the head piece of Infinity's new bridle and stitched into it were infinity symbols linked into a chain. I lifted the bridle up so I could see the rest of it. The black browband and noseband gleamed with their recent conditioning, and stitched into the middle of the brow band was yet another infinity symbol. The reins hung separately from the bridle, with no bit to attach to as yet.

'How did you... I mean, when did you?' I said.

He chuckled and his big belly lurched up and down. 'Been up all night, since you ask. No, don't you apologise, Amarilla, I was all for startin' it today like we said, but my Diligence wouldn't hear of it. All of a buzz she is with what you're doin', you, Rowena, Justin and your horses, wouldn't let me sleep she wouldn't, kept on at me that the sooner your horses have their bridles the sooner, well actually she wouldn't say what would happen, just kept on and on until I knew she wasn't goin' to let me rest. So, I took a lantern, got my measurin' tape and went down to the paddocks to do some measurin' and get some bridles made.' He chuckled again. 'Your Infinity wasn't too sure about it to begin with, messin' around in the dark and all, but once Oak stood quietly for his measurements to be taken, she decided she'd allow it.'

I smiled. 'But how did you know what to make? You haven't seen my drawings yet.'

'It seems that your mare isn't the only one who knows what a bridle looks like. Dili led me through it step by step.'

'Mason, this is beautiful, I don't know what to say,' I said.

'Say you'll go and show Dili the result of her night's mitherin' so she'll give me some peace. I need to sleep,' he replied. 'Ah, Justin, there you are.' He handed Justin a brown bridle and reins. 'Here you go. I must say, Gas was much more cooperative about being measured than I thought he would be. Spider was a pain in the jacksy though, all over me he was, kept tryin' to push his head in front of mine so I couldn't see the tape and it was difficult enough as it was, bein' dark. Anyway,' he thrust a second, much larger black bridle in Justin's direction, 'give this to Ro when you see her, will you? I'm goin' to bed.' He gave a huge yawn and shuffled off towards the door.

'What's this all about?' asked Justin.

'Sit down for a minute,' I said quietly, aware that most people sitting nearby were now listening avidly to our conversation and many more were sneaking looks at the contents of Justin's and my hands. He nodded and took the chair next to mine. I told him what Diligence and Mason had done for us and he examined his bridle. It was larger than mine and gleamed a deep chestnut brown. There were the tiniest stitches of the thinnest silver thread stitched into the top of the headpiece, so tiny and numerous that one had the impression of something finer than the finest of mists. It was a beautiful piece of workmanship. Shaking his head in wonderment, Justin put it on the table and held up Rowena's bridle. The oak tree stitched into the headpiece matched the one on the back of the cantle of Rowena's saddle, and stitched into the brow band was a single oak leaf. It was difficult to conceive of a man with hands and fingers the size of Mason's, performing such intricate work.

'These are fantastic, no wonder Gas is so full of himself this morning, he couldn't contain himself long enough to tell me what had got into him but now it all makes sense. When is Newson due to measure them for their bits?' Justin said.

'After breakfast, that's if he hasn't been up all night as well. Morning, Ro, I could hear you splashing around in the bath, sorry I didn't wait for you but I needed more tea,' I told an approaching Rowena.

'Heartburn still playing you up?' she asked. I nodded and gave Rowena her bridle, explaining once more about Mason's sleepless night.

'Poor Mason. It's nice to know Dili's on board with what we're doing though,' Rowena said as she inspected her bridle. 'This is amazing. Right, we need to get a move on. We'll go and see to clearing the dung from Dili's paddock to save Mason doing it later and I'll go and look at the rota and see what chores he's down for, we'll do them for him today as well.'

It was decided that I would meet Newson and go with him while he measured all three horses' mouths for their bits, since Infinity was likely to be the one most likely to refuse to cooperate in the absence of her bonded human. Rowena would clear Dili's paddock and field shelter and Justin would take on Mason's share of log splitting for the day.

Newson was waiting for me at the gate to Infinity's paddock, a chilly wind buffeting him as he stood wrapped in his cloak. I greeted him and explained why I was alone.

'So, Diligence is with you all on this. Interesting,' he said. 'I have to admit to you, Amarilla, I'm not sure about what you're doing here – going against Feryl's experience and knowledge, putting harness on your horse's head in order to ride her, a piece of metal in her mouth, flaming lanterns, I'm just not sure about it, but Integrity says I must keep an open mind and so that is what I will do.'

'Do you think I want to use a bridle when I ride Infinity for my sake? For something to hang on to because I can't really ride?'

'That isn't the reason?'

I explained the problems Infinity was having carrying me and why she had requested that I ride her in a bridle, and Newson listened attentively, sucking in his cheeks so that his thin, pock-marked face appeared even thinner. 'And you told all of this to Feryl?' he said.

'Some of it, he wouldn't really listen to me enough for me to get all of it out. He doesn't know anything about the bridles.'

'Well, he soon will. We'd better get these mouths measured, hadn't we?'

All three horses were very cooperative about having string laid in their mouths until Newson was satisfied that he had a length he could work from for each of them. 'I've not much on this morning so I'll aim to have them done before you're due to ride. Stop by my workshop and pick them up, alright?' he said.

'You can really do it that quickly? It won't tire you too much?'

He smiled. 'Amarilla, I've been a Metal-Singer for most of my life and I'm among the strongest of them. Something to do with a cast iron will, according to Integrity, if you'll excuse the pun. They'll be done on time, have no fear and then I suppose I shall be answering to Feryl about it.'

'I'm sorry if it causes you problems, doing this for us.'

He chuckled. 'You only have to consider the name I gave my horse to realise that I do have to risk causing offence to people every now and then.'

My morning passed tediously. I continued to plough through the different combinations of herbs in my collection and by the end of the session, I was none the wiser as to those that I could combine to help cure insomnia. Adam was nowhere to be seen, so I couldn't pop in for a chat to give myself a break. It was just me, my plants and the pain of heartburn – after two days of it, still no amount of tea or water was having any effect.

I made my way to collect the bits from Newson at the appointed time and as I walked, I thought about Infinity's assertion the previous day, that the discomfort I was experiencing was in my heart. Could she be right? I wondered to myself.

Your tendency towards denial is understandable in this instance. You are capable of diagnosing and healing your symptoms fully by yourself but hearing some of what you need to hear from another human will help you to accept your situation far more readily.

Another human? My situation? What do you mean?

Silence. Infinity waited patiently in my mind. I was nearly at Newson's door when I asked, *Shall I ask Adam if he can help?*

He Who Is Peace is a suitable choice.

Newson was as good as his word and all three bits were ready and waiting for me. 'I've coated the mouthpieces with a thin layer of honey,' he said, handing them over by the bit rings. 'I thought it might take the taste of the metal away to begin with, help them get used to having it in their mouths, so take care, they're sticky.'

I thanked him for both his work and thoughtfulness and he told me to be sure to return the bits if any of the horses found them uncomfortable or needed to have adjustments made.

I found Rowena and Justin in the tack room. We hung our bridles from the backs of our saddles as we attached the bits and reins, trying to avoid getting covered in honey as we did so. Infinity and Oak were waiting for us at their gate and Justin ran on to saddle and bridle Gas, saying he would meet us at the riding paddock.

I bridled Infinity first. I had the cheek pieces set too long to begin with and the bit clanged around against her teeth. I wasn't sure what to do about it until she demanded that the bit be lifted higher into her mouth immediately. She opened her mouth for me to see the natural gap between the incisors at the front and the molars that were set well towards the back of her long mouth. There, the bit could sit comfortably, so I adjusted the cheek straps until she was completely satisfied that the bit would indeed rest in a comfortable place. Oak was equally helpful in indicating where different straps needed adjustment – albeit in a less demanding way than Infinity – and we soon had him comfortable in his bridle.

As I stood back from him and registered the image in front of me, my heart lurched painfully in my chest. The two horses standing side by side, fully saddled and bridled, brought back to me with full force the scene from the previous life that Infinity and I had shared, of the horses lined up and ready to charge before being gunned down. Emotion flooded me.

Immediately, Infinity's nurturing energy enfolded me, reassuring me that the increased pain I was now experiencing in my chest was nothing to fear. She loved me. Her energy eased its way through my whole being, caressing my soul and I knew that she loved me with all of herself, unconditionally. Her love enfolded me and held me together as my pain and emotions risked spinning out of control. She only relaxed her support when the pain in my chest had subsided and my emotions were stable once more.

'Right, ready to go?' asked Rowena. She had just finished girthing up, which meant that what felt like a mountain of pain and emotion had arrived and departed within less than a minute.

'Um, yep,' I said, rubbing my face vigorously with both hands.

What just happened? I asked Infinity.

Do not concern yourself with it at present. You are stable for now and we have work to do.

But you helped the pain go away?

Temporarily. It will return. It is necessary. All is as it should be. For now you must concentrate on our work together.

We made our way to our riding paddock. Once Infinity had pulled a small amount of my awareness in to share her body with her, I held the reins while Rowena and Justin called out suggestions as to how to have a contact with her mouth without restricting the movement of her head and neck as she walked. I found it difficult to concentrate whilst being so acutely aware that the longer I faffed around, the more compromised were Infinity's body and emotional state. When I finally managed to find a contact with Infinity's mouth with which she seemed comfortable, I squeezed her sides with my legs.

Infinity lifted a little in front and tried to express relief and excitement, but her feelings bounced back in on themselves, unable to push past the heavy pressure that bound them within her chest. She lifted more and then leant on the reins for support as her body began to overbalance forward. A tiny surge of relief at the extra support was almost expressed, but then the support wavered. I was dually aware of my own body as my hands, followed by the rest of me, were jerked forward and I was pulled out of the saddle, ending up on Infinity's neck, and of Infinity's body as she lost her balance and stumbled heavily.

My friends appeared immediately on each side of me, pulling me back into the saddle while Infinity found her feet.

'I think you need to be able to stay upright when she does that, so that she can lean against you rather than pull you forward,' said Justin.

'And I think you need to be aware when you're stating the bleeding obvious, Jus,' said Rowena. 'Maybe don't squeeze so hard with your legs this time, Am, just help her to lift a tiny bit and work out how to balance her with the rein before asking her to lift more.'

'What, you mean try it again?'

'Does Fin want to stop?' she challenged me.

As Oak and Gas once more helped Infinity to recover, she mustered up a feeling of anticipation and readiness for what we would do next.

I sighed. 'I don't think so, okay, I'll give it a go.'

Our next attempt was slightly more successful in that Infinity didn't stumble, but as she began to lift up in front, I panicked and took a strong hold on her mouth, which caused her to jolt to a halt.

'That was a better effort, you just need to get your timing better so that as she leans on you, you take a steady pressure rather than grabbing at her mouth like that,' Justin said and Rowena rolled her eyes, grinning at me.

'Keep going, Am, you're doing great,' she said.

By the end of the session I was marginally happier as I'd managed to improve my timing slightly and Infinity had been able to take a few steps whilst lifting a little. Rowena found a rein contact with which Oak was more than happy in their session, though he hardly appeared to need to lean on the rein at all for support, unlike Gas, who took a hold on his bit and when asked to lift from Justin's legs, leant on it mercilessly.

'Blimey, that was a bit of a workout,' Justin said as he slid to the ground afterwards. 'I can't say I enjoyed it but Gas is ecstatic.'

'Well done, Justin, he looked much better, more connected, somehow and not just physically,' said Rowena, and I nodded my agreement.

We arrived in the dining room for lunch to find Feryl and Newson having a conversation just inside the door. Judging by the bread roll Feryl was waving around in his hand, he'd been watching for Newson and had accosted him the second he walked in.

'He knows about the bridles then,' muttered Justin. He moved to walk past them and I followed, trying to catch Newson's eye apologetically.

'It isn't a case of taking sides, Feryl,' Newson was saying, 'I was asked to avail them of my Skill and I agreed to make what they wanted, just as I would for anyone else.'

'But they don't know what they're doing, you might as well give a knife to a baby,' Feryl said, glaring at the three of us.

'Integrity has counselled me to remain open to what they are doing and I have every intention of taking her advice. I'm sorry, Feryl, but that's just the way it is, now you really will have to excuse me, I only have time for a short lunch break,' Newson said.

Rowena spoke quietly to Newson as he followed us to the food table. 'Thanks, Newson, the bits are perfect.'

'Well I'm glad someone's happy. You've stirred up a proper hornet's nest, the three of you and your horses, I hope it's worth it,' he replied.

I decided to try and speak to Adam over dinner about my unresolved physical discomfort. When I saw him sitting up near the food table by himself, I quickly got myself a bowl of stew and took the chair next to him. I was just about to ask him for his advice when a pot full of a foul-smelling substance was slammed down onto the table in front of us. A solidly-built, fair-haired woman stood opposite us both with her hands on her hips.

'I've done it, Adam, finally, I've done it. It's passed all the tests I can think of to try and it definitely works, but will Verve let me put it on him? Even have it near him? No. He. Will. Not,' she hissed.

Adam said, 'Amarilla, I'm not sure if you've been introduced to
Vickery yet, one of our fellow Herbalists? She's been spending rather a
lot of time in the woods recently. Verve is her very dashing white
stallion.'

I smiled and nodded at Vickery, and she nodded back briefly before
glaring at Adam. 'Can you believe it? Can you countenance that he could
possibly be that stubborn?'

'Has Verve given you a reason for his decision?' he asked her.

'Wait right there,' she said and dashed off to the food table, returning
shortly afterwards with a bowl of soup. She sat down and slurped a
mouthful. 'Horse dung in my bed that's hot,' she spluttered, reaching for
Adam's glass of water. He passed it to her and she drank the lot. 'That's
better. Verve is of the opinion that he has never smelt anything so foul
and has no intention of undermining his scent by wearing it. Never mind
that it could save his life, and mine come to that.' She took another
mouthful of soup, giving Adam the opportunity to fill me in.

'Vickery decided to work on producing a paste that could be smeared
onto the horses to deter or poison the Woeful,' he said.

'Not poison, Verve wouldn't hear of it,' Vickery said. 'He told me
never to work on producing a poison, not for anything. Damages the soul
or something.'

'Poison would damage the soul of a Woeful?' I said.

'No, mine apparently,' she said.

'Well quite,' said Adam. 'Do you think that if you could maybe refine
it so it didn't smell quite so strongly, Verve would alter his decision?'

'Nope, the smell wasn't the only reason. Verve has assured me that
although he'll do his best to escape any danger to his body and stay here
with me, if he is caught by a Woeful then it will be his time to go and
he'll leave his body and return to "All That Is", whatever he means by
that. Have you ever heard anything quite so ridiculous?' She looked from
me to Adam.

'Um, well, yes I have actually,' I said. 'Infinity said pretty much the
same to me when I wanted to take a long route around some woods to
avoid meeting any Woeful.'

'And wouldn't you have felt more comfortable knowing that you and she were coated in something that would have repelled Woeful from you? Kept you safe?'

'Definitely, but I doubt Infinity would ever agree to it,' I said. Infinity increased her presence in my mind briefly, confirming that I was right.

Vickery gave a sharp sigh. She stood up and banged her hands on the table until the hum of conversation in the dining hall quietened. 'Sorry to interrupt your conversations, folks,' she said, 'but I would like to announce that I have managed to produce a paste that will repel Woeful. It's not the sweetest smell you'll ever have the pleasure of experiencing, but it works. I've left pieces of fresh meat smeared with it in numerous places in the woods, and not one has been touched, despite tracks of more than one Woeful showing that they have visited and considered it. I would like some volunteer horses to trial it, so I can see how long the smell lasts once it is smeared onto the horse's coat.'

'Is your Verve not up for having his looks tarnished by it, Vic?' someone called from a nearby table.

'Er, no he isn't actually, that's why I need volunteers, but I'd need them anyway as I need to see if it stays smelling fresh for the same amount of time on different horses.'

'Fresh? Pungent I'd call it. Sorry, Vic, Astral's no more interested in having that smeared over her than Verve is,' said another voice.

Quinta waved from a few tables away and called out, 'Sorry, Vic, Noble's having none of it. Quite shirty with me for asking, actually, not like him at all.'

Norieva appeared at Vickery's side and said, 'I'm terribly sorry but Dragonfly won't have it anywhere near her. Something to do with being a slippery slope to The Old, she's very put out about the whole idea. Good luck though, I think it's a terrific idea.' Vickery nodded, forlornly.

A man with long, white-blond hair tied back into a tail, took the chair next to her. 'Vic, I'm sorry but Candour says that no horse will agree to wear your paste, the very concept is repellent to them.'

'Oh, Jack, I only wanted to keep them all safe. The light knows how many Woeful are out there and we all have a duty to travel around from time to time, not to mention the fact that there are woods just the other side of the river. I know Woeful don't swim but just knowing they could be so close gives me the jitters.'

I felt thoughts from Verve dart past me to Vickery, like butterflies flitting around in the sunshine.

'I know, I know, so you've said,' Vickery murmured and then said to Adam and me, 'Verve just told me that he's always safe, no matter what happens to his body.'

'But you worry what would happen to you, yourself if he were to die?' Adam said gently.

'Well of course I do, don't we all? Oh, sorry, Adam.'

'You have absolutely no need to be. Peace is safe, just as Verve tells you he will be when his time in a body is at an end. Trust your horse, Vickery, and if you are considering following his advice to ditch the paste, do you think you could do it sometime soon? Everything I put in my mouth is starting to taste like it.'

We all laughed and Vickery made a big show of taking her pot and hurling it from the nearest window, to much applause and laughter from the other diners.

We were leaving the dining hall before I had a chance to talk to Adam on his own. I related how I had been out of sorts for the past few days.

'By the wind of autumn, Amarilla, why didn't you tell me you weren't feeling well before?' he asked, as he marched me to his consulting room.

'I just thought it was heartburn and it would pass.'

'Heartburn? For two days straight? And what do you mean you thought it was heartburn, didn't you check?'

'It feels just like any other time I've had heartburn so I didn't think to.'

His eyes twinkled. 'My my, this will be a funny story to tell when you're a celebrated Healer – of how you once drank endless water and greenmint tea for a heart problem.'

My stomach turned over. 'My heart? So, it definitely is my heart? That's what Infinity said.'

'And do you mind if I ask why you didn't listen to her?'

'I was just so sure it was heartburn,' I mumbled.

'Well then let's make today the first time you perform a self-diagnosis. Proceed when you are ready.' Adam slipped into his role as my Master.

I tuned into my body and could detect no problem with my stomach or digestive tract. I became aware that the pain that was slowly increasing in intensity again was indeed emanating from my heart, but I couldn't seem to pinpoint an exact location or cause. I related my findings to Adam, who nodded and said, 'My findings concur with your own. I think it would be wise to go and seek Thuma's knowledge about this, I saw her light on as we passed her door and I know she'll welcome the opportunity to meet you. Come on, let's go and see what she thinks.'

Infinity was monitoring the proceedings closely but hadn't ventured any opinions or advice, so I went along with Adam to knock on the door of Thuma's consulting room. Thuma was one of the Tissue-Singers, a middle-aged and very serious woman with a shock of short, black, spiky hair. Her green eyes were placed closely together on her small face and as she listened intently to what I told her about the symptoms of my condition and my and Adam's findings, she reminded me of the black cat that lived next door to my family's home in Rockwood.

'How very interesting,' she said. 'Let's have a look at you then, shall we? Just relax now.'

She bade me recline on top of a huge pile of soft cushions while she knelt on the floor beside me with her eyes closed. Candles flickered in sconces that were attached to the red-painted stone walls, and their warm glow was both calming and immensely soporific. I was midway between sleep and wakefulness when I felt Thuma's hand on my arm. She gave me a very gentle shake. 'Alright, my dear, up you get when you're ready.'

I went to join her and Adam at her circle of comfy chairs as she threw off her slippers and curled her legs around herself in one of them. 'I agree that your pain is emanating from your heart, yet I can sense no tissue that is damaged or otherwise unhealthy,' she said. 'It's enthralling – your heart is being inhibited from working at full capacity because you are carrying something that weighs on it so heavily that it can't contract and relax fully as a healthy muscle should.'

Infinity made her presence known more strongly until I picked up her sense of calm confidence that everything was as it should be.

'What is it that I'm carrying?' I asked tentatively.

'Amarilla, you carry an extraordinary amount of emotional pain. There is something about the way it feels that leads me to believe it has always been there, but it seems that it has been newly awakened. I would suggest that there is nothing any Healer can do for you to rid yourself of your physical pain. You must identify the cause of all the emotion you are holding and then find a way to release it. Once your heart is free to work unhindered, I think the physical pain will subside.'

Infinity let me know that Thuma's advice was sound.

'Have you come across this before?' I asked Thuma.

'A couple of times. In both cases my patients had deep wounds that refused to heal fully, despite my best efforts. I could sense that the wounds were loaded with something that festered and the first time, it was a good few months before I realised that it was emotion rather than anything physical. The second time, I recognised it more swiftly and with you it would have been difficult for me to miss. Amarilla, you carry a heavy burden and it is my strong advice to you that you make it a priority to find a way to release it. Your heart will only be able to struggle for so long,' Thuma said gently.

'Do you mean that my heart could give in? I could die?' I said.

'I'm sure it won't come to that. Any time you need my support, you come and see me,' Thuma told me. Feeling numb, I nodded and thanked her.

Infinity's warmth infused me. *You will resolve this. I shall assist you. Everything is as it should be.*

Adam and I left Thuma's room and Adam said, 'Amarilla, I know you must be feeling overwhelmed. You're so young and it seems that you are taking on so much. My feeling is that Infinity wouldn't be allowing it if you weren't capable of rising to the challenge, so take confidence from that. Trust her. Okay?'

I nodded. 'She keeps telling me that everything is as it should be.'

I left the building and headed straight for Infinity through the still, clear evening. She was waiting for me, watching me intently but quiet in my mind. I climbed through the fence and she whickered softly. I put my arms around her neck and buried my face in her fur. I have no idea how long we stood so.

Eventually, I asked, *You know the source of the emotion that's hindering my heart, causing me this pain?*

Of course.

Will you tell me?

You allowed the situation that led to our acquaintance in our previous lives to affect you very deeply.

When I was a Government Advisor?

I felt her assent. *You were a long way ahead of most other humans in your thinking at that time. You knew how to resolve the conflict that arose without need for physical force but you were unable to make yourself heard. Your knowledge would have saved millions from suffering had you been able to use your influence to full effect and sway the opinions of those who were in charge. You allowed your inability to do this to weigh heavily on you and the manner of your subsequent punishment by your peers only compounded your torment.*

But why does this mean I have pain in my heart now?

You allowed the extreme anguish you suffered to imprint onto your soul. You have carried it with you into this lifetime as an issue to be resolved.

But why is the pain in my heart?

The heart is at the core of your ability to express yourself. You adopted the view that everything that befell the human race at that time was as a direct result of your inability to express yourself strongly enough. You held all of the emotion from that and the events that followed in your heart. You still do.

I leant my cheek against her warm neck, watching the mist of her breath in the moonlight.

Why has the pain only started now? If I brought it with me from my previous life, why has it waited until now to bother me? I asked.

Like resonates with like.

I made the connection. Back then I had seen a way to avert a war that would take countless lives. I had been unable to express myself strongly enough to make what I knew of use to anyone; exactly as was happening with the knowledge I was gaining and trying to express now. As soon as I was faced with someone who questioned or discounted what I had to say, I crumbled. Everything was beginning to make sense.

The pain is here because I am in a similar situation again?

Because you are in a similar situation and responding in the same way as before. The difficulties you are experiencing with some of your fellow humans have presented you with an opportunity to face the same challenges as before but to respond to them differently. If you succeed then you will be able to release the emotion that you hold and that holds you back.

I have to be able to stand my ground and say what I know to be true in the face of opposition, I thought to myself as much as to Infinity. I felt weak at the knees just thinking about it.

SEVENTEEN

Attacked

*A*utumn passed me by in a blur of swirling leaves, rain and misery; I hated feeling like an outcast among my fellow Horse-Bonded and I was in almost continual pain.

Knowing that the pain was emanating from my heart made it seem more intense somehow. There were times when it seemed to spiral out of control and my breath would become shallow and raspy while I fought down panic. Was this it? I'd ask myself. Had I run out of time to clear the issue that was causing it? Was I going to have a heart attack and die? What if I died all by myself at night-time? What if the pain got even worse?

Every time I was on the verge of losing the plot completely, Infinity would draw me to her. Sometimes just being with her was enough to calm me, but usually she would instruct me to get my saddle and bridle and go with her to the riding paddock. As soon as I was on her back, she would take up all of my concentration. No part of my attention could be spared to dwell on my pain and I would notice after a while that my breathing had returned to normal, the pain in my heart had subsided to a more manageable level and another panic had been overcome.

I told Rowena and Justin that I had a problem with my heart and would be dealing with it by myself, and they were both incredulous.

Rowena demanded an explanation, which I found myself unable to give; whenever I thought of the cause of my heart problem and the hurdle I would need to overcome in order to clear it, it felt as if a sore spot very deep in my soul were being prodded. It was too personal, too painful for me to talk about and for a while, I avoided even thinking about it. I asked my friends if they could understand that as soon as I felt I could say more, I would, and further I asked if they would cover for me if I were ever too ill to do my chores.

Rowena went to Norieva and arranged that her chores would always be alongside mine. More than a few times, she had to make excuses for me and work longer hours as I left what we were doing to hurry off and ride my horse, in order that I could cope with yet another attack of extreme, heart-clenching pain. I know Justin and Shann both helped her when they could and I felt awful at the burden I was being to them all.

It wasn't long before word got around that I was leaving my chores for others to do whilst I went to ride my horse. To those who were already feeling cool towards me for my rebellion towards Feryl, I was now a very credible target at whom to direct their hostility. I was either ignored, glared at, or openly berated for my behaviour and not once could I find it within myself to explain my actions.

On one occasion, I was hurrying from the tack room with my saddle and bridle, my heart lurching painfully, my breathing erratic and sweat pouring down my face despite the frost that crunched beneath my feet. I was focused on getting to my horse, knowing that once I was with her, my symptoms would begin to ease and that once I was riding, Infinity would fill my senses sufficiently that the pain would subside to a level that was necessary, rather than debilitating. I didn't notice Feryl and a group of his admirers coming towards me, all on horseback, until they were almost on top of me. As I sidestepped around Liberal, I noticed briefly that the hollows above his eyes were more pronounced.

'And here she is again,' Feryl sneered. 'I expect that your deluded, long-suffering friends are, yet again, doing your work for you while you go and snatch some extra practice at riding terribly, are they, Amarilla? Just how do you get them to do it?'

I looked at the ground and hurried on. I could feel my heart straining against the shackles of my emotion and every now and then it lurched sickeningly as it managed a few stronger beats before the vice that I had subconsciously placed around it tightened once more. I ground my teeth together, concentrating on keeping my feet moving in the right direction. Infinity's calm reassurance drew me to her, providing a focus that prevented me from slipping into hysteria.

'Don't want to tell us? No, I didn't think so, you hurry off, little Amarilla, go and play,' Feryl called and laughed an empty laugh that was echoed by some of his companions. I increased my pace even more, knowing that I should calmly defend my actions, but knowing also that I was further than ever from being able to do so.

I was practically gasping when I reached Infinity, and had allowed fear to assure me that I would faint. Infinity ignored my predicament and held her head out to be bridled. Once I had her tacked up, she turned and gave me a gentle nip on the outside of my thigh in reprimand for tightening the girth without pulling her legs forward to remove any trapped wrinkles of skin.

As soon as she was out of the gate, I was on her back. Immediately I could feel, as always, that she needed my help to balance; I needed to get myself into position and then support her with my legs and reins. Infinity focused on what she was doing and I was drawn completely and utterly into an awareness of her body and her needs, leaving my body to calm itself back down without the hindrance of my mind's agitation.

My riding did seem to be slowly improving. I could now help Infinity to lift a little without falling, but if I lost concentration even momentarily, she would either stumble due to a lack of support, or grind to a halt due to a yank in the mouth from me as I grabbed at the reins.

Rowena and Justin were faring much better. Rowena had learnt to help Oak to lift in both walk and trot and was beginning to work on his canter. Justin was at a similar level with Gas, though the chestnut stallion, thrilled at the support he could get from Justin's rein contact, continued to lean against it.

We began to draw spectators to our riding sessions. They were from the crowd who often sat watching Feryl teach and as we passed them with our horses on the way to our riding paddock, they would follow us and then sit on the fence and amuse themselves by calling out less than helpful suggestions while we rode. I could feel thoughts whistling past me from Oak and Gas, and my friends remained silent, even Rowena. I was aware of her fury, but she didn't say a word. It seemed the horses were all in agreement that if anyone was to be responsible for explaining and defending our actions, it was going to have to be me.

We took the initial measure of moving our horses to one of the far paddocks, just beyond the riding paddock we liked to frequent. That way, we could take our gear across the paddocks to our horses, tack up and go straight into the riding paddock without having to pass Feryl's teaching paddock. It wasn't long before our avoidance tactics were discovered, however and when the heckling started up once more, we resorted to riding during lunchtime. The lovely Turi agreed to save us some food, so that we might eat it when the lunch sitting was over.

Rowena was initially furious at the way we were "sneaking around, as if we were doing something wrong," and Justin admitted to feeling uncomfortable about it, but I managed to persuade them to go along with it for the time being. Aside from my aversion to confrontation was my reasoning – that the others eventually admitted was sound – that the people who were threatened by the fact that we were going our own way would never be talked around. We would need to show them the results of what we were attempting and we would work towards achieving that much better and quicker if we could work with our horses in peace.

And so it was that by the time winter set in, our horses found themselves in one of the furthest paddocks from the buildings. I hated being so far from Infinity, but I knew that she liked her new paddock; it was much larger than her previous one and it had a high hedge sheltering it down one side and an enormous stone field shelter that she, Oak and Gas could share with plenty of room to spare when they needed somewhere to escape from the weather. The fact that it was one of the furthest paddocks meant that it was used much less than the others and still had a good amount of grass, and it was in close proximity to our riding paddock, which suited all of us.

It wasn't long before Spider joined the herd; he had apparently badgered Shann for several days and nights without break, not only to move him back in with Gas, but to ask if he might join our riding sessions too.

It was unfortunate that we then experienced one of the harshest winters for decades. The snow arrived a few weeks before the Longest Night Festival and then the weather closed in on us all, refusing to permit even the hardiest of us to be outside for more than a few hours at a time. By day, the sun was hidden by thick clouds that either spilled yet more snow or threatened to. By night, the temperatures plummeted and froze everything to everything else and it seemed that the cold, biting wind would keep blowing until it had stripped the hide from every living creature unfortunate enough to be out in it for too long.

Thankfully, hay and shelter were in plentiful supply, so all of our animals fared relatively well but it was hard work looking after them, especially for those of us who had to lug hay and water to the furthest paddocks over tracks that were soon trampled to hard-packed ice.

Riding was miserable, as our hands and feet became numb and painful within minutes. We persevered, although Rowena and Justin were soon limited to restricting their work to walk with just a little bit of trotting once the ground froze and became too hard and slippery for any faster work. Rowena concentrated on helping Oak to stay lifted as he made transitions between the paces, whilst Justin was attempting to find a way to persuade Gas to stop leaning quite so heavily on his reins. Shann and Spider spent a good amount of that bitterly cold winter observing our sessions rather than joining in, as Shann explained that he was still having trouble understanding exactly what we were attempting to do and why. Rowena was of the firm belief that it had more to do with Shann not wanting to get his hands cold.

My apprenticeship had ground to a halt somewhat, as my pain levels fluctuated unpredictably and I found myself unable to follow Adam's rule and leave all of my concerns at the door. He was kind and understanding, but I felt I was letting him down. He occupied me with sorting through the vast herb stores, putting to one side any that I could sense were too old to be of any use, and making a careful inventory of what we had, so that we could fill any gaps by gathering more once spring arrived.

The Longest Night Festival was difficult for me as I missed my family desperately, but I made an effort to join in the festivities alongside my friends. I twisted small conifer twigs into a crown to wear to the midnight ceremony – where we would welcome the days becoming longer once more – and decorated it with holly berries and the tiny horseshoes my aunt had sent; it was customary for the Horse-Bonded to wear the tiny ornaments from their Quest Ceremonies in their crowns. As I sat between Adam and Shann, attempting to keep up with the rowdy verse we were all singing, I wished I could have been with my family. I pictured them all sitting around the kitchen table, laughing and joking with the fire roaring in the hearth.

You are closer to them than you think, Infinity informed me. I managed to find new strength in my voice for the next few lines about the Weather-Singer who took on a hurricane and battled it for three days and nights.

It seemed that winter would never end. The Weather-Singers refused to attempt to influence the weather even the tiniest bit and anyone who went shivering to them to request it was firmly reminded that whilst they were happy to influence short term weather patterns, attempting to change the course of a whole season was grossly inappropriate. There was much grumbling about the Weather-Singers' "obstinacy", "inconsideration" and "arrogance" and I felt slightly guilty at my relief that I was no longer the sole target of ill feeling.

As the end of that bitter winter drew near, a day arrived that was forever afterwards referred to as "that day".

There had been a definite lessening of the bite in the wind and a perceptible softening in the snow and ice underfoot, and the general mood at The Gathering was improving. I had been having one of my better days. I'd spent the morning helping Adam make up jars of poultice whilst he told me anecdotes from his own time as an Apprentice, some of which had had me in tears of laughter. My riding session afterwards had gone well; Rowena had worked out that by closing her thighs around Oak and pulling back with them slightly, she could stop him from leaning against the bridle when he moved from walk to trot and I found that her discovery was the missing ingredient for which I had been searching.

Infinity had become more used to her thoughts and feelings having to struggle to be expressed when I rode her and she tended to concentrate on feeling the hope that was trying to surface. When I asked her to lift a little and then closed my thighs around her and pulled back, her front legs immediately carried less weight and her chest opened a fraction, enough for her hope and a surge of delight to break through!

Justin, Rowena and Shann all clapped. I asked Infinity to halt and flung my arms around her neck, laughing with joy but slightly disbelieving of what we had just achieved. Then I took the reins back up and tried again.

This time, I squeezed harder with my lower leg, creating more lift, and then instantly pulled back even harder with my thighs. The front half of Infinity's body lifted up and came back towards me, something I'd never felt before. Her chest opened more and she expressed pure, unadulterated joy. My friends roared with delight and I found myself overcome with Infinity's emotion as well as my own.

'Hang on, Am, don't drop her, thunder and lightning, don't you drop her now,' shouted Rowena. 'Pull back further and see if you can help her to stop like that.'

Through tears and laughter, I asked my already screaming thigh muscles for more, leaning back in my saddle to add more leverage to my request for Infinity's body to stay up and back off its front end while we slowed to a halt. We made it. I slid to the ground and landed on shaking legs. I looked at my horse and realised what we had done. She looked completely different from how she had ever looked before. Her front end now stood higher than her rump and her front legs almost appeared to be out in front of her. Her neck was arched and her blue eyes shone bluer than ever as she batted her long white lashes at me. I cried and I laughed, and as my friends joined me in a group hug I realised that their faces ran with tears also.

As I stood with my arm around my horse's neck, watching my friends ride, I felt buoyant and more at peace with myself than ever I could remember. When we walked our horses back to their paddock, however, I noticed that Infinity's posture gradually returned to what it had been before I rode her and sadness filled me.

Worry not. My body has neither the strength nor awareness to achieve balance without your body to support it but this we will achieve over time. Together. She was happy, so happy and my elation returned and remained with me all afternoon as I mopped floors.

As I tucked into my dinner, listening to Rowena telling Adam about what we had achieved with the horses that day, I still couldn't wipe the smile from my face. I caught sight of Quinta standing with a plateful by the food table and waved her over, eager to tell her what she and Newson had missed – they had recently moved their horses to the paddock the far side of ours and sometimes brought their lunch out to eat while watching my friends and me ride. We felt that it was only a matter of time before they would ask to join us. Quinta grinned and began to make her way over. I turned back to my plate and had just loaded my fork with a large piece of buttery potato, when I felt it. The hairs on the back of my neck stood up and I wanted to squirm in my seat.

Fin?

Hunted! A surge of panic.

A plate smashed just behind me and Quinta screamed, 'NOBLE! OH, NO, NOT NOBLE, NOOOOOO. WOEFUL! WOEFUL ARE ATTACKING MY HORSE!'

I looked up to see Rowena's face frozen in fear, her own fork held in mid-air as Oak's frantic thoughts reached her. We both threw our forks down and ran, with Quinta close behind us. A shocked silence hung over the room as we ran for the door, followed by questioning voices which escalated to shouts. I could feel Infinity's sheer, unadulterated panic and I nearly lost my mind. I ran blindly, not knowing what I could do but knowing that I needed to get to my mare as fast as I could.

'Weapons,' said Rowena. 'We need weapons, get the shovels from the dung pits in the paddocks.'

I ran next to her, trying desperately to keep up as we slid on the ice. I could hear horses screaming in the distance now and could feel that Infinity raced around and around her paddock at break neck speed. She was alone! Where were the others? As I reached through the fence of the first paddock that we came to and grabbed a shovel, my question was answered. Hooves thundered on the ice and Gas appeared, ice chips flying in his wake, followed by Spider and then Oak, who had blood pouring down the front of his forelegs. They had jumped out of the paddock, leaving Infinity, who was smaller and not balanced enough to clear the fence, on her own.

'OAK! OAK!' shouted Rowena as he tore past her, but he was beyond reason. The whites of his eyes showed, his nostrils flared and sweat poured down his flanks. Rowena turned and began to run after him.

'Let him go, he's safe,' I panted. 'Infinity can't get out, she's on her own. Please, Rowena, please, HELP ME.' I screamed the last few words as my panic levels rose to match Infinity's.

Suddenly, a calm strength stole over me that I would never have known I possessed. My horse was in danger and I would save her. That was all there was to it. How I thought I might battle a Woeful, who stood over six feet in height and had toughened skin, fangs and slicing talons, with only a shovel, I have never managed to reconcile in my mind, but I knew absolutely and completely that I would save my horse or die trying. I drew a deep breath as I ran.

We passed more horses who had jumped out of their paddocks and were making their way towards the buildings, towards safety, and we had to run along the fence line so as not to get trampled. I ran on, adrenaline giving me the strength and endurance I needed. We were nearly there when Newson's horse, Integrity, passed us with a gash in her chest and numerous cuts on her front legs. She was lathered with sweat and lame on one of her hind legs but she flew past us in her terror.

All of a sudden, Quinta, who was running behind Rowena and me, let out a blood-curdling scream that shook me to my core. I will never forget that heart-wrenching noise as long as I live. 'NOOOOOOOOOOOOO!' she screamed. 'Noooooo, Noble, no, please don't go, please don't, no, please don't…'

I glanced behind me to see her sink to her knees. A largely built man caught up with her and crouched down by her side, pulling her against him and holding her head against his shoulder as she wailed her grief.

Newson, Shann and Justin all tore past her, each carrying a shovel and I turned back to run to my horse, holding the horror of the situation away from me. I was going to save my horse. That was all there was to focus on. I would get to my horse.

Our paddock came into sight and time slowed down as I took in the scene in front of me. Three enormous, brown-pelted Woeful were climbing the far fence of Noble and Integrity's paddock, with Noble's black body hoisted onto their shoulders. Infinity was galloping around the perimeter of her paddock and yet another Woeful, this one even larger than the others and with black fur, gambolled awkwardly after her.

Fin, we're here, just keep going a little longer, we'll get him away from you. Keep going, my heart, just keep going.

She didn't register my thoughts. I could feel her exhaustion. She had strained and torn multiple muscles from galloping so fast in a relatively tight space, and even that pain couldn't penetrate the total fear and panic that overwhelmed her every sense.

It was a miracle she had managed to stay upright as long as she had, travelling over snow and ice at that speed. Just as I climbed through the fence, I saw her slip. My heart lurched as I saw her trying to keep her feet underneath her. She made it; with a scrambling of legs she stayed on all four feet, but it was the chance that the Woeful had needed. He caught up with her as she fought to get a purchase on the ice to get herself moving again and just before she could galvanise her tired legs back into action, he leapt onto her back and brought her down.

'NOOOOOOOOOOO!' My scream rang in my ears and tore at my throat. 'GET OFF HER! GET OFF! INFINITY! NOOOOOOOOO!' I was running flat out with my shovel raised above my head. Running footsteps overtook me as Shann shot past, yelling at the top of his voice. I saw the Woeful lift his arm for the slash that would end my horse's life. No. This couldn't be happening. Not to Infinity. Not to me.

Shann reached them and brought his shovel down on the Woeful's back. The Woeful's knees buckled briefly under the impact and then he leapt off of my horse with astonishing agility and turned to face us. He was monstrous. Hunched in his posture as he was, he still towered over Shann and me and the huge fangs that protruded from his mouth were thick and yellow and dripped with saliva. He had long talons at the end of each of the hairy fingers that he flexed open and closed in readiness for the attack he anticipated. His face looked largely human, but was covered by a thin layer of fine, black hair. His eyes were those of a cat. Green with slitted pupils, they broadcast his hunger and as his gaze met mine briefly, I felt it as if it were my own; he was starving, as were his mate and his youngling. He was desperate. Hungry, fearful and desperate.

Shann had already begun to bring his shovel down in a heavy swipe at the Woeful's head but I saw the instant that he felt what I'd felt from the Woeful. Shann faltered and tried to take the power out of his swing but it was too late. The Woeful raised an arm and lashed out to defend himself, and I heard the break of Shann's arm as the shovel was diverted from its target. The Woeful's arm continued its swing and I saw a talon brush against Shann's neck. The gash that opened sprayed thick red blood all over me and Infinity as Shann fell wordlessly, landing with the upper half of his torso on my horse. I looked back at the Woeful, stunned with shock and disbelief. I saw immense sadness in his eyes, before he turned and fled as more people arrived behind me.

I sank to my knees in a pool of blood beside Shann's lifeless body. Infinity lay unmoving on the ground in front of me; a tangled mess of white, black, red and the purple of her rug. Someone screamed, I think it was Rowena. I was aware of people shouting everywhere and Shann's body was pulled away from where it had fallen. Broad hands clasped my shoulders and I heard Justin's shaking voice behind me saying, 'Am, are you hurt? Amarilla?'

I couldn't speak. *Infinity?* I ventured. Nothing. I felt for her in my mind. Nothing. I could feel my mind slipping away from me in despair but caught hold of it and anchored it firmly. My horse needed me – at the moment, that was all that mattered. Everything I wanted to feel, to think about, to try and make sense of, would have to wait. I saw my trembling hand reach out in front of me and touch her through a rip in her rug. I closed my eyes and tuned into her body. Her heart was beating weakly, but it was beating. The relief that washed over me with that realisation was nearly enough for me to lose my concentration, but I grabbed hold of it before it fled, and began a careful inventory of her body. I was suddenly aware that her life force was slipping away. But why? How? Justin's hands still rested on my shoulders and I was glad of their strength.

Help... not time to leave... need your help, Infinity mustered all of her strength to focus her thoughts to me, and then slid back into unconsciousness.

I fought away dread and consternation and refocused. If I didn't find the critical injury very soon, it would become a fatal one and I knew I didn't have the time to scan her whole body in depth before I would lose her. What to do, oh if only she could tell me what to do.

I felt the weakest breath of a whisper in my mind and to this day I couldn't say for sure whether it originated with Infinity or me. *We are one... trust yourself.*

I brought my awareness back to my own body. Where is it? I asked myself. And I knew. Her life force was leaking out of the underside of her neck; I could feel it as if it were happening to me. Immediately, I tuned back into her body, to the area I now knew needed my immediate attention. She was lying on a gash caused when the Woeful had clung to her as he brought her to the ground. His talons had slashed through one side of an artery, which was now pumping her blood onto the snow.

I began to hum. The vibration of the noise I made resonated exactly with the damaged artery wall. I sent my intention of knitting the damaged tissue together down the path created by my humming, then as the tissue of the artery wall came along with my intention and began to heal, I gradually changed the hum to one that was smoother and more high-pitched. I put everything into my humming; my profound love for my mare, my energy, my pure, solid intention that she would heal, that she would live. I changed my humming once more, softer now, and the artery wall strengthened until it was fully healthy. The main bleed stopped. I tuned into Infinity's heart, which still beat its weak but steady rhythm. I moved on. Three of her ribs were broken. I was just composing myself to sing them back to wholeness when Feryl's voice interrupted me.

'Right, everyone, stand aside. You too, Amarilla, I've organised the Healers, we'll just move Infinity into the field shelter and then they can get to work. Come along now, Amarilla, she'll be in the best hands, up you get, move away now.'

Justin's hands squeezed my shoulders more tightly, but I brushed them aside and stood up to face Feryl. 'You get away from me and get away from my horse,' I spat at him.

'Amarilla, I'm here to help, someone needs to organise this chaos into some sort of recovery...'

'And you think that person is you, do you? You, who thinks he has all the answers, you, who won't listen to a word anyone else has to say, you, whose fault it is that our horses were in this paddock in the first place?'

'Well, I...'

'How dare you take it upon yourself to tell me what's best for my horse when you haven't the first clue of what she needs? You need to get away from us, Feryl, and you need to do it RIGHT NOW, AND TAKE ALL OF YOUR SYCOPHANTIC CRONIES WITH YOU.'

Feryl gaped at me in shock before turning and walking away.

'Way to go, Amarilla,' Justin said quietly. 'Can I help at all?'

'I don't know,' I mumbled. 'She's got broken ribs and torn muscles and I haven't even done a complete inventory of her body yet. She's weak and I have to get to work.'

I dropped back down to my knees, shivering, and concentrated on calming myself down in preparation for singing Infinity's ribs back to wholeness. I was aware of Justin organising people around me. 'Please could someone run and get some blankets for Amarilla and Infinity, and something to make a stretcher to roll Infinity onto? She can't stay out in the weather all night. Has Adam gone back with Rowena and, well, you know, Shann?' His voice broke. 'Okay, well he'll look after her. Where are the Healers, can anyone...'

I tuned in to the first of Infinity's damaged ribs. The broken bone screamed its disharmony to the energetic world, and I soon found the exact droning tone with which it resonated. I sent my intention along the pathway of sound, willing the bone to become whole once more. As I felt it respond, I adjusted the droning noise from a nasal to a smoother tone, encouraging the rib to come along with me and strengthen. I was so, so tired. The terror for my horse, shock at what had befallen Noble and

Shann and fear that I would fail my horse were all taking their toll on me.

A hand rested gently on my shoulder and Holly's voice whispered into my ear. 'I'm not interfering, Amarilla, I'll follow your lead, I'm just lending you my strength. Okay?'

I nodded and then felt a foreign energy feeling its way around the intention I was sending to Infinity's rib. Holly added her voice to mine and I felt her intention resonate completely and utterly with my own, amplifying it. The first rib quickly reached full strength and I began to heal the second, taking Holly with me.

A hand appeared on my other shoulder and a voice I didn't recognise asked permission to join his strength to Holly's and mine. I nodded and the second and third ribs were healed in no time. The hands remained on my shoulders while I searched through Infinity's body for any more broken bones. A cracked spineous process was swiftly dealt with and then, mercifully, I could find no more bones that broadcast anything but health and vitality.

I opened my eyes and thanked Holly and the man, whom I recognised as the one who had comforted Quinta. He introduced himself as Marvel.

I was so cold but I had so much more to do. I composed myself and tuned back in with Infinity's body. The bones inside the hooves of her two hind feet had twisted around, tearing all of the connective tissue that held them to the hoof capsule – I could see in my mind the spin around of her body while her hooves remained stuck in the snow, which had caused the terrible injury. Multiple tendons, ligaments and muscles were torn and each would need singing back to health, and the list of muscles that were bunched and strained to their limits was endless. They would be easier to heal as they didn't need knitting back together, merely reminding how to relax back to their normal state of being.

Thuma knelt down beside me. 'Amarilla, Holly has told me of the fantastic job you have done with Infinity's ribs and I find myself in no doubt that you will be able to tissue-sing as you clearly intend, but you must be tired. Will you allow me to add my strength to yours?'

'Thank you, that would be great, she's badly injured,' I said.

'Where are you going to start?'

'Her feet. Ready?'

Thuma nodded and rested her hand on my knee. As I tuned into the first of the damaged tissues and began to whistle through my teeth, she added her whistle and joined her intention with mine.

At some point, blankets were piled on my shoulders and on top of my hands as they rested on my horse's side. A fire was built up nearby and a tiny part of me was aware that my discomfort at the cold was lessening.

Thuma and I had healed both feet and had begun work on Infinity's back muscles when Thuma squeezed my knee in warning before another added her strength to ours. I nodded gratefully, but could spare no more attention than that for the new Healer. Two more Healers added their strength shortly after as we worked into the night.

At one point, a different energy arrived to add strength to our efforts. I was just encouraging a tendon to come along the path my intention was showing it, when I was aware of a low level, constant source of energy that was available both to me and the other Healers, and to Infinity. It reminded me of Infinity and as I allowed a small part of my mind to wonder at it, I decided that it was love. The horses had arrived to help.

We healed everything apart from some surface wounds where skin was missing, which would need attention from a Herbalist. The irony wasn't lost on me that after having done all of the healing for which I had no training, I would have to ask Adam to help with the part for which I was almost qualified to perform; I was exhausted. I opened my eyes and took in my surroundings.

Someone sat next to the fire that blazed nearby, feeding it with sticks and poking the embers constantly as if trying to give it the will to stay alight. Lanterns surrounded Infinity as she lay, still unconscious, on the ground. There were four people to the side of me, all wrapped in blankets, who were beginning to stretch and rise to their feet – my fellow Healers. Over on the far side of the fire sat another group of people and with them stood the horses who had supported our healing. Oak stood closest to the fire, with white unguent coating the front of his forelegs. Gas stood next to him and then just behind I could make out Spider, Diligence, Integrity and two other horses I had never seen before. Poor Spider, his human was dead and yet here he was, helping

Infinity and me. I thanked them all silently and each one whickered to me in response. I stood up and thanked the Tissue-Singers for their help.

Justin threw another stick onto the fire and got to his feet. 'Amarilla, would you like us to move Infinity into the field shelter now? We've put a deep bed of straw down in there for her to have to herself at one end and Rowena and Lexi have cobbled together a stretcher that should be strong enough to drag her on, if we can roll her onto it?' The small voice didn't sound like the Justin I knew and I noticed how he swayed where he stood.

'Yes please,' I said. 'I'll sleep with her. Please could someone ask Adam to come up when it's light, to see to her surface wounds?'

'I'm here, my dear. I'll begin work as soon as we've moved her.'

I think it was the combination of exhaustion, shock and reassurance at the sound of Adam's voice, that made me let go of my own consciousness. I remember feeling dizzy and then thinking that the fire was rising up in the air very suddenly, before I felt a thump and everything went black.

As I drifted in and out of sleep I could feel the fire roaring close by and was comforted as well as warmed by its heat. Snatches of conversation reached me at different stages through the night but I couldn't bring myself to sufficient wakefulness to stay with any of them for long.

'... shouldn't still be out here, if exhaustion from performing that amount of healing in one session doesn't kill her, the cold will...'

'... to be near Infinity and I don't blame her. At least she's by the fire, just keep it blazing and she'll be alright...'

'... managed to get her rug off, we had to soak it off in places but Adam's confident he's found all of the wounds that needed dressing. Are there anymore...'

'... Newson's body. Integrity has asked Oak to tell me she needs to be near it. Something about him refusing to move on...'

On one occasion I managed to organise my mind enough to try and reach Infinity, but she was still unconscious, her mind as spent as her body. I mustered as much love as I could and flung it in her direction, vaguely aware as I drifted off again, that I could feel some of the horses supporting her in much the same way.

When I completely came to, it was light. It was cold and there was an argument in progress nearby.

'I'll just have to explain my reasons to her when she wakes. I'm not going to leave her there in the cold a moment longer. Look at her. She'll be no use to Infinity if she dies of hypothermia, will she?' Justin said.

'For the last time, she won't thank you for it. Think how you would feel if it was Gas lying in there, you'd want to be near him, wouldn't you?' retorted Rowena.

Justin sighed. 'Well, I'll move her in with Infinity then, at least she'll be under cover. I'll build another fire in the doorway and hopefully that will warm her up a bit. Where's Turi with that cursed soup? She went to make it ages ago.'

Rowena said tiredly, 'Jus, you haven't slept. I've at least had a few hours in a warm bed, why don't you go and rest? I'll stay here with Amarilla, I've got to see to Oak's legs anyway.'

'I can't face it, Ro. If I rest, I'll see it all. What happened. To Noble, to Newson, to Shann...' Justin's voice broke.

I couldn't open my eyes as my lashes seemed to be frozen together. I sat up and rubbed them until my lashes came free of one another, allowing me to see Rowena and Justin crying into their embrace. I looked past them to the field shelter where I could see a mound that had to be Infinity, and someone wrapped in blankets sitting nearby. Diligence, Oak, Gas and Spider stood in the shelter, all facing towards where my horse lay, their heads drooping. They supported her still.

The full horror of the previous night's events hit me. My mind replayed Noble's limp body being carried off by Woeful; an exhausted Infinity being brought down and pinned to the ground with a huge black Woeful on top of her; Quinta's screams; horses racing wild-eyed towards the square; Shann slain in front of me; my own terror; and what was that I heard in the night about Newson's body? I got to my feet and began to keen as I stumbled over to Rowena and Justin. Each put an arm around me and pulled me close as my keening turned to sobs that came from deep within.

'I need to see Infinity,' I said at last. My friends walked me to where Infinity lay. It was Mason who sat with her and once I could see that she lay peacefully and covered in blankets, I nodded to him gratefully and managed a weak smile, which he returned.

Infinity had green paste smeared on her in multiple places and there was a swelling above her eye that had what I recognised as starflower paste smeared on it. Her belly rose and fell in an even rhythm and as I tuned into her body, I could feel that her heart now beat strongly in her chest. I sat down by her head and stroked her cheek gently.

'Marvel and Adam cleaned her wounds and Adam is confident that everythin' will heal well,' said Mason.

Rowena added, 'And Oak says she'll just need time now to regain her strength. The healing you did last night used up her energy as well as your own and though the horses supported you both as best they could, it will take some time for her to fully recover from it all.'

I looked up at my friends and noticed how truly dreadful they both looked. Rowena's face was grey and she had dark patches under both of her red-rimmed eyes. She appeared to be wearing her whole winter wardrobe at once. Justin was standing completely still for the first time I could remember. He stood with sagging shoulders and tall as he was, somehow, he looked very small. He had soot smeared down one side of his face with clear tracks through it where his tears had run.

'Where's…' I had to swallow before trying again. 'Where's Shann?'

Justin looked upwards and appeared to be holding his breath. Rowena clenched both fists and looked at the floor as tears ran down her cheeks. Oak moved up behind her and rested his chin gently on her shoulder.

It was Mason who said, 'Shann's body is in his bedroom. When Spider has finished here, he will take it somewhere that will make it easy for Shann to fully leave it behind and move on.'

'Oh. And Newson?'

Mason said, 'He's in the field shelter nearest the buildin's. Integrity has insisted that she stay there too. Apparently, Newson is havin' difficulty acceptin' that his body is dead and she's tryin' to help him.'

I heard the words but I couldn't gain a purchase on them, I was so tired. I asked, 'How's Quinta?'

'Restin'. She's refused sedation as she wants to make the most of every second that Noble is still with her. She says he won't be stayin' long. This whole business is goin' to take some gettin' over, no doubt about it.'

Rowena, Justin and I all nodded numbly.

EIGHTEEN

Aftermath

I spent the days and nights that immediately followed "that day" with Infinity in her field shelter. I insisted on tending to all of her needs myself and refused to listen to my friends' pleas for me to go and rest and let them take a turn at sitting with her. I slept under the blankets with her at nighttime and was always close by during the day. It was partly my way of distancing myself from the horror of what had happened – if I kept my mind focused on Infinity's needs and recovery then I didn't have to think of anything else – but I also felt extreme dread and anxiety whenever I thought of leaving my horse to go and wash or change my clothes. I was terrified that something would befall her while I was gone and I couldn't cope with being separated from her, not even for a few minutes.

My friends took turns in staying with me and helping. They kept the fires roaring and they brought hay and water for the horses, and food and extra clothes for me. They also helped me to assist Infinity when she needed to change the side on which she was lying. She could just about heave herself onto her feet, but then needed people to lean on each side of her to keep her upright while she had a drink and then lay down on her other side. It broke my heart every time. Her legs trembled, her head hung low and when she made it back down to the ground safely, she would let out a long sigh before lying flat out and sleeping once more. She would half wake at times and then munch hay whilst lying down, and I managed to tempt her to eat a few handfuls of warmed mushy grain every so often, but mostly she just slept. I missed her dreadfully. I yearned to feel her presence in my mind again, so strong, so calm, so constantly reassuring.

Twice, when I was missing her most keenly, I felt her stir in my mind. The first time, she reached out weakly to me, just long enough for me to take comfort from her before she receded again. The second time, she stayed with me for a short while, wrapping me in a weak veil of her energy in an attempt to ease my anxiety. Then she was gone and as she faded again, I felt what her effort had cost her. I felt shamed by my selfishness and resolved to stop pining for her and give her the space she needed to recover her strength.

Oak, Gas and Diligence maintained a constant supportive presence; there was always at least one of them making their energy available to Infinity as she recovered from her ordeal. Integrity and Spider were otherwise occupied.

Spider left The Gathering with Shann's body on the second morning after "that day". According to Oak, Shann had adjusted very well to his situation and was ready to move on. Spider was taking his body to a place where Shann would feel comfortable leaving it, so that he could move on completely and in peace. Rowena told me about it in a matter of fact sort of a way, but the way she shifted about on her feet, holding her arms tightly about her, gave an indication of the pain she was desperately attempting to hold in check.

Integrity was apparently still with Newson's body, in a field shelter down near the buildings. I learnt that Newson had gone after the Woeful who had been carrying Noble's body away from The Gathering, whether in a mad attempt to retrieve it for Quinta, from guilt that his own, larger horse had jumped out of the paddock and left Noble on his own, or whether it was just something he did without any rational thought, no one knew and none of the horses would provide enlightenment on the subject. What they had passed on, however, was that Newson had been killed by one of the Woeful and was refusing to accept what had happened. A part of him was still anchored in his dead body and he was refusing to let go of either his body or his bond with his horse. He was confused, angry and afraid, and Integrity had refused both hay and water as she concentrated all of her energies to try to help him.

On the third morning, Quinta came to see me. I was by myself, Mason and Justin having helped me to support Infinity as she changed sides, and then gone to get some breakfast. I had reapplied Adam's ointments to all of the injuries on Infinity's newly exposed side and was gently lowering her blankets back down over her, when I perceived movement. I looked up to see Quinta carrying a steaming bowl of porridge towards me. She looked even smaller and more delicate than normal. Her face was drawn and her long, dark hair was uncharacteristically untidy, with thick chunks of it hanging loose from her ponytail and curling around under her chin. She looked up, saw me watching her, and hesitated. She took several deep breaths before setting her shoulders down and walking over to where I stood. I ground my teeth together. Having had to endure the agony of losing her own horse in such appalling circumstances, I couldn't even begin to imagine how she must be feeling at seeing Infinity safe, albeit wounded, at my feet.

'He's gone,' she said quietly. 'He stayed with me afterwards for a while, but now he's moved on.'

I couldn't speak. I took the porridge bowl from her, put it on the floor and then put my arms around her. She gripped me into a hug, but no sobs came from her, only long, deep breaths. When she let go of me, she said, 'How's Infinity doing today? I'm so glad she's still with you.' Her voice was calm and sincere.

'She's... um... well, she's still very weak and she sleeps most of the time, but she's as comfortable as I can make her.'

Quinta bent down and retrieved the bowl. 'You should eat this while it's hot. The moon knows you must need the warmth from it, staying out here day and night.'

I took it from her and sat down in the straw. Quinta sat down beside me.

'Quinta, h... how are you?' I asked.

'I'm alright, I think. I wasn't, as you probably know. It was all such a shock and seeing Noble carried off like that was horrific, but he tells me that the Woeful killed his body very quickly once they caught him and he left it behind immediately. It was his time to go and things happened as they were always meant to. He's been with me constantly since his body died, helping me to come to terms with the loss of his physical presence and when I finally felt at peace last night, I slept. When I woke this morning, he'd moved on.'

My porridge stuck in my throat. 'I'm so sorry.'

'Amarilla, you have nothing to feel sorry for. It will take some time to get used to him not being around, but I only have to feel for him with my mind the way I used to while he was here and I can find a sense of him. It's not possible for him to move away from me completely.' She smiled faintly.

'Not possible?'

'No. Having named your horse as you have, I imagine that at some point, you will come to understand what I mean.'

My throat loosened at her words and I continued eating my breakfast. Quinta waited for me to finish, then said, 'Amarilla, you are young and I'm sorry to burden you with this, goodness knows you've already had your share of problems since you've been here, but I have to tell you, to prepare you, to ask for your help.'

'Me?'

She nodded. 'There are dark days coming here at The Gathering, I can see the momentum building already. You and I and anyone we can persuade to listen to us, will need to hold firm to what our horses have taught us. We must help our fellow Horse-Bonded not to follow the path their fears will try to lead them down, otherwise the human race faces repeating mistakes of the past and returning to the ways of The Old.'

'W...What do you mean?' I whispered.

'From time to time, when the Woeful have killed animals that were held dear by villagers, or when they've injured humans, there has been talk of hunting them, as I'm sure you know. The horses have always counselled their Bond-Partners to intervene and advise against that course of action and so far, their advice has always been heeded.

'The Woeful are largely human. Noble has always counselled me that the fact they were bred in the first place, then left to fend for themselves when the people of The Old destroyed themselves, and then shunned by the humans of The New, is a reflection of what is lacking in the human race. He has spent the last few days helping me to understand that the Woeful attacked out of sheer desperation. They were starving and so were their kin. Despite their terror of water, they built a raft and crossed the river, leaving their families in the safety of the woods. When Noble first sensed them, he was terrified and his prey instinct took over as he tried to flee. Once they caught him, he felt their desperation and hunger but also their great love and respect for him as he left his body for them to take to feed their young.'

'I felt it and so did Shann,' I said and was flooded with a rush of emotion. I fought to steady myself.

'Felt what?' Quinta asked gently.

I told her what had happened when Shann was killed, adding, 'The Woeful never meant to kill him, it was an accident. I felt his desperation and sadness before he fled.'

Quinta nodded. 'Noble told me that the same happened with Newson, but Newson still refuses to accept it. His anger and fear hold him here and it seems he is still refusing to move on. I think Integrity plans to leave and move on with him. It's the only way left for her to try.'

'Leave? What, leave her body?'

Quinta nodded. 'Noble told me last night that the only way she will be able to get him to release his hold on his body is to leave her own body and help him to move on with her. He's just too confused and frightened.'

'But surely if he knows what Integrity intends, that will be enough to make him let go? He can't want his horse to give up her life for him, surely?'

Quinta shrugged. 'I think he's too frightened to be able to think that calmly and logically. Integrity feels that if she goes with him, she can help him to accept what has happened. Better that than to allow his fear to prevent him taking everything he's learnt and achieved in this lifetime, with him.

'And now we've arrived at the crux of what is threatening to overwhelm us all – fear. What happened the other day frightened everyone very badly and there has been talk of what can be done to prevent it happening again. Some have gone to Vickery saying that they will smear her Woeful-repelling paste over their horses whether they like it or not. Others are all for going after the Woeful that attacked us and hunting them down and it seems that their argument is beginning to gather some momentum. Already there is a team guarding the riverbank in case the Woeful show themselves again. They have long poles and if there is any attempt made to cross the river, the plan is to upend the rafts before they reach our side, in the hope of drowning them.'

'But what about what the horses think? Aren't they listening to their horses?'

Quinta sighed. 'Not all of them, no. It seems that some are ignoring their horses and allowing their fear to guide their thoughts. Ever since the first horses chose to bond with the humans that began The New, they have been helping the human race to make their decisions not from fear, but from what is healthy for their souls. So far they have succeeded, but if the Horse-Bonded ignore them now and hunt the Woeful, it won't be long before the rest of the human race follow their example. Once decisions are made out of fear, out of an attempt to protect what we deem to be important, then we will truly be back on the pathway to The Old.'

A shiver ran down my spine as I remembered my previous lifetime with Infinity. When I had tried to intervene and prevent conflict on that occasion, not only had I failed but I'd been heavily punished. 'What do you want me to do?' I asked Quinta, dreading her response and feeling so alone without Infinity's presence in my mind.

'My horse was killed and yours came very close, so if anyone should be calling for a course of action to be taken against the Woeful, it should be us. And that is why it is so important that we stand together and hold firm to what Noble advised me, and I am sure Infinity will advise you once she is able; that rather than rise against the Woeful, we should help them. We have to stop the others from acting on their fear and dragging the human race back towards the ways of The Old.'

The thought of having to speak out not just about what I was trying to do when I rode Infinity but now also about listening to the horses and opposing the hunting of the Woeful, scared me almost witless. My heart – which I had barely registered over the past days – lurched sickeningly.

Infinity stirred. *Together,* reached me before she faded once more. It took all of my self-control not to reach after her. Together. I would do this and she would help me. Together. I focused on her thought and my mind became resolute.

'I agree. Of course I'll help. We both will,' I said.

'Well, that's two of us in agreement. I guess it's a start,' she said.

'We'll be more than two before long,' I said. 'There's Rowena, Justin, Adam of course, Mason, and I'm sure…'

'Don't count on Rowena agreeing with us, Amarilla, she's not herself at the moment,' said Quinta.

'I know she's hurt and upset, but she'll listen to Oak even if she won't listen to us, she always listens to him,' I replied.

Quinta shook her head. 'You've been removed from it all, staying up here with Infinity as you have, and those who've been up to help you have been treading carefully, trying not to upset you while Infinity recovers. But things aren't as they were, Amarilla, trust me.'

When Quinta had gone, I didn't know what to do with myself. I replenished Infinity's hay and water needlessly, as she hadn't touched either since I had last done it. I poked around and found a single pile of dung near Oak that I could clear away, then flicked the straw of Infinity's bed around with a pitchfork until there wasn't a strand out of place. I sat and stroked the soft, velvety, pink skin of Infinity's muzzle, allowing her exhaled breath to warm my hand. I just about managed to stop myself from willing her to wake up.

Hot breath warmed the top of my head and I looked up to see Diligence's pale grey muzzle above me. She nuzzled my cheek and then I felt her make her energy available to me, much as Oak was doing for Infinity at that moment. I received it gratefully. It wasn't the nurturing energy in which Infinity would have cocooned me, it was more as if something caught my mind as it struggled to cope and gently held it together, giving me the feeling that there was a safety net through which I wouldn't be allowed to fall. And then, what was that? Something was there at the edge of my mind, a similar feeling to when I could feel horses' thoughts whistling by me to their Bond-Partners, but this felt more tangible, closer somehow.

Open... try... Foreign thoughts came into my mind.

???????????

Try...

Try what? I asked.

I heard footsteps behind me and turned to see Mason approaching with a look of wonder on his face. He held out a mug of steaming tea to me. 'Dili?' he said softly.

She turned to look at him. *Hear me... help...* Her thoughts touched me and I frowned, trying to make sense of what was happening.

'Amarilla, can you hear Dili? She says you can but you won't believe it and so you're blockin' her. She wants me to help. Help her, Dili? How?'

It was like catching the odd word of a conversation between people in the next room. *Open... straining... relax.*

Mason said, 'Dili says you need to be open to different possibilities with your mind. You're strainin' to hear her now and there's no need, she's right here. You just need to accept it and...'

'Relax,' I said. 'I caught that bit.'

He slapped his thigh and guffawed. 'You can hear my Dili? Well I never. Can you hear any of the others?'

'I don't know. I can sense when they're communicating with their Bond-Partners, but I've never heard what any of their thoughts were.'

Dili's thoughts whistled by me. Mason raised an eyebrow. 'Catch that?'

'No, sorry.'

'She said you'll be able to hear her when she decides to communicate with you.'

'But why me?'

Young... flexible... others... open... possibilities.

I repeated the words as I perceived them, and Mason chuckled. 'You've got the gist, you're young and your mind is flexible, not like me, fat, hairy old codger that I am, eh, Dili. She said that once the others realise what you can do, it will open them to further possibilities. She's not wrong, either; what you did when you healed Infinity the other night, bit o' bone-singin', bit o' tissue-singin' and you trained in neither, we've never seen the like before and from the sound of it, you did a right good job of it too. Properly thrown the wolf in with the sheep that has, I'd stay up here a while longer, my little Am, if I were you – once you show your face down there, they'll be leapin' on you to know how you did it.'

'Haven't they asked Adam?'

'Adam? Why would they?'

I shrugged. If Adam was keeping it to himself that he was dabbling in the other Skills, I wouldn't give him away.

Mason began to groom his mare. I sat down and watched him as I sipped my tea, taking time to gather my courage before saying, 'Quinta said people are talking about hunting the Woeful.'

'Did she now.'

'Yes. What do you think about it?'

'I think that you need to get your horse well enough to move down nearer the buildin's and then have yourself a hot bath and a good night's sleep before you start worryin' about anythin' like that.'

'But do you think they're right?' I was desperate to hear that he disagreed with them.

He let out a long, deep breath. Dili stood peacefully and as her gaze caught mine, I knew with absolute certainty that it would be alright. There was something about her demeanour and her relaxed confidence with her Bond-Partner that told me he would listen to her. All of a sudden, images of Liberal's face flashed into my mind and in that moment, I understood the hollows above his eyes and his slightly downcast demeanour that couldn't completely be hidden by his magnificence. I realised that it wasn't just Infinity and me that Feryl wasn't listening to.

Mason spoke. 'When I saw our horses frightened and injured, I wanted to go and hunt those beasts with every livin' fibre of my body. And then to see Shann and Newson lyin' there, just lyin' there, well, I don't want to admit what went through my mind. To answer your question, yes, in a lot of ways, I think they are right. But it's what my Dili thinks that matters and she says they're not.'

'Then will you stand with Quinta and me? And with Infinity?'

'Stand with you? My little Amarilla, stand with you about what?'

I didn't feel belittled that he spoke to me that way; I think it had the same effect on me as his words to Infinity always had on her. I relaxed a little and told him what Quinta had told me.

Mason said, 'I've always taken heed of my Dili's counsel, Amarilla, and this time is no different. I won't be joinin' in any plans to hunt the Woeful, but try to stop the others? I'm not sure. Dili is waitin' for me to make a decision on that by myself, so I have a lot of thinkin' to do.'

My heart sank. I hadn't realised how much I'd been counting on knowing that Mason would stand with me, until he refused to give his decision. Infinity chose that moment to stir. She raised her head and neck and rested on her elbows as she picked at the pile of hay in front of her. I rushed to sit next to her, leaning against her shoulder to support her while she ate.

'Hello, my beauty, that's it now, you eat as much as you can. From the sound of it, our little Am here is going to need you more than ever over the comin' months,' said Mason. 'I'll be up to see you both later. Amarilla, you practise what Dili told you, accept that you can hear her and relax. Got it?'

I nodded and smiled weakly.

Getting up. I was overjoyed to hear Infinity in my mind.

Wait, Fin. Rowena and Marvel are coming, I can't support you on my own. I beckoned frantically to my approaching friends and they broke into a run.

'What's happening, is she alright?' asked Rowena.

'She wants to get up. Help me?'

Rowena rushed around to Infinity's right side with me and Marvel stood ready on her left.

Okay, Fin, up you get.

Infinity lurched up onto all four legs and the three of us leant our weight against her.

Hungry. My beautiful mare began to tuck into her hay.

'She's hungry! She said she's hungry!' I said. 'Oh, I haven't got any grain up here. Why didn't I think to have some ready for when she wanted to eat more?'

'Don't worry, Amarilla. MASON,' shouted Marvel at Mason's retreating back, 'GET SOMEONE TO COME UP WITH A BUCKET OF WARM GRAIN, WILL YOU? INFINITY'S HUNGRY.'

'Curse the clouds, Marvel, she may be hungry but she's probably deaf as well now, like Am and me. Where'd you learn to shout that loud?' complained Rowena and I couldn't help but smile to hear Rowena talking more like her old self. But then it brought back memories of her frequent scolding of Shann and my smile disappeared.

Marvel chuckled. 'Comes from having big lungs, so I've been told and going by all accounts, I'm guessing your lungs take up a fair bit of room themselves.'

'Hurrumph. Am, this is great that she's up and eating, we'll have her walking down to where she'll be safe in no time now, you'll see,' said Rowena.

'Ro, I've told you, she's safe up here,' said Marvel. 'It'll just mean that Amarilla can live a bit more normally herself when her horse is in a shelter nearby.'

'She's not safe up here, none of us are. Sorry, Am, but it's true. Two men and a horse were wiped out in a heartbeat within spitting distance of where we're standing.'

'Well, we don't need to discuss that now,' said Marvel.

'No. Sorry, Am, pay no attention to me,' said Rowena.

'It's alright, I know what's going on, Quinta told me,' I said.

'WHAT? She had no right to. You don't need to be worrying about anything other than getting Infinity well and keeping yourself warm at the moment.'

'I don't need to be worrying that some of the Horse-Bonded are talking of going against the advice of their horses? That they're willing to risk everything that the horses and the people of The New have been working towards?' I said quietly.

'I won't discuss this with you now,' she said.

'Ro, please just tell me that you'll always listen to Oak. Please?'

'Of course I'll listen to him, but I do have a mind of my own, you know, and I will see that Shann didn't die in vain.'

'What do you mean?' I asked her.

She refused to answer me. I tried everything I could think of to provoke her into talking to me, but she set her mouth into a thin line and kept her gaze down at the floor. When footsteps approached, she said, 'Marvel, ask whoever it is to come around this side and relieve me, will you, I'm meant to be helping to make the shroud.'

I heard Adam's voice. 'Well, Infinity, you're a sight for sore eyes, fancy a bit of warm grain? Have some water first, that's it. Not too much, now, how about a bit of this? It's all warm and mushy, you won't have to chew too much. Just a little, or you'll colic. Slowly, that's the way.'

Adam came around to where Rowena and I leant against Infinity. 'She's just had a small amount, otherwise she'll colic when she lies back down. Best that she has mainly hay. I've brought a big bucket of it up and a flask of warm water so you can give her small amounts whenever she wants it. Move over, Rowena, I'll pop in beside Amarilla. Are you still alright on your own, Marvel?'

'Doing fine, Adam.'

Rowena shuffled along until Adam could take her place and then left without another word. Adam said, 'We'll need to keep Infinity upright a bit longer. That's more food than she's had in days and lying down immediately after won't help her at all.'

I nodded. *Fin, you need to stay up for a while longer. We've got you.*

She didn't reply. All of her attention was taken up by her effort to stand while picking wisps of hay to eat.

'Is everything alright?' Adam asked me.

I told him about my conversations with Quinta, Mason and Rowena.

'Well, you've no need to worry about asking for my support,' Adam said. 'Peace isn't here to advise me but he doesn't need to be. Three times, he asked me to intervene in villages where there were murmurings about hunting the Woeful and each time, both I and the villagers concerned paid him heed. I have no intention of doing otherwise now.'

'But will you speak out to try and stop those who are talking of doing it?' I asked him. 'Please, Adam?'

'If I didn't, then all of my years of learning from Peace would count for nothing. And don't you be worrying about Rowena. She's been through tough times before and she will again, but she always listens to Oak.'

'I'm not so sure this time, Adam,' said Marvel. 'From what I can make out, she's among those who are the most adamant that a hunt in the spring is necessary.'

'In the spring?' I asked.

'Yes, they're not planning to go while winter still has a hold on us,' he replied.

'That means there's a goodly amount of time for us and the horses to talk them out of it then, doesn't it?' said Adam cheerfully and I could have wept with relief.

'Count me in with that,' said Marvel. 'Broad's been having to focus a good deal of his energy on his foot, but not so much that he couldn't put what happened into perspective for me.'

'Is the poultice working?' asked Adam.

'He says it is, the splinter should be out soon but he's fighting infection now.'

'Hmmm. I'll bring a draught along to him as soon as we've finished here and once the splinter's out, we'll use a different poultice to draw out the infection.'

'Broad's your horse?' I asked Marvel.

'Certainly is, great big bugger of a horse he is too, you'll know him when you see him. Only problem with a horse his weight, if he stands on anything even remotely sharp, it either gets driven into his foot or causes a mother of a bruise. Trod on a buckthorn twig this time, the clot,' he said, affectionately.

'Do you mind if I ask what he said to you about what happened?'

'Not at all. He said it wouldn't have happened if we'd seen fit to help the Woeful through the winter before they became so desperate. He also made the point that distressing as the events were, they would act as a catalyst to either propel the human race forward in its evolution, or backward.'

I will lie down now, Infinity advised me, her legs trembling violently.

I just had time to warn Adam and Marvel, before her front legs buckled and she lay down with a thump. I thanked the two men for their help and they told me they would send more people up to help later, in case Infinity wanted to get up and eat more once she had rested. 'And don't you worry too much, Amarilla,' Adam said. 'Things will work out, they always do.'

I felt much better for a while, but my relief was short-lived. Of those who came up to help me with Infinity, Justin was the only one who would tolerate my even broaching the subject of a spring hunt. Even then, it was just to tell me that I would understand more once I was involved in the discussions down in the buildings and that for now, I should just focus on Infinity and myself. The others who came changed the subject immediately and Rowena didn't come up at all. When Quinta appeared later that evening with my dinner, I told her about my day.

'I'm sorry to say I'm not surprised,' she said, 'but I'm glad you had a chance to talk to Adam and Marvel. I've been so busy helping with the shroud and checking on Integrity in case she needs anything, I haven't really had the time to start a discussion with anyone about it. I should have known those two would take a sensible view.'

'A shroud? Rowena said she was working on it too. What's it for?'

'It's for Integrity and Newson. According to the horses, Integrity is sure now that Newson will leave his body behind if he knows it will be alongside her own and in what he still believes is the safety of The Gathering. The problem is that the ground's too hard to bury their bodies once they've gone, so we are having to make a sealed shroud that will contain the... you know, the smell, and repel any animals from trying to, well you know, until we can bury them.'

I shuddered. 'Where will they be kept until the ground softens?'

'There's an old stone building just along from the workshops. Integrity plans to carry Newson's body there herself, stand on the shroud and then leave and take him with her.'

'When will she go?'

'The shroud's finished and in place, so I should think sometime very soon. She doesn't want anyone else to be there, so Mason and Marvel will assist with lifting Newson onto her and then leave her to it.'

'How is she?' I was completely in awe of what she was about to do.

'She's tired and hungry, but the horses say she's stopped taking much interest in her body now. She's ready to go.'

Integrity left her body during the night, Marvel told me the following morning. Apparently, he went to the stone building at dawn and found her and Newson's bodies atop the shroud, as if they'd both lain down to sleep. The shroud had subsequently been stitched together and sealed by the Tailors, and the building had been made secure. Broad told Marvel that Integrity and Newson had successfully moved on and Integrity was now confident that Newson would be able to retain everything he had learnt in his lifetime. I breathed a sigh of relief for him.

During that day, a shift took place within me; the immediate aftermath of that terrible day had passed and I felt a keen sense of anticipation, strongly coupled with one of dread, for what now lay ahead.

That evening, Infinity returned to the land of the living.

NINETEEN

Change

I was sitting with a hand resting on my horse's neck, concentrating on breathing slowly due to a particularly intense bout of pain in my heart, when Infinity came back to herself.

You have done well. Her energy flowed around and through me, steadying the painful lurching of my heart.

Fin? I allowed myself to reach for her and she was there! *Oh, Fin, thank the stars, you're back.*

She heaved herself up onto her elbows, and I moved to sit in the warm spot that had been vacated by her head and neck. I cradled her head in my arms and hugged her, crying with happiness, with relief, with all the love in the world for my horse.

Fin, I've missed you so much, you've no idea, I've been completely lost, thank goodness you're back with me.

You have been far from lost. You have demonstrated to your fellow humans that the Skills are something anyone can perform. You have been able to see past your fear and have realised the path you must take despite little support from those to whom you feel closest. In addition you found the courage and strength to speak out when necessary. It has been an uncomfortable time for you but at no time were you lost.

But I don't really know what I'm doing. I feel as if I'm groping around in the dark and I have no idea what to do next.

If you knew what to do next then you would not need to do it.

Oh, Fin, you've no idea how much I've missed you. And poor Quinta will never have this again with Noble.

She Who is Noble no longer needs this level of interaction with her horse. If she did then he would not have left.

But he had no choice, the Woeful...

Played the part they were meant to. Cease struggling. Your mind rushes from one thing to the next and you prevent yourself from realising what you know.

But...

Walks A Straight Path. Cease. I must eat and you must sleep. She got to her feet and began to munch her hay.

Do you need support? Shall I go and get the others to help me support you?

I will eat and rest as necessary. I require no assistance. Sleep.

I felt as if my world had come back into focus. Infinity was thin and weak, but she was back with me. I fell asleep to what will always be one of my favourite sounds – the munch, munch of a relaxed, hungry horse.

I slept well that night and awoke feeling refreshed and happy. I sat up to the sight of Infinity tucking into a vastly depleted pile of hay and noted that for the first time since I had healed my mare, the other horses were all at the far end of the shelter. Oak and Gas lay flat out as they slept and Dili stood with one hind leg resting, giving the appearance of being asleep on her feet although I knew that she would be alert for anything out of the ordinary as she took her turn at watch. So, the horses felt that Infinity no longer needed their help, I realised and smiled with fresh relief that my horse was now well and truly on the road to recovery.

Fin, there's some grain here, I can add warm water to it if you want some?

Hay will suffice.

How are you feeling this morning?

You are as aware of my body as I.

I grinned as I realised that in the absence of Infinity's thoughts, I'd once more grown used to the human social requirement for chatter. I felt her amusement at my thoughts and gathered them together. There was so much I needed to ask her.

No. You do not.

????????

You do not need to ask me. You know.

But what about what happened? With the Woeful? With you? What if Shann hadn't got to you when he did? And what about the other Horse-Bonded planning to hunt the Woeful? Quinta said you'd advise me as Noble counselled her. Will you?

Infinity munched on in silence.

Fin? Please, Fin, I've waited and waited for you to wake up, I've felt so alone, please help me?

You do not require my assistance. You have no questions to which you do not already know the answer.

I pondered everything that had happened, how I had reacted and how I thought that she would have advised me had she been conscious. She was right; I knew that I had behaved in exact accordance with everything she had taught me. Mild approval washed over me from Infinity, but the majority of her attention was focused on satisfying her appetite.

Infinity and I received many visitors as the news spread that she was now fully conscious and able to stand by herself. The Healers who had helped me on "that day" all came to see us, thrilled that Infinity was back on her feet and eating well. Holly hugged me and told me excitedly that she was looking forward to my return to normality when Infinity was strong enough to make it down to the buildings. Apparently, she and the other Healers were desperate to know how I'd done what I'd done, but had been requested by Adam not to ask me about it until Infinity was well on the road to recovery. My heart sank slightly at the thought of having to impart yet more controversial information, but a pulse of energy from Infinity reminded me that I wasn't alone.

When Adam came to see us, I asked him why he was keeping it secret that he was using Skills other than the one in which he'd been trained.

He smiled, his eyes twinkling. 'Ahh, with me, it's just a case of an old man tinkering around and having some fun. You, on the other hand, have a job to do and I wouldn't dream of muddying the water.'

'Sometimes, Adam, I think you speak in riddles as much as Infinity does. Can't you just tell everyone you can tree-sing before I get back down there, maybe take some of the attention away from me?'

His smile broadened. 'Now why in the name of all that is natural would I want to do that?'

'To make my life easier? Please, Adam?'

'Would that I could, Amarilla, but this old man is long enough in the tooth to know when to keep to one side and allow another to tread the path they were meant to, even if, sadly, it means having to watch them struggle.'

I sighed, recognising the finality with which my friend and mentor spoke. There was a wisdom about his words that was reminiscent of how Infinity counselled me.

Rowena remained conspicuous by her absence and when I questioned Quinta, and later Justin, about her, they had little to tell me; Quinta had seen little of her and Justin was a shadow of his former self and had little to say about anything. I tried to engage him in conversation, telling him how Infinity was doing, how Gas and the other horses were now resting away from her, and finally resorting to talking about the slowly improving weather. Nothing I could say seemed able to pull him out of his depression.

Infinity munched hay almost constantly for the next couple of days and then announced that she was strong enough to walk down to a shelter nearer the buildings. I tried to talk her out of it, wanting her to gain more strength first, but she was adamant. Apparently, she was in the best position to judge how strong she was and she deemed it beyond necessary that she move closer to the buildings in order that I would resume taking care of my own body's needs satisfactorily. I soon realised that there was little point in arguing with her and so organised for people to walk on both sides of her, leaning into her to help support her if her strength failed at any time.

The pathway was a layer of slush on top of ice and negotiating it with Infinity was a slippery and nerve-racking procedure.

'There we go, my sweet, just slowly now, we don't want you slippin', do we? That's it, just take your time.' Mason talked quietly and non-stop to Infinity as she stepped tentatively along the path. I had a feeling it was as much to ease his own concern for her as to try and provide her with reassurance.

We slipped and slid our way slowly towards the warm bed and mound of hay that waited for Infinity, according to Mason's continuing discourse from just behind me. Holly and Justin were in front of me and on Infinity's other side were Jack, Quinta, Marvel and Vickery. Gas, Oak and Diligence stepped along carefully behind us all, already having made it clear that they expected to share Infinity's new paddock and shelter. I was grateful to them as I knew I would find it easier to be apart from my mare knowing that she wasn't alone.

As we neared the buildings, I realised that things were definitely not as they had been. Mason's dialogue became louder and more urgent, but he couldn't distract me from noticing that something extremely unpleasant pervaded the atmosphere. It wasn't dispelled by the high-pitched and not quite real laughter that emanated from a group of people who stood chatting nearby. I felt acutely uneasy as we peeled away from Infinity to allow her and the other horses through the gateway of her new paddock.

'That was a mission well accomplished, well done, everyone,' said Mason. 'My little Am, you'll be needin' a good feed, a hot bath and then some sleep in a nice warm bed. We can settle the horses in, don't you worry about your girl, Dili'll watch over her.'

'Um, I'd like to stay with Infinity for a little while first, thanks, Mason. Thank you all very much for your help, it's such a relief to have her down here,' I replied.

'Right, well I'll stay with you and then we can go and find Turi together. She promised to have somethin' special prepared for your first meal back in the land of the livin' and you never know, she might have made extra for me,' Mason said.

Justin said, 'It's alright, Mason, I know you have loads of work to do, so I'll see to the horses with Am. I missed breakfast so I was going to go and beg some grub from Turi anyway. Amarilla can come with me.'

They held each other's gaze and unspoken words appeared to pass between them.

Mason nodded slowly. 'If you're sure? There shouldn't be much to do, I hauled plenty of hay for all of them first thing and that should see them through to this evenin', when I'll bring another load. Maybe just shake up some straw in the far shelter in case any of them have a mind to use it?'

Justin nodded. 'We'll see to it.'

Mason put a meaty hand on Justin's shoulder and gave it a brief squeeze, before giving me a nod and a wink and then departing. Everyone apart from Marvel traipsed off after him.

'I'll be fencing in that paddock over there all day, Amarilla,' said Marvel, 'so I'll check on Infinity regularly. You rest easy when you've eaten.'

'Thanks, Marvel. You will let me know if there's a problem? Do you know where my room is if you need to find me?'

'I'm sure it won't be hard to find. There's probably a queue of Healers waiting outside it as we speak. Joking!' He laughed and walked off towards the livestock paddocks.

I grinned. A glance at Justin revealed that he didn't share the humour.

'How do you do it, Am?' he said.

'Do what?'

His brown eyes bored into mine desperately. 'After everything that's happened, everything that you've seen, what you've been through with Infinity and what's going on here now – and you can feel it, the fear and anger that's leaching from just about everyone here, I know you can – how can you still smile? I'm ten years older than you and I feel about the same amount younger. I'm a mess.'

'Justin, you've just lost your best friend. It's understandable that you need time to get over it. You're grieving, just like Rowena is.'

'It's more than that, Amarilla, much more; I feel hate. Real hate. And when you start talking of helping those... those monsters, I feel like I hate you too. I'm sorry, I don't want to, but I do. How can you possibly want to help the creatures that caused all of this?'

I took a deep breath and climbed through the paddock fence. Justin followed me and we passed Dili and Oak pulling hay from a manger attached to the fence, and carried on towards the field shelter into which Infinity and Gas had disappeared. We found Infinity lying down in a deep, clean straw bed, while Gas munched hay from a pile nearby. The sight of my horse resting peacefully calmed me.

'What are Gas's thoughts on all of this?' I asked Justin.

'I don't know, I haven't asked him.'

'WHAT? You're in all this turmoil and you didn't ask Gas to help you?'

'I could feel Gas supporting Infinity when you were healing her, and afterwards, and I felt I should leave him to focus his attention on you and Fin. I've been so preoccupied with my own thoughts that there's been no room in my head to process anything from him anyway.'

'It's fear that makes you like that,' I said. 'Maybe you just need to stop focusing on everything that's happened and bring your attention back to the part of you that's aware of Gas, and then you'll know everything you need to?'

'It's not that easy. How can I stop thinking about what happened to Shann? What the Woeful did? What they could do again?'

'Infinity says they played the part they were meant to. Justin, please, listen to me. Infinity was nearly killed. Don't you think I should be the one who's angry and afraid? You asked me why I can still smile, well it's probably because I live by what Infinity's taught me. I may not have been bonded as long as the rest of you but I listen to her over everyone and over everything I ever thought I knew, because she's better than me. You and Gas are the closest bonded partnership here, I can't even see you as being separate when you're together, you know that, and that means of everyone here, you should find it easiest to get over all of this. Stop struggling. Stop focusing on what's happened and find yourself again through Gas.'

'But Shann…'

'Wouldn't want you to suffer like this. You know he wouldn't.'

Justin sighed and leant back against the wall. Gas was at his side in an instant and they blurred together. Infinity was already asleep, so I quietly left the shelter.

Some of the rails had been taken down to allow the horses into the adjacent paddock and its field shelter, as Infinity's shelter was only large enough to accommodate two horses lying down. Remembering Mason's instructions, I wandered over to the field shelter and began to shake loose the straw that had been dumped inside. I was just finishing when Rowena appeared in the doorway.

'Hi, Am, I'm glad Infinity's better, here's a new blanket I've made, since her old one got shredded,' she said cheerfully. 'Is that ready for Oak? Thanks, I should have been down earlier to see to it myself, only I thought I'd better get this rug finished if Fin's going to be on her feet more of the time now.'

I decided to follow Rowena's lead and pretend everything was normal. 'Er, thanks, Ro, she'll definitely be needing that, I'll put it on her next time she stands up.'

'She looks very peaceful sleeping in her new shelter, I've just been in there,' said Rowena.

'Is Justin still there?'

'Yep, he's a bit emotional. Gas is with him so I thought I'd better leave them to it and come and see to Oak.'

'Oh, thank goodness,' I said.

She gave me an odd look. 'Right, well I'd better get on with grooming Oak, his coat's been looking a bit dull these last few days.'

'Want a hand?'

She handed me a brush and then removed Oak's rug. I was shocked to see that his normally gleaming coat had indeed lost a good deal of its lustre. Oak turned to face me and gave me my second shock. How had I not noticed his eyes during all the time he had spent in the field shelter helping Infinity? Was it the dull light in there or had I really been so preoccupied with Infinity that I'd failed to notice anything else? He had the beginnings of the hollows above his eyes that Liberal had and behind his gaze I could see that he suffered. I took an involuntary step back.

'Ro, what's wrong with him? It's not just his coat, look at his eyes.'

She sighed. 'He's alright. He'll be alright.'

'But what's wrong? Is it anything I can help with? He's been helping

Infinity and me enough… oh no, it's not that is it? Has he worn himself out helping Fin?'

'It's nothing to do with you or Infinity,' Rowena said sharply, 'and it's nothing that he and I can't sort out by ourselves.'

Liberal's face flashed into my mind along with the realisation I'd had about his demeanour and appearance being connected to Feryl's attitudes and behaviour, and I suddenly knew what was wrong with Oak. He stared deeply into my eyes with his huge, sad, brown ones, confirming to me that I was right. My heart lurched painfully as I plucked up the courage to speak.

'Ro, you're not listening to Oak, are you.'

She put her hands on her hips and said, 'How dare you? You who stand there all goodness and light while Shann's dead because of you and your horse, how dare you try and lecture me about my relationship with my horse?'

I was horrified. 'I don't blame you for being angry, for being hurt, I know what Shann meant to you…'

'YOU HAVE NO IDEA,' she yelled. 'HOW COULD YOU KNOW? YOU WHO'VE GROWN UP FEELING SORRY FOR YOURSELF BECAUSE YOUR FAMILY DIDN'T *UNDERSTAND YOU*. YOU HAVE NO IDEA WHAT IT FEELS LIKE TO BE ALONE YOUR WHOLE LIFE, TO FEEL THAT YOU'RE WORTH NOTHING. And then, just as I begin to trust that my life could actually turn out well after all, with my beautiful horse and someone who really cares about me, ABOUT ME! He's taken away from me. BECAUSE OF YOU AND YOUR HORSE. IF IT WASN'T FOR YOU, SHANN WOULD STILL BE HERE.'

'No, he wouldn't.'

'WHAT?'

'He wouldn't still be here, because it was his time to go. Infinity says that everything happens as it should and she's right. She says the Woeful played the part they were meant to…'

There was a blinding flash of light and I was vaguely aware of falling. The next thing I knew, I was sitting in the wet snow and my jaw felt as if it were on fire.

'THUNDER AND LIGHTNING, ROWENA, WHAT DO YOU THINK YOU'RE DOING?' Justin rushed over to where I sat, dazed and confused. Hands appeared under my armpits and I was hauled to my feet before Justin took one of Rowena's arms and spun her to face him. 'YOU JUST PUNCHED AMARILLA TO THE FLOOR. WHAT ON EARTH HAS GOT INTO YOU?'

'It was my fault,' I said absent-mindedly. My mind was spinning. Part of me stood next to Justin as he angrily continued to demand that Rowena explain her actions, while the other part leapt back to a scene in my previous lifetime; I stood in an office of government, while a colleague I had liked and trusted looked at me with scorn in his eyes as he told me I would be sent to the frontline to help fight a war in which he knew I didn't believe. My heart alternated between spasming painfully and calming down almost to a normal rhythm.

Everything happens as it should, came into my mind as the slightest of whispers.

'Justin, let me speak,' I said. 'Rowena, whether you want to hear it or not, everything did happen as it was supposed to. It was Shann's time to go – just as it was Noble's, Newson's and Integrity's. Infinity, being injured as she was, gave me the chance to prove what is possible with the Skills. The Woeful that killed Shann was just trying to get food. He and his family were starving and he was sad, frightened and desperate. Shann saw it too and tried to avoid hitting him but his shovel was already coming down and the Woeful tried to defend himself and caught Shann by mistake. They never would have attacked in the first place if we had offered them help to get through the winter and that's what we have to take away from this.'

'Help?' said Rowena. 'Help the Woeful? Are you mad? Why on earth would we do that? They're dangerous.'

'They're living beings who were created by us, abused by us and then abandoned by us.'

'No,' said Rowena.

'Yes.'

'NO! They're monsters and they killed Shann and for that they need to pay.' Rowena threw Oak's rug onto his back, fumbled with the fastenings and then stormed off.

Justin's unshaven, tear-streaked face appeared in front of mine as he gently turned my face so he could see where Rowena had hit me. 'She's gone way too far. Are you alright, Am?'

'Yes, I think so, it's nothing that a bit of starflower can't fix,' I replied. 'You look better.'

He grinned sheepishly. 'As soon as I let go of it all and allowed Gas in, it was as if everything that has happened just fell away.'

'As if even the most horrible parts all make sense?'

He nodded and then drew me into a warm bear hug. 'Thanks, Am.'

As I hugged him back, I remembered back to when Infinity and I had been on our way to The Gathering and I had been so afraid, and how it had taken Infinity knocking me to the ground and threatening to kick me before I had allowed her back into my thoughts to help me. I understood exactly what Justin had been through.

'Come on,' he said, releasing me, 'let's get something to eat.'

We checked in on Infinity and Gas, and found them both snoozing peacefully, so I left Infinity's new rug in a corner, ready to put on her when she woke up. We then made our way to the kitchens where Turi provided us with a welcome meal of her hot pot.

'What do I do about Rowena?' I asked Justin.

'Mop muchoo camboo,' he replied. He swallowed his mouthful. 'If I know her, she'll be mortified at her behaviour once she calms down. Mind you, I've never seen her that angry, I mean she actually hit you.'

'It's not just how she is with me that worries me, it's how she is with Oak,' I said. 'He looks terrible and judging by the way Liberal looks because Feryl isn't listening to him, it's only going to get worse.'

'What's this about Oak and Liberal?'

I explained my observations about the two horses and also how I had known by Diligence's demeanour that Mason would listen to her.

When I'd finished, Justin nodded slowly. 'Makes sense, but if Oak can't get through to her at the moment, she's not going to appreciate anyone else trying to talk to her. I know I wouldn't have appreciated anyone trying to stick their nose in before I was ready.'

'One friend punches me, the other one calls me a sticky beak,' I said. 'I'm so glad I came here.'

He laughed. 'Never that, Am, and I asked you for help in a roundabout kind of a way.'

'So, we just leave her alone for now then?'

'I think so. We'll see enough of her because Oak's in with our two, but just leave the dust to settle and see what happens. She's going to have to look at that work of art on your face every time she sees you now, maybe that will be enough to make her stop and think.'

'Work of art?'

'It's a beauty. Our Rowena packs a punch, there's no doubt about that.'

'Well, next time, you can be on the receiving end and then we'll see how funny you think it is. I'm going to see Adam, I think I'll try one of his starflower combination creams as a face pack after I've had a bath, you never know, it might be gone in a few days?' I said.

'I like your optimism, my friend, I really do. Rest well, and I'll see you up with the horses later.'

I left him still eating and went to find Adam, who listened to my explanation about the state of my face without comment.

'And how do you feel about it all?' he asked.

'Shocked, upset, but strangely, now you come to mention it, better,' I said.

'Better? In what way?'

'My heart feels better. Calmer.'

'Interesting. Now I think your idea to use this as a face pack is a good one, just make sure you fall asleep on your back otherwise you'll have most of it on your pillow and it won't be doing any good at all there. Starflower, arnollia, mennawort and my secret ingredient, all in there,' he said, his eyes twinkling.

'Secret ingredient? Secret from me too?'

'Only until you can identify it. That's if you still intend to finish your apprenticeship in between teaching everyone else how to multiskill.'

'Stop teasing me, you wicked old man, and stop making me smile, it hurts,' I said.

I left him chuckling to himself, and walked back to my room. I peeled off the many layers of clothing I had accumulated, put on my dressing gown and then ran a bath. I lowered myself into the stingingly hot water and as the heat seeped into my body, muscles that had been clenched with cold and stress for so long began to relax and waves of fatigue swept over me. Worried that I would fall asleep in the bath, I scrubbed myself all over, washed my hair and then dried myself and returned to my room. Now that I was clean, I could smell my dirty clothes and I wrinkled my nose. I kicked them to the corner of the room furthest from my bed, applied my face pack and then as it sank into my skin and a sense of calm began to infuse my body, I lay down to sleep.

The next thing I knew, I was waking in the dark to the sound of pounding on my door. I hadn't closed my curtains, so the fact it was dark meant that I had overslept. Infinity! I leapt out of bed and rushed to open the door.

Marvel stood there. 'Um, I'm looking for Amarilla, haven't seen her have you, good lady?' he asked with a grin.

'Infinity! Is she alright? I mean she must be otherwise I'd know, but I've overslept. Thunder and lightning, what if she's run out of hay? What is it, Marvel? What's happened?'

He began to laugh and couldn't stop.

'Marvel, what is it? Please stop laughing and tell me.'

'Sorry, Amarilla, but you are a sight. Don't worry, Infinity's fine, I just came to tell you not to hurry. Justin and I have mucked her out, given her fresh hay and straw and put her rug on her and you can just go and see her when you're ready. Skies above, Justin said you'd wake in a panic and he wasn't wrong.'

'Oh, thank goodness. Thanks, Marvel. And, look, no queue of Healers to be seen.'

He chuckled. 'Give it time, Amarilla, give it time. Oh, and by the way, Justin said you'd want to know that Spider's back.'

I washed off my face pack, dressed at lightning speed and then ran all the way to the paddock, stopping only to pick up a lantern from the tack room. When I reached Infinity, she was indeed rugged, warm and munching from an enormous pile of hay. Diligence munched alongside her but the other horses were nowhere to be seen. Infinity whickered to me and I felt her contentment.

... in time... caught the edges of my mind and I spun towards Diligence.

Fin, what is Diligence trying to tell me? I asked.

Infinity expressly ignored me.

Fin, Diligence has been trying to communicate with me but I can only catch snatches of it. Mason helped me last time – can you help me?

No response. I thought back to when Dili had been communicating with me before. What was the advice I'd been given? Accept I could hear her and relax, that was it. I tried to still my mind, but found it difficult as I was curious to know what was "in time". I didn't have to wait much longer for my question to be answered, but it wasn't from Diligence that the answer came. I heard footsteps running past the entrance of the field shelter and caught sight of Quinta.

'Quinta,' I called out, but she carried on running. I ran after her as she made her way towards the other field shelter, and entered just behind her.

Oak and Gas were tucking into hay that Justin was shaking into large piles for them by lanternlight. Rowena stood by Spider, her hand resting possessively on his neck, but Spider's attention was locked on Quinta. He looked rough. He'd lost weight, his coat stood up with the cold and he had twigs matted into his mane and tail. His eyes, though, appeared bright as they stared into Quinta's. Rowena looked from Spider to Quinta questioningly.

'Quinta, is everything okay?' I said quietly.

She nodded, but her eyes remained locked with Spider's and all of a sudden, I was aware of thoughts whistling between them. I stepped back involuntarily. Quinta could communicate with Spider? Was it like with me and Dili? I wondered.

At the sound of footsteps behind me, I turned to find Adam approaching at speed. The light from his lantern revealed a look of wonderment on his face. He hurried past me and stood next to Quinta. Spider looked from one to the other and his thoughts continued to flutter at the edge of my mind.

Adam looked at Quinta. 'Both of us?' he said.

A broad smile lit up her face. 'It would seem so.'

Spider dropped his head and began to eat his hay.

'Does anyone feel like telling us what is going on?' Rowena said thornily.

Adam said, 'Spider called Quinta and me to him. It seems that he would like us both to continue the ridden work that Shann started with him.'

Rowena took a step back. 'What?'

'Do you mean he tugged you?' asked Justin.

'It wasn't like that really, not like when Noble tugged me, at least not for me,' said Quinta.

Adam said, 'No, it was more of a request, really, took me completely by surprise. I never thought to hear another horse in my mind after Peace moved on. There I was, chatting to Norrie about, well you don't want to hear what two old men were nattering about, I'm sure, anyway, all of a sudden, Spider asked if I would come to him and here I am. Then he asked Quinta and me if we would learn to ride him as you are with your horses, as there is more he would like to achieve and he would like to do it with us.'

I caught Justin's eye and he flicked his gaze to Adam and then back to me and grinned. Rowena was as white as a sheet and said nothing. As Adam and Quinta began to discuss their experience and what it would all mean, Rowena walked quickly out of the field shelter. I looked over at Justin and saw the concern on his face. He read my unasked question and shook his head. He looked at Oak and then back to where he had last seen Rowena. I nodded my agreement. She would need Oak to help her with this and if she wouldn't let him, then there was no way she would let either of us.

Justin finished what he was doing and then left the field shelter with me. Adam and Quinta were busy untangling Spider's mane and tail whilst chattering excitedly.

'Things just keep bending around on themselves, don't they?' Justin said.

'Don't they just,' I replied. I could feel a sense of satisfaction emanating from Infinity and... something else from Diligence, I thought.

TWENTY

Surprise
---

*I*t was a beautiful, crisp, sunny morning and I'd had a sound night's sleep. I should have been feeling on top of the world as I made my way across the slushy square to the dining hall, after all Infinity was doing well, winter was on its way out and I was expecting to tuck into a cooked breakfast. Instead, I fought against the waves of fear and anger that lashed around The Gathering, I worried about Rowena and I dreaded walking into the dining hall alone, to the mercy of all the Healers who would now be wanting answers from me.

After leaving Adam and Quinta the previous evening, I'd gone straight to my room and Justin had brought my dinner up to me once he'd eaten. I'd felt a coward, but my face was sore and I just didn't feel up to going into the dining room and playing host to all the questions I would inevitably face regarding healing, or the source of my bruising. Justin had been descended upon in my stead and had apparently thoroughly enjoyed laying false trails as to my whereabouts.

I arrived at the dining hall more quickly than I would have liked and the minute I set foot through the doors, a multitude of eyes focused upon me. Just as I caught sight of a miserable-looking Rowena sitting by herself, pushing fried mushrooms around her plate with a fork, the Healers descended.

Holly reached my side first. 'Amarilla, at last. What on earth happened to your face? Never mind, come and sit down and I'll fetch you some breakfast.'

'Amarilla, we need to sort out a proper meeting so you can tell us how you did what you did,' said Vickery. 'Your knowledge will be invaluable if we are to fight the Woeful, just think, if you can manage to teach all of the Healers how to multiskill by the time we go to hunt, so many more lives will be saved...'

'Honestly, Vickery, let Amarilla move,' said Thuma. 'We all want to speak to her, but ambushing her in this way is no way to behave.'

'Oh? Well I notice you seem to have pushed your way alongside me easily enough, do you think you have the right to speak to Amarilla first and it's the rest of us who should wait?' retorted Vickery.

There was some pushing and shoving, and angry voices began to argue all around me. Holly took hold of my hand and attempted to force her way past people who now blocked our way.

I couldn't believe it. I had looked up to the Horse-Bonded since I was a child, revered them as people who were wise and worthy of emulation and here they were, behaving no better than a group of over-excited school children at snack time. As voices were raised even higher, I fought hard to remain immune to the atmosphere of disquiet that seemed to be fuelling the behaviour of those around me.

Do not attempt to fight fear, volunteered Infinity. *To fight it you must first acknowledge it and then you are vulnerable to its influence. Better to focus on who you are and what is contained within you. Exude light until it surrounds you and no harmful energy will be able to reach you.*

I closed my eyes and turned all of my attention towards doing as she suggested. Gradually the atmosphere around me lightened and the horrible unease that had been battering at me receded. I reopened my eyes to find that the situation around me was much the same. I looked around for a way to escape the throng of arguing Healers. It was hopeless; there was no way of escaping them without undertaking some pushing and shoving of my own, which would only draw more attention to myself. An intention formed in my mind. Infinity sensed it immediately.

You will need to stay within the space you have created for yourself. Do not allow yourself to succumb to what ails them all, she advised me.

I took a breath and composed myself, then shouted, 'STOP.'

All of those in my immediate vicinity stopped talking and looked at me. There was nudging and some angry shushing and finally everyone around me fell silent. I focused on radiating my own positivity again and then opened my mouth to speak.

Vickery got in first. 'You name the time and place, Amarilla, and we'll all be there. Make it soon though, this is important for all of us, not just to save lives here at The Gathering but to help everyone in the village communities. Once they hear what's happened and realise the danger they're in, they're sure to want to hunt the Woeful down. The light only knows how many injuries their Healers will be having to deal with once that happens.'

Someone shushed and Vickery looked furious.

'I won't be holding a meeting and I won't be teaching you anything, because there's nothing to teach,' I said. My heart beat violently in my chest, but it was the normal beating of a heart in response to an uncomfortable situation, rather than the wild lurching that it had been performing of late. I had a small surge of confidence that I was heading in the right direction.

'Explain yourself please, Amarilla,' said Jack, his blue eyes glinting dangerously.

'I don't have anything to teach you because you can already perform all of the Skills by yourself, and not just the Healing Skills – all of them.'

'That's preposterous,' said a voice.

'Don't be ridiculous,' said another.

'How did you come by this knowledge?' asked Jack.

'Infinity told me. I broke my arm on the way here and she told me to heal it, so I did. Salom told you all about this, I know she did.'

'We thought Salom was, um, exaggerating,' Holly said.

'No, be honest, Holly,' Vickery said, 'we all know that Heralds tell exactly how it is. The truth is that none of us believed you had done what you told Salom you'd done, Amarilla. We thought it was you who was exaggerating.'

'Well now you all know that I wasn't. I healed my arm on the way here and I healed it because Infinity told me I could. She's also told me that when the Woeful attacked our horses, they played the part they were meant to. Rather than hunting the Woeful, we should be learning from what happened and making plans to help them. If you have any questions, ask your horses, they'll be able to answer you much better than I can.'

I made to walk away through the shocked silence, but Jack caught hold of my arm and held me back. 'You really mean that we Healers have the ability to perform any of the Skills? Weather-singing? Metal-singing? Any of them?' he whispered. 'We simply must have a private meeting about this, just the Healers, away from everyone else, to discuss what to do with this information.'

And there it was, displayed openly – if not consciously – by Jack's hunger for the knowledge that would set him apart. The human need to feel special. Shock pierced the positive armour I had been managing to hold around myself and I succumbed to the anger that seeped in through the hole.

I raised my voice. 'It isn't just Healers who can perform all of the Skills, anyone can do it, they just need to know they can. That's all there is to it, knowing you can do it instead of believing you can't. The Skills are all the same. Ask your horses, all of you, ask them and for the sake of us all, LISTEN TO THEM. LISTEN TO WHAT THEY SAY ABOUT THE SKILLS AND LISTEN TO WHAT THEY SAY ABOUT THE WOEFUL.'

'How dare you lecture us about our horses,' said an angry voice.

Jack and a few others stared at me with an intensity I found unnerving as another voice said, 'She's not going to tell us how to do it. Can you believe it? She wants to keep all that knowledge to herself just so she'll make a name for herself and go down in the Histories.'

'She's been nothing but trouble ever since she got here, always flying in the face of how we do things, always having to do everything her own way, but this selfishness, well, I've never come across anything like it in my life,' stormed someone else.

Thuma watched me thoughtfully and with sympathy written on her face, but made no move to defend me. When I sought Holly's gaze, all I found there was disappointment. I was aware of Infinity's calm support, but it wasn't enough. My courage failed, I lost all ability to hold a positive shield around myself and as my heart began its protests anew, I felt totally overwhelmed. I looked around desperately for a way to escape all of those angry and disapproving glares, but I couldn't see one. The pain in my heart escalated.

Adam's face appeared in front of mine. 'Here you are, Amarilla. It's no wonder you can't reach the breakfast table with all of these people standing in your way, now just clear a space for us to move if you would be so kind,' he said, taking my arm gently and turning to lead me through the gap in the crowd that was forming in front of him. 'Thank you, Thuma, I'm glad I saw you, would you be so kind as to pop in to see me this afternoon? Lovely, thank you so much. Vickery, I have some large bell jars that are empty and clean, I know you were wanting some more, I'll leave them outside your door, shall I? Oh, Jacob...' he chatted amiably to many of the people as we made our way past, until somehow we had exited the throng. 'Come and sit down now, Amarilla, and I'll get you some porridge, if that will be enough for you this morning?' he asked.

I nodded, gritting my teeth together at the pain in my chest. He led me to the table where Rowena sat. She glanced at me briefly and I thought I saw a glimpse of sympathy, but it was quickly replaced by anger before she looked away. Adam pulled out a chair for me to sit on and then patted my shoulder gently before heading off towards the food table.

Justin sat down beside me. 'What're that lot doing over there? They look like a load of bees whose hive has just been turned upside down. Are you all right, Am? What's happened? Rowena, what's been going on?' Justin demanded, but was answered with only a silent glare from Rowena. As her eyes turned in my direction, the hurt and anger they hurled at me was too much. I ran.

I don't remember how I got to Infinity but the next thing I knew, I was standing by her as she stood in her field shelter, munching hay. My heart was agony with every arhythmical beat and I felt dizzy and overwhelmed with fear. I closed my eyes and leant my head against Infinity's neck. I smelt sweat and smoke, and opened my eyes in confusion. My gnarled, dirt-encrusted hand rested against my mare's dapple-grey neck and I couldn't stop it shaking. Soon we would ride to our deaths; I knew it and she knew it. The sound of gunfire jolted me into action. I managed to lift my foot to the stirrup iron and pull myself onto my horse's back. 'HOLD THE LINE. CHARGE!' The words echoed around in my head and then we were moving, my horse and me. My beautiful, beautiful horse. She enveloped me warmly with her love and reassurance. I was with my horse. Everything would be alright. I became aware once more of my present life and my heart settled into a more steady, albeit painful, rhythm.

Why didn't you do that when I was surrounded by the Healers? I demanded of Infinity. *You left it until now to help me get control of myself? Why?*

I supported you as much as was helpful.

But I couldn't stay in my positive space, I turned into a quivering wreck. You could have helped keep me steady like you just did and then I would have been able to defend myself. You say that you wouldn't have been helping?

Infinity didn't reply.

But why? I felt so frustrated. I had been presented with an ideal opportunity to vanquish the demons of my past, to voice my truth and stand my ground when challenged about it and I had barely managed to get two sentences out before deserting my post.

Infinity was gentle with her thoughts. *You and I have both chosen this lifetime to clear issues that we have been holding on to but no longer need. Only I can clear my issues and only you can clear yours. We may facilitate each other in this task but anything more than that will result in the issues remaining unresolved.*

But why would giving me the extra reassurance have stopped me being able to stand my ground?

There are different layers to the issue that you have chosen to resolve. The outer layer is the rejection you feel when your fellow humans refuse to listen to you. This has occurred regularly since you were very young and you have become accomplished at dealing with it. The next layer involves having the courage to speak your truth when you know it will be ill received. The layer which is buried most deeply relates to defending your ideas with confidence when you are challenged over the truth you have spoken. Had I protected you from negativity and fuelled your sense of yourself then you would have been better able to defend yourself but your confidence would have come from your bond with me and not from within yourself. I would have been shielding you from your own insecurities and this is not help. I will always provide support but only you can learn where to find the confidence you seek.

But can't you tell me where to find it? Surely that isn't doing it for me? Just pointing me in the right direction?

Infinity's attention was fixed now on her pile of hay. I sighed and sank down to sit in the straw beside her. How was it that I'd been awake for such a short time and already felt so tired?

Footsteps squelching through the slushy mud outside announced that someone approached. Justin appeared, carrying a steaming bowl of porridge in one hand and a huge pile of toast in the other. He handed me the porridge. 'I gather you've been upsetting people again, Am, so early in the morning too, I don't know why I like hanging around with such a trouble maker,' he grinned. 'Adam said to tell you that you are excused from your apprenticeship this morning as you and he have far more important things to do. He's having something to eat and then he'll meet you up here. From what he told me, you handled yourself pretty well with the Healers, so why did you run?'

'Fin told me to make a positive shield around myself to keep that angry, scared feeling out, otherwise I wouldn't have been able to say anything at all. I was doing okay until I saw the problem with humans, how ridiculous we are. Infinity has told me about it and I've seen it in myself at times, but today I saw it in the worst possible way, in people I look up to. I got really angry and shouted at everyone, then my heart went mad and I didn't know what to do. Adam rescued me and then Rowena fired all her emotion in my direction and I couldn't cope, so I ran.'

'And dare I ask what the problem with humans is, that unhinges you so completely when you see it?' Justin's mouth twitched.

'We have a need to feel that we're special and more important than other people. It's because we only feel worthwhile if other people think we are.'

Justin frowned. 'And you've seen it in yourself?'

I nodded. 'Haven't you?'

He shrugged. 'I was never much good at school because I couldn't concentrate for very long, and I didn't show aptitude for any of the Skills when I tested – and before you say it, don't – so I trained as a Carpenter. I was an indifferent one though, I just couldn't settle. And then when Gas tugged me, I was so shocked, I didn't have time to process what was happening before I'd had my Quest Ceremony and was off looking for him. He's been showing me up ever since, so I can say with all honesty that I've never had the chance to feel special.'

'But what about at your Quest Ceremony? Didn't everyone look up to you? Didn't you feel good about yourself, knowing you'd be joining the Horse-Bonded?'

'All I remember feeling was a desperation to be off, to find the source of what was pulling at my mind. I could feel this raw energy that knew no limits, just how I feel most of the time, but from Gas I could feel a sense of knowing that accompanied the wildness of his energy. It was such a relief to feel that there was another out there who was so like me, yet so much more than me and I felt like I'd never have to feel alone again if I could find him, so that was pretty much all that was on my mind, sorry.'

'Well, you're obviously doing better than the rest of us,' I said. 'Except Adam, he seems to have things pretty well sorted.'

'He had a long time to learn from Peace. It's my guess that Adam managed to learn pretty much everything that Peace wanted to teach him before he moved on.'

I nodded. 'Infinity calls Adam "He Who Is Peace". She calls Quinta "She Who Is Noble" too.'

Justin said, 'I wonder if maybe that's why Spider wants to work with both Adam and Quinta?'

'Huh?'

'Well, the way Infinity refers to them suggests that they managed to become what they saw in their horses when they bonded – they achieved the full potential of their relationships with Peace and Noble. And it's never been heard of before for a horse whose human has died to work with any other humans, they usually either stay at The Gathering if they've formed attachments with other bonded horses, or they go back to find their original herds. So maybe Spider wants to work with them because...' He stopped as Gas's thoughts whistled by me and Infinity let me know of her disapproval.

'We're invading Adam and Quinta's privacy by talking about this,' Justin said.

'What's this? Privacy? I don't entertain the idea myself,' smiled Adam as he entered the shelter.

'Sorry, Adam, Am and I got to talking about you and Quinta in the course of conversation and we didn't notice we were beginning to intrude into things that are nothing to do with us, until Gas and Infinity pulled us up.'

'No apology is necessary. I imagine you were only voicing what Quinta and I are already thinking. Spider was tired last night and after he had called us both to him and made his request, he could think only of eating and sleeping, which is more than either of us have been able to do since then. Now, who have we in here? Infinity, Diligence and Oak, ah Spider must be with Gas, it didn't take those two any time to pick up old habits, did it? Quinta will be here soon, I hope you don't mind, Amarilla, I think both you and I would be better served this morning by not pretending we'll have any success at being able to focus on herbalism. Spider tells me he's feeling rested and is eager to begin working with Quinta and me, and we were rather hoping that you, Justin and Rowena would consent to helping us make a start?' His eyes shone with excitement.

'Of course we will,' said Justin. 'I'm not sure about Rowena but Gas and I can show you where we started and how far we've got and Amarilla can help from the ground.'

I was distracted by a feeling that was slightly familiar and yet not. It was coming from behind me. I whirled around to find Diligence standing there, staring at me. I recognised what I was feeling; Dili was trying to make herself heard in my mind again.

'Everything alright, Am?' asked Justin.

I nodded, my mind racing. I had to accept that I could hear her and relax. Infinity receded rapidly in my mind and I panicked and tried to grab hold of her and pull her back. *Fin, what are you doing? Where are you going?*

You know that it is not possible for me to go anywhere. I merely make space so that you may find Diligence in your own way.

But why? Can't you stay as we always are? Can't you help me to hear her?

Your mind would find it confusing. For now you will find it easier to communicate with horses other than me if you interpret them as being separate from me.

A lump was forming in my throat and I found myself remembering my first day at school and the anxiety I had felt when my mother kissed me and I knew that she was going to leave me there. Then I felt Diligence providing gentle support. Her energy was there, at the edge of my mind if I needed to draw on it to steady myself. I wanted to push it away like a child having a tantrum, because it wasn't her support I wanted, it was Infinity's, but then I realised how much Infinity would disapprove if I did so and that was enough incentive to get a hold of myself.

I forced myself to calm down, aware that Adam and Justin now leant against the wall of the field shelter a short distance away, watching. I reached for Infinity and felt her familiar presence sitting very small at the back of my mind. Reassured that she was indeed still there, I focused on breathing deeply and clearing my mind as I tried to find a way to hear Diligence.

Nearly... relax... fluttered into the outer reaches of my mind and I felt a brief sense of triumph before my mind shut her out again. Aaaaaargh! I drew on Diligence's energetic support to help me relax more, but I still couldn't seem to find a way to allow her mind to touch mine. My mind flicked back to when Infinity told me I could heal my arm. It was about going beyond believing I could do it, I had to know I could. I took another deep breath. It had to be the same. I turned my attention to where Infinity waited quietly within my mind. I felt our bond, my total trust in her, and I knew.

Greetings Walks A Straight Path. You find this difficult yet you have succeeded. Dili wasn't a presence in my mind in the way that Infinity was, she was at the edge of my mind, politely waiting for my response.

Diligence, I can hear you! How will this work though? It doesn't feel the same as my bond with Infinity.

I am aware of everything you think and feel since I am a horse and it is not possible for me to be otherwise. I am not your Bond-Partner however and will offer no counsel unless you ask for it. If I wish to communicate with you I will nudge your mind and if you do not wish to hear me then I will not intrude.

Will I be aware of Mason now, through you?

I will ensure that does not happen. It would not benefit our proposed endeavour.

What endeavour? I asked.

You and I may be of great assistance to one another. I am aware of your efforts to help your Bond-Partner to utilise her body in a different way. It is hard for you since you must learn to ride whilst attempting something which is difficult. I ask that you ride me whilst Infinity recovers from her injuries. You will have the opportunity to become a stronger and more confident rider.

But what about Mason? Won't he mind?

He is excited by the notion. Once you feel confident enough we would ask that you help me to improve my own balance. He will find it too difficult to help me begin to make the changes I require but once I have made a beginning our hope is that he will be able to help me to continue. I offer you the use of my body to aid you in your quest. We ask for the use of yours to aid us in ours. There was a depth of feeling that Dili attached to the word "he" that made it refer specifically to Mason and I had a sense of the strength of their bond.

My mind raced. *Fin? Will this be okay?*

Infinity remained purposefully neutral and I grimaced at my need to apply human manners to a situation that didn't require them.

Dili, I'd love to ride you, thank you. And I'll try my very best to help you and Mason once I know what I'm doing a bit more, I told her.

I shall require a bridle and bit such as the others have. We should visit the workshop immediately so that I may have my head measured, Dili replied.

I turned to where Adam and Justin waited patiently. 'Can you start without me this morning? Dili's asked me to ride her while Infinity's recovering and we need to go down to Mason's workshop to have her measured for a bridle.'

They both began to speak as I felt the faintest push against the edge of my mind. I raised my hand up to stop them both. *Dili?*

He has informed me that he knows my body as well as his own and will not require me to visit him to be measured. He has already begun work on my bridle and will visit a Metal-Singer with a request for my bit. He is of the opinion that He Who Is Peace can show you which saddle is mine. That way we may begin our work together immediately.

'Cancel that, Mason doesn't need us, and he thinks you'll be able to show me which is Dili's saddle, Adam? Is that alright?'

'Well of course it is. I take it we may now assume that Spider isn't the only horse to be side-stepping convention by communicating with someone other than his Bond-Partner?'

I explained what had transpired between Diligence and me. Adam's grin widened and Justin shook his head slowly in wonder. I got the giggles. All I had wanted was to be with my horse and fit in, yet I seemed to be totally incapable of preventing myself from flouting all normality and tradition. As I realised just how little control I had over the course my life was taking, I saw the humour in my human struggle to keep my life on the straight and uncomplicated path that I had envisioned for myself. My giggles turned into full-blown, unstoppable laughter that drew my friends to laugh alongside me.

When my laughter finally subsided, Infinity increased her presence in my mind once more. *Your awareness increases. This will help you greatly,* she informed me.

But how am I supposed to be now, Fin? I always thought I was in charge of the direction my life took but now I know I'm not really, what do I do?

You have merely become aware that your soul and your personality do not necessarily want the same thing.

But how does that help me, aside from giving me a good laugh every now and then?

Your personality differs in each life you live but your soul endures. You know this. Your personality in this lifetime has been shaped by your upbringing and experience of life so far. Choices made at the level of your personality tend to be made with the primary aim of self-preservation and often are not in harmony with the choice of your soul. When there is a conflict between personality and soul your personality will experience life as being difficult. When choices are made that allow the soul to express itself fully through the personality then life seems easier even when circumstances are not straightforward.

How do I make sure it's my soul that is making the choices? How will I know if I'm doing it?

You could have refused to ride Diligence.

No, I couldn't.

I sensed Infinity's satisfaction and realisation dawned.

I couldn't refuse because everything within me said it would be a good thing to do. My soul and personality were aligned.

Your choices are always yours to make but now you have seen both the humour and the futility of allowing your personality to attempt to thwart your soul's purpose. Your challenge now will be to allow your soul to influence more of the choices made by your personality. It will not always be easy.

'Oh good, another challenge, it's not as if I don't have enough of those already,' I groaned.

TWENTY-ONE

Progress

*D*iligence's saddle hadn't been ridden in for a long time by all accounts, yet we found it recently oiled, conditioned and sitting atop a brand new sheepskin saddle pad. I smiled, realising that Mason and Dili had been plotting for some time.

Once we were all gathered at the riding paddocks, we decided to take it in turns to ride. Quinta and Spider went first. It was strange to see someone other than Shann riding Spider and I was fascinated by how different he was in personality with Quinta aboard; gone was the goofy clown, Spider was quiet and focused as he responded to his equally quiet and focused rider. With a little help from Justin, Quinta soon found a rein contact with which Spider was happy. She and Spider made their way over to us but Adam made no move to go over to them.

'Spider needs a rest now,' he and Quinta said at the same time. 'This is going to take some getting used to,' grinned Adam.

'You go next, Am,' said Justin and gave me a leg up.

I was just arranging myself in Dili's enormous saddle when the sound of thundering hooves made me look over towards the path. I wasn't hugely surprised to see Oak cantering with Rowena on his back; I'd wondered if he'd call for Rowena to come and ride when we took all of the horses except Infinity from the paddock. He didn't slow down as they neared our riding paddock though and I realised with a sinking heart that they weren't coming to join us. Rowena looked over in our direction and gave a brief nod, which I was pretty sure wasn't aimed at me, and then urged Oak on faster in the direction of the river. I sighed.

Dili nudged my mind. *I am ready to begin. I await your signals.*

Right, sorry. Shall I practise everything that Feryl taught me while we walk around, and then try it in trot?

As you wish.

'If anyone can see me doing something wrong, or if you think I need to do it better, can you shout out please?' I called out. 'Dili's going to bear with me while I practise all the basics.'

There was a murmur of agreement, so Dili and I set off. It felt strange to be riding a horse whose body I couldn't be instantly aware of with my mind as I could with Infinity's; I could tune into various parts of Dili as I would if I were preparing to heal her, but it wasn't the same as being able to share her own awareness of her body as I could with my own horse. I had to rely purely on what I could feel physically from Dili when choosing which signals to use and when to alter them. I became engrossed in trying to make my body do as I asked and feeling how Dili's body responded. I was surprised to notice that Dili didn't feel massively more balanced than Infinity. True, she didn't feel as low in front of me as did my own horse, but it was a bit like sitting astride a plank of wood with legs that moved very heavily beneath.

You now understand why we have asked for your help.

Oh, Dili, I'm sorry, that was rude and insensitive of me.

No need. Your observations are accurate and it pleases me that you are aware of the task that lies before you. Shall we trot? Do not answer with your mind. Your body requires the practice.

I obediently gave a little nudge with my heels and Dili obliged me by trotting. My friends roared with laughter as I bounced around in a saddle that was too large for me, on a horse with an unfamiliar way of moving. I persevered, holding onto the front of the saddle to help keep myself in it and trying fervently to keep my heels down to give me some anchorage.

The laughter turned to cheering when I finally managed to rise and sit to Dili's two-time rhythm. I whooped out loud as Dili and I trotted around the paddock and when I became aware that her breathing was beginning to sound a bit too loud, I closed my thighs around her and pulled back, as I'd learnt to do in my last session riding Infinity. She came to an abrupt halt and I was launched up her neck, where I lay panting as my friends once again filled my ears with their laughter.

You helped me to stop more quickly than I have been accustomed, Dili told me.

Dili, I'm sorry but I need to get off before I fall off, is that alright for today's session?

We have made a promising beginning.

I slid from her back, landed on my feet and then promptly fell back onto my bottom.

'We should be selling tickets for this, honestly, I haven't laughed so much since Shann... well for a long time anyway,' said Justin, offering a hand and then pulling me back onto my feet. 'Well done, that was a good start.'

I loosened Dili's girth and ran the stirrups up to the top of the leathers so they wouldn't bang against her sides. We made our way back to where the others waited.

'I don't think I'm going to be able to walk tomorrow,' I groaned to yet more laughter. 'Are you going next, Adam?'

'No, we were just saying that after having watched you helping Dili to lift in front and stop like that, it would be good if Justin could show us exactly what you did. Hello, here comes Mason in rather a hurry.'

I spun around to see Mason attempting to jog up the path towards us in the slush, his arms flailing as he fought for his balance. Panic shot through me. Infinity! I reached for her and found her dozing peacefully. So why was Mason in such a hurry? Was I meant to wait for him to come before I rode Dili? She'd told me that Mason was keen to complete her bridle, but I must have got that wrong, I decided and ran to meet him.

'Mason, I'm sorry, I didn't realise you wanted to come and watch, I thought you wouldn't need to, to begin with while I'm learning to ride better...'

'What did you do?' he gasped.

'Oh, well, I practised using the signals properly in walk and then we did some trotting and I nearly fell off. I was just getting the hang of it when I could feel Dili was getting tired so I asked her to stop by closing my thighs around her and pulling back, and Adam just said she lifted a little before she stopped, but I didn't feel that, I was too busy trying to stay on,' I said, confused; he would have been aware of this through Dili while sitting in his workshop.

He nodded. 'When you asked her to stop, she felt different. If I wasn't so hot and sweaty, I'd hug you, my little Amarilla, because what you just did has just made my Diligence very happy.' He rubbed Dili's forehead. 'Well, Dili, by the look of things, our Amarilla isn't goin' to be hangin' around, she's started work on you already. You're goin' to have to let me know when you plan to ride, Amarilla, I'm goin' to need to start watchin' sooner than I thought.'

I settled into a routine as winter finally gave way to spring. As soon as I woke in the morning, I would sit on the side of my bed and check in with Infinity. Immediately, I would be filled with a warm, calm feeling as if everything was alright with the world. I'd use that feeling to muster as much positivity and light within myself as I could and I would project the light out from my body in all directions, to form a sort of shield that would protect me from the fear that still gripped The Gathering. I would then practise holding it around myself for as long into the day as I could, before taking myself off somewhere quiet to recreate it. I found that as time went on, I got quicker at manifesting my little light cocoon, as I thought of it, and was able to hold it longer into the day before needing to recreate it.

I saw to Infinity's needs before breakfast, after which I focused my attention on my herbalism apprenticeship; Adam and I had agreed that being able to perform all the Healing Skills didn't negate the need to complete my herb journal.

Adam, Justin, Quinta, Mason and I ate lunch together and then had a riding session afterwards – we were soon joined by Marvel and Broad –

before attending to the chores we had been allocated, until it was time for dinner.

Feryl and his cronies appeared to have decided against interfering when we rode and I wasn't sure whether it was because of how I'd spoken to Feryl on "that day", or because I was in the constant company of people in front of whom he didn't feel comfortable bullying me. Whatever the reason, it was a relief.

We were all working hard. Adam and Quinta quickly became used to riding Spider in his bridle and were enthusiastically helping each other to support him with their reins and legs while he lifted in front more. Justin was able to help Gas lift in all three paces now and was focusing on improving the timing of his signals so that Gas could maintain his improved balance more consistently. Marvel and Broad seemed to find things as easy as Rowena and Oak had and approached everything they tried with a huge amount of gusto.

My sessions with Dili were paying dividends. For the first half of each session, Dili would allow me to concentrate on reminding my body what I needed it to do, so that I could build up muscle memory and strength. Once I felt that I was ready, I would ask her to lift with a squeeze of my legs against her belly, and then support her in her new position with my reins and my thighs.

Mason was a great help to me, watching quietly when I was practising what I could do already but ready to answer any questions I had, in conjunction with Dili, if I wasn't sure whether I was doing things quite as she needed me to. He was fascinated by what he could feel happening to her body. 'She's no spring chicken, is my Dili, but you know she feels a lot less stiff in her front legs since you've been showin' her how to balance better,' he told me one day. 'This means the world to her, my little Am, the whole world, you've no idea.'

Your Bond-Partner is nearly back to full health, Dili informed me one afternoon. *She will require that you are confident in your balance in all*

three paces if you are to be of utmost use to her. We will work on the third pace today.

I felt nervous. This would be the first time that I would be attempting something I hadn't already tried with Infinity. Infinity remained quiet at the back of my mind as Dili's thoughts trickled into it. *I shall look after you. You will not fall.*

I took a deep breath. Dili was right, Infinity would need me to know how to ride in canter by the time I tried it with her, as she would be feeling even more vulnerable with the increase in speed. I needed to do this.

Mason gave me a leg up and then Dili and I worked through our usual routine. Once we were both thoroughly warmed up, and after I had run out of reasons to delay it, I asked her to canter, trying to remember everything that Mason had told me I would need to do. Dili launched herself into a steady canter and as soon as I felt the rocking sensation, my instinct was to clamp on with my legs to keep myself in the saddle.

Adam and Spider appeared next to us, also in canter. 'Relax your legs away from her sides, you won't fall, just relax your lower back. That's it, that's better. Look everyone, Amarilla's enjoying her first canter.'

They peeled away from us and everyone cheered as Dili cantered slowly and carefully around the outside of the paddock. Adam was right, I was enjoying it. It was easy once I did as I was told and relaxed so that my body could follow Dili's movement.

I will trot now, Dili warned me briefly, and then I found myself bouncing around in the saddle as she changed gait. Immediately, she slowed to a walk, breathing heavily. Mason was by our side in a flash, rubbing her neck.

'What's wrong, Mason? Is she alright?' I said.

'She's fine, she's fine. Just feelin' her age a bit; she isn't as fit as she used to be, are you, Dili? But don't be lookin' so worried, little Am, by the looks of what I've just seen, you'll be workin' a lot more in canter now and her fitness will soon improve. And maybe it won't be too long before...' He mumbled something that I couldn't catch.

'Sorry?' I said.

'What? Oh nothin', nothin' to worry about, I'll take Dili back to the paddock and give her a good groom if you've finished for today? She's a tired old bag o' bones.'

'Thanks, Mason, and thanks, Dili,' I said, rubbing her neck affectionately. I went over to where Quinta was sitting on the fence, watching Adam and Spider work on their transitions.

'Well done, Amarilla,' she said. 'Your first canter. Looks like Diligence will be improving her fitness quickly now, good for her at her age. Mind you, she and Mason are so excited about all this, there's no stopping either of them at the moment.'

'What do you mean? What's Mason doing?'

Quinta flushed. 'I assumed Mason would've told you, still I'm sure he won't mind me letting on... have you noticed anything different about him recently?'

'He's been wearing different clothes from the ones he normally wears, is that what you mean?'

Quinta nodded. 'His old ones are too big. He gets up before anyone is around and runs laps around the riding paddocks, and the weight's falling off him. He's really pushing himself.'

'He's getting ready to ride again,' I said.

'Yes, he is. He can feel the difference you're making to Dili by riding her as you are and he's determined to try and do as good a job when you're back riding Infinity, so he's put himself on a fitness regime. He doesn't want to let her down.'

'Why would he think he'd let her down?'

'I've not seen him ride but he's always said he was never very good at it. Personally, I think he was probably as good as the next person, just not as good as he thought he should be. I think that watching you has inspired him.'

'Me? I'm not exactly a shining example of a good rider.'

'And that's the point. You've only been riding a matter of months, but you try as hard as you can and you're making a difference to her. As far as he's concerned, if you can do it, he can do it. I've never seen him so determined.'

I was so glad. I'd grown close to both Dili and Mason as we worked together and the thought that they both appeared to be experiencing a new lease of life left me with a very warm feeling. I was still smiling while I groomed Infinity later that day, as she stood dozing in the spring sunshine.

Everything happens as it should, she reminded me. I was understanding more and more what she meant.

~

As spring bloomed in all her glory, the atmosphere began to lighten at The Gathering; fear was gradually being replaced by a sense of purpose as a large group of the Bonded set about making serious plans to hunt the Woeful.

Their relief is ill found, Infinity informed me one morning while I was discussing the situation with Quinta.

I relayed her comment to my friend, who nodded and said, 'They feel better because they think that making plans to remove the cause of their fear will stop it from returning.'

'But what do we do? They won't listen to us and they won't listen to their horses,' I said.

'For now, I think we do what we're doing. Our horses are giving top priority to the work we're doing together, so we have to trust that somehow, what we're doing will help with what we're going to need to do in the very near future.'

I hoped she was right. I was able to relax my light shield without feeling battered by the storm of fear that had been present over recent weeks, however I found that I felt somewhat naked without it. I felt more at ease with myself, more confident, when I had my light surrounding me and I decided it was a practice I would continue. Infinity approved.

My heart was still bothering me, but the pain seemed to have stabilised at a lower, more manageable level. I often found myself wondering why it was better. Was it because I was settled in a routine that I was finding comfortable, where I wasn't finding myself constantly challenged or ridiculed? Was it my light shield that was making the difference, helping me to feel less vulnerable to the negative opinions of others around me? Or was it maybe because of the fact that I'd managed to make myself heard when I'd challenged everyone in the dining room to listen to their horses – maybe I'd managed to clear some of the emotion I was holding that was affecting my heart so much? I wasn't sure and Infinity hadn't seen fit to enlighten me, so for now I was enjoying the respite from the full-blown symptoms for as long as it would last.

I was thrilled when Infinity announced that she would like to have more freedom to move around than her paddock was allowing her. She began coming up to the riding paddock with us all, walking purposefully around the perimeter while we worked.

After a week of walking, I noticed that she was experimenting with brief spells of trot. I had to fight back the tears as I saw how stiff she was. I couldn't concentrate on riding Dili, so I asked Infinity to wait until I'd finished with Dili before she did any trotting, so that I could run around with her as she worked through her aches and stiffness. Although she agreed to my request, Infinity made it clear that indulging my sentiments wasn't something she would be doing on a regular basis, which made me smile.

Diligence reached the point where she was fit, strong and confident enough in all three paces that I was having to step in less to help her to maintain a better balance and I knew that Mason itched to be able to learn how to help her himself.

The change in him was staggering. He would always be a big man, but he had shed a lot of weight and now looked a great deal younger. I suggested to Dili and Mason that I rode Dili at the beginning of each session and helped her to find the balance we had been achieving so far, and then Mason could ride after me and I would help him whilst I walked and ran around with Infinity. My suggestion was met by, *I agree it is time,* from Dili and a bear hug from Mason, which turned into him lifting me off the ground and twirling me around him in the air.

Quinta's assumption about Mason's riding ability turned out to be accurate. He sat with a natural ease and balance in the saddle and learnt rapidly how to help Dili to balance better, but he put a lot of pressure on himself. I'd see him shake his head to himself if his timing to give a signal was a split-second too slow and sometimes he'd ask Dili to stop while he sat with his eyes to the sky in frustration at his own perceived shortcomings. I could feel that Dili communicated with him, so I said nothing.

I was overjoyed to be working with Infinity again, even if only from the ground. I'd loved riding Dili and had got so much from it, but having Infinity back up at the riding paddock with me made it feel like everything was in its rightful place again. When Mason and Dili began to need me less, Infinity and I moved off on our own more. She was feeling better with every exercise session and she soon was able to trot for longer than I could run. I wanted to stay with her, as I could feel how hard she was pushing herself and wanted to give her as much energy and encouragement as I could, but I was constantly being left behind. An idea occurred to me.

Fin, do you think you could circle around me? If you work on a big circle and I work on a smaller one inside yours, I'll be close to you all the time without getting left behind when you trot.

She immediately began to walk a circle around me, but it wasn't long before she stopped, her ears flickering back and forth uncertainly.

Fin? What's wrong?

I cannot walk forward whilst you are in front of me.

???????? I'm not in front of you. Are you alright? Have you had enough for today?

We will try once more. She resumed walking on her circle and I went back to walking my circle inside hers. She seemed happier for a while and then stopped again. *It is too difficult to overcome.*

What is? I don't understand.

I will show you.

Immediately, I saw images of other horses in my mind. They appeared to move at random as they grazed, played or moved off as a herd, but Infinity showed me how she moved in response to their movement and body language so that conflict in the herd was avoided. When a horse of higher status moved in her direction and wanted her to move out of his way, she would move backward if he approached from in front of her shoulders, and she would move forward if he approached from behind her shoulders. It was as if there were an invisible line drawn vertically down her body that affected the direction in which she would move in response to the approach of a horse of higher status in the herd than herself.

I felt her inability to overcome the instincts of her species and move forward if my body were positioned in front of her shoulder line, even though I was a distance away from her. *What shall we do, Fin, shall I just run around with you again and try harder to keep up?*

This way of working is beneficial. Your focus provides me with energy I can utilise and your observation of my body provides us both with information that is useful. You must improve your body language so that it does not conflict with my instincts.

Right, bear with me and I'll try. Hold on though, if you are affected by the position of my body relative to yours, does that mean you see me as higher than you in status?

At the level that my soul is aware of yours there is no hierarchy. In this incarnation I have chosen to live as a horse and you as a human. I have given you permission to sit on my back and give me signals to which I respond and the instinct of my species tells me that you are therefore of higher status. This is something with which we must work.

Right, so where exactly is the shoulder line I need to stay behind?

Infinity walked her circle, leaving me to figure it out.

TWENTY-TWO

Resumption

A marked difference began to form between the horses of our working group and the rest of those at The Gathering. Our horses grew summer coats that gleamed on even the dullest of days. Their eyes were bright, their bodies were toned and supple and they had a zest for life that was infectious. We had to move them to much larger paddocks that could accommodate their frequent desires to canter around, bucking and squealing like yearlings, and even Dili and Infinity were joining in. Infinity only allowed herself very short bursts of canter, but Dili, despite her age, was often the one to initiate the joyful proceedings as well as being one of the last to calm down.

The other horses ranged from those who looked pretty much as they always had, albeit that they seemed a toned-down version of themselves compared with ours, to those who were miserable and a little off colour, to some who looked downright unwell.

We realised that the condition of the horses bore a direct relation to the feelings and behaviour of their Bond-Partners; those whose horses suffered the most were in the group most actively involved in planning the hunt for the Woeful. Oak, thankfully, wasn't included in that group, but he was still a shadow of his former self. He hadn't asked to move to the larger paddocks with our horses and I missed his mellow presence, but I continued to take Justin's advice of leaving him to try to help Rowena come to terms with Shann's loss without interference.

Infinity's strength and fitness were steadily improving.

Will it be much longer before you feel strong enough to carry me? I asked her as she circled around me one afternoon.

She gave me the sense that the time was fast approaching but hadn't quite arrived yet. *I would test my body further,* she whispered in my mind.

I had an idea. 'Hey, anyone fancy a ride down by the river?' I called to the others.

'Love to, mind you, whether I actually get to ride or whether I end up on the floor is anyone's guess, Gas is feeling particularly full of himself this morning,' laughed Justin.

We made our way down to the river with me, Infinity and Quinta walking at the rear of the ridden horses. Gas and Spider pranced along with Justin and Adam laughing astride them. Broad and Dili were more sensible, but both had a spring in their step and Infinity began to be drawn along with the other horses' joy and anticipation. As the path opened out onto the river bank, the water hurtled past in front of us, goading us to race it on its turbulent journey. Gas responded immediately, launching himself into a flat-out gallop, with Justin crouched low in his saddle. Spider was close behind, followed by Broad. Dili danced on the spot as Mason turned to us.

'Comin', my beauty?' he asked Infinity as she stood quivering beside me.

I gathered all my love for my horse and sent it to her. *Go, Fin. Go on, you're ready, I know you are. Go!*

Infinity walked a few paces and then broke into trot. Dili stayed beside her as she turned along the river bank and eased herself into a slow canter. She looked stiff and ungainly, which I could feel was more due to a lack of confidence in her body than anything else. I sent a surge of love to her and also to Dili, thanking her for supporting Infinity with her gentle company. As they moved further away, Infinity seemed to loosen and she increased her pace a little. They got smaller and smaller in the distance and eventually I had to rely solely on my awareness of Infinity's body to gauge how she was faring.

Little by little, she was allowing the tension to leave her muscles as she began to trust that her body was fit and strong once more. She was out of sight now but I could feel her slowing to a trot before she turned back in the direction of home. She moved back up to a canter, feeling more confident.

Go, Fin, go, I urged her and felt her send a new intention to her muscles. She picked up speed as Dili caught up and came alongside her, then pushed herself harder into a fast canter, her hooves thrumming now against the turf. As she came back into sight she was at full stretch and was pulling away from Diligence.

'Wow, look at her go,' Quinta said excitedly.

Tears streamed down my face as I felt Infinity's joy at being able to move as she had before her body had been so badly injured. She tore along the river bank, her silver-white tail streaming out behind her and the spring sunshine sparkling off her mane as it rose and fell against her neck. Her muscles rippled as she pushed her body to its limit, her head reaching forward with each stride and her nostrils flaring as she drew in air and then forced it back out ready for the next urgent breath. My strong, beautiful, brave horse.

Infinity slowed as she approached Quinta and me, and I could feel her tiredness behind her jubilation. She dropped down to a trot and it looked as if her legs were everywhere at once as she fought her weariness to keep them under control.

'I'm going to go back with Fin straight away so I can rub her down and get a rug on her before she gets chilled,' I said to Quinta, who nodded.

I waved to an approaching Mason and Diligence and turned to walk in the direction of The Gathering. Infinity trotted past me, whickering, and I saw that Oak stood where the river bank met the path, with Rowena on his back. He replied to Infinity's whicker of welcome with a deep whicker of his own.

Rowena smiled at Infinity. 'Hello, Fin, it's good to see you back to your old self, just look at you, beautiful girl.'

I decided to take Infinity's lead. I walked up to the three of them and held the back of my hand out for Oak to sniff. 'Hey, mate, how're you doing?' I said. As I raised my eyes to his, I saw the pain they held and had to take a deep breath to avoid exclaiming out loud. He held my gaze with purpose; he wanted me to help him get through to his Bond-Partner. My heart lurched in my chest – just when I'd been enjoying the break from it all.

Infinity stood beside me, wet with sweat and breathing heavily. I needed to get her back to her field shelter before she stiffened and got a chill, so there was no time for me to dither.

'Rowena, come back and ride with us. We miss you. Infinity's going to be ready for me to ride her soon and I don't know how I'll do it without you and Oak,' I said.

Rowena looked into my eyes and I stepped backwards as I felt the depth of her emotion. I took a deep breath and cocooned myself within a stronger barrier of light. As my energetic protection settled into place around me, I found myself less susceptible to Rowena's agony. She said nothing.

'Please, Ro? We ride after lunch every day in the far paddock. Marvel and Broad ride with us too, and Broad finds it easy, like Oak does – you and Marvel could probably both get on with things much faster if you helped each other. Mason's riding Dili now too, you should see them, well I mean you probably just did, but I mean, you should see them working together, it's really lovely to watch. And you could just watch if you wanted to, to begin with I mean, but come back, Rowena? Please?'

I felt Oak's thoughts streaming towards her and was aware of his desperation. Rowena's eyes filled with tears and for a moment I thought she would agree. But then she blinked furiously, radiating her fury so that I could feel it battering at the light cocoon I was just about able to maintain around myself.

'There are things I need to do first,' she said icily. 'Just because the rest of you can carry on as if Shann never existed, it doesn't mean that I can.'

As my heart began to lurch more violently in my chest, I looked from Oak, a physical embodiment of a soul in pain, to Infinity, who was beginning to shiver. Anger began to boil in my stomach. None of us had the time for this. There was far too much to do, helping the horses, the Woeful, not to mention stopping the other Bonded from going on their hunt and risking all of the progress that the humans of The New had made. Shards of anger pierced my light cocoon from the inside and then as my temper exploded, I lost the ability to radiate any light at all.

'How dare you,' I said. 'Get off of Oak right now, you don't deserve the honour of sitting on his back.'

'What did you say?' Rowena's dark eyes blazed.

'How dare you call yourself his Bond-Partner. Look at him.'

Rowena dismounted and took a step towards me.

'And don't think that hitting me again will stop me saying what you need to hear. Go on, do it if you need to, but I'll get straight back up and carry on until I've said what Oak needs me to say.'

Rowena recoiled. 'Oak needs you to…? How would you know what my horse needs?'

'Because I have eyes and a willingness to pay attention to others besides myself, unlike you. How can you be so selfish? How can you see your horse looking worse by the day and not care? Look at the state of him, Rowena, you should be ashamed of yourself.'

'You have no idea…'

'Yes, yes, we've heard it all before. You're the only one who's suffering, the only one who's ever lost anybody, the only one with the right to treat her friends as if they're her worst enemies and to treat her horse, her Bond-Partner, as if he's merely her servant, someone to carry her around when she doesn't feel like walking because yes, Rowena, that's how you're treating him and it disgusts me. Oak came for you when you had no one else. He took you away from everything you hated and gave you the chance to grow into the best person you can be. And what do you do? You wallow in your own self-pity and act as if you're the only one who's ever grieved. Spider lost Shann too and is he storming around like the world owes him a favour? No, he's helped Shann to move on and now he's working with two new souls who need him. Quinta lost Noble and what's she doing? Oh yes, that's right, she's working with Adam and Spider, as well as trying to help the rest of you to see what happened "that day" for what it was… an opportunity to learn and move on with things differently.'

Rowena opened her mouth to speak but I didn't let her.

'I DON'T WANT TO HEAR ANYTHING YOU HAVE TO SAY. I have a very tired horse who has suffered worse than any of us and who needs me to take care of her, but instead, I'm standing here talking to you and to be honest, at the moment, you're just not worth the effort. Look around you, Rowena, some of us down here have faced difficulties every bit as harrowing as the ones you're facing, but we're getting on with things because what we're doing here is bigger than any single one of us. If you can find it in your heart to put your horse before all your wallowing and self-pity, then we'd love to have you back working with us. If not then, Oak, I'm so sorry, I don't know what else I can do. Now I'm taking my horse back to her shelter as I should have been doing ages ago. Come on, Fin, I think you'd better trot slowly for a little bit, you're getting cold. I'll jog at your shoulder.'

I was breathless as I started to run. My heart hurt, but had ceased its wild lurching part way through my tirade. I couldn't quite believe I'd just done what I'd done. What had got into me?

Your body has strengthened and you have begun to open at the chest as a result of helping Diligence to begin to open hers. It was mainly your temper that gave you the strength to speak however, Infinity volunteered.

What do you mean?

Anger gave you the strength to say what was necessary as it has on past occasions. As your chest opens more you will be better able to express yourself from a place of confidence.

How do I get my chest to open more?

We will change as we work together. I shall need a short while to recover from my exertions of today. Then we shall begin.

I can ride you soon? When?

Infinity didn't answer. She was tired to the point of exhaustion. Exhilaration at the return of her confidence in her body had resulted in her pushing herself way past the point she should have, and standing around getting cold whilst I tore Rowena off a strip hadn't helped at all.

Fin, just walk now, come on, we'll walk the last bit, we're nearly there.

Once Infinity was rugged up and warm, I fetched hay for her and then set about mucking out the straw bed with vigour. I would soon be riding my horse again! I was desperate to see how much more use I'd be to Infinity when riding her now. When the others returned from their ride a short time later, I was still buzzing.

'Remind me not to get on the wrong side of you anytime soon, little Am. Is Infinity alright?' said Mason.

'Sorry about the shouting, but there were some things that needed to be said,' I said. 'Infinity's fine, just tired.'

'I'm not surprised she's tired, took me and Dili by surprise, she did, steamin' off like that. Can't say we didn't enjoy the race though, we've not run like that for many a year.'

Justin came in. 'I think it's safe to say that Gas is feeling good, he's normally pretty quick but pheweeeee, we've never been that fast before. And it was so much smoother when he needed to slow down, a slight pull back with my thighs and he slowed down in balance, instead of feeling like he was going to fall on his nose like he used to, he's seriously pleased with himself and with me. And you should have heard Adam, he's never been that fast before as Peace was so much heavier than Spider. He was yelling and whooping the whole way.'

I grinned. 'That's great, Jus, um, did Rowena and Oak pass you on your way back?'

'Yes, but they didn't stop for a chat, not that I really expected Rowena to. She had a face like thunder, and Oak looks terrible. I'm starting to think that maybe we ought to try and have a talk to her.'

'One step ahead of you,' I said and told him what had happened.

'Blimey, you weren't in the mood to hold back, at least you managed to stay on your feet this time,' he said.

'Do you think she'll come back and join us?' I asked.

'Who knows, but you managed to subdue Feryl with that tongue of yours, so hopefully you've got through to Rowena.'

～

I carried on working with Infinity from the ground for the next few days, as her muscles ached after her wild canter along the river bank.

Oak and Cloud In The Storm rejoin us, I was informed as Infinity circled me one afternoon. I saw that the others had congregated around Oak and Rowena.

Cloud In The Storm? You call Rowena that?

No response.

Realisation dawned. *Oak calls her that. Why have you told me?*

Oak requested help with his Bond-Partner. This will help.

How will it help?

Patience and compassion arise from understanding.

???????? My brow furrowed. Cloud in The Storm? I tried to remember what I'd learnt about storms at school. I visualised storm clouds forming in an area of low pressure, as a result of high pressure on all sides. The resulting clouds were then hurled around in the high winds, discharging part of themselves at intervals as thunder and lightning raged around them, only to be broken up and dispersed once the energy of the storm was spent. I understood.

Feeling nervous, I followed Infinity over to where everyone was gathered. I breathed deeply and surrounded myself with more light, and by the time we reached our friends, I was feeling calmer.

'We're all thrilled you're here,' Marvel was saying to Rowena. 'I've heard how well you and Oak were doing, and Broad and I could do with some sensible help, you've no idea what a struggle it's been having to find our way with only this lot to guide us.'

Justin and Quinta booed him playfully and Justin retorted, 'Ro, you're welcome to him, see if you can get him to quieten down, will you, the rest of us can hardly think with all his hollering and yelling.'

Marvel dipped his head with a smile.

'Right, well, let's carry on then, shall we?' said Quinta. 'Amarilla, Rowena and Oak are going to watch today so they can see where we've all got to. Okay?'

I nodded and smiled at her, and then everyone peeled away, leaving just me, Infinity, Rowena and Oak. It seemed as if we stood there forever with Rowena and me looking everywhere except at each other.

'I'm sorry I hit you,' she said at the exact moment I said, 'It's good to have you back.' We both hesitated. 'It's okay,' I said at the same time she said, 'Thank you.' We both laughed nervously.

Rowena said, 'Am, everything you said, you were right and I'm sorry. I've just been finding it so hard.'

'I know. Look, I know Marvel wants you to help him, but why don't you come over and see what Fin and I have been doing first?'

She smiled and nodded. I glanced at Oak and was relieved to see his eyes looking softer than the last time I'd seen him. Infinity's revelation as to the name Oak used for Rowena stabbed at me.

'Rowena, before we start, I know the name Oak uses for you and as I know that, it's only fair that you know that Fin calls me Walks A Straight Path.'

Rowena chuckled. 'I can see where that comes from. It's probably not hard to see why Oak chose Cloud In The Storm for me? I suppose Infinity told you?'

'Yes, she did. She seems to think it will help.'

'Help? With what?'

'Me being more patient and compassionate, apparently.'

We both laughed and some of the awkwardness between us lifted.

'Hey, Rowena, where are you going? I thought you were going to… Ouch!'

'Oops. Sorry, Marvel, I didn't mean to pass that close to you, Spider sort of slipped,' Quinta said. 'Can you come over here with me and show me how you and Broad managed to go from trot to canter without the trot speeding up first? I think my timing's a bit off.'

We laughed even louder and I made a mental note to thank Quinta for her diplomacy later.

'Men,' said Rowena.

'Men,' I agreed, as Justin passed us and winked at me.

The following morning, as I mucked out the field shelter alongside Mason and Quinta, Infinity announced that she was ready to be ridden. My heart sang. I didn't think I'd be able to focus on anything meaningful that morning, so I explained to Adam that I felt I should sit out of the patient consultations with which I was meant to be assisting. He agreed and set me the boring job of re-ordering his filing system. I tried to concentrate as I sorted Adam's patient files into alphabetical order whilst updating the list of which patients were taking which herbs, so that we could ensure we kept enough in stock. As the morning went on, I began to notice something strange.

Adam was meticulous in noting down exactly which herbs in which amounts he was prescribing, even for very common ailments where he must have prescribed the same herbs and doses a thousand times over. In addition to prescribing the herbs with which I was familiar for some of the conditions, he was prescribing the leaves of suncatcher, a very common herb for which I had never been able to find a use. Why was he doing that, when he was already prescribing the herbs which would heal the various conditions? I frowned to myself, wishing that I had worked closely with him more regularly, so that I might have picked up on this before.

A thought occurred to me, immediately followed by a surge of guilt. Should I re-test suncatcher for use with the outstanding ailments I had? I knew I'd already tested it, but maybe I should try harder with it, maybe there was something I'd missed? But that would be cheating, taking a hint from his patient notes when I was meant to be making my discoveries by myself.

Infinity made her disapproval known. *Choose to feel differently.*

I was interested that she had no concerns about me cheating, only about me feeling guilty about it.

Everything happens as it should. Did that come from me or from her? I wasn't sure, but I remembered that I believed it. I had stumbled across this information for a reason and guilt had no place in the proceedings. I pushed it to one side and chose to focus, noting Infinity's approval.

There would be dried suncatcher leaves in the store room but I wanted a fresh sample, which would be easier to tune into. I rushed out of my room and ran full pelt out of the square, scanning the verges as I ran, for the long-lobed leaves of suncatcher. There. I pulled at a few and then ran back to my study room, my anticipation building.

I put the leaves on my desk and then took deep, even breaths as I cleared my mind. My awareness sought and found the leaves. I conjured up the feeling of tired alertness typical of insomnia and took it to the leaves. Nothing. No lessening of the symptoms whatsoever. Frustration crept into my mind and I withdrew my awareness from the leaves. I hadn't really expected it to work, had I? Having tested all of the commonly growing herbs for the potential to help with insomnia already, had I really expected that suncatcher's ability to help would have changed just because I knew Adam had found something unique in it?

Infinity increased her presence in my mind.

Fin? What is it?

She offered no assistance, yet she seemed keen that I continue along the route my thoughts were taking me. What had I been thinking when she showed interest? I was pondering my insanity in thinking that the potential healing power of suncatcher could have changed because it had captured Adam's interest. Infinity caught hold of that thought and held it in my mind, refusing to let me move past it. When it felt as if the thought was actually a physical part of my body, Infinity let go.

AAARRRGGGGGGGHHHHHHHH!! Flaming lanterns, Fin, what are you trying to do? Drive me mad? I sat holding my head in both hands.

No response, just a feeling of intense satisfaction. She made her presence smaller in my mind again, giving me space to mull things over. The healing ability of a herb could change as the result of attention from a Herbalist? How? I'd given my attention to hundreds of herbs but had only ever picked up the healing ability that was already present within them. What had Adam discovered?

I thought back to when Justin and I had witnessed him using tree-singing to affect some potted plants. He hadn't sung though, had he? He said that he had, but just not out loud. He'd obviously found some way of just tuning in to them with his mind and then affecting them with intention alone. It felt as though something had dropped into my body and plummeted all the way down to my feet. Intention? Was that it? The healing power of suncatcher had changed as a result not of just Adam's attention but his intention?

Infinity's jubilation rang around in my whole being as the thought settled into my mind. Suncatcher could carry the intention of a person who tuned into it? How was that possible?

Everything is connected. Nothing can avoid being affected by an observer, Infinity volunteered.

But what about all the other herbs that are already useful to us in healing? I didn't create their abilities to heal, did I? I only discovered them, as have hundreds of Herbalists before me.

There is little difference between discovery and creation.

WHAT?????????? How can that be? Something has to be there already for me to discover it.

Your certainty comes from your beliefs and nothing more.

My mind reeled. Was my horse actually trying to tell me that when I thought I'd discovered something, I'd actually just created it?

I do not merely try. You will need to allow this to settle in your mind.

Hold on, Fin, I can't just accept this like I do with everything else. Are you saying that I created Rowena? Oak? Adam? How is that possible?

Everyone and everything is connected. We all dream the same dream.

You can't answer one riddle with another one. What do you mean?

Infinity diverted her attention to grooming with Dili.

I sat for what seemed like days, trying to make sense of everything that I'd learnt that morning, with no success. When I heard the gong for lunch, the thought that it would soon be time to ride Infinity shot through my mind.

Fin? If I create everything I come across, then surely I can just create you in a better balance and we won't need to work to achieve it this afternoon?

We all dream the same dream.

I wished I hadn't asked.

TWENTY-THREE

Threshold

*a*dam's door was shut as I passed it on my way to lunch, indicating that he was still with a patient, so I went on without him. The others were already seated at a table and I was thrilled to see that Rowena had joined them.

'They still haven't agreed how best to go about killing a Woeful, that's the only thing holding them here now,' Rowena was saying. 'None of their horses will agree to go, so they've built litters they can drag behind them to carry their stuff, and they've been gathering food supplies. Some of them want to use weapons against the Woeful but others think it would be best to use tissue-singing to kill them.'

'WHAT?' thundered Marvel. 'The Skills should NEVER be used that way and for any Healer to even consider it is an abomination. Ro, I had no idea that's what they were considering and they'll do it over my dead body.'

'Have they gone mad?' I said.

Quinta said, 'They're not mad, just frightened. There's really no predicting what they're capable of.'

'On the bright side, some of the Healers have dropped out of plans for the hunt since you told them all what for in the dining hall, Am,' said

Rowena, 'but the others are willing to try anything to get rid of the Woeful and prevent what happened "that day" from happening again.'

'I don't understand how people who are Horse-Bonded can have so completely lost the plot,' I replied. 'They've always listened to their horses and been able to calm villagers talking of a hunt in the past, why won't they listen to their horses this time?'

Mason sighed. 'Because this time, it was a direct attack on a settlement, not just a chance encounter in the woods. And this time, a horse died. Not just any horse neither, but a horse that was bonded to one of us. They don't feel safe here and they fear their horses being taken from them. It's stripped them of all reason and I have to admit that I understand how they feel. The thought of my Dili being savaged... oh, Quinta, I'm sorry. You too, little Am.'

'Two horses died, actually, and two people,' said Rowena.

'So, they're terrified of losing their horses to the Woeful but they're quite happy to see them looking dreadful as a result of their own thoughts and actions,' I said bitterly and then felt heat in my cheeks. 'Rowena, sorry.'

Marvel chuckled. 'We're a sorry crew, aren't we? Can't speak without offending someone, you know the horses have the right of it, a dirty look or at worst a bite or a kick and then it's all over and forgotten.'

'Rowena's already tried that approach but Am just got up and carried on,' grinned Justin.

Marvel guffawed. 'That's the spirit. Who wants to go next? Come on now, don't be shy, let's really cause some offence.'

'It's hard to say who resembles a pea on a mountain more when they ride, Quinta on Spider or Amarilla on Dili,' chuckled Mason.

'Well at least neither of us blow the leaves off the trees with our sighs just because we didn't get a perfect walk to trot transition,' countered Quinta and Marvel slapped his hand on the table, laughing heartily.

Rowena smiled. 'I don't know what you're laughing about, Marvel, I've never seen anyone faff around like you do. The rest of us have groomed, saddled up and been out for an hour's ride and you're still adjusting Broad's saddle pad so it sits in the perfect spot. And I'm glad you can laugh too, Amarilla, The Gathering's biggest troublemaker and owner of the world's toughest jaw, you nearly broke my hand.'

'It's marvellous to hear all this hilarity, it seems I've arrived not a moment too soon,' said Adam. 'Might I be included in the joke?'

'Oh, Adam, you're going to wish you hadn't said that,' I said.

Justin said, 'Adam, my dear, you've nearly missed lunch. Come along now, eat up and then we'll all hurry along to the riding paddock, shall we, that's right, because it won't be a proper session without you. Move up a little please, Amarilla, so Adam can sit down, that's the way.'

Adam chortled. 'Well, I think I might just do that, Justin, and might I suggest that you eat more slowly. Inhaling food the way you do while jigging around in your chair is enough to give anyone indigestion – I'm beginning to think there's very little that's deep about where Gas got his name from.'

Justin saluted, laughing.

The rest of the diners in the hall were silently watching us.

'No hilarity allowed in here, this is a place of fear and anger,' whispered Marvel, shaking a finger at all of us in mock reproach.

'At least if they're wondering what we have to laugh about, they're not deciding how to kill Woeful,' said Rowena, bringing us all back down to earth with a bump.

My hands shook as I saddled and bridled Infinity and I couldn't seem to stop talking. 'Thank goodness the canopies are still up, otherwise Infinity might have found it a bit slippery. Have the Weather-Singers said yet which day we need to bring them down? Is Oak going to help again? He was great when we put them up, wasn't he? Where's Adam? I thought he was coming as soon as he'd finished eating, do you think he'll be long? Should we wait for him?'

'Amarilla, Adam's more than capable of making his way up to find us by himself, I think it's time to face the fact that you've run out of reasons to loiter here and you need to just come and ride your horse,' said Justin.

Balks From What Is perceives with accuracy, Infinity informed me.

'Balks from…?' *Are you intending to tell me the names that all the Bonded are called by their horses? What's going on, Fin?*

Your group of humans has reached a stage where more information will enable you to be of more help to one another. Should they deem it helpful the other horses will now provide their Bond-Partners with the same information about you.

I nodded. Justin turned his head to the side and half closed his eye, still smiling at me. He knew. Well at least I'd been distracted long enough from my nervousness that I felt a bit calmer, I realised as Infinity and I set off at the back of the group.

There is nothing to fear.

Oh, Fin, I'm just worried I won't be able to do as well as the last time I rode you, because it was ages ago and I've been riding Dili and she's so different from you. What if I get my timing all wrong and you fall? Maybe I just think I'm a better rider now because Dili doesn't need as much help from me as you do, maybe we should wait a bit longer before I ride you again?

I will make mistakes and so will you. That is how we shall learn. If you seek to avoid the disappointment of making an error you will never progress. Step aside from your fear and ride.

Instantly, I felt calm. I realised that however much I'd enjoyed working with Diligence, there was just nothing like working with my own horse. It was more than just the familiarity of her thoughts or the fact that I trusted her so implicitly, it was a feeling of completeness, a feeling that together, there was nothing that we couldn't do.

Remember that when we encounter difficulty. It will help. Infinity placed her thoughts gently into my mind as I settled down in my saddle.

'Am, do you want me and Oak to ride around with you, or do you want me to stand and watch you from the ground for a while in case you need help?' asked Rowena.

'Thanks, Rowena, I think we'll be okay for a bit, could I just call out if I need you?'

'Atta girl,' she said. 'We'll stay nearby. Right, Marvel, let's be having you. And keep the noise down today, Amarilla needs to be able to make herself heard if she and Infinity want any help, so you'll have to keep your hollering to a minimum.'

'Does that mean I won't need these today then?' Justin made a big show of removing the bright green ear plug he had just put in his ear, cleaning it on his jumper and putting it into his pocket along with its partner. We all laughed and I felt a surge of affection for my friends. 'Have fun, Am,' he called, 'just yell if you need us.'

I nodded. *Ready?* I asked Infinity.

I felt her assent and gathered up my reins until I could feel her mouth at the other end of them, took a deep breath and then squeezed her sides with my legs.

It was easy. I was fitter, stronger and more balanced than the last time I'd ridden Infinity and in no time at all, she was lifted up in front of me and supported there by my reins and my thighs. Her chest had barely had time to close down when I felt it begin to open, accompanied by a rush of satisfaction and joy from Infinity.

This is it, well done, Fin.

We hadn't gone far though, before her steps faltered.

I cannot maintain it, came her urgent thought as she ground to a halt.

What's wrong? What do you need me to do? Fin? Fin? Please, tell me what happened? What did I do?

No reply. And she was cross.

Infinity, I don't know what happened and I don't know what to do differently, please tell me?

She was rooted to the spot and fury now coursed through her. My mind raced. What was happening?

'Everything alright, Am?' asked Rowena, but I didn't have time to explain; frightened as I was rapidly becoming, I needed to think fast and do something.

Infinity trembled beneath me and I sensed that she wasn't far off exploding with what was fast becoming an all-consuming rage. I asked her to move on, clamping my mouth tightly shut in order to stop my lips from trembling. There was no room for my feelings now, this was about Infinity. She moved forward, but she didn't feel secure, I could feel it. She couldn't stay in her new balance for any length of time and I wasn't doing enough to help her; my legs and reins alone weren't enough. Her tail swished angrily and she gnashed her teeth so that I could hear the bit clanging around in her mouth. How could I help her to feel more secure? I wondered, desperately. Then I remembered something that Dili had told me she'd found helpful when I rode her.

I lifted my chest and immediately something shifted in both me and Infinity. I felt stronger and more stable, and I sensed a glimmer of hope from Infinity. She tentatively took a step forward and as she leant against my reins, I could feel her take heart from the extra stability that she could feel down them. My heart lifted. I had her!

Fin, I've got you. You won't overbalance, I've got you.

Her left ear flickered back towards me uncertainly. She didn't trust, not yet, but I knew I was right, and that knowledge gave me the confidence to relax completely into my riding. I gave her a firm nudge with both of my heels, which shocked her into taking a few hasty steps before grinding to a halt again. We were still in balance. My heart thumped with excitement.

I nudged again, which produced another few steps and then before she could stop, I nudged yet again. After a short while of feeling as if Infinity balanced on a knife edge, making tentative, small steps, I felt her emotion begin to subside a little. I carried on asking her to move forward, keeping my chest lifted as I caught her with my reins and thighs when her balance faltered, bringing her back to that beautiful place where everything felt light and easy for a second or two, before she faltered and I needed to step in and help her find it again.

My back muscles screamed. They were on the verge of cramping, as were the muscles in my legs, but there was only a small part of me that registered the fact. Most of my awareness was with my horse, as moment by moment, I fought with her for her balance. This was of enormous importance to her and I was under absolutely no illusion to the contrary.

I reached the point where fatigue overwhelmed everything else and I couldn't even say whose fatigue it was – mine or Infinity's. I waited for one of the moments when she was balancing by herself and then closed my thighs around her and pulled back gently. We slowed to a graceful halt. Thank goodness. I dismounted immediately and applause erupted all around us.

Infinity stood as she had after the last time I had ridden her; higher at the withers than at her rump, her front legs seemingly out in front of her and with her neck beautifully arched. She blinked incessantly and I could feel her trying to make sense of how her body was now organised and how it affected her emotions and her sense of herself. She was tired, but a sense of wonder and intense satisfaction emanated from her.

'Thunder and lightning, Am, what was all that about? Infinity looked as if she was about to explode,' said Rowena.

'Whatever it was, it was something meaningful, even Gas went all still and thoughtful,' said Justin. 'At times you both looked fantastic and the two of you kind of melded together, and then it was like there was a war going on between you. Are you both alright?'

'We're fine thanks, just fine,' I said and agreed to tell them about it later when they'd all finished riding.

I loosened Infinity's girth, threw her rug over her to keep her warm and then settled onto the fence next to Adam to watch everyone else. Infinity stood with her head by my knee, giving the outward impression that she now dozed peacefully, but I knew differently. I began to feel a little concerned about the degree of introspection in which she was engaging, but then I remembered back to how she had been after I had last ridden her under Feryl's instruction. Then, her chest area had been compressed and she had been less able to express herself, and the other horses had been concerned for her. This was different. Her mind was a frenzy of activity as she processed what we had just achieved. I could feel that a whole range of emotions roiled within her, each steadily rising to a crescendo before the next one bubbled up and took over. The other horses in our group showed no concern for her whatsoever as they and their riders worked on as usual.

I told Adam what had just happened. 'She was furious, yet she knows I'm still learning myself and she wouldn't tell me what the problem was, I had to work it out for myself.'

'And how do you feel now that you have?' he asked.

'Stronger, now that you mention it and not just in my body, in my mind as well.'

'More confident?'

'Yes, that's it, more confident.'

'So then, you both gained from the experience. It seems to me that you and your lovely girl have a very productive partnership. I wasn't aware of you melding together as Justin described, but I think I have a glimmer of understanding as to why he saw you both that way. Just keep going as you are, Amarilla, I have a feeling that you and Infinity are at the threshold of something that will affect us all quite significantly.'

I had the same feeling myself. A rush of anticipation shot through me and caused Infinity to jerk out of her reverie. *Sorry, Fin.*

A faint wave of love and... something else wrapped around me by way of her reply. What was that? There was only one word I could find to describe it – strength. Infinity was feeling stronger too. What was happening to us?

We have both opened more at the chest. You lifted and opened your chest in order to support me and my chest opened more as a result, Infinity told me.

But why were you so angry?

My body was in neither the unbalanced organisation that feels safe by its familiarity nor in the fully balanced organisation for which I yearn. I was stuck betwixt. The emotion I expressed came unbidden.

Fin, why don't any of the other horses get angry? They seem to just gradually get more balanced, I haven't seen any of them react the way you did.

They are willing to accept making the small improvements to their balance which will enable them to carry their riders more easily. You and I must go way beyond that and achieve The Ultimate. It is much more challenging for us both. This is what we agreed to do. Everything is as it should be.

The Ultimate? What's that? Do the others know about it?

Helping a horse to carry a rider without harming itself is only part of what is possible. The other riders have yet to realise this except for one. He knows yet balks from it.

Fin, what's possible?
You know. You have already seen it.
What have I seen? When?

She didn't answer. Balks From What Is. Justin. He knows, I thought to myself, and he isn't going to balk from telling me. I realised suddenly that I wasn't thinking like myself. My newly emerging confidence felt strange, as if there were a whole new part of me unfurling and filling my sense of myself. I decided that I liked it.

As Infinity and I made our way back to her paddock just ahead of our friends, I felt vibrant with energy. Things had changed this day, and were about to change even more, I could feel it.

Justin's voice reached me over my shoulder. 'Well then, Am, sooner or later, you're going to need to come out with it and I'd rather it was sooner.'

I turned towards him and smiled. 'Balks From What Is, you have some explaining to do.'

'I do? Well, At The Cusp, you can go first.'

'What? That's not what Infinity calls me, she calls me...'

At The Cusp, Infinity confirmed.

'Oh. How did you know that before I did?' I asked Justin.

'Possibly because I asked? I didn't for a minute think Gas would tell me even though Infinity had obviously told you Gas's name for me, but he told me as soon as I asked. You mean you didn't know her name for you?'

'I know the one she used to call me, it seems to have changed though. Justin, what exactly is it you're balking from? Infinity says you know what The Ultimate is, she says that she and I have to strive straight for it and miss out all the little steps you're all taking with your horses, but what is it?'

'I'm not sure I know exactly what she means by...'

'Yes, you do, if Fin says you know then you know. Come on, Jus, don't hold out on me, you can help me here, you can help all of us. What is it that we're aiming for?'

He sighed. 'Okay, how did you choose Infinity's name?'

'When she showed me all of herself, I felt that she was all there is, that there was no beginning and no end to her, that she was infinite.'

'She is. They all are. We all are. We're all just parts of the same infinite whole. The difference between humans and horses is that the horses know it and we don't. Well, some of us are waking up to the fact. As soon as I heard the name that you had chosen for your horse I knew you were one of them.'

'And you're another. So why isn't Gas called Infinity?'

'He is, in my own peculiar way. Think about it, Am, and while you're there, consider why Shann may have named Spider as he did.'

My mind spun. 'You're going to need to explain it to me, Jus, sorry, I don't get it.'

'We all saw the same thing when our horses revealed themselves to us, you, me and Shann,' Justin explained, 'but we chose different names for what we saw. The closest word I could think of when I saw All That Is in my horse, was the word for something that has the capacity to expand endlessly. Shann saw Spider as sitting at the centre of a vast network, connected to everyone and everything else, like a spider sitting at the centre of its web. We all saw the same thing, Am, we just chose different words for what we saw.'

'But if Shann knew, why did he leave? Why was it his time to go? Surely he should have stayed to do what we're all doing with the horses?'

Justin sighed. 'As far as Gas has been able to help me understand, Shann became He Who Is Spider in the moment that he felt from the Woeful why it was there. He fully realised that we are all connected, that we are all one with each other and with All That Is. The moment he had that feeling of oneness that Infinity calls The Ultimate, he achieved his potential and didn't feel the need to be here any longer; the Woeful gave him the opportunity to leave.'

'Does this mean that when you and I achieve our potential, we'll die too?'

'That is what I don't know, Am, and Gas refuses to enlighten me. Call me a coward, but I know what is possible and I hold myself back from it because I don't want to die. I'm not ready to leave this body, this lifetime. There it is, I've told you.'

'How is this connected to helping the horses balance better?'

'I'm not sure, but I think the fact that you can't distinguish me from Gas when we're together, and now the same thing is happening when you ride Infinity, points to the fact that we're going in the right direction. One minute I feel happy about it and the next minute I'm terrified.'

A small stab of fear announced itself in my stomach and Infinity increased her presence in my mind in a flash. *Everything is as it should be.* My fear disappeared as quickly as it had arrived.

'Justin, do you trust Gas?'

'Well of course I do, how can you...'

'Then go with it. Neither of us knows what's going to happen, but I know above everything else that I trust Infinity and if she thinks we're going the right way, then whatever happens, I'm carrying on.'

'It's not that easy, Am.'

'Yes, it is. Come on, Jus, what are you going to do otherwise? Creep through life trying to be safe, then sit waiting to die, regretting that you never had the courage to trust your horse and explore what's possible?'

He was silent as Gas's thoughts whistled to him like dart after dart being thrown at a gaming board.

'Right, everyone, see you at dinner when Amarilla is going to tell us all exactly what she and Infinity were up to back there,' Rowena yelled.

'Oh blimey, where will I start?' I whispered to Justin. 'How much do I say? Do you want me to leave you and Gas out of it?'

'I'm not sure of anything at the moment. I'll see you later, Am,' he replied and wandered off towards the field shelter, his horse at his shoulder.

'Yep, see you later,' I said to his retreating back.

Fin, why have I always had trouble seeing Justin separately from Gas? He's only started seeing me that way since I've been riding you, and even then, only in the moments when you're better balanced?

Balks From What Is has been aware of his connection to All That Is for most of his life and instantly connected with his horse at a much deeper level than any other bonded human. You are more sensitive than most and can see how little he holds himself apart from his horse. You currently experience moments of truth only for the few moments at a time that you and I achieve a better balance.

Why only then? Why aren't I aware of it all the time as Justin is, now that I know what's possible? I saw it in you, so why don't I feel it all the time?

There are obstacles which stand between you and greater awareness. Have patience. Everything is...

... as it should be, I know.

TWENTY-FOUR

Clearing

*T*he next few weeks were a bit of an anticlimax. Far from being the exciting time of revelation and discovery that I had envisaged, I found myself as much in the dark as ever and extremely frustrated about it.

Adam had given me his undivided attention for a short time during the morning after I'd discovered his use of suncatcher – enough time for me to explain what I'd discovered and about Infinity's assertion that creation and discovery were pretty much the same thing, anyway – before informing me that my apprenticeship was coming along very nicely now, and politely instructing me to go away and carry on. I insisted that he tell me whether he was indeed using suncatcher as I thought he was, all the while finding it impossible to be angry at his refusal to either confirm or deny that I was right.

Eventually, he took pity on me. 'Amarilla, please remember back to yesterday when you were forced to work out for yourself how to help that glorious mare of yours, and trust me when I tell you that if I truly thought it would help you, I would answer the questions that burn within you now. I have absolute confidence in you, and I would like you to return now, please, to your studies.'

I did as he asked and spent many fruitless hours during the following days and weeks, trying to persuade suncatcher leaves to carry my intention to alleviate insomnia symptoms. Whenever I tuned into them after one of my attempts, however, they felt just the same as ever to me and I couldn't see that I'd managed to alter them one bit.

My riding sessions with Infinity settled into a predictable routine. I would get on, ask her to move forward and then we would alternate between being unbalanced and precariously balanced, until we were too tired to carry on. We appeared to have reached a plateau on which we were now stuck and I didn't know what to do about it.

Infinity barely communicated with me when I rode her. Her attention was always fully taken by the interaction between our physical bodies and how her own body was responding as a result, and she didn't appear to have room in her thoughts to volunteer anything that would help me figure out how we could progress further. She had no more to say on the subject in between riding sessions either.

'You're probably doing all you need to do, otherwise she'd tell you,' Rowena said as I complained of my frustration one evening over dinner. 'She looks amazing when you ride her, I know it's a bit stop and start but it must feel strange for her, moving in such a different way. I should think she'll need to build up the muscles in all of the right places before you can move on more. That's what Oak says he's doing anyway.'

'At least he tells you what he's doing so you know what's going on,' I grumbled.

'Oh, come on, you can be aware of what's going on in Infinity's body any time you choose, she knows it and so do you. She concentrates so hard when you ride her, Am, you can't see her face, but I can and those blue eyes of hers take on this burning look, as if there's nothing more important than what she's doing at that moment. You're doing what she needs you to do and for now you're just going to have to be content with it.'

I sighed. 'But there's just so much to do. Now I know we're aiming for "The Ultimate", I just want to get on and achieve it, even though I don't know exactly how riding will help us to reach it. And we need to be able to do it before the other Bonded finally get themselves organised and set off on their stupid hunt, if we're going to be able to stop them.'

'How do you mean?'

This was something that Justin, Quinta and I had concluded during a discussion earlier that day. 'They're not going to listen to what we say, but if we can somehow show them what the horses know, what we know now, that everything and everyone are all just parts of the same whole, maybe it will be enough to halt them in their plans, make them think about what they're doing.'

Rowena thought for a moment. 'Hmmm, I see what you mean. It wouldn't hurt to give Salom something other than just the events of "that day" to spread around either.'

'Salom? She's back here?'

'Yup, she and Pete arrived after lunch and she's revelling in all the drama. She's just going to love spreading it all far and wide.'

My heart sank. A Herald taking advance news to the world at large of the fear and hate that the majority of the Horse-Bonded now felt for the Woeful would be a disaster; there would be campaigns against the Woeful springing up everywhere and everything the Bonded of the past had achieved in helping the people of The New to stay on the path of human advancement would be at risk. 'Where is Salom? She needs to hear a different side of the story,' I said.

'Just find the crowds and Salom will be there, soaking up all the news and attention at the centre of it all.'

At that moment, the door burst open and Salom marched into the dining hall. 'Right, folks, the bandanna's coming off. I'll be staying in my usual room, so please feel free to drop in to collect or deliver messages after breakfast tomorrow, but for now, I'm tired, hungry and officially off duty.' She caught sight of Rowena and me, and made her way over. 'Amarilla, Rowena, how lovely to see you again. Amarilla, I have letters for you from your family and I must hear all of your news, it seems you and Infinity have continued to create a stir since my last visit.'

'I thought you were off duty,' said Rowena, leaning back against her chair and folding her arms.

'To the world at large, I am, but I always have time for my friends, and Pete and I both count Amarilla as one of those,' replied Salom, cheerily.

'It's funny how your friends always seem to be the people you think can give you the most gossip, isn't it,' retorted Rowena. 'I'm off to finish up in my workroom before bed. See you in the morning, Am.' She left before Salom had the chance to reply.

'I'll just grab some shepherd's pie and then I'll be back, if that's alright with you, Amarilla? Pete'll be along soon, he's just checking that the donkeys have everything they need for the night.'

I nodded, my mouth full of stewed apple. I wanted to finish my dessert before Salom returned, so that I could make her understand that on no account could she take the news of the planned Woeful hunt around to the villages.

Focus rather on the information that is beneficial to your fellow humans, Infinity advised me.

What do you mean? It was good to feel her attention back with me after all of her introspection and silence of the past few weeks.

That on which you focus your attention will flourish. Dwell not on that which is negative to human development. Devote your energy towards highlighting that which will enrich the human experience.

What, you mean I shouldn't mention the hunt? I shouldn't try and talk Salom out of spreading the news that will encourage everyone else to do the same?

It seemed that Infinity had said her piece and no more counsel would be forthcoming, however she fuelled my mind with love and, what was that I could sense, hope?

My mind raced as I saw Salom making her way back towards me. Focus on the positive, not the negative and then that will be the thing that gains momentum. The idea settled well within me. There was a lot of positive news to give Salom. I smiled to myself.

'I'm glad you're here, Salom, there's so much brilliant news to tell you, it's hard to know where to start,' I said as she sat down opposite me.

'Brilliant news? That's not what I've been hearing and I have to say, I'm more than a little surprised to find you so upbeat after what happened to Infinity, Amarilla. You've had a terrible time.'

'We had an incident here that was frightening and shook everyone up, but so much good has come out of it,' I replied. 'Shann was given the chance to reach his potential, I was given the opportunity to demonstrate that the Skills are all the same and that ANYONE can do them – just think of the excitement that will cause when everyone knows what's possible – and on top of all of that, we've been given the push that we needed to reach out to those who've been neglected for way too long. And you must come and watch what some of us are doing with our horses, we're just realising what's possible as a result of bonding with them and riding them, it's so exciting. You really couldn't have timed your visit here better.'

Salom had broken into a smile, but when I finished speaking, she shook her head and said, 'I'm sorry, but didn't Shann die? And when you talk of "reaching out to those who've been neglected", you can't, surely, mean the Woeful?'

I nodded. 'If they hadn't been forced to raid The Gathering, we'd never have had to face the fact that they suffer from living the way they do. Rather than seeing them as dangers to be feared, we need to see them as victims of The Old, and victims that we should be helping.'

'You can't be serious! After everything that happened? Your own horse was nearly killed for goodness' sake, how can you possibly be thinking of approaching them, let alone trying to help them? They're dangerous animals and the bane of my life as a Herald. Two donkeys I've lost to them in the last five years, Amarilla, that's two members of my family, not to mention all the extra distance we have to travel to avoid woodland. And wasn't Shann a friend of yours?'

I nodded, noticing that my heart had begun to beat arhythmically and slightly painfully in my chest. I could do this. 'He was. And I'm happy for him and grateful to the Woeful who not only helped him reach his potential, but helped him move on when it was his time. But just think, Salom, if we'd seen fit to welcome the Woeful into our communities generations back, given them a way to live that doesn't depend on hunting and raiding, then you would still have your donkeys and the incident here would never have happened.'

Salom shook her head. 'I can't believe I'm hearing this. Welcome them into our communities? They're dangerous. If they're capable of being civilised, why haven't they set up communities of their own, villages, like the people of The New had to when they first struck out on their own? Answer me that?'

'I don't know. But I can imagine how confusing it must have been for them. They were bred from different animals that all have different ways of living and different impulses, and in The Old, they were tightly controlled by their handlers. To be suddenly free, with no experience of having to find their own food and shelter, no experience of making decisions for themselves, and living according to their own instincts for the first time, it's amazing that they managed to survive at all. And the Woeful who killed Shann didn't consciously intend to do it, he was defending himself. I felt his regret and I KNOW we share common ground with them. They are mostly human, after all, everyone always seems to forget that.'

Salom looked searchingly into my eyes and shook her head slowly. Finally, she said, 'I'm probably going to regret asking this, but what exactly is it that you're doing with your horses?'

I winked cheekily. 'You'll just have to come along and see for yourself. The far riding paddock after lunch every day is where you'll find us. In the meantime, have a wander around and look at all the horses here. See if you can see any difference between the horses of Infinity's herd, and the others. See you tomorrow, Salom, I'll come for my letters once you're on duty.'

Was it my imagination, or was I having to help Infinity a little less today? I thought to myself. I counted her strides. One, two, three, four, five, six, seven, eight, nine steps before a little help from me was needed, that was four more strides than her previous best. Infinity was definitely keeping her balance for longer at a time. Her silent concentration of the past weeks had given way to suspense as she, too, registered that today was the day that things were feeling a little easier.

I had an increasing sense that she was waiting for me to do something. My mind worked its way around her body. She was gaining the strength and confidence now to lift her front end and hold it back off of her front legs more, but she still felt quite precarious, as if without me she could still topple forward. I thought back to one of my lessons with Feryl. Maybe some of his advice would work now? I waited a few seconds to see if Infinity would let me know what she thought, but she remained silent. Right, well I'd just have to give it a go then, I decided.

My heels nudged her firmly and then stayed pressed against her sides. Her ears flicked back towards me uncertainly as she tried to understand what I wanted from her, and then something jolted me from below... it was one of her hind legs! It had come further underneath her and I actually felt it pushing into the ground underneath where I was sitting.

Again, Fin. I nudged and held my heels against her sides again and her ears continued to flicker as she responded with another increased stride with her hind leg. *Again.* Another nudge. *And again.* I was asking every stride now, and as her hind legs repeatedly came further underneath her, it was beginning to feel as if Infinity was almost sitting on her hind end.

My chest was lifted and my thighs were now closed around her and pulling back firmly, hopefully giving her the assurance that I could help her to stay in balance as we moved forward with the increased momentum generated by her hindlegs. It wasn't quite enough, Infinity wasn't feeling secure. Fury began to roil within her and her ears flicked back and forth, broadcasting her anger.

There was no time for thought. I instinctively allowed my body to copy Infinity's; as she sat on her hindquarters further, I sat down more on my own. I sat into my pelvis and felt my body gain the extra stability and strength that would give my horse the security she needed. She was immediately aware of it and I felt her willingness to push herself further now that she knew my body was stable enough to support her own. Another, firmer nudge with my heels... and we had power.

Infinity's hind legs pushed into the ground beneath me with strength and intent, and as I felt her back lift and the power transfer along the length of her body, I realised that now her hind legs were far enough underneath her, she was sitting all of her weight and mine on her hindquarters; she was in perfect balance!

Infinity's anger was replaced abruptly with complete and utter joy as she bounced along in a new, powerful, balanced walk. Curiosity soon rose within her as she became eager to explore what her body could do. With no warning to me, she pushed herself up into a trot.

We were lighter than the spring air that moved in its gentle currents around us. I was distantly aware of birds singing and of Infinity's hooves landing lightly on the ground, but time slowed down as we trotted slowly, powerfully, effortlessly around the paddock. Infinity's body and mine were parts of the same beast, moving together, responding to one another and sharing awareness of something that I recognised but couldn't seem to place. Tears streamed down my face. I could hear cheering, but it seemed to come from somewhere that Infinity and I were only vaguely a part of. I lost awareness of it altogether when I felt something heavy and noxious begin to lift from my chest area and dissipate into the ether. My heart changed from beating uncertainly and uncomfortably, as it had been doing since my conversation with Salom the previous evening, to beating more strongly in my chest. More strongly and more confidently. I had a split second to register that Infinity's chest had opened in concert with my own, before Infinity roared.

I'd never heard a horse make a noise like that before and the emotion that accompanied it almost unhinged me. A small part of me was aware that we still trotted around and that my body acted seemingly on its own as it stepped in occasionally to help maintain the perfect balance Infinity was achieving. But most of my attention was taken up with the emotions that lashed at my mind; fury, disappointment, love, shame, self-pity, hope, worry and helplessness took hold of me in turn as they were released from Infinity's chest, like pus spurting from a freshly lanced boil.

All of a sudden, I was dragged back to full awareness of my physical body, as Infinity began to buck and heave beneath me. I was thrown forward onto her neck and then jolted back into my saddle as she followed her buck with a rear, roaring and shrieking in emotional agony. Then her head disappeared down between her front legs and she bounced around on all four legs, kicking out with her hind legs every so often as if trying to defend herself from an imaginary foe.

Infinity, stop it, let me help you. Calm down, I thought to her, grabbing large handfuls of mane in an attempt to stay on board. She paid me no heed. Her head came back up abruptly and we shot forward at speed, before she leapt up into the air, performing a powerful fly-buck. I remember feeling the power in her hindquarters as I was catapulted over her head. As I landed on the back of my left shoulder I felt her hooves thump into the ground by my head, before she thundered away. Excruciating pain shot through my shoulder and I thought I would vomit. My physical hurt paled into insignificance, however, compared with the emotional agony that wracked my horse.

'Amarilla, can you sit up? Justin, go after Infinity, she's going to do herself an injury,' said Rowena, kneeling down by my head.

'NO,' I yelled. 'LEAVE HER ALONE, PLEASE LEAVE HER ALONE.' I rolled onto my uninjured side, gasping with the pain. 'Help me up, Rowena, don't worry, we'll sort me out later, just help me up. NOW, PLEASE.' Hands helped me into a sitting position.

Marvel said, 'I can sort this right now, and then you'll be more use to Infinity. Lie back down and take a deep breath, Amarilla.' His huge hands guided me down onto my back and then enclosed my shoulder. There was a brief pressure on the front of my shoulder and light shot across my vision as the pain increased a hundred-fold for an instant. Then it was gone, and a dull ache took its place. 'Okay, let's help her to sit up.'

Infinity was still roaring. I got to my feet.

'Steady now, you're no good to Fin if you faint,' said Rowena, putting an arm around my waist. 'What on earth is wrong with her?'

My mare was throwing herself around over by the fence. She dripped with sweat and her eyes bore a look of pain such as I hoped never to see in her again. Not ever. Her reins were hanging down by her front legs.

Justin said, 'Amarilla, I need to try and get near her or she's going to get her legs caught in her reins and injure herself. Okay?'

I shook my head, knowing that Infinity needed her space. 'No, leave her, this is something she needs to do.'

Gas's thoughts whistled past me and Justin raised his eyebrows, but nodded and stepped back to stand beside his horse.

Infinity jerked her head up, throwing the reins further back up her neck and out of the way of her front legs. She screamed and lashed out with her left foreleg. She was a war horse, trained to obey her rider's demands instantly, whether that be kicking out behind, striking out in front, biting or galloping over anything in her way. She had suffered numerous injuries in her career to date, all of which had been tended and healed so that she may fight another battle, another day. This battle was the most ferocious she had experienced yet. She twirled at the slightest rein pressure on her neck from her rider, lashing out at anyone in her way as her rider hacked his sword at anyone she missed. Suddenly, the way in front was clear and she was spurred harshly on towards the next group of fighting men. Pain exploded in her chest as a spear found its way into one of her lungs. Her rider jumped clear as she fell, and continued to fight on foot, leaving her to die in fear and agony.

She was in a dark tunnel, pulling something heavy. She was thin, hungry and exhausted, and her harness had rubbed her raw in several places. She tripped on a stone in her path and faltered, and then felt acute agony as a whip lashed at her hindquarters. In the past she would have bucked or kicked out with a hind leg in protest, but now she had neither the will nor the energy. She merely lay down in her traces and left her body, feeling nothing but exhaustion.

Now she was being ridden at a flat-out gallop, panicked by the sound of dogs barking as they got closer and closer behind her. Her rider was someone with whom she was familiar but for whom she held no affection. He kicked her hard in the ribs to keep her going and she felt his own panic mirroring hers. She was at her limit. Her front feet and legs were painful and she couldn't get her breath. Blood flew from her nostrils but her rider kept pushing her. She collapsed mid-stride, crushing her rider, and left her body, feeling relieved.

She was carrying a heavy load of bricks in immense heat. She had a piece of wire through her mouth so that her handler could indicate where he wanted her to go, and it hurt her lips and her tongue. She was thirsty and her cracked feet hurt. But she stayed in her body as long as she possibly could, for love of the family who worked her. They lived in as much discomfort as she and depended on her to earn the meagre wage that they needed to survive, but above everything else, they loved her.

She felt the father's heart break every time he was forced to overload her so that he would be paid for the day's work. She felt the love of the children as they groomed her with their small hands at the end of every day. They rubbed sweat from her, washed the blood and flies from the many shallow wounds inflicted by her badly fitting harness, and hugged her before bed. When the day came that she was too weak to stand up, her family gathered around her, the father cradling her head, the mother stroking her muzzle and the children hugging her neck. Without her they would be destitute, yet their immediate concern was for her. She sent them all the love she could, but they couldn't feel it even as they sat and loved her back. She left her body, wishing she could have made them understand that everything was as it should be, that she would be alright, and that, when their times came, so would they.

She was being ridden by someone who loved what she could do for him but had no concern for her beyond his own ambitions. Crowds of cheering people scared her but she was held firmly in place by a harsh rein contact and a strong pair of legs at her sides. As the crowd went quiet, music started up and she responded to signals from her rider to move around and perform as she had been trained. Hope that she would be able to get her rider to pay attention to what she, and he, needed, rather than what he wanted, was long gone. She colicked in her stable later that day and left her body, feeling despondent.

The images came one after the other. She was being ridden by rider after rider, all day, every day, as they learnt to ride for their own enjoyment with no thought as to what she would like to get out of the interaction… She was put in foal too young to an enormous stallion and when she fell desperately ill after giving birth, her foal was taken from her and she was left to die… Lifetime after lifetime was spent carrying riders into battle… She was in front of cheering crowds once more, this time jumping obstacles for a rider who loved her but had no idea how to support her body so that she could jump without injury to herself… She was a wild horse, living on vast plains in a large herd. She had freedom from the shackles of living with humanity and it was a mostly serene existence, but she felt restless and unfulfilled and she left her body long before it would have expired naturally… Image after image flooded my mind and I began to grasp the enormity of how many lifetimes Infinity had lived and how many she had shared with humans, playing a long list of different roles as she waited for the time when humans would be open to the influence of horses – when they would realise that she and her kind could be of far more help than merely as beasts of burden, weapons of war or objects of pleasure.

In each and every lifetime that she had spent with humans, her chest area had been shut down as a result of being constantly pushed onto her forehand by her burdens, trapping unexpressed emotion which her soul then carried with it from lifetime to lifetime... until now.

I felt immense sorrow as I watched Infinity, who was now whinnying shrilly whilst trotting madly around. I tried to reach her with my mind, but she didn't register my thoughts. Her emotions ran wild and she didn't seem able to regain control of herself, either mentally or physically. My mind flicked back to all of the times when I'd been in a state of panic over my heart. I remembered how she'd drawn me to ride her, to lose myself in her calm concentration until I was grounded again. I knew what I needed to do. I left my dumbstruck friends where they stood with their horses and made my way over to Infinity. I noticed that the paddock fence was now lined with people.

'Amarilla, can Dili and I be of any help?' Mason called.

'Thanks, but we'll be alright,' I said over my shoulder.

As I approached my mare, I sent my love to her, enfolding her in it as she had done for me so many times. She snorted and came to a halt, trembling, her nostrils pink and flaring, her eyes wide and her head held high as sweat dripped from every inch of her.

Infinity, I can help. I let you help me, now you have to let me help you. You've waited so long to be able to do this and now I'm here for you. I concentrated on keeping myself calm and my thoughts even as I sent another wave of love to her. I took hold of her reins and she flinched as if I'd struck her. Hurt shot through me and my lip trembled before I got myself under control. *I'm going to get on your back, Fin, okay? I'm going to lead you over to the fence and then I'm going to get on your back.*

Her eyes looked at me but she didn't seem able to distinguish me from the images that were still replaying in her mind, one after the other after the other.

Come with me, Fin, come on. I began to lead her towards the fence, noticing that of all people, Feryl leant against the exact spot for which I was aiming. I found that I didn't care. Infinity and I were in the middle of something that mattered to her, to me, to all of us, and Feryl's opinions and insecurities were simply irrelevant.

'I see you've finally managed to drive that horse of yours mad, Amarilla,' he said loudly.

'Excuse me,' I said, and waited for him to give me space to climb the fence.

'No, I'm afraid I won't excuse you and I can't allow this to go on any longer. By all accounts, you've already suffered one injury and it's my responsibility…'

'I don't have time for you right now, Feryl, I just need you to move so I can get on and help my horse,' I said calmly.

'Help her? You call this helping her? You drove her to the point where she threw you, Amarilla. Now I'm very happy to get on and ride her myself, that way I can show you…'

'How to produce a shut down, unfulfilled horse like Liberal? You don't have a clue what's happening here, Feryl, and I don't have the time to explain it to you because my horse needs me, so if you'll excuse me…' I began to climb the fence, forcing him to take a step back. 'There's my girl, it'll be okay, Fin, just stand for me,' I said softly to Infinity, forcing Feryl out of my mind. If I were to be of use to my horse, there was no room for irritation, self-doubt, anger, or indeed any emotion from me.

I sat down in the saddle and when Infinity shuddered beneath me, I almost reassured her. No. When I had been the panic-stricken one, she had merely drawn me into our work with no reassurance, no emotion, not even acknowledgement of my anxiety. I took a slow, deep breath and made sure my body was ready and able to support hers. I nudged her forward and she responded hesitantly. I nudged her more firmly. We were going to move forward and back into balance, and that was all there was to it. She moved forward again and whinnied shrilly. After a fleeting internal struggle, I regained my calm composure and repeated my request, even more firmly this time. I felt a hind leg underneath me, then the other. I pushed her on, my intention firm now, my concentration absolute as my body stepped in to support Infinity's when needed. Haltingly and with a little prancing to the side at one point, we moved back into a precarious balance. A thought tried to take hold of me, that once we found the place where she was in perfect balance once more, when her chest was fully open, she could very well explode again, but I pushed it firmly away. No room. A drop of sweat ran down my face, tickling me, but I couldn't spare a hand to wipe it away. I asked for her to push just a little harder with her hind legs… and then she was back in her perfect balance.

Just for a little longer, Fin, then we'll finish.

We bounced along in a powerful walk, two parts of the same being, just as we'd been what seemed like hours earlier. There was no distinction between me and Infinity, or between us and anything else. We were all there ever had been and all there ever would be. I smiled as I remembered where I had first experienced that feeling. We were All That Is… we were… *infinite,* my horse agreed and slowed herself to a halt. *I am tired.*

I dismounted immediately. We had achieved The Ultimate! I stood by my horse with one arm over her neck, trying to relive the feeling of oneness I had just experienced. I was oblivious to the total silence that hung over the paddock, until the cheering and clapping erupted from all sides. Infinity and I both jumped at the noise, and she snorted. I stroked her sodden neck, noticing the pink of her skin showing beneath her wet fur, and came fully back to myself as I realised that my horse needed me to take care of her.

Rowena appeared by my side. 'That. Was. Amazing. I haven't got a clue what it was I just saw, but it was beautiful. You and Fin almost looked like, well like you were joined somehow and it made me all emotional.'

I nodded. 'I had no idea.'

'No idea about what?'

'About any of it. Rowena, you and the others, you have to push yourselves harder, you have to work harder to help your horses move in a better balance. Much better than they already are, I mean. They have to be able to open at the chest in order to clear...' I couldn't continue past the emotion that choked my throat.

'Clear what?'

Mason threw Infinity's rug over her back and Justin enfolded me in a warm hug. 'You're a brave girl, Amarilla,' he whispered, 'and in front of all these people too, but you did it. You really did it, I saw you and Infinity become one.'

I felt a squeeze on my arm as Rowena said, 'We'll talk later, Am, I'll wait for you by the gate.'

'We didn't do it in front of everyone on purpose,' I said to Justin, 'but then, everything does seem to happen as it should.'

He released me. 'Yes, I guess it probably does, doesn't it?'

I said, 'You know what Fin and I just achieved, yet I'm still here, aren't I?'

'You have more to do though, don't you? The two of you? More that stands between you and achieving your full potential?'

'I think so, I think today was just the beginning. But, Justin, even when we're nearly there, I won't be afraid, how could I be? What's there to fear about being aware of my place in things and feeling at one with my horse, with everything? After all, it's the truth, isn't it?'

He looked uncertain.

'Please do this with Gas, Justin, he deserves your best and you're not giving it to him. If you won't do it for yourself, do it for him. Infinity needs to rest now, are you and Gas coming?'

'No, we're going to stay here and work awhile. Will you be okay on your own?'

I nodded. 'Besides, I'm not ever on my own am I, not really?'

He grinned. 'No, I don't suppose you are.'

TWENTY-FIVE

Strengthening

$\mathcal{O}$ver the following weeks, our joint balance, strength and confidence improved with every riding session. Every now and then, another memory or emotion – to which Infinity's soul had held fast during lifetime after lifetime – found its way to the surface of her being and evaporated into the ether as the physical imbalance that had trapped it was corrected. Each release was accompanied by a buck, rear, spin, shy, or a combination of any of those manoeuvres, which was never comfortable for either of us, but I knew that I had to sit her cavorting as best I could and be there for her, calm and sure, so that once her outburst was over, she could use me to ground herself, just as she'd done for me so many times.

My friends increased their efforts at pushing their own horses to lift and sit back onto their hindquarters more after hearing my full account of what had happened with Infinity, and Salom didn't miss a single one of our riding sessions. Whatever the weather, she was there, watching and asking questions. She seemed oblivious that she was a constant source of annoyance for Rowena, but the rest of us were pleased at her interest – it meant that she was still at The Gathering, rather than spreading negative news to the villages and we hoped that she was beginning to understand what it was that we were trying to achieve.

We were all delighted when Norieva, Holly and Thuma asked if they and their horses could join our sessions, and we took it in turns to help them. None of them had been there when Infinity first began to release her past, but each told the same story; their horses, like all of the others, had been aware of what our group was attempting and as soon as they had felt Infinity progress to the point she had, they had informed their Bond-Partners that they wanted to join us. We all suspected that many other horses were making the same demands of their own partners, as increasing numbers of people were coming to watch us ride.

Adam made a point of riding around the perimeter of our riding paddock at the end of each session, talking to everyone who had been watching us and making sure they knew that anyone who wanted to come and ride with us would be very welcome. Every few days after the first three came to join us, one or two more horses and riders arrived to ride with us and the paddock, large as it was, began to get a little crowded – a fact of which I was possibly the most keenly aware, since Infinity and I needed the most space to allow for her periodic explosions.

'How are we supposed to concentrate with all these people making all of this noise?' complained Rowena one day.

'I find that... ooooof... Infinity keeps me from getting too distracted,' I replied as Infinity sidestepped and bucked. As I felt another previously trapped trickle of emotion leave her, I forgot all about Rowena and gave her all of my attention.

Infinity's latest release was over almost as soon as it had begun and we moved on to practise being able to maintain a powerful, balanced trot. It fascinated me that balance could be such a precarious thing; Infinity was now capable of reaching such a perfect physical balance that the toxic emotions of her past were fast running out of places to hide within her – and judging by how my heart function was steadily improving, my own balance wasn't far behind – yet something as innocuous as a bump in the ground was enough to throw us both off balance completely. But we worked on, trying our best to stay on our circle as we worked around the other riders.

Justin and Gas crossed in front of us and I realised with a jolt that Gas was looking better. His neck was arched, his withers lifted and he walked forward powerfully and purposefully, a world away from his old, joggy walk. My heart leapt. With Infinity taking up so much of my attention, and all the new riders teeming around in the paddock, it had been a while since I'd really noticed how any of my friends were doing. I turned Infinity alongside Gas and asked her to slow to a walk.

'Gas is looking fantastic,' I told Justin.

He grimaced. 'I'm doing my best, but Gas is frustrated that we're not moving on with this faster. I'm trying, Am, but I'm only asking of him as much as I dare and it's not enough, I know it isn't. He wants me to push myself and him further, he wants to achieve the same level of balance as Infinity but I'm too much of a coward.'

'You're asking more than you dared to ask before, aren't you? You must be, or else Gas wouldn't have changed so much. And as time goes on, you'll push yourself and him harder, and you'll get there, I know you will.'

'Get where though? I don't have your courage, Am. You don't hold anything back when you help Infinity to move like that, but I can't do it. I'm terrified I'll lose myself if I give everything the way you do, and I'm letting Gas down.'

'Stop letting him down then, it's that simple.'

'No, it isn't.'

'Yes, it is. You're choosing to see being in balance with your horse and truly being at one with him as a threat to your individuality and to your life. Choose differently.'

'I can't just…'

A roar interrupted him. Infinity and Gas both stopped in their tracks and I could feel Infinity's heart thumping against my left leg. It was a horse's roar, similar to the one Infinity had issued weeks back, but deeper. All of the horses and riders around us had also come to a halt, and each and every horse had their ears pricked, eyes bulging and nostrils flared. Then, to a horse, they all relaxed and turned their attention back to their riders.

'That's Spider,' said Justin and nudged Gas in the direction of noise. Infinity and I followed them.

All of the other horses and riders had moved away from Spider as he bucked, spun, reared, kicked out behind, struck out in front and occasionally shot forward before grinding to a halt and leaping around again, roaring and screaming all the while. Adam, though, stuck fast. Wherever Spider launched his body, Adam's body went with him, seemingly without effort. He sat in his saddle wearing an expression of relaxed concentration and I felt my shoulders, which I'd hitched up in tension when I'd first caught sight of what was happening, relax back down. It seemed that Adam had helped Spider to reach the same level of balance as Infinity, with the same result and he appeared to have grasped instantly what he needed to do to help his horse. Spider would be okay. I looked around for Quinta and saw her standing over by the fence on her own, her face wet with tears. I jumped down from Infinity's back and we went to stand with Quinta.

'I h-had no idea,' she said.

I put an arm around her shoulder. 'The main thing is, we're helping them to release it all now and Adam's doing brilliantly, much better than I did. He's really amazing, isn't he?'

'Yes, he is. I'm glad it was him that helped Spider get to this point, he's a much better rider than I am. I'd have either sat there panicking or been thrown by now. I don't know why Spider asked for me to ride him as well, really.'

'There'll be a good reason for it, you know that,' I murmured, mesmerised by Adam's capability to maintain his balance, physically and emotionally, as Spider's explosions showed no sign of letting up.

Rowena appeared. 'He's really something, isn't he?'

'Spider or Adam?' said Quinta, trying to smile.

'Well, both I guess. I tell you what though, I think we're about to see a bit of an increase in riders asking to join us.'

'Really?' I said.

'Think about it, Am. Those not already riding with us are either in firm denial, or are sitting on the fence, literally, dithering about it. Now they've seen that you and Adam, the two most unlikely people here, have had the guts to go for it and support your horses through the discomfort of making changes, they've got absolutely no excuse for not taking the plunge and doing the same for their own horses.'

'Two most unlikely people?' I said, amused.

'You're the youngest and least experienced rider here, and Adam is the oldest and most likely to really hurt himself, yet neither of you have let that hold you back. I think you may now have to get used to your new status as an inspiration.' She grinned wickedly at me.

'Give it time, I'll be back to being the resident troublemaker before you know it,' I said.

Spider was tiring now. Adam stroked his neck with one hand, talking quietly to him as he easily sat the half-hearted bucks and leaps to the side that Spider still gave every now and then. Spider's coat was dark with sweat and his nostrils flared pink as hot breath and droplets of water were expelled in regular, violent bursts.

Adam smiled at Quinta as he and Spider jogged past. 'Just a little while longer, the worst is over now,' he said. He set about helping Spider to find his perfect balance once more. It didn't take long before he reached it and instantly, I was unable to distinguish Adam and Spider as being separate from one another. Judging by the collective gasp that emanated around the paddock, I wasn't the only one who could see it. Adam slowed Spider to a halt and dismounted.

Quinta ran to them, quickly hugging Adam before throwing a rug over Spider and rubbing his neck muscles with her hands. There was clapping and cheering all around.

'Adam, that was beautiful to watch. You and Spider merged together and everyone saw it, not just me,' I said.

'Well, now that they've seen two of us reach that state, let's hope it spurs more of them to do the same with their own horses. It's truly a privilege, isn't it?' His eyes filled with tears, and he was unashamed as one broke free and traced its way down his old, weathered cheek.

My own eyes filled in response. 'Yes, it is. Everyone saw me and Fin blur together like that?'

He nodded. 'Did no one mention it?'

'Justin did, but he's been able to see it before as he's...' I stopped, suddenly unsure if I were about to share information that was private.

'... close to being there already and has been for a very long time, I think,' Adam whispered. He gave my arm the gentlest of squeezes and then followed Spider as Quinta led him back to his paddock. I saw many people leave the fence to follow him and chuckled to myself.

'That was a spectacular sight to behold. What gives, Amarilla?' Marvel asked, arriving with Justin, Mason and their horses.

'I think Adam's about to find himself much less able to lurk in the background,' I said. 'He likes to play the part of an old man messing around and having a little fun in the years he has left, but after that display of talent, I don't think his little charade is going to wash with anyone anymore. Spider's well and truly exposed him.'

Wicked grins spread slowly across the faces of all three men, but Rowena merely nodded. 'It's scary, isn't it?'

'What is?' I asked.

'There's nowhere to hide. That's twice I've seen it now and it scares me.'

'I'm not with you,' I said.

She sighed. 'Adam isn't the only one who's been exposed, Am. When you got back on Infinity after she threw you, you gave her all of your focus, all of your energy, everything you had. It was obvious to everyone who saw it. And in doing that, you lost all ability to hide anything of yourself, just as Adam did just now. You both gave everything and in doing so, revealed yourselves as you really are. Adam's at complete ease with himself. He's strong, confident, capable and balanced. You aren't any of those things yet, at least not completely, but your determination and love for Fin override anything you lack, and you'll push yourself way past your capabilities, way past your knowledge and experience, past your fear even, to give her what she needs. It took me a while to really understand what it was I saw when you and Infinity had your episode, but now I do, especially after seeing Adam for who he really is, and it scares me.'

Justin, Marvel and Mason had all dismounted and come closer so as to hear Rowena better. I looked pointedly at Justin and raised my eyebrows.

He took a deep breath. 'I'm scared too, more scared than I've ever been about anything. You worry about people seeing who you really are inside, Rowena, I worry about losing myself altogether.'

'It's a right wasp's nest we've disturbed, ain't it,' said Mason, 'and I'll say one thing for nothin', I think we need to go back to ridin' in our own little group and we need to split that lot,' he hiked a thumb over his shoulder, 'into groups of their own, if we're goin' to be of help to them. I'm thinkin' that we and the horses are all goin' to need more space than we've had of late.'

~

We all agreed that Mason's idea was a good one, although some of us confessed to being nervous; helping other riders by offering hints and suggestions as we passed each other in the riding paddock was one thing, but putting them into groups and helping them from the ground in a more formal way was something completely different.

It was decided that Justin and I would take one group, Rowena and Marvel another, Quinta and Mason the third, and the remaining riders and their horses would be taught by Adam alone. He protested at the idea when we put it to him, saying that he'd barely ridden in years and no one would want to listen to a silly old man, but his objections were met by silent, amused stares from all of us and then Marvel said, 'Brilliant, so we're all in agreement then.'

Adam threw his hands into the air, pretending to be offended at being ignored. The twinkle never left his eyes though and after we'd finished our own riding session the following day, I noticed that he walked with a very definite purpose as he made his way to the paddock in which he would be teaching.

Justin and I were to be teaching in the farthest paddock by my request, as I hoped that by doing so we'd draw the fewest spectators. As we passed the other riding paddocks, we saw that Adam already had his students riding in a large circle around him, Rowena was talking animatedly to her and Marvel's group while Marvel stood nodding in agreement, and Mason and Quinta appeared to be checking the fit of their student's bridles before beginning their own session.

'They'll never listen to me, I'm too young and inexperienced and hardly any of them even like me,' I said to Justin.

'They've seen what you and Infinity are capable of. They'll listen,' said Justin firmly.

You merely need speak of what you know. You are ready, Infinity assured me.

My heart twinged uncomfortably, a mere echo of the pain and wild lurching it had performed in the past, but enough to remind me that I still had cause to push myself as firmly as I'd been willing to push Infinity. *I'm ready,* I attempted to affirm to her and to myself, but when my heart gave another twinge, I knew that I didn't completely believe it.

'How are we going to begin?' I asked Justin.

'I think you should talk about what you've done with Infinity, as they won't have heard the full story. Then we'll check their bridles look okay and get them riding, shall we? I think we'll probably be able to see where we need to go from there.'

'Can't you do the talking?' I said.

'I feel a fraud even attempting to help them with their riding, let alone telling them they need to be aiming for something I haven't got the guts to do myself. No, Am, I'm afraid it's going to have to be you.'

I sighed and my heart twinged and then began to thump madly as I saw how many spectators we had, on top of the ten riders who waited patiently with their horses. I attempted a smile and noticed that my lips were trembling. They seemed to do that a lot these days.

You are ready, Infinity whispered in my mind.

I found myself entering the paddock to stand in front of our students. My mind went blank. I reached for my horse and found her sitting quietly at the back of my mind, much as she had done when I'd needed space to converse with Diligence. She was there, I reassured myself. I could do this. My heart twinged again and my confidence faltered.

Thankfully, Justin stepped in. 'Afternoon, everyone, it's good to see you all here. Amarilla and I will do our best to help you and your horses as much as we can, but I think before we start, it would be good if each of you would tell us what made you ask to join us and what you and your horses are expecting from us. Aleks?' He motioned with his hand towards a slim, curly-haired man of middle years who looked rather nervous as he stood next to a rangy grey mare with a dull coat and pronounced hollows above her eyes.

'Oh, um, well, I kind of didn't have a choice. Not that I'm not glad to be here of course, it's just that without Nexus telling me…' He paused and then continued, 'To tell you the truth, I've been interested in what you've been doing ever since you took yourselves off and started doing things your own way, but, well, Feryl's always been really good to me. Anyway, I think it's fair to say that Nexus has been waiting for me to realise what my priorities are and when I saw you and Infinity do what you did a few weeks back, Amarilla, something just clicked inside me. Nexus felt it and told me that we were to ask you to help us, so here we are.'

Of the remaining nine riders, five had a similar story to Aleks's, two of them had been impressed by what Adam had had to say on his and Spider's rounds of the paddock fence and the other two had only recently returned to The Gathering from their travels, and had asked to join our group as soon as they had caught up with everything that had been going on. They all looked from me to Justin expectantly.

'Okay, well before we start, Amarilla is going to tell you all exactly what we've been attempting with our horses and more specifically, the stage she and Infinity have reached. Am?'

My heart twinged more strongly. I clenched my fists and began to sweat. Infinity did no more than increase her presence in my mind slightly. No reassurance, no nurturing energy enfolding me to keep me safe, no advice. She was confident I could do this.

'Well, um, it's hard to know where to start, really,' I said.

'It all began when Infinity wasn't happy in your first riding lessons, didn't it?' Justin said.

'Er, kind of, I mean things felt all wrong from the first time I sat on Infinity, when we were chased by a Woeful on our way here and she ended up falling, but I just thought that happened because I didn't know how to ride. But then when we started our riding lessons, Infinity still couldn't carry me without being pushed down onto her front legs and when that happened, her chest area became compressed and she shut down…'

I talked and I talked and I talked. Miraculously, I found that as soon as I was talking about something I cared about so much, speaking my truth was easy. When I finally stopped talking, I looked over at Justin, who gave a hint of a wink and said, 'Any questions, anyone?'

In the silence that followed, I felt for Infinity and sensed her satisfaction. No one spoke for what seemed an eternity. Finally, a red-haired lady called Sonja, whom I knew to be a Weather-Singer, said, 'Amarilla, thank you for telling us what you have. I am ashamed to say that I came to my own, mostly false, conclusions about what your group was up to, without knowledge of all the facts, and that has been to my and Bright's detriment.' She rubbed the neck of her dark bay stallion who responded by leaning into her touch. I sensed his thoughts, light but direct as he communicated with her. 'I know, everything at the right time, hey boy,' she said, hugging him. 'Anyway, I was wondering if you could explain what exactly is happening when you and Infinity seem to kind of meld together? I've been watching you closely over the past few weeks and I've noticed that it happens at the times when Infinity is high in front and has her hind legs really underneath her, when she's in perfect balance, if I understand you correctly. She looks, well you both look... beautiful.' Sonja's lips trembled. I tried to swallow the lump that had formed in my throat as Sonja's emotion stimulated my own.

Infinity increased her presence in my mind. *Your tendency to be overly emotional is not helpful at this time.*

I grinned and retorted, *Given your own emotional tendencies at the moment, I'm not sure you're in the best position to criticise, Fin.* I sent her a wave of love that I hoped would soften my teasing.

As my attention returned to Sonja, I found her looking at me with a confused expression. 'Oh, sorry, Infinity had something to say that made me smile,' I said and Sonja smiled warmly at me. 'To answer your question, you're seeing exactly what I feel. Infinity can only be balanced in her body when I'm balanced in mine. When we're both in balance within our own bodies and with each other, there are no barriers between us, it's as simple as that. We're at one with each other and with everything else. The problem we're having is that we can't maintain it for very long at a time.'

'Why not? What happens?' asked Aleks.

'Sometimes Infinity releases something and gets emotional and then she loses concentration and we have to start again. Sometimes she loses her balance when she doesn't quite step underneath herself enough, if she's worried about going down a slope or something. Sometimes I lose my balance a bit and then Infinity doesn't feel supported enough to maintain her own.'

The twinges in my heart were very faint now. Infinity increased her presence in my mind until her expectation and absolute confidence that I would know what to say next was all I had room to be aware of.

I said, 'You need to understand that this isn't all just about learning how to ride your horses better. It's about developing a partnership with your horse where you will help each other to find balance and strength, and not just physically, but mentally and emotionally as well. When you find it, you and your horses will release the negative aspects of yourselves that you don't need anymore. You will evolve.'

Infinity was triumphant. I looked around at the riders and spectators and saw that my words appeared to have hit home. Everyone looked thoughtful, some looked frightened and some were tearful, but on a lot of faces I saw eyes bright with excitement. The air was thick with all the thoughts that flew around as horses and their Bond-Partners communicated. I looked over at Justin and held a hand up at hip height, hoping he would understand that I thought we should be quiet for a while. He moved to stand close to me and I felt his hand envelop mine.

'Nice one, Am,' he murmured and then his touch was gone.

Our first teaching session passed in a blur. After a brief bridle check, we had everyone riding a circle around us while Justin explained about experimenting with the rein contact until they found one with which their horses felt comfortable. We watched half of the riders each and called out anything we thought might be helpful. By the end of the session, everyone had managed to find a contact that their horse felt was supportive without being restrictive.

'Okay, so if you can all practise by yourselves tomorrow, we'll see you back here in two days, same time,' Justin called out and was met by agreement and thanks from everyone. He turned to me. 'Well, I think that went well, don't you?'

'Better than well, it was fantastic. Did you see how hard all the horses were concentrating? They're so happy to be doing this, they'll all be looking better in no time.'

'Excuse me,' a voice said from behind me. I turned to find four people standing there, none of whom I knew. 'We were wondering if we could join your group?'

'We've got another five starting tomorrow and I think once they start, there'll be another ten or so that will follow. I know their circle of friends and the others won't be left out for long,' said Quinta as she sat down that evening with her dinner tray. 'I can't believe how well this is going. Thank goodness, it'll be so much harder for any of them to be involved in the plans to hunt the Woeful once they're focusing on working with their horses, and it'll be impossible for them even to think of it when they start getting close to the stage where Amarilla and Adam are. Everything seemed so impossible back in the winter and only a few months on, I'm starting to think we can really turn things around.'

The other lessons had all gone every bit as well as ours. It seemed that we would now be teaching a session every day in order to keep the groups small enough that everyone would get enough help, and soon we'd have to teach two sessions some days. It would mean that we'd be sorely pressed to get our share of the chores done, but none of us minded. We were all high on the excitement of knowing that we were doing something that really mattered to the horses and their riders.

By agreement with Adam, it had been some time since I'd done any work on my herb journal; I'd found Infinity's comment that I'd need time for her statement "there is little difference between discovery and creation" to sink in, to be a gross understatement and had seen little point in continuing with my studies until I had a clearer understanding of what she meant. I therefore began to use my mornings to do as many chores as I could, both mine and those of my fellow instructors, who weren't able to forego their skilled jobs to catch up with chores as easily as I could. Whether I filled in one hour or three for one of my friends, I felt that I was helping at least a little, and repaying what they had done for me every time I'd had to run to my horse when my heart had been giving me so much trouble. And it gave me time to think.

While I scrubbed pots, mopped floors, unloaded supply wagons, carried clean towels to the bathrooms, fetched firewood to the kitchens, laid food out at mealtimes, chopped vegetables and fed the sheep, I spent time considering each bonded pair under Justin's and my instruction, thinking about where they were in their training, what help they might need in their next lesson, and who of the two of us was better placed to do it.

I also got into the habit of running through my latest riding session with Infinity in my head, analysing what I'd been doing when we were in balance, how I'd been feeling about things, how my body had been functioning and what I needed to concentrate more on in our next session, in order to achieve more of that blissful oneness with my horse – with All That Is – that I now craved.

And when I'd run out of horse-related things to think about, I thought about all the outstanding problems in my apprenticeship. I still had no idea which herbs would help either insomnia or stomach ulcers. So far, I'd failed to identify the secret ingredient in Adam's combination cream he'd given me for my face after Rowena had punched me, and I couldn't think where to start. Adam's use of suncatcher still eluded me and yet seemed to be so close to my grasp, and Infinity's assertion about discovery and creation was driving me nuts.

As I churned all of these things over and over in my mind, day after day, an inkling formed in my mind that the answers to all of my dilemmas were connected. Sometimes I felt as if I were just on the verge of realisation and I would stand bolt upright, dropping whatever I was doing as I waited for the answer to become clear in my mind... only to find that all thoughts disappeared completely, leaving me angry and frustrated.

You try too hard to remember what you already know, Infinity informed me on one such occasion.

But how will I know what I know without trying to remember?

Trust yourself. When you and I find balance you lift the veil that you pulled down when you incarnated as a human and you experience the truth. You know what the horses know. You know we are all one with everything that is. We have all of the answers to all of the questions. You will remember what you need at such time that you can truly understand it.

It'll be when I'm riding you, won't it?

Maybe. Not necessarily. Your body is changing. It will not be long before you can clear the last of that which holds you back. When that happens you will be able to experience truth at will without needing me.

I'll always need you, Fin.

Your thought comes from emotion rather than truth.

Right, well, while we're on that topic, how come it's ok for you to be emotional but not me?

Emotion can be necessary at the appropriate time. Fear can provide the body with motivation to protect itself. Anger can signal that a boundary needs to be established for the good of all. Joy signals that a worthwhile experience should be repeated. All animals make use of emotion in order to gain the most from their bodily experience. Humans alone choose to experience excess emotion as a form of indulgence.

Oh. Well how do I know when I'm experiencing appropriate emotion and when I'm just indulging myself?

It is a distinction most humans find difficult. It is useful to ask yourself whether your emotion is serving a purpose. If you fail to think of one then it is an indulgence best foregone.

I brought the thought of not needing Infinity to the forefront of my mind and once more felt fear and sorrow. I'd be alone. Never mind that I wouldn't need her, I'd always want to be with her. The thought of going back to life as it had been before I found her was intolerable, and tears filled my eyes.

There is yet much work to do, Infinity noted.

TWENTY-SIX

Infinity

a few weeks on, and Infinity and I were going from strength to strength, literally. Infinity would achieve perfect balance within her first few strides and I was becoming used to the gasps that would emanate from onlookers as my beautiful mare powered her way around the riding paddock. She committed everything that she had to each powerful stride, as did I.

I sat deeply into my pelvis now and revelled in the feeling of security that gave me, not just in the saddle but within myself. Occasionally, the tiniest trickle of emotion would still leave Infinity's body, but she no longer felt the need to perform any of her explosive accompanying manoeuvres.

The same couldn't always be said, however, if a spectator happened to cough as we passed by, if a bird flew out of a nearby tree, or if a leaf dared to rustle in the wind. One minute we would be trotting with purpose and concentration, the next we would be airborne, before landing somewhere else entirely. I had to use all of my strength and balance in order to stay on board when she spooked like that and she would snort her affront if I wasn't quite where she expected me to be by the time she was ready to carry on.

Uncomfortable as it was when she reacted that way, I couldn't blame her; when she and I were in perfect balance, we were so absorbed in our connection with one another that we were far less aware than usual of what was going on physically around us. With any small loss of balance, we would be jolted fully back to the physical reality and it was at these moments that any sort of disturbance nearby seemed magnified a hundredfold.

The day arrived when we finally managed to achieve our perfect balance whilst cantering. We also experienced our first major spook whilst travelling at increased speed, as a result of Feryl choosing to pick the fight that had been brewing ever since my friends and I had taken it upon ourselves to give riding instruction.

We had been expecting it for a while. Feryl was Master of Riding and we were now not only going against his instruction, but giving our own to students that were formally his. We had agreed that there was going to be a tantrum of epic proportions at some point, and none of us were under any illusions that the focus of that tantrum would be anyone but me.

'Let him say his piece until he's exhausted himself and then just carry on, Amarilla,' Quinta had advised.

'No way, you know how he'll speak to you, give him as good as you get, Am,' Rowena argued.

'It's a shame the man's too pig-headed to sit down and talk about this with us,' Mason said. 'He looks terrible and so does his horse, and those of all his friends, I just don't understand any of them.'

'I think he's way past the point of reason. He's hurt, angry and he's lost most of the kudos he's so dependent on. We're all here to support you, Am, you know that, but, if I were you, I'd be practising with that light shield thing you do,' was Marvel's advice. 'Focus on protecting yourself while he has his rant. You have no need to justify what we're doing, the results we're getting with the horses are doing that.'

The human need to feel special has a lot to answer for, I thought to Infinity. She carried on her mutual grooming with Oak without comment.

'The chances are he'll do it while you're either riding or teaching, and I'll be alongside you during both, so don't worry, we'll face him down together,' Justin said.

'What do you think, Adam?' Rowena asked.

'I think that whatever needs to happen will happen,' Adam replied, winking at me.

Feryl did, indeed, pick his moment. I was revelling in the strength and balance of Infinity's body as the three-time beat of her canter stayed rhythmical and sure beneath me. I felt the tiniest hint of emotion leave her and realised that she was finally free of all the elements of her past that had been trapped within her for so long. Infinity's forequarter began to drop very slightly as we went down a slight incline, and as my body effortlessly corrected her small loss of balance, I felt my chest open the fraction it needed to for my body to be able to reach its own perfect balance. We were a part of everything, and yet everything ceased to exist. We were one, we were infinite and we needed nothing other than the blissful awareness of that truth.

Just then, someone began to clap loudly, directly in front of us. Infinity stopped dead in her tracks and spun to the right, her heart thumping wildly, and I came close to leaving the saddle. We turned back to see that Feryl was spreading his hands far apart in between each clap so that his movements were unmissable and so that the resulting noise was as loud as possible.

He looked dreadful. His hair was now shoulder length and greasy, and greyer than I remembered. He was clean shaven but his face was drawn and he had dark circles under his piercing blue eyes. Judging by the way his clothes now looked baggy on him, he had lost weight. As soon as he saw me looking at him, he climbed through the fence, still clapping. Salom was standing next to the spot he had vacated with an avid expression on her face.

'Am, do you need me?' Justin called out worriedly behind me.

'I'm fine thanks, don't worry,' I replied.

Feryl stopped halfway between Infinity and the fence and I realised that his words were going to be as much for the spectators as for me. 'Well, at least this time you didn't fall off, let's have a round of applause for Amarilla, everyone.'

A few people clapped, but other than that there was silence. I waited for the terror to begin; the tightness in my throat, the shaking, the sweating at the thought of having to stand up for myself, but nothing happened.

'Now tell us, Amarilla, in front of the captive audience that we all know you crave, tell us all, what gives you – who hadn't even sat on a horse this time last year, and who, let's be honest, still finds it hard to sit on one for any length of time without hitting the deck – the right to TEACH MY STUDENTS?' He was hysterical, there were no two ways about it.

I still didn't feel scared or underconfident and I didn't even feel angry that Feryl had given Infinity such a fright. I was aware of Feryl as if he were me. I felt everything he was feeling. He was angry, he was tired and he was lonely, oh so lonely; he had held himself back from Liberal so as to protect himself from the things he couldn't face and he missed his horse desperately. But above all, he was frightened. Frightened that he was wrong. Frightened that he wasn't everything he thought he should be. Frightened that he didn't know as much as one in his position should. My heart went out to him.

I dismounted and walked over to Feryl, Infinity at my side. Feryl fidgeted where he stood and then took a step back. I mustered as much light as I could and pushed it outside of me, but instead of surrounding myself with it, I sent it to Feryl and allowed it to settle gently around him. I was surprised at how easy I found it and how natural a thing it seemed to do. His shoulders lowered slightly and I saw his jaw relax.

'Feryl, there's no need to be frightened,' I said quietly. 'Everything you've always taught was right and is still very much needed by everyone here, it's just that we've found a few extra things that can really help the horses. I know you can see how Infinity can balance now, and the effect it has on us both, and we couldn't have got there without some of the things you taught me. We couldn't have done it without you, Feryl.'

His anger faded visibly, allowing exhaustion to take over. His piercing eyes flicked constantly between my own and he looked desperate to believe me.

I tried again. 'Feryl, please come and ride with us. Between your knowledge and what we've learnt from our horses, we can help so many more people and horses so much more quickly, including Liberal. He misses you as much as you miss him, you know he does.'

At that, Feryl's shoulders sagged and all the fight left him completely. Infinity moved close to him and rested her head on his shoulder, blowing softly into his ear. He slowly lifted a shaking hand to her muzzle and rubbed it gently. 'What have I done?' he whispered. 'Liberal, what have I done?'

Immediately, Infinity lifted her head, her ears pricked, and turned in the direction of the buildings. A horse was whinnying loudly and soon hoofbeats could be heard pounding against the ground. Infinity whinnied back so shrilly that I was forced to block my ears. *Liberal comes,* she informed me.

People who had been watching from the gateway moved to make way for Feryl's tall, black stallion.

Liberal looked a shadow of his former self, but even though he was underweight with a dull coat and eyes that looked too prominent in his beautiful, delicate head, he made an impressive sight as he jumped the gate and cantered up to where Feryl stood looking utterly defeated. Infinity whickered in her throat, but Liberal ignored her. He came to a graceful halt in front of his Bond-Partner and then proceeded to sniff each of his hands in turn, whilst communicating with him at what felt like hurricane speed. Feryl looked at him with misery in his eyes. I continued sending him as much light as I possibly could.

Silence hung over the paddock but the air was charged with anticipation. Eventually, Feryl reached a hand up tentatively to rub the side of Liberal's face and I saw a glimmer of a smile on his lips. He took a step closer to his horse and put both arms up around his neck, burying his face in Liberal's mane. I heaved a sigh of relief. Everything was going to be alright.

All of a sudden, my heart lurched violently in my chest and an indescribable pain seized me. At least it tried to. My heart continued to lurch and it was as if it dodged the pain, giving it nowhere to anchor itself. It wasn't really a physical pain, I realised as I clutched hold of my chest with my left arm. It was the pain of a hurt that had lasted ages but now had no place to be. I didn't need it anymore! As soon as that thought came into my mind, I felt the pain begin to leave.

Infinity's love infused me as I screamed. I felt the hurt in all its ferocity as bit by bit, it left my body. I wanted to run away but my legs were so weak that I had to put an arm over Infinity's neck to steady myself. The pain continued to leave my body like a deep breath being slowly exhaled and I didn't know what to do with myself. I wanted to knock myself out, anything to avoid having to feel what I was feeling.

'Am, what is it? Tell me?' Rowena's frantic voice was by my ear. All I could do was scream.

'Ro, leave her, she's alright I think, well she will be, Infinity's all she needs right now. She's just doing what Infinity and Spider did. Leave her,' I heard Justin say urgently.

The last of the pain left me and my knees buckled. It seemed an eternity before I hit the ground and, on my way down, as the blurred images of my surroundings seemed to pass my eyes in slow motion, realisation hit me. I had reached the point Infinity had told me I would. My body had changed to the point where I could maintain my physical and emotional balance on my own and as such, I'd been capable of seeing how things really were when I spoke to Feryl. I'd known what the horses know; he was as much a part of me as I was of him and of everyone else. We were all part of the same... part of the infinite, we WERE THE INFINITE.

All of this time, I'd thought I needed to be able to stand up for myself, to be able to make myself heard, but now I'd reached a place of understanding, of knowing that it wasn't about any of that. It was about knowing the truth for myself, knowing it so deeply, so unequivocally, that being right and being heard didn't matter. Instead of arguing with Feryl, I had loved him and given him what he needed... and it had been enough. I was aware briefly of Infinity's pride, her love for me, before I hit the ground and everything went black.

I was floating in a vast greyness and I could feel Infinity very close by. Cords of varying thickness seemed to be running from where I floated to where my body lay, and I probed at them with my consciousness. The thickest one felt strong and seemed to be pulsing.

Do not disrupt that one until you have decided where we go from this point forward, came Infinity's thought. It resonated throughout my consciousness and I wondered at how I'd ever been content with the muted connection we'd had whilst in our bodies. I turned my attention to the next thickest of the cords, which ran from me to my body's heart and appeared to be wavering in and out of existence. *That one you can clear. You have done everything you needed to resolve the issue that gave your physical heart so much pain. It is no longer needed.*

Why was I so hesitant? Thought was all there was and as a result, my confusion was all-consuming.

She Who Is Infinity. You do not need that any longer. Clear it. Infinity's warm encouragement eclipsed my confusion and I turned my attention towards the cord, at the point where it was attached to my body's heart. I wrapped myself around it and pulled until it came free. It flickered and reeled back to me. I welcomed it and as it became part of me, I felt stronger and more whole.

I noticed now that the remaining cords were more like threads, thin and weak, but they were consistent in their existence.

You will resolve those swiftly but they are for another time. Another lifetime if you so choose, Infinity advised me.

For the first time, I thought about the significance of the fact that my body lay somewhere else and I didn't appear to be in it. *Are we dead?*

We are never dead. You know this.

Well, I'm not in my body, are you in yours?

Partly as is always the way for my kind. Worry not. Your body sleeps for now. You have a choice. You have reached the potential you set for yourself before incarnating into your human body this lifetime. All you need do is sever the tie to your body and you will be free to move on.

But what about you?

If you choose to leave this incarnation then I will leave also.

Do you want to?

I have no preference.

And if I choose not to leave?

Then you and I will return to our lives as Bond-Partners. There is much that we can achieve. You will be one of the first humans capable of fully expressing your soul through your personality. It will be interesting to witness the consequences.

I allowed myself time to consider. I was feeling the deep sense of fulfilment that I remembered experiencing hundreds of times before. It was the feeling of leaving a lifetime having accomplished what I'd set out to do. Immediately, I remembered all those other times when I'd left feeling despondent or full of regret after having done just the opposite, and grief at those memories overwhelmed me. I felt a gentle pulling of my consciousness.

It always takes time to readjust and remember how to direct your thoughts once they are the whole of you once more. Come away from there and concentrate on your decision, Infinity instructed me lovingly.

My decision. To move on with Infinity, or to stay with her in the physical plane and see what came of that. What would we do in our bodies though? Nothing that I had thought mattered, did matter in truth. Knowing that now, what would be the point of going back? I pondered. My family. They would be very upset if I left.

The situation would be temporary. When they are ready their times will come. Then they will remember and understand.

I knew she spoke the truth. The same would apply to my friends. Rowena flashed into my thoughts. She had been devastated by Shann's loss at the hands of the Woeful and she was scared about progressing with Oak. Her fears were groundless, I knew that and at some point so would she, but she didn't know it yet and I did. I could help her. The Woeful. Something nagged at me about them. What was it? I tried to remember but I was finding it difficult to move from one thought to the next.

Some of your fellow humans plan to hunt them, Infinity reminded me.

Yes, that was it. And I had been opposed to the hunt. It had seemed so very important to oppose it whilst I was in my body, yet now I couldn't seem to remember why. None of it mattered.

Not in reality. But in the dream it matters greatly.

Why?

You glimpsed the effect of allowing your soul to express through your personality when you chose to love a fellow human instead of attempting to be right. If you return to your body and use it to change the way The Sorrowful are seen and treated there is enormous evolutionary potential.

Why is that important?

It will move more souls closer to being able to choose whether to continue dreaming the shared dream.

Whatever stance I take, you provide an argument against it. If I think I should stay because of my family, you dismiss my concern. If I consider moving on, you tell me why I should stay. I'm more confused than ever.

I merely ensure all information is considered.

I pondered further. There were those threads that were still linking me to my body. Issues to be resolved.

They are minor. If you choose not to return they will be resolved in a future incarnation. If you return they will be ready for release shortly after.

I examined one of them. It was the concern for the Woeful. I shifted my focus to the next, which held the frustrations associated with my apprenticeship. If I'd been in my body I would have smiled. I knew the answers to those. They came to me now as easily as breathing came to my body. So why bother going back to work on them? I knew them. None of it mattered.

You know them but you have not yet expressed them. The frustration you manifested in your body has not yet been resolved.

Infinity waited patiently as I attempted to wrench my thoughts away from the threads. When I finally succeeded, I felt Infinity's approval. *You are adjusting rapidly. Should you choose to move on your transition will be the easiest you have experienced yet.*

How much time do I have to make the decision?

Time does not exist. You will reach a decision when you are ready.

I decided to stop thinking for a while and see if an answer became apparent. It was so blissful here, wherever it was that we were. We and everything and everyone else, I realised. I thought of Shann, Newson, Integrity and Noble and was instantly aware of their presences, and those of... Infinity enveloped my consciousness before I had a chance to put names to two other presences that were very familiar, cutting me off from them. *Do not be distracted. The decision you must make should remain foremost in your thoughts.*

What to do. If I wanted, Infinity and I could move on, away from all the pettiness of human concerns and I could always resolve the few remaining issues I had in a future lifetime. What would I be then though? Where would I be? Would Infinity still be with me? Would I be with any horses at all? With any of the friends whose support I'd valued so much and whom I'd been able to help in return?

As my friends and their horses flitted through my mind, I felt those familiar presences again. Justin, that was who it was, and Gas. A jolt shook my consciousness. How were they here...? Immediately Infinity pulled me back and surrounded me once more. *No distractions,* she reminded me lovingly but firmly.

But how did I just sense Justin and Gas like that? With the same intensity I can sense you and the others, I mean?

Infinity wove her way through my consciousness, pulling it tighter together. She was all I was aware of now. There was no room for any thought of anything else. No need for anything or anyone else.

The decision, we thought together.

If we returned to our bodies, we could continue the work we had started with the other Bonded. We would be working together with our friends to move humanity on past the point where they would feel the need to make decisions based on fear and insecurity again. We could help to make life easier for those incarnating as Woeful. We could clear the remaining threads that tied us to a need to continue incarnating, dreaming the dream. Infinity gently disentangled her consciousness from mine and left me to consider by myself. The more I thought of returning to my body, to my life as Infinity's Bond-Partner and my friends' friend, the stronger my feeling became. I reached my decision.

About time too, Justin's thought blasted into my mind.

???????????? Justin? There was amusement and jubilation all around.

You know it's me. Gas and I were on the verge of creating beds to lie down on while we were waiting.

But how...

Are we here? That's something of a story. As his consciousness resonated with mine, my question attracted the answer instantaneously and I witnessed his experience.

I felt his concern when he saw me collapse on the ground next to Infinity. He'd been so sure that I'd been releasing past hurt and emotion in the same way that he'd seen Infinity and Spider do, but when I lost consciousness, he worried that he'd misunderstood. Gas reassured him that he'd been right and that what was happening was entirely as it should be. He lifted me into his arms and carried me back to my bedroom, laying me gently on my bed. I felt the depth of his feelings for me and was astonished.

Infinity went back to her field shelter with Gas, falling instantly into a standing sleep. Two days passed. Gas and Oak stayed with Infinity as she dozed and slept, waking briefly to drink, eat or relieve herself before returning to her slumber. Justin stayed at my bedside. Our friends brought him food and drink and repeatedly encouraged him to leave me and rest while they sat with me, but he refused. He hammered repeatedly at Gas to tell him what was happening to me, why I wasn't waking up despite Adam's assurance that there was nothing wrong with my body, but Gas withheld the answer from him, telling him only that if he considered deeply, he would find that he knew.

Another day passed and my condition was unchanged. Feryl came to see me and Justin had an uncharacteristic loss of temper, blaming Feryl for what had happened to me. Feryl looked utterly miserable, took everything Justin said without comment and then fetched a chair and sat at Justin's side. He asked Justin questions. Hundreds of them. He wanted to know everything about how I'd reached the stage I had with Infinity and what Justin thought was happening now. When Justin had told Feryl everything he could, including admitting what was holding him back from pushing Gas as far as I'd been willing to push myself and Infinity, realisation struck him; Justin was more concerned for me than he was afraid for himself. He made a decision. Wherever I'd gone, he was coming after me.

Feryl offered to help and at first, Justin refused, saying he knew what he had to do and he knew that he and Gas could do it. Feryl pleaded with

Justin to allow him and Liberal to work alongside him, even if it were only to provide moral support. He wanted to help.

Gas and Liberal agreed to do three riding sessions a day with their riders, with time to rest in between. Our other friends took it in turns to help Justin and Feryl from the ground. Feryl learnt quickly and was very soon helping the others in pushing Justin and Gas ever harder. I felt Justin's muscles screaming at the end of each day as he took his place in the easy chair by my bed. I felt the determination that coursed through him and knew that it was beginning to overshadow the fear that tried to take over him each time he rode. I felt his love for his horse and for me. He always gave Infinity's neck a rub before and after each riding session and I felt him trying to reach me through her. She didn't acknowledge his presence.

It took them eight days. I was astonished. I couldn't possibly have been here for over a week! It was only an hour or so, surely? But Justin's memories were firm. Gas achieved perfect balance eleven days after I'd collapsed. He bellowed as his frustration at Justin's previous reticence left his body, and snorted and bucked a little as a few other more minor concerns were released... and then he was free. He was a young soul who hadn't incarnated many times and had correspondingly little to release. He was the opposite of Justin. Justin had incarnated over and over, learning and growing with each incarnation. The one issue he had never conquered, never managed to release, was his fear of death and perversely, it was that fear, and that fear alone, that tied him to a need to continue incarnating. Each time he incarnated, he feared losing himself, being no more, and each time he left his body and realised his mistake, he resolved to lose the fear in his next incarnation... so far with little success.

This time, he had chosen to incarnate as someone who would share a bond with a horse. This time he hoped to find the courage to live his life without his constant fear of death, of losing his individual personality. After all, he would be bonded to a horse, and the horses know the truth of existence even whilst they are incarnate in the physical plane. He was giving himself his best chance yet to conquer his fear... yet once again his fear had arisen and held him back.

I felt his jubilation as his beloved horse achieved perfect balance beneath him. He felt Gas release what he needed to in a few short bursts and then realised that he could do the same. He was balanced and strong. He was at one with his horse, with everything that is, was and ever has been. As he and Gas had worked together over the previous days, he had felt his fear receding. Like me, he'd had glimpses of the truth when he and Gas had had moments of balance and as they'd worked on, he had felt his old worries gradually lose their hold over him. Now he had the opportunity to release the last of his fear.

He and Gas trotted powerfully and majestically around the paddock, with Feryl's encouragement and jubilation ringing in their ears. He felt Gas begin to falter and knew that if he released the last of his fear, he would be strong enough and balanced enough to maintain his balance and stop Gas losing his own. If he held on to fear, even the tiniest amount, they would have more work to do. He thought of me and Infinity and his resolve stiffened. He was coming after us, wherever that may be and whatever it meant for him.

He released his fear and found that his body responded immediately. He resisted Gas's slight loss of balance with ease and felt his horse regain his power. They moved up to a canter. It was light, effortless. It felt as if he and Gas were balanced lightly on Gas's hind legs. Time slowed down until it failed to exist. There was only Justin, Gas and... an awareness of absolutely everything else! He felt me, briefly and then felt Infinity put herself between us. He slowed Gas to a halt and dismounted. He was vaguely aware of shouting and clapping erupting around him, and someone patted his back. None of it mattered. He walked Gas back to his shelter, untacked him and brushed him down. Justin left Gas dozing and came back to my room. He sat down in my easy chair and went to sleep, focusing his thoughts on me... and then he and Gas were with us.

His joy at being with us was matched equally by his joy that the cord that was his fear was already flickering doubtfully between him and his body. At Gas's prompting, he cleared it, welcoming his energy back to himself and wondering why it had taken so long for him to be able to do it. It was so easy.

Infinity pulled at my consciousness and I found myself drawn towards her. She once more enveloped me until I was aware of myself as a discrete entity. *You must maintain more of an awareness of yourself in order to be in a position to return to your body,* she informed me gently.

How is Justin able to do it?

He Who Is Gas is assisted by his partner in the same way I assist you.

Are you ready to go back yet, Am? Justin asked.

Are you and Gas going back?

We are.

Then let's do it. Um, Fin? How do I get back in my body?

Follow that which binds you, Infinity instructed me.

I turned my attention back to the thick, pulsing cord and imagined following it back to my body. Instantly I was part of the cord. I was propelled down it like blood pulsing through an artery and the next thing I knew, my eyes were opening. Sunlight flooded my room, which meant it was early morning. Justin was sitting in a chair by my head, rubbing his eyes and when I sat up, he grinned sheepishly and held out his hand. I took his hand in mine and smiled back as my mind began to make sense of everything I had perceived before returning to my body. Rowena was dozing in a chair by my feet and woke suddenly as I began to laugh.

'What the...?' she began.

'He Who Is Gas. That's what Infinity called you, He Who Is Gas,' I said to Justin. He began to chuckle as Rowena looked from one of us to the other, her eyes wide with shock and disbelief. Justin and I laughed until we cried.

TWENTY-SEVEN

Resolution

*S*o, can you hear what I'm thinking right now?' Rowena asked. I'd told her everything that had happened since I passed out at the riding paddock, with the exception of what I'd felt from Justin.

I nodded. 'Yes, and I have a sense of how you're feeling, like I did with Feryl. It all feels so muted though, compared with… the other place. It's like my mind's trying to wade through thick, gloopy mud.'

'Go on then, how'm I feeling?' Rowena said.

'You're tired but relieved, and a bit…' I hesitated.

'What? Go on, what?'

'Envious. Sorry, but you asked me.'

Rowena flushed and looked from me to Justin and back again. 'I suppose I am a bit. But there's only one person who can do anything about it, isn't there and I'm not going to help myself by sitting here. You owe me, my friend,' she said, pointing at Justin as she heaved herself up out of the chair. 'I expect all of the encouragement, cajoling and downright bullying that I gave you, returned to me ten-fold. Oak and I have a lot of work to do and we're going to need help. I'm going to get some breakfast and then I expect to see you at the paddock, to help me find this perfect balance that's so important. You,' she pointed at me, 'get one day's grace in order to feed yourself up after your insane, what was it? Twelve day fast? And then I expect you to join him. Got it?'

We both chuckled as she flung her hair over her shoulder and left the room. I suddenly felt acutely embarrassed. Justin and I had shared an experience where nothing was hidden and I had been aware of things that he may not have wanted me to know – and presumably the answers to any questions he'd wondered about me had been similarly answered for him. Confusion added to my embarrassment. Justin and I had shared the experience because we knew the truth. We knew that nobody is really separate from anyone else and that it just appears that way when dreaming the shared dream. So why was I embarrassed? Justin and I were two parts of the same whole, I may as well be embarrassed at my own thoughts as at his.

Having awareness of your soul and knowing the truth does not mean that your humanity ceases to exist, Infinity informed me.

Meaning?

You have chosen to return to your body with the intention of allowing your soul to express itself through your personality. Not to replace it. She Who Is Infinity you are living as a human. Allow yourself to be human.

I looked at Justin, to find him watching me. 'This is weird, isn't it?' he said. 'Everything seemed so easy, so simple and now we're back here it seems just the opposite. I can't decide whether I'm mortified, happy, daft for feeling anything at all when we both know it's not necessary… I'm not sure how to feel really.'

'According to Infinity, we're meant to be feeling all of those things, because we're living as humans,' I replied. 'Justin, thanks for coming after me. I was alright, you know that, but thanks anyway.'

His cheeks flushed below his intense brown eyes. 'No need to thank me, Amarilla, you gave me the incentive to finally… well, you know what I had to get past. I'm not sure I would ever have had the courage if I hadn't been so worried for you.'

'Oh, I think Gas would have found a way to worry you if I hadn't,' I said. 'There's no way he'd have let you pass a lifetime bonded to him without getting through to you somehow, although he's more patient with you than Infinity is with me.'

I almost felt Infinity's snort in a physical way and saw the shock on Justin's face before we both laughed. 'You felt that too?' I said.

'Yes, I did. She's got a feisty way about her, hasn't she?' he replied.

'Did you hear her when she was helping me just before?'

He nodded. 'Just about, but it didn't feel like it does when I hear Gas. Maybe it's just that she doesn't feel familiar, maybe as we both get used to how we are now, things will change. I guess we'll find out. We're in for an interesting time, aren't we?' He grinned. 'Are you ready to set foot outside the door and be the focus of curiosity yet again?'

I nodded. 'I'm fine, but before any of that, I need to see Adam.'

Adam opened his door wearing his dressing gown and rubbing his eyes. His face broke into a wide smile. 'I wasn't sure you would come back, my dear, but I'm glad you did. And Justin?'

'He's back too. He's gone to get some breakfast. Adam, there are things I need to tell you. I haven't been able to find the herbs that will cure insomnia or stomach ulcers because I've been coming at it from the wrong angle. I've been trying to cure the symptom, whereas I should have been looking for herbs that will ease the cause. They're both caused by stress and anxiety, so I need a herb to provide a sense of calm – chamomilla will do nicely I think – and then I need another herb to carry my positive energy and intention for the person, to help give them strength to deal with whatever's causing the problem. You've been using suncatcher for that and I may well too, I know it works because it was your secret ingredient in the healing cream you gave me to put on my face after Rowena punched me, and I felt it soothing the anger and upset that would have slowed my healing.

'That's all I was missing in order to complete my herb journal, but while we're here, I want to tell you that I know why Infinity told me that discovery and creation are one and the same. It had me completely stumped because if they're the same and we're actually "creating" the remedies, then how come Herbalists end up "discovering" the same remedies for all the ailments? But when I thought about it when I was out of my body, away from all the distractions and illusions that go with being here, I knew the answer. It's because we're all dreaming the same dream, just like Infinity told me, only then I didn't know what she meant. Now I do – we're all one. We believe the dream that we're all separate beings, just like we believe dreams when we're asleep, but the horses know the dream for what it is, and so do I now.'

Adam was now leaning on the doorframe, his eyes alert and exuding their usual twinkle. The more I talked, the wider his smile became. When I finally came to the end of my discourse, he nodded and said, 'Well, I've never said this while standing in a doorway in my dressing gown before, but, Amarilla Nixon, by the light, I declare that your apprenticeship is at an end and you may now consider yourself a qualified Herbalist.' He winked. 'Not that it matters one jot in the grand scheme of things, does it?'

I laughed. 'No, not in the slightest.'

Adam ushered me into one of his armchairs and then pulled a small table in front of me, on top of which was a tray of bread rolls, cheese, jam and a variety of cold meats. He gestured with his hand. 'Tuck in, tuck in. Turi noticed I wasn't making it to breakfast in the mornings, so she's acquired a habit of delivering a tray to my room for when I get back from sitting with the two of you; she always leaves enough for three or four people. You haven't eaten for, what, nearly two weeks? Not that your body appeared to need nourishment while you were gone.'

'You haven't been making it to breakfast because you've been sitting with me at night,' I said.

'Yes, yes, but not just me, we've been taking it in turns to sit with you and Justin, he's been, well he's been…'

'I know.'

'Yes of course you do.' Adam sat quietly in the armchair opposite mine whilst I ate. I had so much to tell him, yet, now I was with him, I felt no need to rush. He put his kettle on to boil and then made some tea. When I'd eaten my fill, he placed a steaming mug in my hands. 'What was it like?' he asked me.

I told him everything, once again leaving out any details that were personal to Justin, and he listened quietly, nodding occasionally as he sipped his tea. 'So, Infinity now calls Justin "He Who Is Gas",' I finished, still tickled by the fact. 'I mean at least I get to be "She Who Is Infinity" and you're "He Who Is Peace" – poor Justin.'

As Adam chuckled, something struck me. 'Infinity calls you "He Who Is Peace" and that means you achieved the potential you saw for yourself when you bonded. Did you consider leaving with Peace when he died?'

Adam nodded slowly, smiling. 'It took me a long, long time before I finally found the peace I'd sought for so long and my dear old boy fought hard for it alongside me. He knew I was close to finding it at the time his body was nearing its end and he gave me a choice. He said that when I took the final step and reached my potential, he would be ready to pass on and he would help me to leave with him if I wished, but that if I did so I would be missing an opportunity. I would have achieved the potential I saw for myself back when we bonded, but I would be missing out on achieving a greater potential for myself. He told me that if I stayed, I'd not only advance myself further, but I would be able to assist others in doing the same.

'It was the hardest decision of my life. I'm an old man and Peace had been my whole world for a very long time. I so much wanted to leave with him, but I felt what he wanted for me and I felt I owed it to him to push myself further. And so, when the day came that he laid down his body and moved on, I stayed. A few years passed and several dear friends made it their business to keep an eye on me, Rowena among them. And then you landed on my doorstep. You and Infinity opened the door to the opportunity Peace foresaw for me and I've been having the time of my life ever since. I'd never have believed it possible.'

'You're close, aren't you?' I said quietly. 'You have to be. We've all seen you ride Spider. Adam, are you going to leave us soon?'

'Yes, Amarilla, I believe I am.'

I didn't feel any need to cry or try and talk him into staying. I could feel how happy he was. He had lived his life and lived it well. He'd achieved more than he'd dreamt was possible and he was almost at the point of achieving that perfect physical balance that would allow him to clear the last few traces of energy from his past, leaving him fulfilled, whole and ready to move on.

'Thanks, Adam, for everything you've done for me.' I put all of my feeling for him into my words.

He smiled the smile of someone who is truly happy. 'Likewise, Amarilla, likewise. Now if you'll leave an old man in peace, I'll be able to get some clothes on before the first of my patients arrives. Unless you'd like to see them for me, my fellow Herbalist?'

'Not this morning, I think Justin is going to need my support. Rowena's on a mission.'

'Say no more, I'll see you at lunch.'

I went to see Infinity and found her grazing peacefully in the warm sunshine, alongside Gas. Liberal stood dozing nearby. He was a different horse from when I'd last set eyes on him; the hollows above his eyes had disappeared, he'd put on weight and he looked muscular, sleek and shiny. It was something about the way he held himself, though, that struck me most of all. I could sense his energetic presence easily and I knew that he was feeling fulfilled. He'd always been admired for his natural grace and balance, but that had been a fraction of what he'd been capable and he'd spent a long time feeling frustrated. Now, he was being pushed and approaching the limits of his physical ability and he was very happy about it. I was thrilled for both him and Feryl.

Infinity pushed at my mind. *I would be groomed.*

I fetched my grooming kit from the field shelter and set to work. Infinity reached around to nuzzle my back in return. I groomed her as I always did, yet something was different. Usually, grooming Infinity gave my mind a chance to wander around and process things that were going on in and around me. This time, however, I found that focusing my attention on my horse gave me a break from my humanity. My hands moved the brushes around, used the comb to untangle her mane and tail, and the hoof pick to clear her feet, while my mind was able to join Infinity in a place of oneness, relaxation and... peace. I was happy. Truly and completely happy.

Liberal whickered. He had awakened from his slumber and was focused intently towards the gateway.

He Who Is Liberal approaches, Infinity told me pointedly.

Feryl's appearance was very similar to how it had been when I'd first met him in terms of being well groomed and tidy, but as he walked over to where I stood with Infinity, I noticed that his bearing, like that of his horse's, had changed. Gone was the jaunty strut that he'd always employed to full effect, he walked with a relaxed confidence and his obvious happiness at the sight of his horse seemed to lighten his step.

He transferred his gaze to Infinity and me, and smiled. 'It's good to see you, Amarilla, I'd have been here before only Rowena accosted me while I was trying to eat my breakfast. Justin and I have just spent the best part of an hour helping her with Oak and we're more worn out than she is.'

I laughed. 'She's really determined now, isn't she?'

'She certainly is. It's a wonderful thing to be part of and I have you to thank for that, Amarilla. I can't for the life of me imagine what I was thinking, shutting Liberal out and refusing to listen to him or to anyone else. That old version of me seems so far away now that it doesn't even seem possible he existed. Can you forgive me for being a stubborn, egotistical idiot?'

'Don't be daft, I didn't exactly make things easy for you. Liberal looks amazing, doesn't he?'

'Wait until you see him in action, although I have to admit to feeling as if I'm letting him down.'

'Letting him down? What do you mean? Look at him, he's happy and he looks the picture of health. Feryl, Infinity just called you "He Who Is Liberal", and that means you've reached the potential you saw for yourself when you bonded to him. You'll be the Master of Riding who goes down in the Histories as the one who reformed the way we ride our horses.'

Feryl rubbed his horse's neck, slowly and gently. 'But I don't push myself as far as I could when I ride, I hold back. It was scary, watching what happened to you, and then when I came to see what had happened to Justin and I couldn't wake him either, I don't think I've ever been so frightened. I don't want that to happen to me.'

'It won't. My potential was to realise the truth about my real nature and about everything that exists. Achieving that coincided with releasing something I'd been holding onto for a long time. It was too much for my body, so I left it for a while and a consequence of that was that I realised I didn't really need to be here anymore. I got to the same point as Shann. He chose to move on, I chose to stay and we both had our own reasons for doing so. Justin reached the same point I did but he didn't have to leave his body, he chose to, because he wanted to come after me.

'The work you're doing with Liberal will take you as far as you want to go in this lifetime, but you've already reached the potential that you saw for yourself, so use it. Use it to help all the other Bonded to help their horses and to reach their own potentials, whatever they are.'

'How is it, that one so young can be so wise?' he asked, half teasing me.

'Infinity, that's how,' I said ruefully.

He laughed. 'You're well matched. See you later, if you'll be at the riding session after lunch? I'd love you to see how Liberal's doing, but don't worry if you need to rest?'

'I wouldn't miss it.'

I didn't feel physically strong enough to ride and Infinity was more than content to snooze and graze, so I spent the afternoon sitting on the fences of the various riding paddocks, watching my friends ride their horses and teach their students.

People kept coming to sit with me, wanting to know what had happened to me and where I'd been, but I found myself reluctant to give details. I wasn't sure how much they'd believe, however much they wanted to and I felt as though I'd be giving them information that would be better discovered themselves, so I merely said that I'd released my past in the same way Infinity and Spider had and my body had needed a little time to recover.

I felt emotional as I watched my friends ride. They and their horses looked so completely different from when we'd all started. Diligence and Mason drew the eye with their combined size and both looked fit, toned and a lot younger than their years. They were completely absorbed in their work together and I didn't think it would be at all long before the horses referred to him as "He Who Is Diligence", if indeed they weren't calling him that already.

Marvel and Broad, likewise, worked on intently together. Marvel's main difficulty was in timing his signals accurately, but Broad – unlike Infinity, I noted – was patient and rewarded him with instant responses when he got it right.

Rowena was pushing herself as hard as she could. Oak was beginning to bring his hindquarters underneath himself more and several times, I saw her smile when she felt the effect of the enormous power contained within his hind legs. But I was aware that her fear of losing herself in their work together still lingered and held her back. She was still terrified that if she gave all of herself to her work with her horse, her barriers would drop and the side of herself that she kept so carefully hidden would be exposed to all. My heart went out to her. She was so good at caring for and organising other people and she put a strong, forceful impression of herself out to the world, but inside she was still the child who had been rejected and unloved and she would protect that child at all costs.

I knew she'd get to the place of peace and inner strength that she'd seen for herself when she bonded with Oak, but I wondered whether to send some light her way to give her some extra help. Immediately it felt wrong. No, Oak was working with her and he was everything she needed. They would get there in their own time and in their own way. Everything was as it should be.

With Quinta on board, Spider didn't look quite the way he did when Adam rode him, but she was getting there slowly and I was excited for her as I knew that the very fact she was now bonded to Spider meant that she had the same potential as Adam, Justin and me. I wondered what she'd do when she got there; whether the pull to follow after Noble would be strong enough for her to release her body and leave, or whether she'd choose to stay. As I remembered how Infinity currently referred to her, I knew instantly which way she would choose.

Feryl and Liberal were something else. They'd made an impressive picture before, but with the increased lift and connection in his body that Liberal was now achieving, they were jaw-dropping to watch. I was interested to see that Feryl, although secure in his seat, didn't sit down into his pelvis quite as much as I'd learnt to do when riding Infinity, and he didn't seem to need to lift his chest and be quite so strong in his core as I did, yet Liberal was still achieving a high degree of balance. Liberal didn't need him to be, I realised; Feryl's reason for bonding to and riding his horse was different from mine. Everyone was different and had different reasons for bonding with their horses, different things to achieve, each as relevant and important as the next.

Everything slotted into place for me. There really was no need for human beings to need to feel better than each other. No need to feel special. *Everything is always as it should be,* I broadcasted as loudly as I could to Infinity and to All That Is and I grinned from ear to ear at the sheer daftness that I ever could have believed otherwise.

Justin immediately looked around from where he was sitting upon his horse, smiled at me and nodded. Infinity continued to graze without comment. Justin turned back to what he and Gas had been doing before my broadcast had interrupted them. It was magical. Gas was a force of nature as he lifted in front, stepped right underneath himself with his hind legs and then proceeded to move in absolute balance, without any apparent effort. Each stride was the same as the last in its relaxed power. He was connected from his hind feet all the way to the tips of his ears and no matter what Justin asked of him, he was able to respond with ease. Justin sat tall and strong, there to respond to and support his horse at any time. It was impossible to tell where one began and the other ended; they were consciousness made visible.

I couldn't resist clapping quietly when Justin brought Gas to a graceful halt in front of me. I couldn't think of anything to say, but then realised I didn't need to say anything – this was Justin and Gas, they would know. Justin leapt across to sit beside me, and put an arm around my shoulders and hugged me as Gas nuzzled my knee.

Feryl took my place teaching alongside Justin in the two sessions that followed and I was overjoyed to see how well the students in our group were coming along.

'It's a lovely thing to watch, isn't it,' Salom said as she climbed onto the rail to sit beside me.

'S'hard to ge' anythin' done wi' all this goin' on, we don' wan' te miss anythin',' said Pete as he settled down on her other side.

'I'm glad you stayed around to see it, this is far more important news to take to the villages than all the stuff that happened before you got back here,' I said, 'especially now Feryl's involved, he's a better teacher than any of us except Adam, so now things'll really take off.'

I was aware of Salom's unease as she perched next to me, swinging her legs. 'What's wrong, Salom?'

'I'm not a gossip and I'm not here to cause trouble. Whatever a certain person thinks, that isn't my role. I just gather information and give it to whoever wants it,' she said.

I noticed that she was wearing her bandanna, which was unusual for when she was watching the riding sessions, as she didn't normally want to be disturbed. 'Salom, please tell me the latest news around The Gathering,' I asked her formally.

She nodded gratefully. 'Those who intend to hunt the Woeful will be leaving The Gathering tonight,' she told me in a low voice.

'Tonight? They're leaving in the dark? Why?'

'They want to leave without drawing any attention to themselves. They know they're in the minority here now and they don't want anyone to try to stop them. Their plan is to get across the river at dusk, camp on the other side for the night and then make their way at first light tomorrow morning.'

'But I thought they were still arguing about weapons? We were hoping we'd be able to attract them to come and work with us and their horses before they reached agreement on how they were going to... you know,' I said.

'They reached an agreement to disagree a good few weeks ago. Some of them intend to use their Healing Skills to kill, and the Metal-Singers among the rest have produced some sort of crossbow. They'll be aiming for the eyes,' she said, and shuddered. 'They aim to kill as many of the Woeful as they can and to recruit from the villages as they go.'

I felt immense sadness. I saw Justin bend his head towards Feryl, who nodded and stepped to the middle of the circle so that he could see Justin's students as well as his own. Justin headed over to where we sat. 'You and I are going to have to find a way to shield one another if we're ever going to be able to concentrate in each other's presence,' he said. 'What's up?'

I whispered what Salom had just told me and I felt his concern.

'We can't let them leave, they'll destroy themselves and cause a great deal of harm,' he said. 'Salom, you didn't just hear that, okay?'

'You know I can't withhold information,' she said, 'but I feel a headache coming on.' She removed her bandanna, folded it carefully and pushed it into her back pocket. 'I'm going to my room to lie down and won't be available for the rest of the day. Pete will bring a dinner tray to my room, won't you, Pete?'

Justin gave a brief nod. 'Thanks, Salom.'

She nodded back and then left. Pete raised his hand in a wave of goodbye and trailed off after her, mumbling about having to see to the donkeys.

'I'd better get back, we've nearly finished. We'll have a chat with the others back at the field shelter where we won't be overheard,' Justin said, and jogged back to join Feryl.

~

Marvel was thunderous. 'This cannot happen. I've said it before and I'll say it again. They'll use Healing Skills to cause harm, over my dead body.'

'Stop being so melodramatic, Marvel,' said Rowena. 'There can't be that many of them left and with those who've had the sense to join us, we far outnumber them. We can physically stop them leaving if we have to.'

'I'm not comfortable with that, Rowena,' said Quinta, and Justin, Mason and I all voiced our agreement. 'Spider's not being much help, anyone else's horses got anything to say about it?'

'Infinity's in agreement that we should stop them from leaving, but she thinks I know what to do,' I said, and then realised that she was right.

I outlined my thoughts to the others, and Justin and Adam concurred immediately, with Quinta and Mason close behind.

Marvel said, 'I've seen it work once before, and I don't think we'll come up with anything better. Okay, I'm in.'

Rowena shrugged. 'I haven't done it before, but I guess I'll give it a go. We'll grab an early dinner and be back here an hour before dusk, shall we?' There were nods all round.

We will help. Infinity's thought was welcome. I knew exactly to whom she was referring. I smiled and saw that Justin wore a smile that matched my own. We knew we couldn't fail.

My friends and I all arrived in the dining hall well before the bell rang for dinner, with the intention of grabbing a quick bite to eat before heading up to fetch our horses before dusk. Adam, however, picked up a bread roll and headed back towards the door. 'I'll see you all up by the river,' he said over his shoulder. 'Spider and I have something we need to do.'

'What was that about?' said Rowena. 'Quinta? Do you know?'

'Yes, I have a feeling I do,' smiled Quinta. 'Don't worry, it's all good.'

I knew too and I gathered all the positive energy I could and willed it Adam's way. Justin sensed what I was doing and raised an eyebrow, before understanding dawned and he added his energy to mine. I knew Adam wouldn't need it, but I was pretty sure he'd sense it and know who was sending it to him.

We all ate lightly, eager to be on our way so as to be in place in plenty of time. As we were leaving, everyone else began to arrive for dinner, Feryl among them. He took one look at us all and left his friends to come over. 'What gives? Is everything alright?' he asked.

Justin said under his breath, 'They're leaving to hunt the Woeful tonight. We're going to stop them.'

Feryl sighed. 'What can I do to help?'

Justin outlined our plan. 'It would be a massive help if you can keep everyone from coming after us. I don't know how much their horses will tell them about what's going to happen and the last thing we need is for everyone to come tearing up to the river bank and then getting in the way.'

Feryl nodded. 'I'll do my best. Good luck.'

We tacked up and mounted our horses in their paddock. Three horses waited for us on the path and I felt a calm sense of purpose from them all. They, along with Liberal, fell in behind us as we headed toward the river and it wasn't long before another five came trotting up behind them. There was some squealing and scuffling as they organised themselves into a formation with which they were all comfortable and then there were a few seconds of quiet, before more horses arrived at the rear and the same procedure was repeated.

By the time we got to the riverbank, we were part of a massive herd. The same calm sense of purpose emanated from each and every horse as they fanned out along the river bank and then turned to face back towards The Gathering. My friends and I rode towards the section of river bank that was directly in front of where the path opened out onto the bank. We were met with the sight of Adam and Spider waiting patiently.

Even in the failing light, we could see what they had achieved. The being that was Spider/He Who Is Spider stood tall and powerful and radiated peace, strength and oneness. I was thrilled as I felt their complete and utter joy. Quinta went over to stand at Spider's shoulder and the rest of us fell in on either side of them to wait.

It wasn't long before we heard voices coming towards us from the direction of the path. We wouldn't be able to see those who approached until they were near the end of the path due to a curve that took them around a small hillock, but we could hear that they were close.

'Okay, everyone, prepare yourselves,' whispered Adam. 'And please remember, however challenging their behaviour may become, that these people are not enemies of ours, or of anyone else. They are frightened beyond reason and their fear is masking their true selves. It is our job to help them remember who they are.'

I nodded and gathered as much light as I could within myself, holding it there until I could see those who approached.

'Right, four of you stand guard at the end of the path to stop anyone following us, while we find the rafts,' said a male voice that I recognised, as the group rounded the bend and came into sight. They stopped short at the sight of us lined up along the river bank. I sent my light towards them and let it settle down among the group. I concentrated on maintaining my flow of light towards them and was aware of it being joined by my friends' efforts.

Mason's light was strong but he kept losing it and having to refocus to generate it again. Marvel and Quinta were producing a weaker flow of light than Mason but were managing to keep their light streams steady. Rowena surprised me with the consistent strength of light she was able to send to the group. The strength of Justin's light matched my own and Adam's was like a roaring bonfire.

Then the horses joined in. I felt the air steady itself with the calm, assured love of ages. The horses' energy was directed at no one in particular, they merely emanated their own sense of themselves for anyone to use as needed. I felt Mason's light steady itself and become consistent. Marvel's and Quinta's light flows became stronger and Rowena put more positive feeling into hers. Justin, Adam and I found the energy to magnify our light streams to the point where it felt as if that was all we were.

None of the hunting group moved. A white haze of light had settled around them and they were looking around themselves in confusion. I saw that it was Jack at the front of the group, with Vickery immediately behind him. I became aware of their feelings and my light faltered slightly as shock reverberated through my being. Their fear of the Woeful, of loss, death and injury had combined with their overwhelming fear that they were somehow not good enough. The result was a highly toxic need to cause harm to others – to somehow prove to themselves that they could feel safe if they could only eliminate anything that they perceived as a threat to their physical bodies, or to their view of themselves.

Infinity gave me a burst of energy that I used to steady myself and refocus, until my light stream was back up to strength.

Jack spoke. 'What is this? You can't stop us leaving, you know. I don't care how you talked all these horses into joining you in your little display, it doesn't impress me in the slightest, now get out of our way.'

None of us replied. We all continued to send them as much positive, loving energy as we could.

Vickery tried next, her voice full of venom as she said, 'Who in the darkest levels of hell do you think you are? You lord it around here as if you're something special, and you can't see everyone laughing behind your backs, I mean look at you all. Wimpy little Amarilla who can't say boo to a goose, Mason, who rides that lice-ridden carthorse as if she's training for the high class in the next Friendlies, Quinta and Marvel who just tag along with the rest of you for no apparent reason that anyone can fathom, Adam who can't seem to realise that he's past it, has nothing to offer anyone and should never have come back, Justin who can't keep his mind on anything for longer than two seconds and is a total waste of space, and then we have Rowena, who should be avenging Shann but is too cowardly to come with us.'

Everyone remained steady except for Rowena. Her light stream faltered and then stopped completely as anger flooded her. I felt Oak focus his energy towards her and was aware of her anger warring with her desire to stick to the plan, to help. A flicker of light sparked within her and then became stronger. I felt her make her decision, and as her light and positivity flared back even stronger than before, she directed it straight towards Vickery.

I noticed that some of the hunting group were now looking uncertain and I could feel that the fear level of the group as a whole had decreased slightly. It was working! I took Rowena's lead and focused my own light stream on Jack and Vickery.

Jack tried again. 'Why are these horses here anyway? Do you plan to use them to stop us getting to our rafts? They won't harm us, so you can't stop us.' He began to walk towards us, although as he got closer, his air of certainty wavered. He turned and marched to his left, further along the line from where we sat our horses. As he neared the horses who waited there, they shuffled closer together, barring his way.

He waved his arms around. 'MOVE,' he shouted. 'I'M NOT BONDED TO YOU, YOU HAVE NO SWAY OVER ME. GET OUT OF MY WAY, YOU FILTHY NAGS.'

I felt Marvel's light waver slightly before he regained control of himself. I leant forward and saw that the horses at whom Jack was yelling stood firm and one put her ears flat back and shook her head at him, baring her teeth. He took an involuntary step backwards and said in a shaky voice, 'You can't do this, you're not my horse. Candour isn't even here.' He took another step back so that he could see all of us astride our horses. 'You see, Candour isn't here, he hasn't seen fit to join you all against me, so they haven't all taken your side.'

None of us spoke. Adam was now directing the majority of his light towards Jack, whilst Rowena and I focused on Vickery and the others combined the strength of their positive energy to form a cloud that continued to permeate the main group, some of whom were now standing off to one side.

Infinity pricked her ears and I felt her muscles tense as I shared her awareness that there were more horses approaching. The hunting group turned at the sound of galloping hooves and a herd of pitifully thin horses rounded the bend. The horses flew past them without pausing and came to a halt in front of us, blowing and snorting. To a horse, they turned to face their Bond-Partners.

TWENTY-EIGHT

Culmination

$\mathcal{M}$y personality wanted to be angry. More than angry, actually. A bitter rage urged me to stand in my stirrups and shout with red hot fury at each and every one of the hunting group who had allowed their horses to get into such a state. The chestnut mare who had placed herself in front of Infinity and me had a dull, staring coat that failed to hide her protruding ribs and I was intensely aware that she was cold, despite the run from her paddock. I felt her love for her Bond-Partner and her sorrow that she had been unable to penetrate his fear to help him. But as I felt her add her energy to that of the other horses, I released the anger that had been trying to take hold within me, and gave prevalence to my awareness of truth. My light stream was strong and steady.

I felt each of my friends except Justin and Adam falter as their own anger took hold.

'Remember,' called Adam.

'Remember,' I echoed him and felt Quinta's light rejoin ours.

Rowena was struggling with herself again, but I felt her remember the grief and fear she had suffered so recently. Understanding settled within her and her light was soon back up to strength.

Marvel and Mason struggled on, both trying to put their anger and disappointment at their fellow Bonded to one side and refocus, but finding it desperately hard despite energy and support from their horses.

'Remember,' said Adam again and I felt a flicker of light in both men, which grew steadily stronger.

It was all too much for seven members of the hunting group, each of whom came at a run, sobbing, to where their horses stood quietly opposing their actions. Immediately, the horses directed their energy solely to their returned partners. I felt their Bond-Partners' fear dissipate and be replaced with relief, love and sorrow for their horses. My heart leapt.

'Candour? Are you here?' Jack stepped back in order to have a better view of the horses standing in line in front of us. There was no whinny, no whicker of greeting in response to his question. 'There you are, you silly old fool, what are you doing here? Candour?' He moved to stand in front of his horse and reached out the back of his hand. No response. 'What have you done to him? Why is he like this?' Jack challenged Adam, who didn't answer but continued to send intense light towards Jack, battering at the barrier of fear he had subconsciously erected around himself. The barrier was significantly weaker now, I noticed.

'Verve? Are you there my boy?' Vickery called out uncertainly and I was aware of movement to my left as a big, pure white horse stepped forward and tossed his head. 'Verve, come here, I know you don't want to go with us, but you don't need to join them. We're only doing it to keep you safe, please try and understand.'

Verve didn't respond. He had given up trying to communicate with his partner.

Vickery walked towards her horse, but stopped well short of where he stood with us. 'Verve, please go back to your shelter and eat, look at you, I've given you your wormer but you still look awful, please eat more? Or at least go back so you can be inside and out of the chill?' She was obviously as aware as I, that her horse was feeling the cold far more than he should for the time of year.

Again, Verve gave her no response.

Her voice shook. 'Verve? Please?'

Rowena and I continued to direct our light streams towards Vickery, and as her fear barrier began to flicker uncertainly, our love, combined with that of her horse, breached it and reached her. She ran towards Verve and flung her arms around his neck. 'Oh, my boy, forgive me, can you forgive me? Never mind about the Woeful, we need to get you better, don't we? Come on, my beautiful boy, let's get you back to your shelter.'

'Vickery, I left Oak's rug hanging over the fence of his paddock. You can take it on your way past and borrow it for Verve, it's thicker than his,' called out Rowena. Vickery hesitated and then nodded briefly, before walking away, her horse at her shoulder.

'Vic, where are you going? You can't leave us, we need you,' Jack called to her.

'Verve needs me more and I need him. That's more important than anything and I can't imagine how I ever thought otherwise. I'm sorry Jack.'

The remainder of the hunting group watched her as she and Verve passed them, and then all but two of them ran to their own horses. As more horses began to leave with their Bond-Partners, our light got through to the final two, both of whom released their fear and also ran to their horses.

'You can't do this.' Jack's voice was little more than a squeak as he ran up to those leaving with their horses, waving his arms frantically. 'We had plans, we were going to rid this world of the Woeful once and for all, we were going to make it a safer place, we were going to show the villages that they need not live in fear anymore, that we have the strength and the power to protect them. And what about all your stuff? The weapons you spent so long working on? Are you just going to leave it all here?' He gestured wildly at the litters that the hunting group had been dragging behind them, dark mounds that now eerily resembled freshly covered graves as they lay abandoned in the twilight.

Soon there was no one left at whom he could rail, apart from us. The air was thick with supportive energy from the horses. My friends and I were now all directing our light streams at the fear that Jack was still managing to maintain around himself. I was amazed at how tough his barriers were, how thick his fear, for it to take us all so long to reach him, but we persevered.

Three times, one of the horses had to warn him physically not to escalate his behaviour; once when he tried to push through their line, another time when he ran at Adam, boasting that he had learnt to multiskill and that he could use his abilities to tear us all to shreds if he chose to, and finally when he picked up a stone and threw it at me, missing me only narrowly. On this occasion it was his own Candour who left the line, nudged him to the ground and then stood over him, refusing to let him stand back up.

Finally, when he'd completely exhausted himself and could no longer maintain his fear barrier against the love that pummelled against it, we got through to him.

He sat on the floor, sobbing, as his horse stood over him, blowing peacefully on the top of his blond head and infusing him with love. I felt acutely Jack's lack of confidence in himself, his anxiety about showing his real, sensitive self to the world and my heart went out to him. His sensitivity, combined with his newfound ability to multiskill, could make him invaluable in helping others to open up to multiskilling and he needed to hear that, I decided.

I was just about to go to him when I saw that Adam was already walking towards him in the moonlight. He spoke quietly to Jack as he helped him to his feet. After a while, Jack began to nod slowly. He lifted an arm and put it around his horse's neck and hugged him as he listened to Adam. I was aware of Candour communicating with him now too, and I knew I could be aware of Candour's counsel if I concentrated on the thoughts that I could sense. I chose not to.

Eventually, Jack and Candour walked off together, back towards The Gathering. Adam came to stand in front of all of us. 'I think we can be pleased with the way that went, well done, everybody,' he said and I felt him send his love to all of the horses, who began to leave, sending thoughts to their Bond-Partners as they went.

'Flaming lanterns, I thought we were going to be here all night,' said Rowena. 'Come on, let's get back, Oak's tired and I can feel a warm bed beckoning to me.'

'That was fantastic,' Quinta said as we followed Oak and Rowena. 'I can't believe we all did it, and the horses were brilliant.'

'It was somethin' else, wasn't it?' agreed Mason. 'I have to admit, I had my doubts it would work, I just thought they were too angry, too scared for us to get through to them. I thought there would need to be some stern words at the very least, but I can't tell you how happy I am to be proven wrong.'

I turned around to speak to Adam and saw that he and Spider remained by the river, making a silvery silhouette in the moonlight. A shiver went over me as I felt their intention. Infinity stopped and turned back to face them both. Justin and Gas appeared by our side.

'Adam?' The slight panic in Quinta's voice told me that she too was aware of what they planned. 'Come back to The Gathering with us? We can talk this through. Please, Adam? Spider?' She ran past us, back to where her friend sat astride her horse.

I was aware of Rowena's voice raised in question from somewhere behind us, but ignored it as I asked Infinity to walk back to where Quinta was now crying into Adam's leg. As I got closer, I could see his hand stroking her hair and heard the reassurance in his voice. She stepped back and looked up at him, then nodded, wiping her eyes with the end of her sleeve.

'You're going,' I said to Adam.

'Yes, I am. Spider is going to take me somewhere that is very special to me and once there, I will leave my body.'

'You're going to lie down with Peace,' said Justin.

'There's no keeping anything from you two, is there?' Adam chuckled. 'Yes, I would like to leave my body where I buried his. Not that it matters where I leave it, but it's something I always planned to do. Spider is very kindly going to take me there. It's not very far away, Quinta, Spider won't be gone long.'

'Do you really have to go now?' Quinta asked.

'Go where? Adam, it's the middle of the night, where's so important that you have to go now?' Marvel asked as he, Mason and Rowena and their horses reached us.

'Adam's leaving us to join Peace,' I said. 'Adam, I'm going to miss you more than I can say but I'm so happy for you.' My personality took over then and my emotion left me as silent tears.

We all dismounted and Adam hugged each of us before remounting Spider. 'It's been a privilege to know all of you, but now, I have somewhere I need to be. Farewell.' Spider turned and moved effortlessly up to a canter. I laughed at Adam's 'WAHOO!' as they tore away from us in the moonlight.

And then they were gone. Gone physically, anyway. As we made our way back to the horses' paddock, I realised that I could be aware of Adam and Spider whenever I chose to be. I could feel their happiness and contentment, and it eased the pain of losing Adam's physical presence.

Quinta was pale at breakfast the following morning. 'They're so happy, I feel awful for feeling just the opposite,' she said.

'You're aware of Adam as well as Spider?' I asked.

'Since he found his perfect balance and they became one, yes. They're close now to where Peace's body was buried, oh why am I telling you, you already know this, I imagine?'

'I'm aware of them as a presence and I know how they're feeling but I haven't probed any deeper than that, it doesn't feel right,' I said.

Justin and Marvel sat down on either side of Quinta. 'What shall we do today, lovely lady?' said Marvel. 'I think we're all going to be feeling a bit strange after everything that happened last night, so my vote goes towards having a day of fun, just as our favourite Master Herbalist would have prescribed for us. Anyone up for it?'

Rowena and Mason joined us. Rowena was pale with red-rimmed eyes. 'Up for what?' she asked. Marvel repeated his suggestion and she said, 'I probably should be keen to honour Adam in that way, but however much I know he's happy and doing what he wants to do, I'm struggling with it all. I hardly slept last night, I'm going to miss that old man so much.' Mason put an arm around her shoulders and hugged her.

'I think we should each go and see some of the members of the hunting group before we do anything else, to make sure they're all okay,' said Justin. 'They need to know that they're welcome to join our riding groups – oh blimey, we need to sort out who's going to teach Adam's groups now as well.'

'And who's going to take over his patients?' I said. 'I could do it, I know all their histories and I've consulted with most of them before with

Adam there, but I don't know if the other Herbalists would allow a newly qualified Herbalist to take over the patients of a Master.'

'You're not exactly a run-o-the-mill newbie though are you, my little Amarilla?' chuckled Mason. 'Mind you, I can't help but think you'll be wasted as purely a Herbalist when we all know you can multiskill, who knows where the future of healin' will be now that everythin's been turned on its head?'

Marvel said, 'It's thrilling isn't it? Everything's been thrown up in the air and has come back down to land in a different place; the way we ride, the reason we ride, the way we look at the Skills, the way we'll be able to use the Skills... And now that, hopefully, the Bonded will be united in our goals and purpose again, who knows where the future lies? Amarilla? You and Infinity have been the catalysts for all this change, what are we all meant to do now?'

'I've no idea,' I said. 'It felt like we were climbing a mountain before, but now we've got to where we were aiming for, there's even more to do. I don't know how we're going to replace Adam as instructor for his riding groups when he's irreplaceable, and then there are all those people out in the villages who either failed their Skills testing or only showed aptitude for one or two Skills – we need to help them to open up to believe they can do any or all of the Skills if they choose to. I don't know, I just assumed Adam would sort it all out at some point. And the Woeful, we need to be thinking about how we go about approaching them. Has anyone seen Salom yet this morning? She needs to know that the hunting group aborted their hunt last night...'

'And... breathe,' interrupted Justin. 'We prioritise and with time, things will get sorted. First things first, we need to speak to Feryl.'

'And he needs to speak to you.' Feryl sat down with a bump next to Justin. 'What in the clouds happened last night? Liberal told me he was needed elsewhere and would be back soon, and then all hell let loose in here when I stopped anyone leaving to see why all of their horses were heading off towards the river in the fading light with minimal explanation. I had to lock the door and bar it with my body, and I'm not exaggerating when I tell you that there was nearly a riot and I am possibly the least popular person around here this morning. Care to explain anyone?'

We all laughed and then Justin filled him in on what had happened. Feryl whistled through his teeth. 'Well done, you guys. But Adam's really not coming back?'

'No, he's not,' replied Quinta. 'We were just discussing how to fill the void he's leaving as the senior Healer and also our senior instructor, which is where your name came up.'

'Right, well can I make a suggestion regarding the riding groups?' Feryl asked. When we all nodded, he said, 'For now, I think Amarilla can take her group on her own and Justin can take Adam's. If you're all in agreement, I'll move between the groups, assess how the riders are doing and put them into streams. Amarilla and Justin will take the top four groups and the remainder will be divided between the rest of you, all of whom will also now be teaching on your own.'

'But what about you, Feryl? You're the Master of Riding and the most experienced teacher, shouldn't you be taking the top groups?' asked Justin.

'I propose myself as a roving instructor for now, moving around between all of the groups to offer help to all of you as you instruct, should you need it. And no, I may have the most experience of riding and teaching, but only you and Amarilla have attained the ultimate achievement and it would be unfair of me to hold back any of our students who have the same potential. In time, more may achieve the same as you two, and then we'll have more instructors for the top groups and you can have a break. How does that sound?'

'Sounds good to me, mate,' said Marvel.

'Nice one, Feryl,' said Rowena.

'Amarilla? Are you okay with that?' Feryl asked me.

'Yes, I think so, so now it's the villages and the Woeful we need to think about,' I said.

Mason chuckled at Feryl's confused expression. 'Amarilla's taken it upon herself to worry about everything for everyone,' he explained.

I giggled. 'Sorry, it's just that... Adam.' I felt him leave. One minute he and Spider were there, a quiet presence at the back of my mind and the next, I could feel Spider's lone presence and Adam was the faintest trace, as if he'd stretched my awareness of him so far that it had thinned to the most delicate of threads. Justin took a deep breath and exhaled slowly.

Quinta smiled, sadly, and said, 'He's gone home.'

A lot was achieved in the days that followed Adam's death. Between my friends and me, we approached all who had been members of the hunting group, and persuaded them to join our riding sessions. Jack was persuaded by Marvel to take up the challenge of organising those Bonded who were now choosing to multiskill, to go out to the villages to confirm and prove the news that Salom would be spreading ahead of them – that anyone could perform any of the Skills. We knew it would be difficult for those who were unbonded to accept the idea, as those of us who'd had the encouragement and support of our horses had found it difficult enough to begin with, but in time, we hoped the concept would take hold.

Feryl was efficient and accurate in his assessments of the riders we were helping, and soon had them organised into groups of matching ability for us to teach. I was daunted at first to be teaching some of the most advanced students, but I found that within seconds of each session beginning, my nerves would disappear. I could feel where each horse and rider partnership was in their training and in their relationship, and I worked hard to make sure my instruction pushed them slightly out of their comfort zone so that they progressed, but not so far that they were overwhelmed and fearful. The horses concentrated intensely and it was a privilege to be part of their quest for balance for themselves and their riders.

I kept feeling an urge to visit my family but my mornings were taken up with healing and my afternoons with chores and teaching; I couldn't just leave my riding students hanging while I took time off to go and visit my home village. And, much as I didn't want to admit it, I didn't want to miss a single thing that was happening with all the Bonded and their horses. The atmosphere at The Gathering was one of purpose and excitement, and it was an exhilarating place to be.

They are always close by. You know this, Infinity reminded me as I lay in bed one night, wondering how my family would react to all the news Salom took with her, as well as to the letters she carried from me; would my father expand his Skill set? Would he even believe it was possible? I had been wondering to myself. I could have kicked myself when I realised what Infinity meant, and immediately set about reaching out to my father. A thrill shot through me when I found him, and then each member of my family in turn. They were all tired at the end of a long day and each had their own worries and concerns, but nothing more than the average person carried around on a daily basis. I was overjoyed at being able to sense them and sent each and every one a surge of love, before I fell asleep.

~

'We're the luckiest girls in the world, Fin,' I said as I groomed her glossy coat before saddling and bridling her. The birds were singing, the sun was shining and there wasn't the faintest wisp of cloud in the sky. I could feel my mare's pleasure as my brush strokes massaged her skin and the underlying muscles, and I lost myself in the feeling of oneness that was so magnified when I was in Infinity's presence.

My friends arrived one by one to get their own horses ready to ride, Feryl included. 'It's been a bit of a busy time, my boy, I'm sorry you've been neglected,' he told Liberal.

'He's the image of neglect, mate,' joked Justin, 'just look at him.'

We all chuckled. I stood back from Infinity to look around our herd of horses as their partners groomed and fussed around them. I was struck by the image they presented. To a horse, they were bright eyed, glossy coated, toned of muscle and simply oozed presence, as if they took up far more space than my eyes were telling me they did. Infinity and Gas had an added lightness about their appearance, almost as if they were using the ground as a point of reference, rather than something to stand on. I just couldn't stop smiling.

We led our horses leisurely up to the riding paddock, laughing and joking as we went, but the minute we mounted our horses, we were quiet as concentration took over. It didn't last long in my case. Infinity and I were immediately in our perfect balance and I couldn't stop myself from whooping as we powered our way around the paddock for a time, before slowing to a graceful halt. I laughed as Infinity then sat down onto her hindquarters and lifted her forequarter up off the ground and held herself there, just because she could. She landed lightly on her forelegs, pushed off into a slow, powerful trot and then acceded to my request to move sideways across the paddock. Whatever we decided to do, we did, easily, gracefully, powerfully. Infinity formed an intention. Why hadn't I thought of it before?

Let's go, I agreed with her and we cantered towards the paddock gate. I was expecting Infinity to slow to a halt so I could ask a nearby spectator to open the gate for us, but as she pricked her ears and gathered momentum, I grinned. We could do this. She checked her stride as we got closer, and then as her neck came up towards me, I folded at the hip and leaned forward. We were airbourne! We landed lightly on the other side of the gate and Infinity turned sharply to avoid having to make another immediate jump into the riding paddock on the other side of the path. She made the turn easily and then set off at a powerful canter in the direction of the river.

'Am, are you finished already? I was going to ask for your opinion on something,' Rowena called.

'Sorry, but we've waited a long time for this and Infinity's not going to wait any longer,' I yelled back and then realised the truth of my statement; Infinity had absolutely no intention of waiting, slowing down, or doing anything at all that I suggested, including slowing to a trot to avoid splashing water from last night's storm over some people walking the other way. 'Sorry,' I called out to them as we thundered past, 'Infinity's on a mission, very sorry.'

I began to giggle and couldn't stop. We arrived at the river bank and Infinity slowed herself to a walk, blowing slightly. 'Okay, good idea, let's walk for a bit then, shall we?' I said, still laughing.

Infinity turned to the left and walked along the bank while she regained her wind. She then turned back on herself to face the long stretch of grassy river bank that positively invited us to indulge ourselves. She came to a halt and my left leg vibrated with the force of her heartbeat. We savoured the smell of the fresh water as it entered her nostrils, the feel of the gentlest of breezes as it disturbed the sensitive hairs at the tips of her ears, the feeling of oneness with each other and with All That Is.

Infinity flicked an ear to the right as we felt our friends coming to join us. She lifted her forequarter into the air and let out an ear-piercing whinny, signalling to all that we were here, we were powerful, we were Infinity. Then we were off. She launched herself into a powerful canter and I folded at the hip slightly and took my weight off of her back, staying almost upright so that I could help her if she needed it. She didn't. We passed the end of the path to The Gathering and I saw a blur of black, chestnut, brown and grey out of the corner of my eye as the other horses burst onto the river bank and fell in behind us.

Infinity increased her pace to a flat-out gallop. She stretched out her neck and for a second, I was worried she'd lose her balance, but then I realised that her forequarters were still back with me and I felt her back rounding behind the saddle as her hindquarters came right underneath to balance herself. We flew. We raced the river as it hurtled along beside us, we raced the horses whose hooves thrummed on the ground behind us, we raced life itself.

By the time I felt Infinity slowing, I couldn't see anything for the tears that clogged my eyes before being whipped off from the side of my face. All I was aware of was the thundering of our hooves, the thumping of our heart and the infinite sense of love and peace that was the truth of our existence.

We cantered slowly and then dropped to a trot, tired but exhilarated. We slowed to a walk and our friends joined us, all of the humans but Justin laughing and shouting excitedly to each other. They Who Are Gas were as lost in their enjoyment of oneness as Infinity and I. A familiar presence touched us. Adam! He wasn't quite the same as when he'd been in his body, he was more – Peace was with him! No thoughts were necessary. We felt their elation, their completeness before they drifted away, and we knew that they were where they needed to be. As were we. Everything was as it needed to be.

'I'd never have believed Infinity could run that fast, never mind jump a flaming five bar gate.' Rowena's excited voice jerked us all back to the physical world. 'Gas could have overtaken you both, and probably Liberal, but the rest of us were pushed just to keep up. There's no stopping her now, is there, Am?'

I laughed. 'No, I don't think there is.'

Marvel suggested untacking the horses so they could graze the river bank while we rested awhile in the sunshine, but gave in with good grace when we all reminded him that our students would be waiting for us back at the paddocks. We made our way back along the river bank at a walk, enjoying the warm sunshine and the sound of the river as it rushed along its path. We revelled in the camaraderie we felt with our horses and with each other.

'This responsibility is most inconvenient, in fact now that summer's beginning to announce itself, I'm thinking of jacking it all in.' Marvel's voice rang out loudly, and he made a show of covering his head with his arms to protect himself from our shouted protests.

'Pick your reins up, you feckless man, you just dropped Broad and left him to balance on his own,' scolded Rowena.

'No, I didn't, I have him with my thighs, see, look at my legs. You really are the bossiest woman...' Marvel's voice was drowned out by our laughter.

'It's good to hear her back to her old self,' I said to Justin as we rode on, chuckling.

He nodded. 'That's our Ro, and Marvel seems to revel in being the focus of her tyranny.'

We were quiet for a time, then I voiced the question that had been going over and over in my mind. 'How long do you think we'll be needed here?'

He shrugged. 'As long as it takes, I guess. You're itching to be off, though. The Woeful?'

I nodded. 'I can't stop thinking about the one who killed Shann, how he was feeling, his worry for his family. We can't let them go through another winter like that, we have to help, and like Marvel said, summer isn't far away. It'll be autumn and then winter again before we know it and there's just so much to do. We have to find them and persuade them to trust us, we have to come up with a plan of exactly how they and humans can share communities and live alongside one another, and then we have to persuade the villagers to cooperate with it all, which isn't going to be easy.'

Infinity increased her presence in my mind, pushing my worries to one side. I remembered. *Everything is as it should be,* I agreed with her and then broadcast it to All That Is, wondering if maybe some of the Woeful would pick up on my thought and know that we would try to make things right. *EVERYTHING IS AS IT SHOULD BE!*

Justin smiled. 'It always comes back to that, doesn't it.'

Infinity pushed off into a slow canter and Gas was soon cantering alongside. Our friends' initial protests at the lack of warning were soon replaced with shouts and laughter as their horses joined ours, and the slow canter became a gallop as our horses egged each other on in the sunshine.

We really are the luckiest girls in the world, Fin.

Luck does not exist. We are who we are and we have done as we agreed. In time we will attempt more.

Other books by Lynn Mann

The story continues in:

The Horses Rejoice (The Horses Know Book 2)

Amarilla and Infinity have been the catalysts for change that they agreed to be, but they know there is more to be done. If they can befriend the Woeful and persuade the rest of humankind to do the same, then the destructive ways of The Old will forever be in the past.

Amarilla, Infinity and their friends set out on a journey to find the Woeful but their search becomes something so much more due to a courageous chestnut mare, a lone Woeful youngling and numerous herds of wild horses who seek their help along the way. But the friends never forget what they agreed to do. They must reach the heart of the Woeful community. And then they must be willing to risk losing everything…

The Horses Return (The Horses Know Book 3)

It has been more than twenty years since the Kindred came to live in Rockwood. Most of the villagers have embraced the Kindred and all that they have to teach, but there are those who fear the Kindreds' influence, and so have drifted away to live as outcasts. The outcasts suffer, living as they do, but they refuse help, even from the Horse-Bonded.

Will is adamant that he can succeed where the Horse-Bonded have failed, and bring the outcasts home. But his forceful personality constantly gets in his way. He is the key to the future, but if he is to play his part, he must allow a herd of wild horses to show him how to be the person he needs to be. Only then will he fully understand the lengths to which Amarilla and Infinity have gone to ensure that he can fulfil his destiny and reunite the human race…

Horses Forever (A Sequel to The Horses Know Trilogy)

It has always been believed that the people of The Old obliterated themselves generations ago, but when horses begin to amass at one of the city sites of The Old, the villagers of Rockwood discover the truth – an underground city, full of people, has survived.

Supreme City's inhabitants have been waiting for the conditions to be right for them to come up to the surface and claim dominion. They believe the time has come. They are genetically enhanced, armed and aggressive, and they are certain that nothing can stand in their way. But they haven't counted on Will, Maverick, the Horse-Bonded and several hundred horses…

The Forgotten Horses (A Sequel to Horses Forever)

Tania is supremely Aware and exceedingly headstrong. Her parents have kept her shielded from the full extent of her Awareness in order to protect her from herself, but now that she is twenty, the time has come for them to relax their guard.

Tania's abilities begin to emerge, striking awe into those around her, but when she disappears in the middle of the night, all in Rockwood are left shocked and grieving. All, that is, except for Will and Amarilla, who know exactly where she is and why. They also know that they will need to follow her if she is to survive long enough to help the horses whose call for help she has answered – and help the horses she must, for they are the safeguards of humanity…

The Way Of The Horse (A Sequel to The Forgotten Horses)

Nathan has survived the years since his parents' murders by visiting an equine assisted therapy centre every day, where a devoted mare provides him with sanctuary from his demons. When she and the other therapy horses are taken from the centre by the police and herded out of The City Of Glory, Nathan is ready to kill or be killed.

But then the enigmatic Tania takes his hand and he remembers another time. Another life. Then, he was one of the Horse-Bonded, one who failed to fulfil his potential. Now, he is a scientific research assistant barely clinging to sanity. The fate of The City Of Glory's citizens depends on him staying alive but in order to do that, he will need to embrace both his memory of who he really is, and the help of the horse who won't allow death to thwart them both…

Prequels to The Horses Know Trilogy

In Search Of Peace (Adam's story)
The Strength Of Oak (Rowena's story)
A Reason To Be Noble (Quinta's story)

Tales Of The Horse-Bonded
(Companion Stories to The Horses Know Trilogy)

Tales Of The Horse-Bonded is a collection of short stories that will take you on a journey into the lives of some of your favourite characters from *The Horses Know* series. The book is available in paperback and hardback, and is also available to download free. To find out more, please visit www.lynnmann.co.uk.

Did you enjoy The Horses Know?
I'd be very grateful if you could spare a few minutes to leave a review where you purchased your copy. Reviews help my books to reach a wider audience, which means that I can keep on writing!
Many thanks.

One of the best things about being an author is chatting with my readers. I love to hear from you!
Get in touch, receive news and sign up to my newsletter to receive free stories, exclusive content, new release announcements and more at:

www.lynnmann.co.uk

I can also be contacted via the Facebook page:

www.Facebook.com/lynnmann.author

Acknowledgments

My heartfelt thanks go out to:

Darren Mann for his never-ending support and encouragement;

Fern Sherry, Leonard & Ann Palmer, Rebecca Walters, Susan Wilkinson and Wendy Evans for editing, copy editing and proofreading;

Dashel, Ivy and the late Sidney, my canine companions who accompanied me on walks whenever I needed a breather;

Coxstone Infinity (stable-name Pie), my beautiful, blue-eyed mare who is the horse I always hoped I would find and the inspiration for this book;

Jon Morris of MoPhoto for generously supplying the wonderful shots of Pie used in the cover design;

Gavin and Annabelle Scofield for all of their help with Pie and me over the years;

The Society for the Welfare of Horses and Ponies (now Redwings SWHP), who rescued Pie from a desperate situation, saving her life and that of her foal;

My readers – not only for reading, but for all of your emails, reviews, messages and comments on facebook posts, they are hugely appreciated!

Manufactured by Amazon.ca
Bolton, ON

29994905R00203